THE
FIRST CENTURY
CHRISTIAN
SAGA

BOOK FOUR

VERONICA'S VEIL

VERONICA'S VEIL

A Catholic Christian Novel by
JOSEPH L. CAVILLA

"For my children."

ACKNOWLEDGEMENTS

Once again, thanks to my son Paul, for his encouragement, and his dedication in formatting, and publishing of this book. Thanks also to my brother Charles for his enthusiasm and the proof-reading of the book.

VERONICA'S VEIL

CHAPTER ONE

THE VEIL

She ran back to her place, in the crowd madly waving her veil, her tearful eyes contradicting the look of exultation and wonder on her face. The condemned Rabbi shuffled uncertainly on, followed by a big man carrying his crossbeam. The bystanders who stood beside her; which included two of her friends and her son, were dumbfounded at what they beheld imprinted on that white veil.

Veronica, realising the treasure she was holding, instinctively folded it with urgency and held it securely on her bosom. Her eyes still tearful and with great sadness, followed the Rabbi whose name she knew to be Yeshua. Her life, which had been truly miserable over the last twelve years; plagued with a constant issue of blood, had been totally changed for the better, when on an earlier occasion whilst following him in the midst of a crowd, she had tentatively touched the hem of his garment in desperate hope of a cure. She shuddered as she remembered him turning and asking who had touched him.

"Woman!" he had said looking into her eyes; a faint smile on his lips. "Your faith has made you whole."

As the escort of soldiers passed, she and her party along with many others who were following the macabre procession, fell in behind them. This journey to Calvary was proving to be a slow and distressing affair.

Yeshua received a taste of the cruel whip whenever his weakness impeded his progress. She could see that the poor young rabbi, perhaps only three years older than herself, had been badly beaten and abused prior to beginning his tragic journey. On spotting the vicious thorns crowning his head she winced involuntarily, mentally feeling the pain that it must be causing him. The knowledge that the big man was now carrying his heavy crossbeam gave her much relief. If he had been carrying it himself, she reasoned, it would have caused him further torment by occasionally colliding with the thorns and driving them deeper into his bleeding, wounded head.

Veronica was a handsome woman of medium stature and elegant in her bearing. Her delicate features were enhanced by her long light brown hair, which having lost the cover of the veil, hung loose and long over her shoulders and back. Her kind, brown thickly lashed eyes searched those of her twelve-year-old son. His eyes were similarly shaped and coloured though they seemed bigger. They displayed an enquiring look.

"My son," she said drawing him to her. "I would you were not here to witness this cruel scene."

She smoothed his thick dark brown curly hair; a glimmer of a smile on her full red lips.

"We will follow the Rabbi to the cross perhaps, but we shan't stay for the crucifixion."

"Why not mother?" asked the boy. Veronica had named him Mezsod, but he was 'Mesi' to his young friends.

"I am almost a man now," said the twelve-year-old boy with disdain. "Surely you will let me see it."

Veronica threw a quick glance at her friends Sarah and Martha, who walked beside them.

"We shall see," she said.

The sun shone cheerfully from a clear blue sky. The day, though intensely hot, was better suited to a happier event than that which the morbid and cruel procession represented with death awaiting at its final destination.

When the Rabbi fell for the third time, it looked as if he were going to die there and then. His acute state of exhaustion and the utter inhumanity of the soldiers filled Veronica and her friends with compassion. Martha, her other friend, suddenly declared that she was leaving; she could not bear it any longer. Likewise, Sarah and Veronica, feeling most distraught by the spectacle, turned around, and despite protestations from young Mesi, directed their footsteps away from the crowd and made their way back to their respective homes.

Veronica's soul was in turmoil as she separated from her friends and made her way to the fruit stall she owned in the marketplace. She had left it in the hands of Jacob; her friend Sarah's son who often helped her out and was like family. Mesi walked beside his mother with a look of disappointment on his face.

'Dear God,' she prayed, her thoughts going back to Yeshua. 'I owe this man my life. I should have stayed there to witness his crucifixion, but I could not let my boy see that horrible execution. He is much too young and impressionable, and I fear the consequences.'

These thoughts occupied Veronica's mind as she walked in silence with her son at her side.

She tried to convince herself that she had avoided the crucifixion for her son's benefit. That was only part of the reason. What she was reluctant to admit to herself, was that she had a strong aversion to dealing with unpleasant things, which she did her best to dismiss from her mind as quickly as possible. Perhaps this weakness in her nature had developed as a defence for the pain she had endured when her husband had suddenly left her ten years before; due she thought, to her sickness with that constant issue of blood which greatly restricted her wifely duty to him.

He had left her the fruit stall and house and disappeared. Mesi was only two years old at the time. The event had been quite traumatic for the child, who for a good while kept waking up with nightmares and often wetted his bed. Veronica had to downplay her bitterness and resentment for his sake. Her malady continued to be a constant concern. Thankfully, it had recently come to a miraculous end; her earlier desperation replaced by a strong faith in Yeshua's power.

She had only met the Rabbi on two fateful occasions, but now she had in her possession a personal gift of his. A gift given her as a reward for her compassion as she had thankfully tried in her own small way, to make some return for his great kindness to her. She felt that a great bond had now been established between them, and the remorse for not having accompanied him to the cross was breaking her heart. She reached her fruit stall; her face wet with tears.

Jacob became alarmed as he greeted her and beheld her troubled face.

"Stay here with Jacob," she said to her son, gently pushing him towards the young man and rushing into her house which happened to be directly behind the fruit stall.

"Mother is upset because of the Rabbi whom they are crucifying," said Mesi, taking an apple from a basket and giving it a good bite.

Veronica having reached her bedroom, unfolded the treasured veil and reverently kissed its cherished image. She laid it on her pillow, and tenderly placing her face on it, wept bitterly.

Feeling a hand gently shaking her shoulder, Veronica awoke to the realization that she had fallen asleep. Mesi looked at his mother with surprise as he beheld both her face and the incredibly realistic face of the Rabbi, there, side by side on the pillow.

"You can come in Jacob," said the boy, addressing the young man waiting in the corridor. "She's awake!"

"Oh! My goodness!" yawned Veronica. "It's late, we must hurry. We must be at Martha's house for our Passover meal. I don't want to be late. It's almost Sabbath."

"No. It's but the tenth hour," said the nineteen-year-old Jacob as he walked into the room. He suddenly froze at the sight of the open veil on the pillow.

"What is that you have there?" he asked; his eyes wide with amazement.

"It was given her by the Rabbi that they were going to crucify; after mother went over to him and let him wipe his face with it," explained Mesi before Veronica could answer.

Veronica reached for the veil and holding it up to allow Jacob a closer look, explained.

"His sweating and bleeding face was imprinted on to this cloth miraculously as if by magic," she said, as tears brimmed once again in her eyes.

Jacob took it, examined it carefully, and rubbing his finger over the imprinted face looked up in wonder.

"It isn't pigment," he said. "It's surely magical. No artist could paint this realistically."

Jacob's face was a picture to see. His gaping, open mouth; his eyebrows dropping in a frown and pressing against his squinting eyes; his long somewhat hooked nose floating over his cropped black moustache and short beard; and his black hair feathering over his brow, gave his face a comical and bird-like expression. Veronica, in the midst of folding the cloth, burst out laughing. Mesi's good sense of humour was similarly titillated and he heartily joined in his mother's laughter.

The veil was reverently placed on a shelf near the bed, and all walked out of the room.

"Is all the fruit in now?" asked Veronica, looking at the two boys.

"Yes, everything is in for the night," answered Jacob, who having reached the front door, wished mother and son a good night and left for his parents' house.

It was the first day of the week. Veronica had had a busy morning at the stall, but a little after mid-day the crunch had lessened and having left Mesi to look after it, she was busy preparing something to eat.

As she carried the food outside she was almost bowled over in the corridor by her son who came charging into the house with a very excited look on his face.

"Mother!" he said, stopping abruptly in front of her. "There is a woman outside who says that the Rabbi has risen from the dead this very morning."

Veronica gave Mesi a suspicious look as she walked past him.

"That isn't possible my son, you are surely mistaken."

She stepped out and slipped in behind the tables that displayed her fruit. The woman facing her shook her head meaningfully.

"Your son is not mistaken," assured the woman. "The preacher is said to have risen this morning. I heard that his disciples found his tomb empty when they went to finish their embalming after the Sabbath. They say that the large stone that enclosed it was lying on the ground well away from the door as if some great force had moved it. Others are saying that it is not true and accuse his disciples of stealing the body before the Sanhedrin had had a chance to set a guard."

Veronica could not believe her ears.

"Risen? How is that possible?" She raised her hands to heaven. "No one has ever done that...My goodness."

The woman bought some fruit and went on her way leaving a stunned pair back at the stall.

"Do you think mother, that what the woman said is true?" asked Mesi, about to bite into the piece of cheese he held in his hand.

"She said he had disciples. I sure would like to talk to one of them," said Veronica nibbling at her cheese with a far-a-way look in her lovely eyes.

"Maybe Jacob can find out," said Mesi enthusiastically. "He knows a lot of people. If you let me go find him after I eat, I shall ask him. He said he would be at his stall today. His father had to go somewhere."

"I can manage on my own this afternoon," said Veronica, "but be back here by the tenth hour. You have to help me put the fruit away. We are going to Sarah's house for today's Passover meal."

Mesi got back in time to help his mother take the fruit into the cellar for the night. It was a nightly ritual. The small but cool cellar was fitted with shelves where the baskets of fruit were stored. When Veronica's husband abandoned them, Solomon, Jacobs father, who had been a friend of her husband, helped her set up the stall in the mornings and strip it in the evenings until Jacob was old enough and strong enough to help her in his stead.

Veronica owed Solomon and his wife Sarah a debt of gratitude which she knew she could never repay. Jacob was not their only son. They had two other younger sons, and a daughter who was a year older than Jacob, named Tobah.

"Mother," said Mesi. "Jacob knows a young disciple of the Rabbi, called John. He was very close to Yeshua. That was the Rabbi's name you know."

"Yes, I know," said Veronica with a smile and locking the cellar door. "How can I find this young man?"

She dusted her dress, locked the house door, and they both went to their rooms to dress for their visit to Jacob's house. Veronica planned to take the veil for the family to see. Only Sarah had got a glimpse of it so far.

"Jacob will tell us more about him tonight I feel sure," said Mesi with a smile. "John is only four years older than me, you know."

* * * * *

A few weeks had passed since the Passover, and Jacob was still trying to find young John the disciple of Yeshua. He had enquired of others who also knew him, but without any success.

Veronica tended her stall and looked after her son for whom she had found a teacher a while back, who was teaching him to read and write. The teacher was a young woman nineteen years of age, very good looking but a cripple from birth. She was an only child and her parents doted on her. Her father who was a very wealthy merchant had given her as good an education as money could buy, and she, being very talented, had responded well. Esther, for that was her name, gave lessons in a number of subjects and could play a few musical instruments. This kept her busy, and because she did not need the money, her fees were very reasonable. Mesi took a great liking to her and studied very diligently just to make her happy.

One day he happened to mention to Esther, the image on her mother's veil. She was most intrigued, and having heard much of Yeshua and his many miracles, asked him if his mother could take it for her to see.

"Yes," said Veronica in answer to her son's request on behalf of his teacher.

"Poor soul, she never leaves the house," said Veronica with pity in her voice. "This will give her something unusual to look at, and I am sure she will appreciate it. I shall go with you this afternoon if we can get Jacob to tend the stall."

"I'll go find him," said Mesi, putting on his cap and running off before his mother could say another word.

As luck would have it, Jacob soon appeared with a smiling Mesi at his side.

"Here he is mother," announced her happy son. "We have to hurry. It's late. We should have been there already."

Veronica hurried into the house to change her clothes and get the veil. She could not go as she was. They were wealthy people and used to dressing well. She would spruce Mesi up as she always did when he went for his lessons.

Soon they were both on their way; the veil tucked under her robe.

Esther's house was not far from the market.

A servant opened the door in answer to their knock, and recognising Mesi gave the lad a warm smile.

"Anna, this is my mother," said Mesi. "Esther asked me to bring her. She has something to show her."

The young woman greeted Veronica with a smile and a slight bow and led the way to her mistress whom they found playing her harp in the lovely interior garden of the house.

Veronica had been there only once before when she arranged for Mesi to take his lessons, but she was stunned once again by the opulence and beauty that surrounded her. The garden which she had not seen on her previous visit, enraptured her in an unprecedented and powerful way. She stood there enchanted by the perfume of the flowers, the colours, the arches, the pool with its beautiful water lilies, and the many plants and flowers surrounding it.

"How nice of you to come!" those words from Esther, snapped her out of her reverie. Mesi prodded his mother's side gently with his elbow to make sure she would answer.

"Oh! please pardon me," blurted out Veronica feeling rather foolish. "I was completely swept away with the beauty of your garden...Lovely to see you again. How are you my dear?"

"I am well, thank you. But please do not apologize for letting the garden capture your attention. It flirts with everyone like some shameless woman. She knows she is spoilt with all the loving tending she receives and takes advantage of all of us mortals. We spend more time here under her spell I think, than in the house." She motioned to an elaborately carved marble bench positioned directly opposite her chair.

Both mother and son sat down and smiled amiably at Esther, as she handed her harp to a nearby servant who apparently seldom left her side.

"Sheba! Please ask my mother to join us," said Esther addressing her servant.

As the latter hastened away, the young teacher took the opportunity to report on Mesi's good efforts and progress in his reading and writing. She suggested that perhaps if he liked the idea, he could begin to learn arithmetic which she assured them would be very useful if he ever became a merchant or an architect.

Mesi was quick to answer.

"Yes," he said, turning to his mother for concurrence. "I would love that."

Veronica looked at him and smiled. "Maybe."

"There would be no further cost involved," assured Esther, who could sense that Veronica might be hard pressed to find the extra money. "He is a very clever and dedicated boy. He deserves to be taught all that he wishes to learn."

Approaching footsteps could now be heard, and a few moments later, Esther's mother wearing a beautiful smile and accompanied by Sheba, stepped into the garden.

"I am so pleased to see you again Veronica. How have you been? It's been quite a while since I saw you last."

Veronica got up and embraced Ruth warmly.

"Lovely to see you again and looking so beautiful. How do you do it? You really must tell me your secret."

Ruth was in her early forties, but still kept her youthful figure and refined features. She obviously spent much time pampering herself. That however did not detract from her warm and amiable personality. Veronica made room on the large bench, and Ruth sat down beside her.

Esther had purposely asked her mother to join them because from the description of the 'veil' that Mesi had given her, she suspected that it might prove to be a work of art, and both her parents loved art. In fact they owned quite a collection.

"Now!" began Esther, once having captured everyone's attention. "Veronica, please show us that imprinted veil of yours. Mesi told me a most extraordinary tale of how you happened to get it. That man Yeshua, who was crucified had, I hear, worked many miracles. He claimed to be the Messiah I believe. There is now a rumour going around that his disciples are saying that he is the Son of God, and has risen from the dead. So you see how keen I am to see the veil."

Veronica took out the veil, and opening it, stood back and held it up for Esther and her mother to see.

Mesi awaited with bated breath. Esther gasped visibly, and Ruth's eyes opened as wide as they were capable, and getting to her feet, went over to inspect the veil more closely.

"My goodness!" she exclaimed with great emotion. "How very realistic. It does not look as if it is painted."

She felt the fabric, to check for pigment much as Jacob had done. There was no stiffness in the fabric, and when she carefully scratched it in one corner with her nail, no marks appeared.

"I cannot understand it," she whispered to herself, but loud enough for all to hear.

"May I have a closer look at it too?" asked Esther who could hardly contain her excitement after her mother's assessment.

Veronica handed her the veil. Esther examined both sides carefully, her eyes betraying the excitement that was gripping her very being.

"What a remarkable face," she said. "Poor man, how he must have suffered." She turned the veil over again and felt it carefully. "No," she asserted, "it certainly is not painted on. It is much too perfect and smooth. If I shut my eyes and simply feel the fabric, it is as if there was nothing on it."

She smiled and said. "I feel like wearing it," and proceeded to cover her head with the veil.

No sooner had she done so than her eyes filled with tears, which overflowed and streamed down her face, soaking her lovely cheeks and making them sparkle in the light of the early afternoon sun. She pressed her hands down on the arms of her chair and with great determination, slowly raised herself. All present stood aghast, as with her feet on the ground, she slowly, very slowly, stood up. The tears stopped. She took a step forward. Sheba moved to assist her mistress, but Ruth put her arm out and stopped her.

All looked on anxiously and expectantly. Esther took a second step. Then she gingerly took a number of steps down the garden path in the direction of the pool. Presently she stopped, lifted up her dress, and looked at her legs. They were normal legs, strong and shapely. The atrophied muscles had disappeared, and they looked just like everyone else's.

"I can walk! I can walk!" She shouted, time and time again. Then, turning back with newly found confidence, she as good as ran into her mother's waiting arms.

Tears of joy filled every eye present, and the sound of loud and repeated thanks to God filled the garden.

"He *is* the Messiah! He *is* the Son of God," cried a jubilant Esther, as she took off the veil and kissing it reverently gave it back to Veronica, who being overcome with emotion, flopped back onto the bench in a state of shock. Mesi, had not moved. He sat there with his mouth wide open hardly believing his eyes. Sheba shook with excitement, and Ruth just hugged and hugged her daughter.

"Your father is going to get the shock of his life when he sees you and hears what happened here today," asserted Esther's mother, wiping away her tears and giving her daughter's flushed cheeks another ardent kiss.

It took a little while for the euphoria to pass. Veronica and Mesi were invited to stay for supper and meet Jesse; Esther's father.

All were seated on their cushions around a very ornamental low table in the sumptuous dining room of the house. That is, all except Esther. Her father arrived slightly later than usual; a delay that often seems to happen when people are eager to experience some great happening.

Jesse made his appearance with apologies for being late. He did not tell them, but he had had a difficult day and was tired and somewhat unhappy.

"This is Veronica," explained Ruth. "And this young man is her son...He is one of Esther's more talented pupils. They have brought us a very great surprise today, for which we are extremely grateful."

The master of the house greeted Veronica with a bow of the head and Mesi with a big smile.

"Welcome to our house," he said, and turning to scan the room, asked:

"Where is Esther?"

"Here I am father," she replied, suddenly appearing at the dining room door, and walking elegantly towards him with a big smile on her beautiful face.

It was difficult to say whether poor Jesse was going to laugh or cry. The expression on his face was indescribable. He simply stood there, unable to move as his daughter reached him and threw her arms around his neck; tears running down her lovely cheeks.

Of a sudden, he burst into tears. He held her in a long and tender embrace, as the reality of her being able to walk registered in a mind that was resigned to seeing her in a chair for the rest of her life. The fact that she could walk struck him with a powerful force.

"What happened my love?" he cried. "I can't believe it. Who has cured you?... Adonai be praised!" He fell on his knees; his eyes to heaven; hands outstretched; his whole frame shaking with overpowering emotion.

Esther also in tears, gave her hand to her father, who taking it, got up and hugged her once more; his eyes still raised to heaven.

They both sat down at table. The story of the veil, which actually was the story of Yeshua's passion, was unfolded, but in a sketchy manner; each contributing what they knew of it. However before supper was over, Jesse, who along with all present at the table now believing in Yeshua, promised to call on his friend Joseph of Arimathea; a merchant; councillor, and member of the Sanhedrin, whom he felt might know something of Yeshua and his followers and could give them much more information.

It was late in the evening when Veronica and Mesi returned home bringing the veil back with them. Jesse had offered her a large sum of money for it since it had changed his daughter's life, and he wanted it in remembrance of that great miracle. But Veronica told him that it was a gift from the Messiah, the Son of God, and that no money in the world could possibly pay for that. He had understood her pious refusal and commended her for her purity of mind and love for Yeshua.

"Who knows," said Veronica to her son, whilst sitting in their family room later that night, "how many people can be cured by this divine image. We must keep it always and help people who need to be cured. When I am gone you will have charge of it, and later, your own first born will carry the responsibility of letting it be used for good. Always without charge. It must never be tainted with money."

"Yes mother, I promise," said Mesi. He hugged and kissed his mother tenderly and went off to bed to dream of Esther for whom he had a great crush.

A few days following Esther's miraculous cure, a well-dressed gentleman appeared at Veronica's fruit stall in the late afternoon. Veronica was serving a customer, and there were two more people waiting to be served. The man paced around the stall studying the fruit for a few moments awaiting his turn so that he might speak to her.

At this point Mesi came out of the house carrying a basket of figs, and seeing the distinguished looking man, asked if he could be of assistance.

"Thank you, young man. I wish to talk to your mother," he said throwing a glance at Veronica, who was now serving her last but one customer.

Mesi went behind the long table, replaced a nearly empty basket with the new one, and whispered in his mother's ear.

A smiling Veronica apologized to the woman last in line. She told her that her son would serve her since there was a gentleman waiting to talk with her. The woman smiled back, nodded in ascent, and waited for Mesi to look after her needs.

Veronica smoothed her work dress and hair and exiting the stall, greeted the man with a polite smile.

"I am Joseph of Arimathea," said the man with a smile and a slight bow of the head.

"I am pleased to meet you. How can I help you," she answered with a sweet smile.

"My good friend Jesse asked me to come and talk to you regarding a matter which would best be discussed in private if you don't mind," he said; his eyes looking towards the door from which Mesi had exited a few moments earlier and which he correctly assumed to be the door to her house.

"Please, won't you come in," she said, leading the way in.

He followed Veronica into her living room and she motioned to a cluster of cushions that lay on the floor around a very simple low table.

"Please take a seat...May I get you some juice? Or wine if you prefer." She turned to go into the kitchen.

"Juice will do very nicely. Thank you," he said, settling down on one of the cushions.

She soon reappeared with an earthenware jug and two cups which she placed on the table and sat directly opposite him.

Following a sip of his juice and a complimentary remark regarding its freshness, the visitor began.

"I am acquainted with the story of your unique and sacred veil, and the marvellous miracle that it worked on young Esther. It staggers the mind. But knowing who the donor of the gift was, and is, it's power to heal is not in the least surprising to me."

Veronica listened attentively but kept silent, nodding for him to continue as she felt that there was more that he wished to tell her.

"Before I go any further," he continued. "I would like you to tell me what your views are regarding the man we call Yeshua." He looked straight into her eyes with a kind, but inquisitorial look. Veronica met his gaze and with a smile, and much love in her eyes, answered.

"I owe him my life."

She went on to explain the twelve years of torment with the issue of blood, and how he had cured her.

"Now," she concluded, "all I want to do is to use the veil to cure as many people as I can, and to find his disciples so that they can tell me all about him. Esther called him the Son of God, and the Messiah, when she felt herself cured. I feel the same way. No man could do the things that I hear he did. Especially his rising from the dead." She stopped and gave him a pleading look.

"Do you know any of his disciples?" she asked hopefully.

"Now that I know I can trust you Veronica," he said, smiling but dismissing her question. I will tell you many things which you ought, and surely want to know about our beloved Yeshua." Joseph smiled again and began his story.

He told her of his visits to Yeshua at night to receive instruction from him; his familiarity with the Apostles, and his role in trying to protect the disciples from the Sanhedrin of which he was a member and councillor. He also told her of the much-expected arrival of the Holy Spirit.

Joseph's narration was well on its way when Mesi entered the room, and after begging their pardon for interrupting, asked his mother if he could start bringing in the fruit for the night.

"Try to manage on your own. I am having a very important conversation with this gentleman. If there is anything you cannot carry by yourself, call me and I will take a moment to help you."

Mesi smiled at the opportunity to challenge himself, and saying he could do it, went back out to the stall.

"He is quite capable," said Veronica. "He is a smart and strong boy."

"Esther spoke very highly of him," commented Joseph taking a sip of his juice.

"Now that you know where I stand," continued the learned visitor. "I am going to give you some advice that I wish you to take very seriously, as not just your own and your son's life may be at stake, but many, many, other innocent lives also." He said this with great gravity in his voice. Veronica became frightened at his words.

"Very difficult times are coming for the followers of Yeshua. There will I fear, be persecutions even. You must not show or tell anyone about the veil." He looked at her meaningfully.

Veronica's eyes opened wide, her thin eyebrows rose, and her mouth flew open.

"No, my dear," continued Joseph, reading her expression of incredulity and disappointment. "You will not be able to use the veil for those wonderful works that you were intending. Enough people are already aware of its existence, and it is in danger of being stolen. For one, the Sanhedrin would love to get their hands on it and either destroy it or hide it where they would be sure that it would never be found again. There are also other people with bad motives who would be quite amenable to stealing it, perhaps erroneously thinking that it is magical and would try to sell it for a large sum to some collector of rarities."

"When may I get to see the Apostles?" she asked; recovering from her shock.

"At the moment, they are all in hiding from the Sanhedrin who are looking for any excuse to incarcerate them. We don't know what is going to happen when the Holy Spirit comes. But we are all praying that something wonderful will occur." The councillor shifted on his cushion and asked.

"May I see the veil?"

"Certainly," replied Veronica, getting up and walking off to her bedroom. Moments later, a distressing scream broke the serenity of the house.

"Ah! It's gone! It's gone! Oh my!" cried Veronica; her heart breaking; tears bursting from her eyes.

Joseph rushed into the room, followed closely by Mesi, who ran to embrace his mother with panic written all over his face. Joseph instinctively looked at the window, and immediately saw that the shutters though closed, were damaged.

"Were your window shutters damaged? he asked, turning to Veronica. She looked at the window and shook her head.

"No," she said. "They were whole and bolted."

CHAPTER TWO

THE CULPRIT

It would be incumbent on me to neglect explaining to you, my esteemed reader, the circumstances that led to the theft of the veil, and how and by whom the crime was perpetrated.

It happened this way:

Sheba, the servant in the Jesse household walked home on her weekly day off. She had been impatiently waiting for the last two days to take the extraordinary news of her mistress' miraculous cure to her family. She had been told to keep it a secret, but she would tell her mother and sister at least. They, she knew, could be trusted.

Salome and Hannah, Sheba's mother and sister, were sitting in the family room finishing their breakfast when Sheba entered the chamber. She slumped on a cushion between them and gave them both a hug.

"Have you had your breakfast?" asked Salome with motherly concern.

"Yes, mother," answered Sheba with a smile. "I have some fantastic news to give you both, and I've had to wait for two days to tell you. I was told to keep it even from you." She gave them both a stern look. "You must swear to me that you will tell no one."

Sheba took their hands, and holding onto them, made them swear there and then to keep the story she was about to relate an absolute secret. They both nodded and said they would.

Sheba began the amazing tale. The other two listened attentively and incredulously to what she was relating.

By a stroke of bad luck, Hannah's son Sadoc, a delinquent young man who was forever getting into trouble, had just woken up and was about to leave his room to go to his ablutions. As he opened his door, which opened into a short corridor next to the family room where the trio were sitting, he happened to hear his aunt Sheba mentioning the word 'secret,' and froze where he stood.

Through the partially open door he could hear every word spoken in the family room.

When the name Veronica was given as being the owner of the veil, Sadoc's ears perked up. His lips stretched in an evil smile when she was described as being the owner of the fruit stand at the market.

He noiselessly closed the door and went back to bed.

Shortly after, his mother knocked at his door and getting no answer, entered. He pretended to be asleep. She went over to him and gently shook his arm.

"Wake up Sadoc," she said. "Your aunt Sheba is here, and she would like to see you."

Sheba had not been aware that Sadoc was in the house. There were nights when he did not come home at all, and so she had spoken freely unsuspecting that he was in his room.

To put her sister's mind at rest, Hannah went back to the family room and announced that her son had been asleep, and she had just woken him up.

"He often sleeps in," said Hannah, shaking her head.

They all knew that he was a lazy eighteen-year-old who tried to do as little work as possible. His father was perpetually promising to throw him out, but somehow never did. The boy was supposed to be learning his father's trade; the leather business. Though he showed aptitude for the work, he was lazy and more interested in spending time drinking, gambling and galivanting with his shady friends than spending time with his father.

Sadoc joined the family a little later and had his breakfast with them. He talked as normally as he could, and then headed out saying that he was meeting a friend but would later go and help his father. His mother who was most gullible where her son was concerned, gave him a kiss and a hug and saw him out of the house.

The deviant youth made his way directly to the market, where he soon enquired after and found, Veronica's fruit stall. Stepping back into the crowd, he observed the stall for some time. He noticed how every so often she or her young helper would go into the house behind the stall and come out with fresh supplies of fruit. Making his way to the street behind the house and carefully counting houses, he soon located the house. The backyard was very small. It only had room for a toilet and a few potted plants. The gate was easy to open. He could see a back door and two windows closed by wooden shutters.

Going around the front again, he slowly walked past the stall mixing with the crowd and continuing to observe mother and son. He had to make sure that there was no one else in attendance there.

He continued his spying for a number of days with a varying time table and discovered that whenever she left, Jacob and Mesi, would stand in for her. However, sometimes she would be there by herself. At such times, Veronica would be too busy and well provisioned to have to enter the house.

Finally, one day, he decided to strike whilst Veronica was attending the stall on her own. He kept an eye on it, and the moment it became really busy he hurried to the back of the house.

He broke in with the aid of a small crowbar which he used to pry the shutters open. He waited a few moments to hear if the noise had alerted her. Hearing nothing, he climbed in through the window. He tiptoed around the room, foraging around the clothe hooks and cupboard where some of Veronica's tunics and veils hung. He soon became frustrated; having found nothing but plain coloured veils. He started towards the window to make his exit.

As he was about to climb onto the sill, he spotted from that angle, a piece of folded cloth covered by a wooden tray containing some trinkets on a shelf near the bed. He went over to investigate. Carefully lifting the tray, he took the piece of cloth and unfolding it, soon realised that it was the veil he was looking for. The imprint of a wounded male face was evident. He quickly refolded it and put it in his tunic.

Suddenly, he heard the sound of footsteps coming into the house. The thief quickly hid behind the open bedroom door and held up his crowbar in readiness to strike. The footsteps however did not reach the bedroom but seemed instead to be descending a staircase. He could feel his heart pounding as he waited. A few moments later he could hear them ascending the stairs, and to his relief died out soon after as they were directed away from him and out of the house.

He quickly made his way back to the window and climbed out; noiselessly closing the shutters.

* * * * *

Veronica was heartbroken. She cried bitterly after Joseph of Arimathea had gone.

'Who could have taken my cherished veil? When had it been taken?' she mused.

She realised that because it had been covered by the tray, it had escaped her attention over the last few days.

In view of the fact that no one in her neighbourhood other than Sarah, Martha and their families knew of the existence of the veil, she never thought for a moment that anyone would want to steal it. She completely discounted Jesse and his family. They, she assured herself, were beyond suspicion. The whole of his family was beholding to her. She would naturally have to let them know if Joseph had not already done so.

Once she had closed the stall for the day, she lost no time in setting out for Jesse's house.

On Veronica's arrival at the Jesse residence, she was soon informed that Joseph had come earlier that day and had given them the disturbing news.

"We were expecting you Veronica," said Esther, meeting her in the hallway with a sad look in her eyes. They embraced warmly.

"Joseph who was here earlier told us all about it, He felt sure that you would be coming to see us as soon as you could close your stall."

"I am absolutely heart broken," sobbed Veronica; her lovely eyes brimming with tears.

"I feel the same way my dear," cried Ruth, suddenly entering the front hall where her daughter was welcoming Veronica. She too, quickly gave the distraught visitor a warm hug.

"We have been thinking all day," explained Ruth, "as to who could have done such a dreadful thing. We have even questioned our servants." She looked at her daughter for concurrence and taking Veronica's hand led her into the reception room where the three of them settled down on the couches.

"Sheba," continued Ruth, "was the only one of them who witnessed the miracle. But of course, all the servants got to know about it. They saw their beloved mistress suddenly cured in a way that could not be explained. We however admonished them in the strictest manner, not to speak of this to anyone outside of this house. If asked, they should say that they did not know."

Sheba was not in attendance, but being nearby, she was greatly disturbed at the sound of Veronica's voice. She wondered if her sister or mother had divulged the news to anyone. But knowing her family, she immediately dismissed the ugly thought from her mind and went on with her housework.

* * * * *

Sadoc sat in his father's shop working on a piece of leather which would end up being a belt. As he worked, his mind was searching for the best way to sell the veil.

'Who would pay a good price for it?' he asked himself.

He had placed the veil in a box which he had bought at the market and hidden it in a favourite hide-away inside an old stone wall near his home.

His original plan had been to get his girl friend to try and interest her Roman mistress in the veil as a piece of art. However the girl had found out in a roundabout sort of way, that her mistress was not particularly interested in collecting such things. He would be meeting the girl that evening and see what they could both come up with in that regard.

Money had been the cause of the theft. His gambling debts were overdue, and he desperately needed to clear them

When his work day came to an end, Sadoc told his father that he would not be going home for supper. He would be eating out with a friend instead.

Aneksi waited for her boyfriend Sadoc outside a hot food shop near the market. It was her day off, and she had spent most of the day at home with her ailing mother whom she dearly loved.

'He's always late,' she said to herself with a touch of impatience.

The bazaar beside the food shop caught her attention.

'I'll browse around in there until he arrives,' she mused.

Aneksi was pretty; small in stature; but well proportioned and graceful. Her large black eyes were vivacious and had a touch of mischief about them. She adjusted her shawl to make sure that all her long back hair was tucked under it and walked into the bazaar.

Sadoc, finally made his appearance, and soon spotted her.

"Sorry I'm late Aneksi, my father made me stay and finish a belt that I was working on," he lied. "Shall we have something to eat at the food shop, and then go for a walk?"

"Yes, that'll be fine," said Aneksi. "I shan't eat much though, I had an early supper today. I didn't know if you would be eating at home before coming."

The pair returned to the food shop and ordered their food. They sat on a nearby bench to eat.

"Have you had any new ideas as to how I can sell that veil?" asked Sadoc between bites of his bread and mutton.

"I have one possibility."

"Tell me."

Aneksi finished chewing the piece of fig pastry she had in her mouth and said.

"One of my girl friends works for the Prefect's wife. She tells me that her mistress is an avid collector of rarities."

"Pontius Pilate's wife?" asked Sadoc with some dismay.

"Yes," she answered with a smile. "My friend promised to find out if her mistress Procula is interested. Are you sure that this friend of yours still has the veil? Maybe he has already sold it."

"No. He still has it."

Sadoc had given his girl friend a false story regarding the veil to protect himself from suspicion.

"That sounds like a good idea," he said with a smile.

"How much money does your friend want for it?" asked Aneksi

"I shall find out and let you know."

Actually, Sadoc had no idea as to how much he could charge for the veil. He needed to give the matter more thought.

Having now finished eating, the pair got up and began their walk.

* * * * *

It was mid morning. Susannah was busy dressing her mistress' long fair hair. Procula sat contentedly looking at herself in the mirror as her young servant's nimble hands arranged her hair with great dexterity. She seldom had to make any comment as Susannah knew exactly the style that she liked and indeed, best suited her.

The servant suddenly remembered what her friend Aneksi had asked of her, and looking at her mistress through the mirror, asked.

"My lady, I know how you like beautiful things; particularly unusual ones."

Procula perked up at those words and smiled.

"Yes Susannah, you know me well. I have always loved beautiful things and I take great pleasure in surrounding myself with them. They add a certain spice to life and often help disperse the unpleasantness that some days bring."

The maid stopped her combing and giving her mistress a smile, said.

"I have heard through a girl friend, that a most unusual and very mysterious piece of artwork is for sale by someone she knows. She says that it is actually a veil, but the way it is painted makes it unique."

Procula put a slender finger to her lips and looked intently at her servant through the mirror.

"A veil? A painted veil? How unusual. You are sure it is not an embroidered veil?"

"She said 'painted,' my lady. I suppose if it were embroidered it would not be unusual at all."

"Precisely," agreed Procula with a flick of her hand. "Would your friend I wonder, give it to you to show me?"

"I shall ask her my lady."

Susannah returned to the combing, and Procula to her mind searching; pondering over the mysteriously rendered veil.

Sadoc sat in his room. Aneksi had relayed to him Procula's desire to see the veil.

'It's great,' he thought, 'that she is interested in it. But is it safe to let the veil out my hands? Aneksi is so innocent that she could be tricked out of it.'

The more he thought about it, the more concerned he became. He had now worked out a price for it. A price that would wipe out his gambling debts and leave him enough to enjoy himself for a while. He really had no ambition in life other than to do the minimum of work and enjoy himself as much as he could. As long as he could keep his father reasonably satisfied with his work, he had nothing to worry about. He had no plans for marriage as yet. That would not happen he felt for a while. When anything required any depth of thought however, he quickly dismissed it. The concern he was experiencing therefore was soon to be dismissed.

'I am a gambler, and this is a gamble that I must take,' he said to himself. 'The odds are with me. I shall just go ahead and get the job done. What are fifteen shekels to a woman who has so much money. It's a bargain for her, really.'

Having made up his mind, he called on Aneksi and gave her the veil.

"Now be very careful," he admonished her. "Do not show or give the veil to anyone other than Procula. My friend told me to ask for fifteen shekels for it and not a mite less."

The girl said nothing to her boyfriend but knew that she would have to give the veil to her trustworthy friend Susannah and leave the matter in her hands.

On arriving at her house, Aneksi made straight for her room and hid the veil under her bed. She wanted to have a good look at it, but first she had to prepare supper for her parents. Her father was a night watchman and would be leaving for work directly after supper. Once she had her mother tucked away in bed, she could then have a good look at the veil that Sadoc had set so much store by.

Having seen her mother to bed, Aneksi went to her room and took out the veil.

'My goodness!' she gasped opening it out on her bed. 'Why would anyone paint a face on a veil? And such an anguished face at that. But there is such kindness in that face. Who would wear such a thing? I hope the lady Procula does not get angry with Susannah for taking it to her.'

Aneksi found a small cloth bag and carefully folding the veil, placed it in the bag, ready to take with her in the morning. She would probably meet her friend in the market whilst shopping for food for their respective employers.

The following morning, just as she had expected, Aneksi bumped into Susannah and gave her the veil. The latter, on reaching the Procurator's residence, deposited her shopping in the kitchen, and made her way to her mistress's bedroom. Procula was up and waiting for Susannah to do her hair before dressing for breakfast. Her husband had already left accompanied by a centurion on some urgent matter.

Susannah greeted her mistress with a happy smile, put the bag with the veil on a couch, and going to one of the clothes cupboards, pulled out two stollas which she held up for Procula to choose from.

"You have not worn these for a number of days now my lady. I think this blue one would suit you well today. It contrasts well with your hair which would show to advantage. The silver edges will accentuate the folds and play well with a silver palla."

Procula confided in her servant's good taste and agreed to wear the ensemble that Susannah had proposed. She wondered how a girl coming from such a humble home could have such good taste and be so talented in the selection of clothes that she herself could never afford to wear. Presently, the lady's attention was captured by the bag that her servant had placed on the couch.

"What is in that bag?" she asked, with unrestrained curiosity.

"Oh. The veil that I mentioned to you the other day my lady. You wished to see it. I have as yet not had a chance to look at it."

Susannah went to the couch and took the veil out of the bag. She unfolded it and held it up with both hands displaying the image for her mistress to see. Procula recoiled, shifting in her seat...totally taken aback. The colour drained from her face, and she became deathly white. Susannah, alarmed at hermistress' reaction, and conscious of her distress, peered around the veil to see what had been painted on it. She too was stunned by the unexpected and unlikely decoration.

The lady, recovering herself, tried to put on a more normal face.

"It is magnificent," she exclaimed, the colour returning to her cheeks. "Bring it here please," she directed...Susannah obeyed.

"This is not painted on. I do not know how this image is imprinted on the veil." She felt it, turned it around, and holding it up again asked.

"How much are they asking for this? It is a fine piece of art."

"My friend said they wanted fifteen shekels for it," replied Susannah.

"It is expensive, but I shall have it." Procula went over to a small but very attractive table with a drawer. She opened the drawer, took out a little bag of coins, emptied it on the table top, counted fifteen sheckles, and gave them to Susannah. The latter, taking out another small bag that she had been given by Aneksi, put the coins inside and placed it on the couch for the time being. She then assisted her mistress with her hair and dressing and left to see to her breakfast.

As soon as Procula found herself alone, she laid the open veil on her bed and studied it. It was the exact image of the man Yeshua whom her husband had condemned to death. It showed blood dripping down his brow and face. Where had it come from, she wondered?

Her eyes filled with tears. 'It is definitely him,' she said to herself; unable to avoid the tears that suddenly ran down her lovely cheeks.

'How could his face have been imprinted on this cloth? It has not been painted on. My goodness this is inexplicable. Perhaps another miracle that he has performed. But for whom? And when?'

She was greatly disturbed. She could not fathom what had happened and wondered why it had come to her attention.

'The fates are at work in a strange way,' she told herself. 'Pontius must never see this. It would cause him great distress, and who knows what he would do. He feels so guilty about having had to sentence him to death.'

She quickly folded the veil and placed it in a small, well worn trunk underneath a pile of old clothes which she never used.

'No one will find it here,' she said to herself, and locking the trunk, made her way to the dining room for her breakfast.

* * * * *

Joseph of Arimathea knocked at the door of his friend Jesse's house and waited with a touch of impatience for a servant to open. He had a lot on his mind and urgently needed to talk to his friend.

"Good afternoon sir," greeted the smiling servant with a bow of the head.

"And to you, young woman," smiled back Joseph, stepping past her into the well-appointed hall.

"Is your master at home?"

"Yes sir, I shall announce you."

So saying, she dashed off to find Jesse whom she soon found in his office which annexed the atrium.

"I shall see him in Hannah," said Jesse walking out into the atrium to meet his friend the councillor.

The two friends embraced warmly. Joseph took a hold of Jesse's arm, and led him back into his office. Concern showed on the councillor's face.

"The Sanhedrin have heard of Esther's miraculous cure," began Joseph. "Word gets around you know. They plan on paying you a visit to investigate the fact. Providentially, you are not yet a follower of Yeshua so you will not be denying him if you need to on being cross examined. You can tell them any story that suits you best. Though it better be plausible. They will probably ask you if Yeshua or one of the Apostles did it. A cure like that must necessarily be miraculous. No physician can reconstitute flesh and muscle."

"Yes," agreed Jesse, "it was too much to expect. The moment that Esther went out of this house the whole street knew that something extraordinary had occurred, and the only one who could have done such a miracle, was Yeshua. All of Jerusalem knows that."

Jesse looked at his friend with a worried look on his face.

"We must get Veronica away from Jerusalem immediately. I may be forced into betraying her, and she must be safe by then."

"That also was another reason for my coming to see you. I shall see to it right away," assured Joseph in his determined but considerate way.

"I owe her a great debt," continued Jesse, and getting up from his chair went into a small alcove behind his office. From there he said in a louder voice.

"I shall give her enough money to get away with her son, and to set up a stall in whatever town she is taken to. Will you take it to her please Joseph?" He emerged again with a bag in his hand, which he handed to his friend.

"That is very thoughtful and generous of you, I shall do exactly as you ask," promised the councillor taking the bag.

The councillor turned to go. "I must hurry away or they may suspect that I have warned you.

The Lord Yeshua protect you. If you should need me in any way, just send for me."

At that moment Ruth appeared, and seeing Joseph, quickly went over and embraced him.

"How lovely to see you! But are you leaving already?"

"Yes, my dear. I have a most urgent matter to attend to ...Jesse will fill you in... By the way, Naomi sends her love to you all. Please visit with us soon and be sure to bring Esther with you."

With these words, Joseph parted from his friends as the ever-watchful maid stood holding the door open for him.

"Thank you, young woman," smiled the councillor walking past her and on to the street.

Joseph made his way directly to Veronica's stall in the market. He was dressed in a rather well-worn robe and tunic, and an old shawl threw a convenient shadow on his handsome features. He did not want to be identified on this particular visit.

Veronica, recognising him however, as soon as he uncovered his face, asked young Mesi to look after the stall and led Joseph into the house.

She received her visitor with joy but was greatly surprised at his attire. He followed her into the family room where she invited him to sit. She was about to offer him a refreshment, when with an earnest look in his eyes and raising his hand, he motioned for her to sit. He immediately related to her the purpose of the visit.

She was overcome with fear as she listened to the news he brought her, and the speed with which she would have to leave her home and disappear from Jerusalem to... God knows where.

"You suggest I go to Egypt?" she asked in wonder and horror with tears in her eyes.

"I would have suggested Antioch in Syria. There are quite a few of Yeshua's followers there now. But it is too far, and the sooner you are out of the country, the safer you will be. The Sanhedrin has long arms, but they are not nearly as effective in Egypt."

"Tomorrow morning just after dawn, I shall have a very trustworthy man come for you, and if you travel as a family you will not be suspect. He will stay with you until you reach your destination and sees you settled." Joseph got up.

"I must leave you now," he said with compassion in his eyes. "Pardon my attire, but I must not be seen as connected with you in any way."

Mesi arrived just then, carrying two practically empty baskets of fruit, and after greeting Joseph with a smile and a quick nod of the head, went down to the cellar to store them for the night. He had just closed the stall.

"Young man" said Joseph, meeting the boy on his return at the top of the stairs. "You and your mother are about to set out on a long journey. I want you to be a man and look after your mother. Don't protest at having to go but help her instead to do what she needs to do. She will explain everything to you."

Mesi looked at the man with an odd look in his eyes. He turned to catch his mother's eyes, which were brimming with tears, but she made no comment.

Joseph walked to the door. "Remember, you can only take what a donkey can carry. Our Lord Yeshua go with you and protect you. I and all the Apostles will be praying for you. Have courage and guard the money I have given you on Jesse's behalf. It has to last you until you can earn your own again."

Veronica and her son followed Joseph out. She asked Joseph to thank Jesse on their behalf and began to dismantle the stall which was devoid of customers as were all the other stalls. All having closed for the day. Veronica made for the kitchen and busied herself preparing their food for their last supper in that house. She explained to her son with many tears in her eyes the cause of their having to flee.

It was just after dawn next morning. There was a coded knock at her door as per Joseph's instructions. Veronica and her son were both up and having had their breakfast were ready to go. She made haste to let the visitor in. A man of about thirty-three years of age, with a pleasant face and big in stature walked in. He had kind light brown eyes and wore a big smile on his thin-lipped mouth. He greeted mother and son with a short bow of the head.

"I am Aaron," he said, looking at Veronica and ruffling Messi's mop of brown hair. "I am a friend of Joseph's and a disciple of Yeshua. I have brought two donkeys, which have to be loaded up with as much haste as we can muster.

She looked at him and motioning with her hand, led him into the family room where she had gathered all the items that she felt would be needed in the course of their journey.

"These all have to go with us," she said, turning to meet his gaze with a hopeful expression in her intelligent eyes.

"We shall soon find out how much of this we can take," he said. "One of the donkeys will only be lightly burdened as it must also bear one passenger. Either you or this young fellow," he smiled, again ruffling Mesi's hair.

'He seems to like children,' thought Veronica with some comfort.

All three got busy carrying the various pieces of baggage out, and Aaron arranged them carefully on the donkeys. Two pieces were left over. Those would have to be carried by hand.

Veronica had hidden the money around her body, and some in a belt inside Mesi's tunic.

"We have to be at the dung gate within the hour to latch on to the caravan that leaves for Bethlehem," said Aaron. "We travel as a family...You, young man, must call me father. By the way, what is your name? You have not told me. How can I act as a father if I do not know your name?" he laughed.

"My name is Mezsod, but everyone calls me Mesi," said the boy with a smile.

"I like your mother's name... Veronica is a lovely name," he said looking at her. She gave him a grateful smile.

"However, you cannot use those names for a while."

Both mother and son stared at the stranger; a questioning look in their eyes.

"No," he explained. "Your names will betray you to the Sanhedrin who will be looking for you here in Jerusalem. The guards at the gates will report back names. We must fool them. Please think quickly what names you wish to use from now on." He looked at them expectantly.

Veronica and the boy searched each other's eyes.

"I can take the name of Miriam," volunteered Veronica.

"I shall be Mathew, and you can call me Mat," said Mesi with a twinkle in his eye.

44

"Very well, family... Let's move," said Aaron. "And my new name... Is Aaron," he laughed and the other two joined in.

The caravan was preparing to leave as the fugitive trio arrived. Aaron checked in with the caravan master; paid him and turned to answer the guard who had approached them and whose business it was to check everyone leaving Jerusalem.

"What are your names?" he asked. His eyes scanning the trio.

"This is my family," began Aaron. "I am Aaron, this is my wife Miriam, and this is my son Mathew," he said pulling Messi to him.

The guard looked the three over and asked. "Are you just going as far as Bethlehem?"

"If I can find work there... Yes."

"What is your trade?"

"I am a carpenter," lied Aaron. He was, in fact, a blacksmith.

"Good luck," said the guard. And looking at Veronica, smiled and said. "Have a safe journey."

* * * * *

Two days after Veronica and party had left Jerusalem and were just starting on their way to Beersheba from Hebron, two members of the Sanhedrin were rapping at Jesse's door, as had been foretold by Joseph of Arimathea.

They were both courteously received by a maid and shown into the atrium. Jesse soon came out of his office and greeted them. One of the councillors was known to Jesse but not the other.

"Good morning gentlemen. What brings you to my house. How may I be of assistance," smiled the host, motioning them to sit on one of the couches in his sumptuously appointed atrium.

"May I offer you a refreshment?"

"No thank you," answered on of them. "We will not be staying long."

The visitors sat down and quickly came to the point.

"We are here on Sanhedrin business," began the 'unknown' councillor without so much as introducing himself. Jesse felt a little annoyed at the man's bad manners. He silently waited for the man to state their business which of course he was aware of.

"It has come to our notice," he said, turning to his comrade, "that your daughter who was a cripple from birth has been miraculously cured by some cloth with an image painted on it." He threw an enquiring look at Jesse.

"Who?" asked Jesse do have I the honour of addressing. Subtly berating the man for his bad manners.

"I am councillor Ruben, and this man I think you know, is councillor Mordecai."

Jesse smiled at Mordecai and turning to Ruben, said.

"Pleased to meet you." He rose from his couch which faced his two visitors, and walking slowly and partly sideways towards the impluvium, so as not to give them his back, said.

"Yes gentlemen, it is a truly extraordinary and amazing story. Quite unbelievable, but true non-the-less."

"Would you please expound on that," said the man he knew. "We have heard many versions of the incident, and we would like you to clear it up for us Jesse." Mordecai crossed his arms and faintly smiled.

"The cloth to which you refer," began the host, "was actually a woman's veil. It was white and had imprinted on it the face of a man who was crucified about three weeks ago, by name of Yeshua. A rabbi from Nazareth so I have heard. The veil was brought by a woman who my daughter knew, and had asked to see it simply out of curiosity for a piece of art. As you can see we have many beautiful pieces here," said Jesse waving his hand in the general direction of those displayed in the atrium. "We are a family of art lovers." The visitors nodded but remained silent.

"The woman," continued Jesse, "explained that she had handed Yeshua the veil which she had been wearing at the time, and with which he wiped his bleeding and sweating face. She said she felt great compassion for him. When she returned to the place in the crowd where she had been standing, she glanced at the veil and discovered the imprint."

At that point in the conversation, Jesse was standing directly in front of the visitors, having been pacing about as he told the story.

"Are you sure you would not like a refreshment?" he asked them again.

"No. No. Thank you. Please continue with your story," said Mordecai, both waving their hands.

The story of Esther's cure was recounted by Jesse exactly as it had happened, without any personal commentary.

As the story came to an end, Ruben asked.

"What was the woman's name?"

Jesse delayed in his answer as if trying to bring the name to mind.

"Veronica," he said.

"Do you know where we can find her? Our man Saul of Tarsus would like very much to talk to her in this regard."

"You say your daughter was a cripple from birth?" asked Mordecai interrupting his friend, whether intentionally or not his host could not determine.

"Yes," answered Jesse, "and it broke my heart to see her imprisoned in a chair all those years. She is presently nineteen years old and quite a beauty I assure you."

"Her legs must have been totally deformed?" continued Mordecai.

"Yes," said the father shaking his head with great sadness in his eyes as he remembered.

"And now, how do they look?"

"As normal and beautiful as you would ever want to see." He threw up his hands in the air.

"Thanks be to God!" he exclaimed with a big smile.

The two visitors also smiled with sincerity. The thought touched their hearts.

"Would you like to see her?" asked Jesse.

"If it is not inconvenient for her. Yes," said Mordecai.

Esther was summoned. Presently, she walked elegantly into the Atrium, much to the admiration of the two men who getting up gave her a shallow bow and a sincere smile, which she prettily returned.

"Would either of you not rejoice at such a miracle. Gentlemen?"

There was no answer to that remark, but in their hearts they realised that Jesse was right, and that there had certainly been a great miracle.

The councillors got up and made ready to leave. Ruben however on reaching the entrance hallway, turned around and asked.

"You did not tell us where we could find this woman Veronica."

Esther, who was on the point of going back into the atrium, was shocked at this question, but left it to her father to answer. He hesitated for a moment, then said.

"I believe she owns a fruit stall in a market near here. Good day gentlemen."

He saw them out, and closing the door embraced his daughter whose eyes were brimming with tears ready to overflow.

* * * * *

Veronica's house was the scene of a great purge. Sanhedrin soldiers headed by a civilian were trampling all over the abandoned house looking for a white veil with a man's face imprinted on it. The soldiers were not told whose face it was, but the civilian by name of Saul of Tarsus knew. He however kept it to himself. The house was badly damaged, as anything that looked like a hideaway was smashed with hammers. The bed mattresses were slashed, and the straw strewn all over the floor. The fruit baskets in the cellar were all emptied, and bags all torn apart. The chimney over the hearth in the kitchen was smashed with hammers, and everything breakable was broken. The stall posed no problem, but the soldiers tore it down for good measure.

A crowd had gathered outside trying to understand what was happening, and those who knew Veronica wondered what the soldiers were looking for and what had become of her and her boy.

Jacob was among the spectators awaiting the outcome of the invasion of his beloved friends' house. 'What had they done with Veronica?' he wondered.

At last the soldiers came out of the house, but Veronica was not with them. The man in civilian clothes followed his men out and stopping outside the door asked in a loud voice.

"Who knows where the woman named Veronica is? Has anyone seen her? We are here in the name of the Sanhedrin." He waited, his eyes sweeping the crowd. No one answered.

"If we find that any of you are sheltering her and her son," he said, "you will be prosecuted in the strictest way. My name is Saul of Tarsus. If any of you have any information to offer that may assist us in her capture, you will find me in the Sanhedrin offices at the temple. There will be a reward for helpful information."

He scanned the crowd once more. Then taking the soldiers with him walked away, leaving one of them behind to guard the house.

The people dispersed. Jacob found his way back to his father's meat stall with a puzzled look on his face. He had no idea as to what had occurred, or where Veronica and Mesi had gone. Then it struck him. They were looking for the veil. It could not be anything else. They had heard of Esther's cure and wanted the veil for its magic.

'I must visit Esther and tell her what has happened here,' he said to himself.

Late in the evening after having closed his stall for the day and finished his supper, Jacob went off to find Jesse's house. Everyone in the neighbourhood knew where that sumptuous house was. He had on various occasions delivered meat orders there at the kitchen door.

That evening however he knocked at the main door and waited patiently for someone to answer.

"May I help you?" The voice came from behind him.

Jacob turned to identify the voice just as the door to the house opened. A servant stood there silently awaiting developments.

"I wish to speak to Esther, I have something of importance to tell her," said Jacob, looking at the well-dressed man who had addressed him.

"I am her father. Can you tell me what it is you want to see her about?"

"Yes, I suppose I can, though she, would be particularly interested in the news that I bring; which are not good by any means."

"Please come in," said Jesse realising that the young man could be trusted.

Jacob entered the hall. The servant closed the door, smiled, and walked away.

"Bring us some refreshments Hannah, we will be in my office," said Jesse as the servant disappeared.

"Now young man. What is your name?"

"Jacob, sir. I am a butcher. I have a stall in the market. I and my family are very close friends of Veronica and Mesi her son."

"I am pleased to meet you. But how would my daughter be interested in your message?"

"She is Mesi's teacher and I also know about and have seen, the miraculous veil which I strongly suspect they were looking for," explained the visitor innocently.

Hannah appeared with a small tray and placed it on the table between the two men.

"Some watered wine? Or would you prefer some orange juice?" asked Jesse with a smile.

"I'll have some juice. Thank you."

The host poured some juice into a silver cup and handed it to his guest. He then poured some wine for himself and taking a sip, asked Jacob to tell him what he came to say to Esther.

Jacob swallowed a mouthful of his juice. He then related the invasion of Veronica's house, and the call for information regarding her whereabouts.

Jesse stroked his beard, took another sip of his wine, and looked his young visitor in the eye.

"I am shocked and sorry to hear that, and I know that Esther and my wife will be too. They are both quite fond of Veronica and young Mesi. I have no idea where they could be. You say it was the Sanhedrin that came looking for her?"

"Yes," answered Jacob. "The man in charge was a civilian by name of Saul of Tarsus."

"I think I have heard of him," said Jesse. He is apprehending many followers of that man called Yeshua, who was crucified about a month ago.

"It was Yeshua's face that was imprinted on the veil," said Jacob with conviction. "I saw it myself. Many people are saying that he was the Messiah, and that he rose from dead. The Sanhedrin do not like that it seems and are trying to silence all his followers."

"I am sorry to hear that," said Jesse with sincerity. "But I advise you to keep all you know to yourself. These are very dangerous times and one must be very discrete. I shall let Esther know what happened, and if you hear from Veronica please let us know. But in the meantime, remember what I have just told you."

Jacob took leave of Jesse with some regret at not having seen Esther, who Mesi had described as being very beautiful, and whom he had so longed to meet.

* * * * *

It was close to mid morning. Hannah, Jesse's maid answered the loud knock at the door.

"Is your master at home?" asked a well-dressed young man of medium stature. His dark beard, piercing eyes, and authoritative voice created in her a sense of caution. She looked at the man and hesitated in her answer.

"Please come in," she said, in a formal tone and with the faintest of smiles.

"I shall announce you.... Who shall I say is calling?

"Saul of Tarsus," he said dryly, stepping into the well-appointed hallway.

She directed him into Atrium.

"Please have a seat," she said, pointing to one the couches. The maid quickly walked through another small, arched hallway into the peristyle where the family were sitting having a conversation.

They all looked at Hannah expectantly. The knocking had been heard throughout the house and Jesse in particular did not like its tone.

"Well Hannah. Who is it? And what is his business?"

"It is a man by name of Saul of Tarsus. He told me nothing else." She made an enquiring gesture with her eyes and mouth and awaited a reply from her master.

"Thank you, Hannah," said Jesse, and getting up, went in search of the stranger. That name he knew was familiar in connection with some high-handed persecution the man was carrying out against the followers of Yeshua. He therefore braced himself for a fight as he walked into the atrium and greeted the man with an enquiring look.

"Good morning," greeted Jesse. The visitor got up and repeated the greeting with a slight bow of the head and formal expression on his face.

"How can I help you?" asked Jesse, himself adopting a look of formality. He sat down opposite Saul and motioned him to sit.

"May I offer you a refreshment?"

"No thank you. I have come on a very serious Sanhedrin matter, and I have a few questions for you to clarify for us." He placed his hands together and threw a steely glance at his host.

Jesse stroked his light brown beard, met his opponent's eyes with resolve, and gesticulated with his hand for him to continue.

"As you may know, we raided the house and stall of the woman Veronica the day before last and found that she had fled.

The host nodded. "Word gets around."

"We feel very strongly that the woman was warned of our intended raid, allowing her to escape." Saul threw another steely look in the direction of Jesse and continued.

"The matter had been kept from everyone, except the councillors in attendance at that meeting, who naturally being free from suspicion, left us to suspect someone on the outside."

"And I take it, that you suspect me," Jesse met Saul's eyes with defiance.

"Since you say so yourself. Yes!"

"Suspicion is not enough. I hope you can furnish some proof. Even witnesses I would suggest."

Saul realised late, that he had moved too quickly. Unlike others that he had dealt with, this man was a confident and self-assured person. He should have been approached in a more cunning manner.

"Are you ready to make a formal accusation against me?" asked the host. If so, I would advise you to arm yourself with the best legal council you can find, because I, shall certainly be well represented."

Saul rose up to go. But Jesse was not finished.

"Do you have a legal directive from the Sanhedrin authorising this investigation? If you have such a document, you should have shown it to me the moment you walked into my house. Please show it to me now," said Jesse, knowing full well the man did not have one.

There was no answer.

"I shall find out before this afternoon passes, if indeed you have been authorised to harass me. And, who gives you the authority to be raiding law abiding citizens in their own homes in any case," said the angry host, and calling for Hannah who promptly appeared. He gave Saul another stern look and instructed her to show him out.

When Saul had gone, Jesse went into his office to think.

'I have to continue to be aggressive with this man,' he said to himself. He is a committed and fanatical trouble maker. His hatred for Yeshua and his followers is without precedent. He will go as far as he is allowed, to do as much damage as he can to many innocent people who are intimidated by him.' His throat felt dry. He called out for Hannah once more and asked her to bring him some juice.

'I must go quickly to the Temple and see if I can find Gamaliel or perhaps Joseph,' he said to himself.

Hannah placed a tray with a small pitcher and a cup in front of him. He poured himself some juice which he quickly drank.

"Thank you, Hannah. Please tell your mistress that I am going to the Temple on business and I might be late for supper."

He was about to exit the entrance hallway when Esther came to him.

"Has that man brought disturbing news?" she asked.

"Yes, somewhat my love. Not to worry, I am on my way to deal with it right now."

He gave his daughter a kiss and left.

Jesse made his way to the temple library where he sometimes met Joseph, or Gamaliel who was also a good friend of his. He walked into the well used room and looked for his friends. The librarian who knew him came to greet him. He told him that Joseph had been in and gone, and Gamaliel might yet show up. As the librarian spoke, he saw a man's head peering into the room, and quickly pulling away after looking in Jesse's direction.

At that moment, Gamaliel appeared.

The friends embraced as they greeted each other and soon found a free bench in a corner of the room where they could quietly chat without being disturbed. Jesse related the mornings events at his house and waited to hear Gamaliel's reaction.

"That fellow," began Gamaliel with a nod of his great bald head, "is taking a lot of liberties with these persecutions that he carries on against those people. The Apostles of Yeshua, are not being molested at the moment, as they are altogether too popular with the people. But this man bullies all those that he can take advantage of." He looked around the room, as if checking to see if anyone was listening and continued in his low and well modulated tone of voice.

"He has absolutely no mandate from the Sanhedrin for such action," he stated with certainty. "However, some of the councillors who despised the Nazarene, encourage him and cover up for him. We do not pay him a single mite, so he does not work for us. You certainly have a case against him for unauthorized harassment and even for civil disturbance. I do not think he will trouble you further. You dealt with the situation well. There are quite a few of us in the Sanhedrin that do not agree with the measures that are being taken against these followers of Yeshua.I shall have a talk with him. He was for quite a while a pupil of mine. He is very smart but tends to be somewhat over-dedicated when he believes in something."

Gamaliel scratched his head and said.

"I have already told him and others, that if this Yeshua affair, which is certainly extraordinary, is a political thing, it will come to nothing. However, if it is something that God is doing, it will gain force no matter how anyone tries to oppose it. He claimed I am told, that his kingdom was not of this world, so why are they persecuting his followers? Neither Herod nor Caesar are being threatened. They are not taking up arms. As I said. There are quite a few of us here that are not happy with the way this whole thing has been handled and is now developing. But we are in the minority I'm afraid."

Jesse reached for his learned friend's hand, and squeezing it, thanked him for his good advice and invited him over to his house.

"Give my regards to Ruth and Esther. I shall see you all soon," said Gamaliel as Jesse walked away.

* * * * *

Gaza had now been left behind, and the caravan that carried with it Aaron, Veronica and Mesi, was about to enter Egyptian soil, or more accurately, 'Egyptian sand.'

The fugitive trio were travel weary and longing to find a resting place that might give their long and uncertain journey a respite, even if only for a short time. Their destination was now Heliopolis where there were campsites to be found. There they hoped to rest for a couple of days before continuing on their journey. From there, the caravan master had told them, they could take a riverboat down to Alexandria where work was plentiful in that great cosmopolitan city.

Veronica had been very adept at shopping for food and assessing their dietary needs during the trip. They had never run out of food or drink, which she bought at the three major towns they had passed. The guarded caravans which allowed them to travel in relative safety had been quite large. In particular, the one that took them from Beersheba to Gaza which proved to be a long and sometimes disorienting crossing; sand storms often obliterating the road. It took experienced camel masters to steer a true course. For that reason, they charged more for that particular run.

The seventh day of their final desert crossing found Aaron and his two dependents entering the much-lauded campsite in Heliopolis. The last phase of the desert part of their journey had passed once again without incident, and the thankful trio rented a tent a little larger than their need in which to stay for the next couple of days. Aaron slept at the front of the tent and left the remaining space for mother and son. Their food was cooked at a communal spit, and public ablutions were made available to them. There was a food shop, and a corral for their animals with grain and water provided. These amenities were at extra cost, but the fees were reasonable.

The campsite was very well kept. There was a central pool with palm trees bordering it. The tents, laid out in groups, were separated by flower beds or plants. All these embellishments were designed to give the weary travellers a feeling of welcome to that vibrant city.

"It is quite lovely here," commented Veronica, as they sat eating their cena (supper) outside their tent. She smiled at Aaron who was busy with his mutton chop.

"You could stay in Heliopolis if you are tired of travelling," pointed out Aaron. "We would have to stay here much longer than just two days though whilst you found a stall to buy in one of the markets."

"I don't think I would feel too safe here." said Veronica wiping her mouth. "We are too close to Judea. They might easily find me if they come looking for me."

She looked enquiringly at her protector. "Do you think they are presently searching for me?"

"Yes, but only in Jerusalem. I doubt whether they consider the veil to be such a threat to them that they would launch a country-wide search. I wish they would believe that the veil was stolen from you. But they would think you were lying, and who knows what they would do to find out."

"I dread the thought," muttered Veronica with a little shudder.

"Will you be leaving us soon now that we are relatively safe?" she asked with some trepidation.

She had grown used to him. Mesi really liked and respected him, and he, having taken a liking to the boy, had behaved just as a true father would behave. He was pleasant and amusing, and he had taught them much about Yeshua and how his followers were expected to live under his commandments.

'Yes, they would miss him,' she told herself.

"I shall not leave until I see you settled. "He took a drink of his newly purchased wine and met her eyes. "I am in no hurry to go back in any case."

"That's great!" cheered Mesi. "Maybe you will take me fishing in the sea when we get to Alexandria."

Aaron had told Mesi that Alexandria was a beautiful city by the sea. And that as a boy, his father sometimes took him fishing in the sea of Galilee.

"The Mediterranean Sea," explained Aaron with a smile, "is much much bigger than the Sea of Galilee. One can sail on it from Alexandria, all the way to Rome or even as far as Hispania.

Two days later, the trio was sailing down the Nile on their way to Alexandria. That typically Egyptian way of travel was new to them. They were well entertained by the activities unfolding on both sides of the river. Mesi's questions kept the pair of adults busy as they themselves were unsure of many of the things that caught their attention in that new and unfamiliar land.

Aaron marvelled at the way the traffic flowed safely up and down the river; the boats and barges keeping clear of each other as they floated in either direction towards their destinations. Veronica was enthralled at the endless chain of people that lined the banks of the river performing their varied chores. The children, all of a darker completion than Judean children, played happily in the water, whilst their mothers busily washed clothes which they lay along the grassy banks to dry in the scorching sun.

The wharf at Alexandria where their boat finally docked was swarming with people awaiting its arrival. A portable ramp was passed down to the boat's crew who quickly locked it into place. The disembarking commenced with urgency. Passengers without animals went off first, followed by those with animals. They all used the same ramp.

Aaron led one donkey and Mesi the other. Veronica carrying their hand bags, followed.

The crowd opened a path for them, and soon they found themselves in a little square where they stopped to decide which way to go. One of the ship's crew had given them directions to a campsite nearby, and they walked away in that direction. Soon however, they realised that they were lost. The river was far behind. Aaron, addressing a passerby in Greek, asked for directions and was told that the camp was near the river. They had obviously missed it.

"Where can we find a house for rent?" asked Aaron of the man, as the thought entered his head. Veronica looked at him with surprise in her eyes.

"I believe there are some houses for rent in that street over there," said the man pointing in its direction. Aaron thanked him and crossed over into the indicated street. Sure enough there were notices on the windows of two of the houses.

"Which shall we enquire about first?" asked Aaron turning to Veronica.

"This first one I suppose," she answered after scrutinizing both facades carefully. "We will not know until we go inside."

Aaron suspected that the neighbour would know how to contact the owner, and so he knocked on the door of the adjoining house. As he had suspected, the neighbour was well versed in the house's layout and explained that it had two bedrooms, a family room, a kitchen, and an outdoors toilet in the back garden, where there was also a stable which would accommodate two horses.

"What do you know of the other house two houses over there?" asked Veronica who had been listening and pointed at the them. "We would prefer three bedrooms," she told the woman.

"Oh. Try the one on the opposite side at the end of the street. I think that one has three bedrooms."

"They thanked the woman and walked further up to look at the house. Again, the neighbour described the house, and confirmed that it had the three required bedrooms. Aaron asked the cost of the rent. It proved to be affordable if they both pooled their resources. After a quick inspection, they took it. It had a large backyard, an indoor ablution, and a well-ventilated toilet just a few steps into the back garden. The stable, also in the back garden, provided shelter for two horses and good storage space.

They paid their first month's rent, and having been given the key to the house, quickly moved in.

By now they had all got used to their new names which they continued to use at least until they felt safer. The house was very scantily furnished, and Veronica was not happy about using the existing bed mattresses. Since the day was still young, they unloaded their belongings, and taking the donkeys with them, set out to buy the required three mattresses, and a few other things including food. By supper time, they were back with the new acquisitions, and made ready to start a provisional new life.

A couple of weeks had passed. The trio were now well acquainted with their neighbourhood and had looked at a couple of nearby market places in search of a vacant stall. They realised however that their neighbourhood was noisy at night and brawling in the street was a common occurrence. They soon attributed that, to being fairly close to the river which brought many drunken sailors and trouble makers.

In the course of the next month they discovered a better part of the city. The people dressed better, the streets were lit at night with torches at almost every street corner, and there were better houses and buildings. The price of renting was higher also. This caused them some concern since they had a limited amount of money, and some had already been spent.

"I think," said Aaron one day. "That I am going to look for some work in a blacksmith shop in the area that we like. I've noticed a couple of them already in that vicinity.

"But you will be leaving as soon as I buy my stall," said Veronica, with what seemed more like question than a simple statement.

"I am running short of money," he said with a tilt of the head, "and a bit of work will help. It will also give me something to do."

Veronica was delighted, but she controlled her emotions. She had grown to like this quiet and gentle man. She would greatly miss his company. He was also teaching Mesi to read Greek, even though he himself could not write it. She could read a little, but in Aramaic, and she could only write numbers, and do some very simple arithmetic. She had had to learn that, to price, weigh, and count her fruit. Aramaic and Hebrew were not used in Egypt. Egyptian, Greek and Latin were the everyday languages.

"I am glad to hear that you are thinking of staying with us a little longer," she said with a big smile. Mesi looked on happily.

"That stall," said Veronica tentatively, is beginning to feel out of reach.

"You still have most of your money, don't you?" asked Aaron,

"Yes. But the fact that we must live away from the stall, makes things more difficult. Here it is difficult enough to find a vacant stall never mind a house nearby to make it practical."

"Well, it's too soon to give up. We shall keep our eyes open," said Aaron.

A month went by very quickly. Veronica had still not found a stall. Aaron however was now gainfully employed with a blacksmith in that better neighbourhood. His employer was an older man who had two sons, but neither of them had wanted to follow their father's trade. The man now in his late sixties, was tiring, and the people who worked for him were lazy. He was quite frustrated and unhappy.

The business had been started by his grandfather, and so it had been established for many years. Aaron impressed the man with his skill and enthusiasm. The latter very soon got rid of his two lazy helpers and employed the Judean giving him a very good salary.

"I have a strong feeling," said Aaron one night to Veronica, that Demetrius (the man was of Greek ancestry), is going to retire soon, and will be looking to sell his business."

"We can buy it then," said Veronica impulsively. "Oh," she gasped, covering her mouth with her hand. "I'm sorry, I had no right to say that."

Mesi was asleep in his room, the two of them were sitting in the living room passing away the time. Aaron moved closer to her, looked into her eyes, and taking her hand said.

"When my Rebecca died, I promised myself that I would not look at another woman again. For eight years now, I have lived up to my resolution. But now that fate or providence has brought us together and allowed me to play the role of father to Mesi, I realise what great joy you have both brought into my stale life."

She did not pull her hand away. Instead, she drew closer and laid her head on his shoulder.

He looked down at her lovingly, gently raised her chin and kissed her luscious red lips tenderly. She returned his kiss ardently; laid her head back on his shoulder; and with tears in her lovely eyes, groaned.

"This is lovely, but impossible. I told you why my husband left me. He is probably very much alive. Not that I wish him any harm, but as long as he lives I am a married woman, and as such prohibited by our law from marrying you, as you well know. If we were to live together as husband and wife in its proper and complete way. We would be guilty of adultery."

"I know my dear," he said giving her a little squeeze. "My new religion as a disciple of Yeshua, also prohibits adultery. The Mosaic law holds good for us too. I spent many hours with the Apostles in the room where they were hiding, and they instructed a number of us in our new faith in Yeshua the Christ. There was a woman who had been caught in adultery, they said, and she was to be killed. She was brought before Yeshua by the Pharisees to see if they could trap him in his speech. They told him that by the law, she was to be stoned to death...What did he think should be done? Yeshua remained seated, but silently began to write with his finger on the sand at his feet. Presently, without looking up, he said...'*Let him who is without sin among you be the first to cast a stone at her.*'

Slowly, they all dispersed. Yeshua then asked the woman where those who were going to condemn her had gone. She replied that she did not know. *'Neither do I condemn thee. Go thy way and sin no more.'* he said.

"Oh, what a beautiful story," said Veronica.

"There are many more stories of wonderful things that our Lord Yeshua did and said," smiled Aaron. "I was told that soon they will be written down so as not to be forgotten, and everyone will be able to read them." His eyes gleamed with enthusiasm.

"We shall continue to live together as a family," he continued, and if any one asks, we shall say that we are married. However, we will hopefully, and by the grace and strength that God will give us, live as brother and sister until He deems otherwise."

"Do you think that the Apostles of Yeshua, will come here sometime?" asked Veronica with hope in her heart.

"Who knows?" he replied. "If you wish to be baptised however, and become a true disciple of Yeshua, I can do that for you. Even though I am only a follower, I am empowered to baptise you in the absence of an ordained priest. It could be quite some time before one comes to Egypt."

Veronica did not need much encouraging. Both she and Messi were duly baptised by Aaron and so became, along with a few other fugitive families, pioneers of the Christian faith in Egypt.

CHAPTER THREE

ROME

Pilate's tenure as Prefect of Judea had come to an end in an unpleasant manner. He had been ordered back to Rome by Vitellius, the governor of Syria, following an incident in Samaria, under Pilate's command which the Jews had strongly condemned and appealed their case to Rome.

Procula and her hapless husband were back in the Eternal City. It was the reign of Caligula; the emperor Tiberius having recently died.

She was glad to be back home. Her husband had never been popular in Judea, and she hoped that he might be able to reorder his life and continue to advance his career in Rome.

The political climate there however, had become most unpredictable. The emperor displayed great inconsistency in his behaviour and policies, and though he did not prosecute Pontius, he did not offer him any new post to fill. He had met with the emperor but once. She had not accompanied him on that occasion, but it was evident from what Pontius had told her, that Caligula had shown no warmth in the meeting. He had instead asked him to take some time for himself, and informed him that when he, the emperor felt that there was a post that would warrant his Judean expertise, he would summon him.

Pilate was not happy with the situation. A politician not constantly in the eyes of the public would soon be forgotten. However, being aware of the emperor's inconsistent moods and cruel traits, he resigned himself to his temporary plight and awaited better times.

Procula, who soon found herself at home in a villa near Pyrgi that her father had given them on their return, began to get her new house in the country in order, and tried to assist her somewhat distracted husband in getting over his ever more frequent grey moods. He was subject to nightmares that were taking a toll on his health. As a result of this, and after much consideration, she decided to look for the veil which she had hidden in the little trunk that held her old clothes. It was she presumed, still among some of the luggage that she had not as yet given her attention to.

She made her way to a room at the back of the house and taking a servant with her, began to review the pieces of luggage which were stored there.

To her great disappointment, she could not find the little trunk.

"Is all my luggage here?" she asked, turning to her servant.

"As far as I know my lady, it should all be here," answered the servant; her eyes scanning the room.

"Great distress befell Procula, as she came to the realisation that the trunk with the veil which she had so treasured was not there.

'I should have brought it with me in my personal baggage,' she upbraided herself. 'I was so scared of Pontius accidentally finding it. I should have risked it. Oh! what a terrible loss.'

She walked around the room once more; her eyes scrutinizing every piece of luggage.

'It must have stayed behind in Caesarea or even Jerusalem,' she silently lamented.

'Or, maybe it stayed on board the ship? I shall have to try and contact the naval authorities at Puteoli ...But how? I cannot ask Pontius to enquire. He will wonder why I would worry about one small, insignificant trunk, that he knew kept only my left- over garbs.'

Procula dismissed the servant and walked out into the garden to ponder over her great loss. She tried to think when she had seen it last and where it could possibly have gone.

'It could perhaps cure Pontius of his terrible nightmares. Who knows? Susannah said something about it being miraculous as I seem to recall.'

* * * * *

Susannah had just returned to the empty Procurator's house in Caeserea. She made her way to her lady's bedroom just to have a last look and see that nothing had been forgotten. Perhaps even to reminisce over her close to eleven years in her lady Procula's service, which she had really enjoyed.

The room was bare except for a small trunk which contained what she knew to be Procula's old clothes, and which she had purposely kept back. She felt it would only encumber her mistress on her long sea trip to Rome with garments that she would not want. She tried to open it. It was locked.

'Why would she have locked this old thing?' Susannah asked herself.

'I better get the watchman to open it for me... No. I shall do it myself.'

She went off to find something to open it with. The kitchen was still well equipped. It had been kept in a serviceable state awaiting the house's next tenant. There were many knives on a shelf, and she, choosing the strongest one, and a meat cleaver, took them back to the bedroom.

After a few tries at prying the lid, the skimpy lock gave way and she opened the trunk. As expected, it was full of old but very valuable and attractive clothes. She began to pull them out and examine them one by one.

'These are all much too classy and large for me.' she muttered to herself as she unfolded each one and held it up to look at it. Just as she was getting to the bottom of the trunk, she pulled out a large piece of white cloth and unfolded it.

"My goodness!" she gasped aloud. "The veil!"

Looking around the room to make sure that she was alone, she folded it up once more and placing it on the inside of the open lid of the trunk. She continued to fold all the clothes she had taken out, carefully putting them back again.

Tucking the veil under her arm, she went in search of the man who was looking after the house. She encountered him as he was entering the peristyle.

"There is a trunk in my lady's bedroom with some of her old clothes," she said.

"I had to force the lock, as I did not have a key. My brother in law will be picking it up later today or, perhaps tomorrow. Please show him where it is."

The man nodded his head in ascent.

She thought of selling the contents of the trunk at the market. It would bring in a good bit of money for her, and she felt sure that her mistress would not have minded. Though Procula would certainly be distraught at having lost the veil.

'What was she going to do with that? How was she going to send it to her mistress?' she mused.

"I'm off now," she said, with a wave of her hand and made her way home.

A soothing breeze was blowing in from the sea. Susannah stood on the terrace of her mother's house, watching the sun set and thinking of the veil.

'Who can I trust to deliver it to my mistress in Rome?' she mused. 'I do not even know where they live. They may not even be in Rome. Perhaps I better keep it. If she ever contacts me in the future, I shall then give it to her.'

Susannah had been able to dispose of the trunk and clothes. She had made a good profit from the sale. Her preoccupation now was to find another prestigious family to serve.

Caesarea was home to a good many wealthy Roman families and she was confident of finding employment soon. Procula, had given her a good gift of money and a scroll lauding her abilities and excellent character which would assist her greatly in finding a position to her liking.

As expected, Susannah soon found herself employed; thanks to the glowing references contained in the scroll that Procula had given her. Her new employer was the wife of a senior centurion who held a high post in the Roman Legion stationed there in Caesarea.

The new mistress' name was Aemelia. She was a handsome woman of average height, slightly on the plump side, with very light brown hair and large well lashed, kind eyes, which by their vivacity, diverted attention from her somewhat wide bridged but otherwise well shaped nose. Her mouth, a trifle on the large side, boasted a good set of teeth advantageously displayed when she smiled.

Susannah found her new mistress less demanding than Procula, but more reserved. She put it down to as yet, a lack of familiarity with her. There were two other servants in the house with whom she began to acquaint herself. Rachel the cook, and Fina; a short but very buxom Greek woman (actually a slave), who took on the more arduous tasks of the household.

There were three children in the family. A boy, six years old named Julius, and two girls; Priscilla, aged five and Meli, three.

Young Julius was an independent little boy, though most endearing when he took a liking to someone. He soon took to the diminutive but well proportioned and handsome Susannah who became very fond of him, and of his little sisters. She loved children but was as yet unmarried.

Gabinius, the father, was often away on account of having to move at a moment's notice to take command of some military assignment or other. There were continual minor disturbances in effervescent Judea that had to be defused before they erupted into more serious situations.

The children were always accompanied by either their mother or a servant whenever they left the house. Rachel often took the two older ones with her to the market to shop for food. At other times, Susannah or Aemelia herself would take them sight seeing or to a park nearby. Most of the time however, they played in the garden which being fairly large, gave them plenty of room to run around.

One morning, whilst Rachel was shopping in the market, accompanied by the two older children Julius wandered off by himself. Priscilla remained at the cook's side, as usual, absorbed in what the latter was buying. On leaving the stall where she shopped, Rachel, not seeing Julius, called out to him. He would normally be nearby and return at her call. She grew concerned when he did not appear,

Julius! Julius! she called again, trying to make herself heard over the noise of the marketplace. There was no answer. With Priscilla on one hand and bag in the other, she began to search the immediate area.

'I'll bet he's is in the engraver's stall,' she said to herself with some exasperation. 'He likes to look at the daggers and swords that the man engraves.'

To her complete distress, she realised on reaching the stall which was close by, that he was not there.

"Have you seen the boy that sometimes comes to watch you work?" she hopefully asked the man.

"You mean young Julius?" said the man.

"Yes," she answered. "His father is Centurion Gabinius, and I work for him."

"No. I'm afraid not. Perhaps you better contact the soldiers on guard over there," he said, and pointed at three soldiers who were talking among themselves nearby.

Rachel lost no time in alerting them. They, learning who the boy was, immediately dispersed and began their search. After a while, not finding the boy by the description given them, they reported the matter to the centurion on duty. A wider search was immediately put into operation.

The cook hurried home with Priscilla. Susannah was in the atrium doing some dusting and keeping an eye on Meli who was trying some dusting of her own. On hearing the knock, Susannah went to answer the door.

"Master Julius is gone!" blurted out a tearful and distraught Rachel, rushing towards the peristyle and calling: "My Lady! My Lady!"

"What is it?" enquired Aemelia, coming out of her bedroom.

"Master Julius is gone. I looked all around for him. I have the soldiers looking for him."

Rachel flopped down on a cushion and covered her face with her hands as she cried in anguish.

The mother was shocked at the disturbing news. She too gave way to tears, as she considered the terrible things that could overtake her boy. His father had many enemies in Judea, as was incumbent on his position as a Roman commander.

"If only your master were home," she said with distress, looking at the servants who had collected around her. All were crying. The girls, impressed by their elders, burst into tears.

There was a knock at the front door. Susannah rushed to open. All made for the door; hope stirring in their frightened hearts.

A tall young tribune accompanied by another soldier stood in the doorway, helmets in hand awaiting to be invited in. Aemelia, arriving at the door, waved them in.

"We are combing the town looking for your son," said the tribune. "We will find him soon I'm sure. Perhaps he is playing a game with us to see if we can find him. Please don't worry, all will be well. He will be learning a good lesson when the Centurion returns home," smiled the tribune.

"How I hope you are right," said the mother wiping her eyes and smiling at the men.

"We shall bring him home as soon as we catch him," assured the tribune as the two of them left.

* * * * *

Julius struggled with the bonds that tied his hands and feet. His mouth was gagged with a piece of dirty cloth that almost made him sick. His eyes were also covered, and he had no idea where he was. The last thing he remembered was the market. He had been on his way to look at the daggers that the engraver usually displayed. He wanted his father to give him one for his birthday. His head hurt badly.

'I must have a huge bump on my head,' he thought, as he cried silently feeling sorry for himself and much afraid as he contemplated his position. 'I have been stolen. I wonder what they are going to do to me? The soldiers must be out looking for me. I hope they find me soon.'

He continued to work at getting his hands free, but he was just getting tired, and the rope would not give way. His wrists were sore and raw. He felt something run over his foot and quickly got up realising that it was a rat. He jumped up and down hoping either to step on it or frighten it away.

"What's all the noise in there?" roared a harsh male voice.

Julius froze with fear as the owner of the terrible voice approached.

The voice spoke again. "I'm going to free your hands, but if you dare to reach for your blindfold, I'll cut off your hand. Do you hear me?"

"Yes... My wrists are sore," cried Julius, stretching out his hands for the man to loosen them. He gave a sigh of relief as the man removed the rope and tucked his sore hands and wrists under his armpits for warmth and consolation.

"I suppose you're thirsty and hungry," said the man.

"Yes," acknowledged the boy. "Please give me some food and something to drink."

"May I feel my head. I think I must have a big bump. It's very sore."

"No! Just keep your hands where they are. Remember what I told you."

The man then tiptoed away for a few moments. He returned very quickly with a hood over his head. He had forgotten to put it on when he first went to check on the boy.

"Now I shall take your blindfold off and give you something to eat."

The boy was much relieved to hear this and waited anxiously. But the man went away again. Presently, he returned with something that he put down on what sounded like a table. Finally, the blind fold was removed. Julius was shocked and frightened to see a hooded man in front of him. He was of medium height but had broad shoulders and strongarms. He wore soiled, rugged clothes; a grey tunic and a dark brown robe. His feet were big and dirty, and though he wore sandals, Julius noticed that he was missing the small toe of the right foot. For a boy so young, Julius was very observant.

The promised food, consisting of a small loaf of bread; a piece of cheese; two figs; and a cup of water, sat on a bench beside him. There was a lighted torch stuck in an iron ring up on the wall. To his disgust, there was a dirty cushion close to the food that had been placed on the bench on which he sat.

The place was a cave. The floor was sandy, and in one corner lay a square piece of wood with a handle. A cracked earthenware jug stood near it. There was no door that he could see, but Julius was aware of a continuation of the cave curving around a blind corner. It too, was illuminated by lighted torches he thought.

After having finished his meal, Julius' hands were tied once again; though this time not as tightly. His wrists were still sore, but he resolved not to cry.

'My Daddy when he was a boy, would not have cried if he had been in my place,' he sternly said to himself.

The man left him and went around the corner to his part of the cave. Julius assumed that it must be night time. There were no openings in the wall anywhere to let him know otherwise.

He hopped over to the bench and lay down, but he could not put his face on the dirty cushion; it stank. He threw it on the ground and laid his head on the bare wood. The bump on his head was too painful to lie on, so he lay on his side and tried to sleep.

Soon, the sound of snoring could be heard coming from the other part of the cave.

Julius wondered whether he could untie himself and sneak out as the man slept.

'But I do not know where the door is,' he mused. "And what about the bolt. I might not be able to reach or slide it.'

Having talked to the man, he felt that as long as he did not try to escape, he would not be harmed. He was still scared however, and did not understand why the man had taken him away from his family? He could think of no reason. He began to dose off. Presently, he fell asleep.

"Wake up boy!"

The words snapped Julius out of his deep sleep, and having forgotten that his hands were tied, he punched his nose as he tried to rub his eyes.

"Ouch!" he yelped.

"Ha ha!" laughed the hooded man. He removed the bonds from the boy's hands and then from his ankles. "I'll take these off too," he said, "cause you're not going anywhere."

Julius winced as he tried to stand. His feet were swollen, and they hurt when he put his weight on them.

"Try to walk around slowly, they'll stop hurting after a little while."

The boy stood up but sat down again. "They hurt a lot," he cried." They feel funny, as if needles were pricking them. Agh!"

"Take your time, you have all day to walk around," he said. "You can't go anywhere. The stone door to the cave is heavy and you can't move it. I'm leaving you some food and water in there." He pointed to the other part of the cave that Julius had not yet seen.

"Why did you take me away from my family?" asked the boy anxiously as he got up again and tried to stay on his little feet.

"I owe your father a debt," he growled. "And I'm about to collect it. You can pee in that hole there." He pointed to the wooden lid with the handle.... Just don't fall into the hole. You'll never get out."

So, saying he left the boy and made his way to his own side of the cave where he collected a number of things he needed and got ready to leave.

"Come here young pup!" he shouted.

Julius slowly made his way to the where the man awaited him. His feet were getting back to normal and the discomfort had almost stopped. He beheld a much larger room lit by two oil lamps. There was a bigger wooden bench than the one he had slept on, and it had a dirty mattress. A table with an oil lamp on it was covered with pieces of parchment cut-outs. On the side of the room there seemed to be a corridor and it was filled with big burlap bags full of something or other. To his amazement, he could see some wooden steps leading nowhere. He glared in wonder at the oddity. He could not see a door.

"So you're wondering where the door is?" laughed the man from under his hood. "I'll show you since you'll never be able to open it."

"Now, listen to me before I go," said the man. I'm leaving you food and drink. It has to last you all day. I won't be back till tonight, so if you eat it all at once you're going to go hungry the rest of the day." He showed the boy a little crack in the rock where he could see out.

"If you look through this crack, you can tell when it gets dark."

He then took a number of empty bags that were stacked nearby and walked up the steps. He put the bags down on the short landing, and then to Julius' utter surprise, took hold of two iron handles embedded in the stone, and using both hands, rolled the stone entrance over.

As the daylight came bursting through, the boy covered his eyes with his hands. A few moments later when he removed his hands from his eyes again, the stone was being rolled back from the outside. The man was gone.

Cleophas, (for that was the abductor's name), climbed down the rocky hill to his hut where he normally lived and where he kept his donkey and cart. He had discovered the cave sometime time back and had reshaped a large stone that was nearby and fashioned it into a cover for the mouth of the cave. He made it similar to those used to seal off tombs, but rougher looking so that it would blend into the rocky landscape and become indiscernible.

He had been planning the kidnapping for two years. The rag business, which he had grown quite good at, allowed him by virtue of the many times that he had entered and exited the city without ever having given the guards any problems, to win their confidence. As a result, they never examined his bags other than occasionally squeezing some of them. The guards all knew him by name and never paid him much attention.

He had smuggled the unconscious boy by covering him with the many bags that he carried. The ransom money would leave the city in the same manner.

Cleophas could not write but could read Greek. He had been collecting scrap parchments written in that language and cutting words to allow him to convey his ransom demands and directions. He had laboriously cut out each required word, and making up crude sentences, pasted them with a paste of flour and water onto a new piece of parchment which he had acquired for that purpose. Every step of his dastardly kidnapping plan had been cleverly and meticulously worked out. His act of revenge on Centurion Gabinius was to be a masterpiece in planning and execution. Ten years in the galleys had given him much time to think and his hatred for his prosecutor to ferment.

He had built the shack he lived in at the foot of the little hill that housed the cave. The whole area surrounding his hut was strewn with the rubble of old demolished buildings, stones and architectural waste, which had been dumped there when the new city was built by Herod some years earlier.

The second phase of the operation, namely the actual collection of the ransom money that he was going to demand was the riskiest part. It would require nerves of steel and a very cool head to carry it off. There was only himself to accomplish it. A decoy or diversion he felt, would greatly assist in the execution of his plan, but such manoeuvres would require a partner, and that was out of the question. In his warped mind, this was his war, and he would fight it himself.

Julius had made himself at home in his captor's absence. He had eaten some of the food that Cleophas had left for him in a wooden box with a lid protecting it from the rats. There was a small covered pitcher with water taken from a large lidded earthenware tub that sat in a corner near the door. Having finished his breakfast he began to take a good look at the cave to see if there was another larger crack that perhaps he could squeeze through.

There were no other cracks in that main part of the cave and going back into the area where he had been sleeping, he diligently examined the cave wall there, but to no avail. He went to where the hole in the floor was located and carefully pulled the lid to one side and taking further care, relieved his insistent bladder.

He returned to the main area again and sat down on a stool by the table. Noticing the pile of parchment clippings, he began to examine them.

Julius was a proficient reader. He had a good tutor who daily taught him to read and write in Greek and Latin. He was soon immersed in the process of deciphering the intent of all those clippings. However, much as he tried, he could not make any sense of them. He took a break, and as a diversion, went up the wooden steps, stood on the little platform, and carefully examined the stone door. He grabbed the iron handles and tried with all his strength to move the stone. It would not budge.

'He was right,' he said to himself. 'I don't have enough strength to move it.'

He gave up and sat down again to examine the clippings once more. He noticed that whole words had been cut out. There was a whole bag of parchments under the table. He pulled it out and taking some out, began to amuse himself by reading them. They dealt with all sorts of subjects. Some fascinated him. He became engrossed in them and time sped by.

Once again, he rested. He was thirsty and hungry. On examining the intensity of light through the crack, he guessed it must be around noon. Going back to the stool, he pushed the parchments off the table, took some more food from the box, and pouring himself some water, began to eat what he felt was his lunch. As he ate, his eyes fell once more on the stack of bags that were stored in an adjoining alcove.

'My goodness,' he mused, 'what a lot of parchments he collected.'

Having nothing else that captured his attention, he finished his lunch, and taking the oil lamp from the table, he approached the smaller cave where the mysterious bags were stacked. He put the lamp down and opened one of them. To his great surprise it was full of old clothes. He tried another... More of the same.

'Why does he have all these old clothes?' he asked himself. He could come up with no logical answer.

He then began to pull all the bags out of the alcove and into the main area. He picked up the lamp once more and slowly walking along, examined the cave wall with great care. It was actually a tunnel, and soon it began to curve. The boy followed it for a number of steps. Suddenly the ceiling height began to decrease. It gradually got lower and lower, as yet he turned another corner. Julius was now forced to slide on his belly to continue. He felt afraid, but he persevered and turned another corner. As he completed yet another turn, a strong ray of light lit the ground ahead of him. He crept into the bright space and looked up. It was actually coming from one side and a little above where he lay. To his great surprise, he looked up and saw an opening through which he might just fit. He got on his knees with great difficulty.

'Yes! He could squeeze through,' he thought. Gingerly, he climbed into the crevasse and poked his head out. Keeping his little body sideways, and after much wiggling, he barely made it through. But he was out, and a big smile of joy appeared on his face, followed by a feeling of elation.

* * * * *

Whilst our little hero was performing his act of bravery, Cleophas was just leaving the city with his bags full of the old clothes he had been gathering all morning. In the course of his rounds however, he had hurled unobserved over the gate of the boy's home, a scroll enclosing the patchwork parchment. He had concocted it in Greek, because if he had done it in Aramaic which was his own language, it would have given the hated centurion a clue as to his nationality, and they could track him down easier.

As he sat steering his cart on his way back to his shack, he rehashed the plan for the collection of the ransom. His instructions were for the money to be carried in a black bag by a woman servant walking around the market in mid morning when the crowds were largest. She was to walk around continuously until relieved of the bag by someone (himself). If the bag was not taken, the whole operation was to be repeated the following morning, and every other morning until the bag was gone. He would observe her until a propitious moment presented itself. Then, threatening her with certain death if she screamed or made any betraying motion, he would give her his black bag containing some stones, and she was to continue her walk, without looking back at him. He fully expected the place to be swarming with soldiers both in uniform and in civilian clothes. His timing had to be impeccable.

'What would I not give for a diversion at the crucial time,' he said to himself.

The exit through the gate would be made riding his cart full of bags as usual. The money, he would hide in a secret compartment which he had constructed as part of the cart's seat. His familiarity with the guards would have to pay off now he hoped. Everything depended on it.

Centurion Gabinius soon became acquainted with the contents of the 'mysterious scroll,' as it was described by the servant who found it on the garden path. He had rushed home from a village on the Antioch road, when he heard the dreadful news of his son's disappearance. Now he knew the reason.

"An old enemy has done this," he said looking at his wife who was at his side anxiously waiting to hear the contents of the scroll.

"He is demanding a very large amount of money, and he wants one of our maids to carry it around the market in a black bag, every morning starting tomorrow morning. A heavy black bag it will be.... which of our servants is strong enough to undertake that chore?" he asked. Again, looking at his wife.

"Fina," said Aemelia without hesitation. "She is very strong."

The servant was duly briefed in what she was expected to do.

"If we catch him before he releases Julius," said Aemelia with some trepidation and tears in her eyes, "my poor boy will starve to death locked up somewhere."

"I have been considering that," said Gabinius. He walked over to a cabinet and pulled out a small bottle. He held it up for his wife and Fina to see.

"This is a powerful and permanent stain?" He looked at his slave girl. "If you Fina, can somehow, without his noticing, put some on the back of his robe, tunic, or whatever outer garment he is wearing, whilst exchanging bags, he will not be able to see it himself. I shall alert all my men including the guards at the gates, to be on the look out for this violet stain. They will be ordered not to apprehend him, but I will have him followed. I have men inside and outside the city in civilian clothes." He took a hold of his wife's arms, and holding her at arm's length, vowed.

"We will get him, and I shall have him crucified."

* * * * *

Whilst the grown-ups were setting up their battle stations, young Julius, having found freedom did not know what to do with it. He had no idea where he was. He finally decided on one direction and ran. Soon however he began to tire, and he felt very thirsty. There was no one in sight, and the heat of the day was causing his head to ache. The bump on his head was smaller but still there. As he trudged along, uncertainly; his mouth parched, he thought he heard voices. He had been climbing for the past half hour as the terrain began to ascend.

'Maybe I can see the town from up there,' he said to himself hopefully; observing the summit of the hill he was climbing.

Of a sudden something frightened him. It sounded like a growl and he increased his pace. Looking back with fear, to see what or who was trailing him, he lost his footing and fell into space. He landed on his back and experienced a terrible jab of pain, then nothing.

The voices that the boy had thought he heard materialised. A group of people emerged from a large cave and grouped around him. None however would touch him. They had seen him fall but they could not help him. They were lepers.

"I wonder if he's dead?" someone said with a sad intonation in his voice.

They drew closer.

"His chest is moving," said one of the women. "He is alive, but unconscious."

"We can't leave him there. The sun will finish him off."

"Poor little boy," sighed a girl.

"We will not be doing him any favour by touching him," said the man who had first spoken and whose name was Eli.

"How are we to move him then?" asked another young woman named Beca, rubbing her hands. "He must be badly hurt. We must get him some water and try to bring him around. He needs to be in the shade."

"Go bring as big a piece of cloth as you can find," said Eli to a little seven-year-old boy who stood beside him, looking sadly and silently at the unconscious boy.

Eli made himself busy snapping off some branches from an old dead tree nearby. With the help of Beca and Mary; another woman that stood there, they rigged up the skeleton for the cloth that young Jonah had gone to fetch.

The little group of lepers soon had the boy under a vital shade.

"Now!' said Eli, addressing Beca. "Go find the goatherd up on the hill. He is normally there at this time of the day. Ask him to come and bring his water skin with him."

"Mary! You must look after things till I get back," instructed Eli with concern. "I must go to town and get help."

Just then Julius regained consciousness.

"I can't move!" he cried as he tried to get up. He could not even rub his eyes. His hands would not respond. He began to wail in frustration and fear. The bystanders were shocked.

Eli came a little closer.

"Don't cry my son," he told the boy. "We will get you some help very soon, and you will be fine. Who are you? What is your name?"

Young Julius tearfully told them the story of the kidnapping and that the man may be looking for him to kill him. Eli was quite disturbed and realised that because this boy was a high-ranking Roman's son, there would be serious repercussions.

"I will go to your father right away," promised Eli. "Stay with him all of you until I get back."

At this point another two Lepers appeared. A man and a woman. She carried a basket with vitals that she had been given in town. The man was big in stature and carried a heavy staff. As was the case with all lepers, they wore torn clothes. Both their faces were covered from the eyes down. As was indeed Eli's.

"You are back just in time 'Ox'," greeted Eli. You may have some guarding to do."

The lepers had a short meeting discussing the boy's adventure and tragic end, and Eli took off as fast he could for the city.

When Eli was approximately half way to the city, he saw a cart coming his way. He pulled away from the road as he was prone to do as a leper. As the cart drew near him he realised that it was full of bags. The boy had told him about the bags he had seen in the cave.

"Good day to you!" greeted the man.

"And to you!" retorted Eli, taking a good look at him and the bags. He had seen this man before. Yes, he was the rag pedlar who lived in the shack about two miles away from his cave. This then must be the man who kidnapped the boy. He continued on his mission increasing his speed as much as he could; his excitement spurring him on. It wasn't every day that lepers had anything of interest happen in their sad and sequestered lives.

"Guards! Guards!" He yelled on arriving at the closest of the town gates. Caesarea had a few of them; all well guarded by both Roman and Judean soldiers.

After a few more attempts, Eli finally got their attention.

"What do you want leper? What are you screaming about?" asked the Judean guard.

"I bring very urgent news which I want you to report immediately to your Roman commanding officer."

"Tell us tell the news," said the Judean guard coming a little closer to Eli.

"We have the son of Centurion Gabinius in our camp. He fell off some rocks and is not able to move. We cannot touch him. You must send help right away."

The Roman guard was immediately informed. The soldier rushed off in great haste to relay the news to his commanding officer, who would in turn alert Gabinius.

* * * * *

Beca, found the young goatherd sitting on a rock watching his flock meandering around looking for bits of scrub and moss to eat in those arid surroundings.

"Hello Mishad," she greeted with a smile concealed by her veil.

"Hi Beca. What are you doing up here?" smiled the boy.

"I have come looking for you. I need you to come with me and bring your water skin. There is an injured boy who needs a drink very badly, and we can't give him water."

"Why not?"

"He's not a leper," she said shaking her head at the boy.

"I can't leave my goats unattended."

Beca had not given this any thought. "I'll stay here and look after them for you," she said as the thought struck her. "You'll be back very soon."

The goatherd hesitated. He did not answer.

"Whoever heard of a goat wth leprosy?" she laughed.

The boy realised that she was right. What he was thinking was really silly.

"Very well, I'll go. I'll leave my staff here." He laid it on a rock beside him.

"Don't touch it though unless you have to use it. If any wolf or jackal appears throw stones at it first. Most of the time they go away. I'll hurry back in any case."

Beca watched the boy disappear at the bottom of the hill and sat down on a different boulder to the one that he had sat on. She kept near the staff just in case. Somewhat frightened, she anxiously surveyed the goats, whilst saying a prayer to Yeshua in whom she fervently believed, and to whom she prayed constantly for a cure.

'You have cured so many other lepers. Why not me also?' she habitually and fervently prayed.

* * * * *

Eli turned around and began to walk back to his cave. He had not gone a mile, when the thundering of hooves made him turn and quickly get out of the way. A detachment of cavalry led by Centurion Gabinius himself was speeding off to his cave. A horseman broke off from the group and trotted over to Eli.

"Are you the man that brought the news to the guards at the gate?" asked a young officer stopping a little distance from the leper.

"Yes."

"He threw him a bag with some money."

"Thank you," said Eli. "But you had best go find the man who kidnapped the boy. I know who it is I think."

Eli explained. The young officer galloped away shouting. "Thanks again!"

The tired leper reached his cave to find it a hub of activity. Young Julius, in a stretcher was being carried by two Roman soldiers. His father walked beside them. The lepers had all retreated and were standing at the mouth of their cave observing the spectacle.

Cleophas, was surrounded by cavalry men. His hands were tied, and he had a rope around his neck which one of the horsemen was holding. Eli kept to one side as the company pulled out.

"Thank you all for your wonderful help!" shouted Centurion Gabinius walking away. "You will all be greatly rewarded for this," he promised.

Eli and his leper comrades climbed up the rocks and watched the soldiers until the dust from the horse's hooves had settled and they could see the city walls away in the distance.

CHAPTER FOUR

THE CUNUNDRUM

Aemelia welcomed her son with great distress; her heart breaking. She hugged and kissed him, missing his little arms around her neck.

"He cannot move his arms!" she cried, her face wet with tears, and turning, sought her husband's arms instead. Gabinius pressed her closer to him, fighting back tears of his own.

"It is not just his arms," he said, his voice breaking. "He cannot move at all. He is completely paralysed my love."

Aemelia went limp in his arms. He picked her up and took her to their bedroom, followed by Susannah who was greatly grieved. She quickly undid the covers of the bed ready to receive her mistress.

"Look after her Susannah," said Gabinius. I must find a good physician to attend to my son immediately. If I cannot find one here, I shall have to send to Jerusalem for one.

"Go Master. We will look after mother and son whilst you are away," she assured him.

Little Julius was laid on a couch in the peristyle, where he could watch his sisters at play and talk to them. Priscilla sat beside him listening to his frightening story, and occasionally kissing him. Little Meli was too busy with her doll to be concerned with anything else but would bring it over to visit her brother every now and then. Priscilla kept sending her away with a modicum of motherly instinct, protecting her sick brother from annoyance.

The days passed into weeks. Julius was no better. A very well-regarded physician had been in attendance almost on a daily basis. But he knew that with a broken spine his young patient would never recover and might well run into complications at any time.

Gabinius who had been well briefed by the physician and knew the dangers involved, kept as much as he could from his wife and the women of the household.

Cleophas had been duly judged and crucified, but the consequence of his dastardly crime, had doomed his innocent young victim to a life of immobility and dependence.

Beca the young leper, faithfully visited Gabinius' house every week, taking care to stay a couple of paces outside the gate and constantly chanting, 'unclean'. The servants had been instructed togive her news of any change in young Julius' condition, and to relay any message that the boy, who felt indebted to the lepers would give them for the girl.

One evening, Julius began to run a fever. It came over him quite quickly, and by the time the physician arrived he was delirious. The latter was totally at a loss as to the reason for this turn of events, and other than having the women of the house keep a cold damp cloth continuously over his brow, he did not know what else to do. The household was in total panic. Gabinius, who following his son's accident, remained in Caesarea; delegating outlying missions to his subordinates, was at home when this change of events put his son in danger of his life.

The following days worsened the boy's condition. The fever ravaged his little body, and because he was not eating, he grew weaker by the day.

Aemelia and Susannah, who alternated their watch on the boy day and night were at their wits end. One evening, the physician declared that the boy would not survive the night.

The boy's breathing grew more and more laboured, and to every one's horror he was slipping away. Aemelia and Gabinius had evoked all the gods they could think of, and nothing had changed the boy's condition for the better. The doctor who stayed the night, shook his head.

"He is going fast," he told the assembled family.

Suddenly, a thought occurred to Susannah. 'The veil.' Perhaps there had been some truth in the rumour that the veil was miraculous. What had she to lose? She quickly went to her room, and into her clothes closet where she kept it. She took it out of its wrapping and carried it into the dying boy's room.

"May I have your permission my lady to place this veil over my little master?" she asked with hope in her tearful eyes.

"What good will that do?" asked Gabinius in a defeatist tone of voice; his head bowed; his hands dangling at his sides.

Susannah did not answer but gave her mistress an appealing look.

"Go ahead, all hope is lost," cried Aemelia sullenly; her eyes heavy with tears.

Susannah opened the veil and carefully laid it over the dying boy. All eyes were on the face imprinted on the veil. A shiver ran down the centurion's spine.

Suddenly, the veil moved. Young Julius sat up and it slipped off him. He looked around and smiled.

Everyone including the physician was stunned. No one moved. No one spoke.

The boy got up and ran into his mother's arms who barely opened them in time to receive him.

"My boy! my darling boy!" wept the mother with great joy. The father took a hold of Susannah and hugged her with tears in his eyes.

"Thank you! Thank you!" he repeated.

Susannah took the veil from the bed and kissed it reverently. "Thank you," she said, "Whoever you were."

"I have never witnessed anything like this in my life," said the physician, taking the veil from Susannah and examining the face. "This face is of a wounded man. There are blood stains dripping down from his brow. How extraordinary. This is not paint, or even stain. This image seems to be imprinted in a most impossible way."

By now jubilation had taken over the inhabitants of that house in place of the sorrow that had enveloped it earlier. Young Julius took the veil and looked at the sad face.

"I wonder who that man is?" he said meeting his father's gaze with eager eyes. "You must find him. I must thank him for making me well."

They were all astounded in the way that the child had said those words. The physician suddenly recalled something that he had witnessed two years or so ago in a little square in Jerusalem. He pointed at the veil in the boy's hands.

"That," he said, "is the image of a Jew such as myself, who was crucified in Jerusalem over two years ago. His name was Yeshua. He claimed to be our Messiah, and the Son of God.

He performed many miracles, and even, I heard, brought people back to life. I saw him once as he argued with some Pharisees outside the temple in Jerusalem. I was on my way to see a very sick patient and so I only stopped to hear him for a few moments." He turned to Susannah.

"How did you come upon the veil?"

Susannah thought for a moment before answering, as she wondered whether Procula would want it known that it belonged to her.

"It was given me by one of the ladies I worked for," she lied.

"I see," said the physician with a smile. "I do not think your mistress would have given it to you if she had known what that veil is capable of doing. Use it well."

The physician congratulated the family on their good fortune, and after receiving a generous monetary compensation, and copious thanks for his attentiveness to them, he left.

Gabinius and Aemelia could not thank Susannah enough.

"You had better guard that veil well," advised Julius. "If people find out that it has miraculous powers, they will surely try to steal it from you."

"Yes," agreed Susannah. And said no more about it.

A few days later, young Julius came to Susannah and asked for the veil. Susannah was most surprised at this and enquired as to what he wanted it for.

"I want Beca to be cured by it too," he said innocently. I saw her outside the main gate, and I asked her to come to the side gate. She is waiting there now.

Susannah was shocked. How could she let a leper touch the veil? It would have to be burnt afterwards. She did not know what to do. After all, it was not her veil. It belonged to Procula.

"Come on Susannah," begged Julius. His large brown eyes appealing confidently.

"Don't you want Beca to be cured? They saved my life too. Father says we owe them a great debt."

"I must talk to your mother young man."

The boy called out to his mother who was in the kitchen with Rachel.

Aemelia came at her son's call. Susannah explained her problem. She made her mistress and her son, promise to keep secret the fact that Procula owned the veil.

"Now what do I do?" she asked.

Aemelia thought for a few moments... then said.

"I don't think that the veil would permit anything bad to happen. Even if it does not cure the leper girl, it won't make anyone else sick."

"I have to agree with you," said Susannah with resignation and a touch of disgust at herself.

"Let's try it," she conceded.

The three of them went to the side gate. Beca was waiting outside a few steps away.

She had come to ask about Julius, and on seeing him well she was delighted. Hearing his story, she was dying to at least get a glimpse of the veil with the man's face on it.

"I am going to put the veil here on the gate," said Susannah, placing it on the horizontal centre bar. "You Beca, take it and put it on."

Beca took the veil reverently and pulled off her rag shawl. Terrible sores were visible on her lips, and a piece of her nose was missing. Julius and the women looked at her in horror.

She took the veil and with eyes to heaven, gently put it on her head and bowed in prayer.

Presently, she looked up again. The sores had disappeared from her lips, her nose was totally restored, and her flesh had taken on a normal, healthy colour.

She fell on her knees, and taking the veil from her head, looked at the imprinted face and with tears of joy in her eyes, said aloud and with great emotion.

"Thank you Yeshua. You have answered my prayers."

She got up, walked to the gate and reverently kissing the veil, held it out for Susannah to take. Julius was beside himself with joy. He tried to open the gate to give Beca a hug. Aemelia regaining her composure, held him back.

"Please come into the garden," said the lady of the house. "We must burn all your clothes. I shall get you a clean tunic and robe to wear. But you must take off those torn things and leave them on the ground here."

Susannah took Julius away, whilst Aemelia got Fina to put the old clothes on a stick and burn them. They then took Beca who as quite naked, to the ablutions so that she could wash herself in readiness for her clean clothes.

Half an hour later a pretty Beca, sat in the peristyle looking lovely in her clean clothes and sharing some tasty refreshments with the family.

"You thanked Yeshua for your miraculous cure," said Susannah. "Is he the man on the veil?"

"Yes," assured Beca with a big smile and tears in her eyes. "I have been praying to him for a cure for over two years. He cured quite a few lepers when he was alive you know. As many as ten in one day on one occasion. He is my God. I am a Christian. That is a follower of Yeshua the Christ," she explained with much love in her eyes.

"Now that you are cured, what are you going to do?" asked Aemelia looking at a very attractive Beca. "You cannot go back to the cave with the other lepers."

"I will go back to my family," she said. "They will be greatly surprised and overjoyed to see me all well again. Thanks to Yeshua, and all of you."

"Is your family here in Caesarea?" asked Julius hopefully. He liked Beca.

"Yes. They visit me often at the cave. My father has a food shop near the new forum."

"Oh, that's great, I shall be able to visit you," said Julius with a happy smile.

Beca giving Julius a loving hug, thanked Susannah and Aemelia for their kindness, and went off to surprise her family.

Susannah did not tell her to keep the matter secret. She knew it would be impossible.

The knowledge that Yeshua was the man whose image had been miraculously imprinted on the veil, as the physician had also vouched for, gave Susannah much food for thought. Firstly, she wondered if Procula had known that all along, and would account for her being so stunned when she first saw the image. Secondly, there were many people who believed in him and were being called Christians. Thirdly she wondered if she was not also a Christian herself, since she now thoroughly believed that he was what he claimed to be...The Son of God.

The news of the two miraculous cures spread like wildfire around Judea. Susannah had left the veil in the care of her employer for safe keeping in his iron box.

One evening after having put the children to bed, she sat in the peristyle conversing with her patrons. She was now considered part of the family; they owed her so much.

"I wonder if I might ask a favour of you," she said addressing Gabinius, who had asked her to call him by his name, as had Aemelia. He smiled and motioned for her to proceed with her request.

"I feel very strongly," she began, "that I must return the veil to Procula; Pontius Pilate's wife. The veil is hers and she should have it back. She may have grave need for it also. I have no idea where they live. She may or may not be in Rome, so I have no way of sending it to her. I was thinking that perhaps if you knew of some trustworthy military officer who might be taking a trip to Rome in the near future, he might undertake as a favour to you, to track down Pontius Pilate and deliver the veil. He need not be told of its miraculous powers. Unless you deem it necessary for whatever reason."

She threw an appealing look at her employer.

"As it happens, I know a young officer who has just finished his Cursus Honorem and will be leaving for Rome within the next week or so. You are in luck. His father who is a senator, happens to be a good friend of mine and knows a good many people. I shall ask him."

Gabinius got up and walked around to stretch his legs a bit, and to think.

Presently he turned and said.

"I think I shall have to tell him. Confidentially of course. I want him to know what he is dealing with. I have heard that our emperor is persecuting Christians in Rome even though there is no persecution here other than by the Jews themselves. Tribune Marcellus will have to be careful."

Centurion Gabinius sat in his office at the Legion headquarters. It was early afternoon, and the day had so far been quite uneventful. He was contemplating paying his friend Centurion Cornelius a visit. He knew that the man was well versed in the new Christian faith that had been gaining strength everywhere over the past three years.

'This business of the veil is driving me insane,' he said to himself. 'That image is not of this world I feel sure. The imprint is inexplicable, and its power is totally astounding. Men do not have such power. Why, the physician was as helpless as a baby, and he is one of the best. I must talk to someone who can help me, and soon.'

He picked up his helmet and going outside, called a soldier over.

"Please go find out if Centurion Cornelius is in town."

He stood there looking at the sea, entertaining himself with the view whilst awaiting the soldier's return.

The messenger returned with hurried footsteps. Standing at attention, he saluted and said.

"Centurion Cornelius is in Caesarea sir. But he is not on duty today."

"Thank you," said Julius, and started off for his friend's house.

The congenial Cornelius welcomed his friend with a warm handclasp.

"Good to see you Gabinius," he said with a big smile on his long, and scarred face.

"I haven't seen you for quite a while. Have you been out of the city?" asked Gabinius, following Cornelius into the atrium. They went into the host's office. The latter lost no time ringing a little bell that sat on his desk. Sitting down, he motioned with his hand.

"Please sit down."

"I had a sticky assignment near Antioch," said Cornelius in answer to his friend's question. "It kept me there for almost two weeks."

"A servant girl appeared wearing a pretty smile."

"Bring us some refreshments please Mary," ordered the master of the house.

The girl went off to the kitchen. Cornelius smoothed down his thick hair.

"I have heard a lot of things about the veil that cured young Julius. Everyone is talking about it."

"It also cured a girl with leprosy who had gone to Julius' assistance when he fell off the rocks outside of the lepers' cave," said Gabinius.

"Really? I had not heard of that one. But you must be accosted by people now all wanting to be cured."

"Yes, and the girl who has it is scared that someone will try to steal it or harm her for it."

"Who is the girl, and how did she get it?"

The servant reappeared carrying a tray with the refreshments and placed it on the table in front of them.

"Thank you, Mary," said Cornelius. He offered some wine and other delicacies to his friend.

Gabinius then embarked on a conversation regarding Susannah and the veil.

"I need for you to tell me about this man whose image is imprinted on the veil," continued the eager visitor reaching for a morsel from the tray. "I am told that his name was Yeshua, and that he was crucified by Pilate a little over three years ago in Jerusalem. He claimed to be the Jewish Messiah and the self-proclaimed Son of their God. He has a large and ever-increasing following who are called Christians and who incidentally are being persecuted in Rome."

He stopped to take a cup of wine that Cornelius handed him.

"I suspect that you have learnt much about him," he said, resuming his narrative... "You entertained his chief Apostle some time ago as we all heard, and surely he must have told you much about his Master." Gabinius leaned back in his chair, took a sip of his wine and awaited Cornelius' story.

The centurion was sceptical about the safety of entrusting the fact of his faith to his pagan friend. He knew Gabinius to be a fair-minded moral man, but as a Christian he had learned to be cautious, especially as he was in the pay of Caesar.

"Before I tell you what I know of him." he began, with a shrewd look on his face. "Please tell me how you feel after witnessing those two phenomenal miracles by that veil."

"That is the reason I came to see you," said Gabinius. "I and my whole household are convinced that this Yeshua whose face is on the veil, could well be the Son of God. The leper girl who was cured had been praying to him for a cure for the last three years, and she was ecstatic when it happened. She thanked Yeshua with tears of joy in her eyes. She said she was a Christian."

"So, you believe in Him?" asked Cornelius leaning forward in his chair, his eye glued to those of his friend's.

"Yes. I do. But now what do I do?"

"You have to be baptised by one of his Apostles," said Cornelius with relief and a happy smile. "Peter, his chief Apostle, who baptised me and my household must do the same for you if you wish it the next time he passes by here. You will then be a Christian. You must keep it secret from everyone. We, being Roman, are likely to find ourselves back in Rome one of these days, and we will surely be persecuted and possibly even be put to death, should an enemy find out and denounce us."

Cornelius took a mouthful of his wine in readiness for his friend's next question.

"Why are they persecuting the Christians in Rome?" asked Gabinius and sipped some of his wine.

Cornelius leant closer to Gabinius. "We refuse to accept the emperor as our god, he is a mortal like everyone else. The immortal Yeshua who rose from the dead is our God." He sat back again in his chair, took a fig from the tray and began to peel it.

"Let me tell you something which is a great mystery and concerns our God."

His eyes squinted as the sun suddenly streamed in through the window and lit up his face.

"It is called the mystery of the Holy Trinity." He stopped; allowing the words to be absorbed as Gabinius exhibited a questioning expression on his intelligent face.

"It consists of three persons in one God," he explained...." Yahweh, the great God of the Jews is God the Father; Yeshua, is God the Son; and there is also the Holy Spirit who constitutes the third person. Still, the three count as One."

Gabinius was stunned. He was trying hard to understand the meaning of his friend's words.

"It is an incomprehensible thing to understand," assured Cornelius, in agreement with his friend's conundrum, "but it is our belief non-the-less. The Apostle's do not understand it either, but by putting together the things that Yeshua taught them, they have come to that logical conclusion."

The two men talked for a long time. Cornelius explained many things to his friend. The Crucifixion; the Resurrection; the descent of the Holy Spirit; Jesus' baptism in the Jordan; and many parables and miracles that he remembered being told by Peter, Barnabas, and other close disciples of the Lord who had visited him whilst on their missionary travels. Gabinius became more and more interested as the conversation progressed, and finally, his head swimming with information, he got up to leave.

"Thank you for your help and wonderful instruction. I must show you the veil before it goes off to Rome," said Julius. "It will be gone next week, if I can keep it safe till then."

"I would love to see it," said Cornelius with a nod of the head.

"Come to my house tomorrow, bring Claudia with you. I am sure she would like to see it too."

The friends shook hands again and Gabinius left; a very different man.

When he arrived at his house, Gabinius was greeted by a crowd clamouring to see the veil.

He forced his way through to his gate which was promptly opened by Fina and quickly closed again behind him. She threw a look of disdain at the crowd.

"They've been there all day, Master, and they won't go away," she complained following her master into the house.

"Petronius!" called out Gabinius.

A young soldier came out of the servant's quarters urgently putting on his helmet and stood to attention in front of the centurion.

"Go down to headquarters and bring back a few men to disperse this crowd. And, he added, see that they leave two on guard."

"Yes, sir," said the soldier and ran off on his mission.

Young Julius came out of his room where he was playing with his toys and ran to his father.

Gabinius picked him up, hugged him, and put him down to make room for the girls who rushed at him with big smiles on their pretty faces, shouting, "Daddy! Daddy!"

"Where have you been Gabinius?" cried Aemelia, coming to him and giving him a resounding kiss.

"That crowd outside scares me," she complained. "They've been out there all day screaming for the veil." She bent and picked up little Meli who wanted to be closer to her father.

"I sent Petronius to tell you about them, but you were gone, and no one knew where."

"I went to see my friend Cornelius. He sends his and Claudia's regards. I asked them to come over tomorrow. They want to see the veil." He finally took his helmet off. The children had not given him a chance to do that. "I have much to tell you and Susannah," he smiled.

The last mentioned entered the peristyle and greeted her employer with a shallow bow.

"Ah, Susannah," he smiled, "I was just saying to Aemelia how much I have to tell you both. I shall do so later after the cena, when Petronius is back at the barracks and we can talk 'en famille'."

The day following Gabinius' visit to Cornelius' house, a messenger arrived from the latter centurion with the news that he had had to leave town on an urgent assignment and would call on Gabinius on his return, hopefully in a few of days. The week however passed, and Cornelius had not returned. Gabinius made enquiries at headquarters and found out that his friend had been sent off to Joppa to quell some unrest which had erupted there.

'God knows when he will be back,' he said to himself. 'It's a good thing that Marcellus's trip has been delayed.'

* * * *

Whilst Gabinius awaited the return of Cornelius, a sinister plot was being hatched which would affect the veil and those involved with it.

The Sanhedrin in Caesarea had heard of the miracles worked through the veil. Being acquainted with the miracle it was credited with three years earlier in Jerusalem; that of the spectacular cure of Jesse's daughter Esther. They quickly took steps to steal it. They posted spies in the crowd outside Gabinius' house in the hope of finding a way to lay their hands on it. They intended to send it to the main Sanhedrin headquarters in Jerusalem where it would surely be disposed of.

When the crowd was dispersed by the Roman soldiers, they posted two men well away from the house to keep a watch on the gates and record all comings and goings.

After several days of spying however, the Sanhedrin had not been able to formulate a feasible plan for achieving their goal. Breaking into the centurion's house would be too risky, and the penalty too severe if the intruder was caught. It was finally decided that they would use a sure and time-honoured way to obtain the veil.

* * * *

The degree of domestic tranquility and wellbeing of an affluent family generally depends on the efficiency and personal traits of their servants. Aemelia was fortunate in that regard. Her servants were loyal, obedient, and efficient. She had no complaints whatsoever. Susannah was now considered a worthy part of the family; Rachel was a charming and caring person; and Fina was a true defender of the family who treated her with consideration and even love, regardless of her status as a slave.

This serene relationship between staff and masters of the Gabinius residence at this juncture of our story, was about to be tested.

The Sanhedrin were ready to put their evil plan into into practice.

Rachel's father suddenly disappeared. He left his house one morning on his way to work (he was a mason), and never got to his destination. His wife panicked when her husband's boss sent a man to the house to ask if he was ill. Soon the authorities began to search the city for him.

Seeing that the man was a Jew, the Roman authorities would not interfere. The Sanhedrin simply put up a front and pretended to look for him. Rachel's mother sent word to her daughter at Gabinius' house. The poor cook, greatly distressed, wondered why anyone would want to harm her father. He was an ordinary working man and had as far as she knew, no enemies. Her answer was not long in coming.

On her way home that evening (she never slept in Gabinius' house), Rachel was accosted by a man who suddenly appeared beside her. His face was partially covered by his shawl which he held in place as he spoke.

"We have your father prisoner," he said. "No harm will come to him if you do what I will tell you to do."

He took her arm and pulled her over to a park bench nearby and rudely sat her down. He sat beside her still holding his shawl over his face. She became very frightened as she listened to what the man told her.

"How can I steal the veil? she asked with a shaky voice, in response to the demand that the rude stranger had made. "It's under lock and key in my master's office.

"You must get the keys when he is sleeping and steal the veil. There are no Roman guards outside the house at night; there are no crowds to control. All you have to do is to throw the veil over the wall once you have it. A man will be there waiting to pick it up."

Rachel shifted uncomfortably in her seat and fidgeted with her shawl.

"I shall have to put the keys back in his room. If I don't get caught the first time, I shall get caught on returning. Besides, as I have already told you, I do not stay the night at my employer's house. You yourself can attest to that if as you say you have been constantly watching the house. So, I am not lying to you. I only work there during the day, and if I should ask to stay the night, my master who is very clever will smell a rat."

She studied the stranger's eyes to gage his reaction to her words. He betrayed nothing.

"Besides," she persisted, "any minute now, the veil will be on its way to Rome." Very quickly she regretted having said those last words.

"Your scheme won't work." she continued. "It is impossible for me to get the veil, so let my father go. I cannot succeed in this, and you will be doing a terrible thing if you harm my innocent father."

"What's that you said about it being taken to Rome?" The man looked at her with great interest in his eyes.

Rachel realised that in her panic she had divulged something that should not have slipped out. But it was too late.

'I'd like to see these people whoever they are,' she said to herself with confidence,' snatching the veil out of a Roman officer's hands. They can try, though, as long as they let my father go unharmed. That is all I am concerned about.'

"I heard that an officer who is retuning to Rome," she said, "will be taking the veil with him."

The man's eyes widened, and his eyebrows arched. She took comfort in this.

"We will keep in touch with you," said the stranger. "The moment you hear of anything I must be told. I shall be here every evening. So, come straight to this bench and sit down and wait for me. If that veil leaves Caesarea without you telling us who is carrying it, you will not see your father alive again. You will have to keep your ears well open."

Rachel burst into tears.

"Let my father go," she sobbed. "I swear to you that I shall do what you ask."

"No. My dear," sneered the man. "Until we are sure that the man you tell us is the man who will be taking it, we will not let your father go. Furthermore," he said putting his face closer to hers, "any little slip on your part, or, if we suspect that you have alerted the Romans, we will give your father a very painful death. We have ways and means of knowing what the Romans are up to, so don't underestimate our powers."

The stranger got up and walked away. She stayed there for a few moments crying and trying to come terms with what had suddenly befallen her.

'That veil,' she mused, 'can bring much joy, but it can also bring much suffering.'

Rachel watched every move that anyone in the house made or commented on regarding the veil or its future. Day after day passed and her evening report to the stranger was of very little use to him. However, he persisted.

One evening, as Rachel was leaving, Gabinius called out to her and asked once again if any thing had developed with regard to her father. He told her that he had checked repeatedly with the Jewish authorities, and that on his last visit with them, they still had no workable clues as to where he might be. There were a couple of new leads they said, which they felt might be promising and that they would keep him informed.

"I did not ask them, but have they demanded any money from your mother? The abductors I mean."

"No," she answered. Shaking her head and wishing she could tell him what their demand was.

"They are very slow in their investigation," he said. "I cannot interfere as you Jew's are allowed to manage your own affairs. I shall keep an eye on them though, so that they know that there is interest in the case." He smiled at her. "Keep your hopes up, and your prayers too."

Having thanked her master for his kindness, she made her way once more to meet the stranger with nothing new to report.

"It seems, that at last, Marcellus's ship is sailing the day after tomorrow," said Gabinius one evening as Rachel was serving the family their cena. Her ears perked up. She listened attentively.

"It was evidently Herod who was holding up the departure," he continued. "He is off to Rome once again. We better get ready for the usual rounds of trouble. No wonder Cornelius is still not back, he must have his hands full down there around Joppa. They are always having problems with those pirate raids. They can be quite troublesome."

"I suppose," said Susannah, whilst helping Meli with her food, "that the young tribune will be coming for the veil soon."

"He might come this evening, or at latest tomorrow," said Gabinius swallowing a mouthful of his fish. "I shall miss him, he is a good officer. He will do well in Rome. A bright future awaits him."

The conversation continued. Rachel became concerned for the young officer who might well be attacked and even killed for the veil that he carried. She went back into the kitchen to think.

She did not feel hungry, but Fina and Petronius did, and so she had to sit and eat something, or they might suspect that she was acting oddly.

While she ate, she pondered over the danger that an unsuspecting Marcellus might encounter on his way to the ship. With the crowd there to see Herod off, he could easily be accosted, and the culprits lose themselves in the crowd.

"You're very quiet tonight."

Rachel snapped out of her reverie, as Fina's words penetrated her churning brain.

"Just doing some heavy thinking," said Rachel in a sad tone of voice which the members of the household had lately become accustomed to.

"You are worried about your father," said Petronius, looking at Rachel sympathetically.

"Of course, she is," retorted Fina; her mouth full of food and nodding her head.

Petronius remained in the kitchen with Fina, when Rachel, having finished her brief supper went to Fina's room where she normally kept her clothes. She dressed and got ready to leave for her daily rendezvous with her tormentor. All of a sudden, things became very clear in her mind.

She went into the peristyle. Susannah was in the girl's room, and Aemelia was playing a game on the floor with young Julius. The centurion sat watching his wife and child at play with satisfaction in his eyes. Rachel approached her master, and with tearful eyes asked to talk to him privately. Aemelia looked up enquiringly, but noticing her cook's distress, indicated with her eyes to her husband, to attend to Rachel's request.

Master and servant went into the office.

"Master," began Rachel, as he motioned for her to sit down. "I have not been honest with you or my lady, and I want to explain something to you which has been driving me mad for well over a week since my father went missing."

Gabinius looked at her with great interest in his eyes. Once again, he motioned to her.

"Tell me. Have no fear I shall be fair in my judgement"

"The people who took my father," she began, "wanted me to steal the veil from you. I told them that it would be impossible as it was guarded by you and locked away and so on. Also, that I did not sleep in the house at night, as they could well see, having placed men to watch the house constantly and had seen me leave. They threatened to kill my father. I seemed to have talked them out of having me steal the veil. However in my panic on meeting one of them that first evening and in hope appeasing his anger, I told him that the veil would be leaving for Rome within a week or so, as I had heard you mention. He then threatened me with my father's death again and demanded I spy for them. They wanted to know who would be taking the veil to Rome, and when." Rachel rung her hands in anguish.

"I promised to do that," she continued, "as it seemed to appease them. I felt with some relief that they had given up on my being able to steal it. They told me that they were very powerful, and nothing was beyond their reach. So now they expect me to go through with their instructions, and I am afraid that the young tribune will be attacked and maybe even killed in their attempt to possess the veil. I had to warn you so that you will have him protected all the time until he is on board the ship." She again burst into tears.

Gabinius got up and going around the table put his hand gently on her shoulder.

"It is a noble thing that you have done. Especially considering the consequences to your father if any of this were to get out... And of course, it won't." He went back to his chair and sat down again. Rachel wiped her eyes with her shawl and looked expectantly at Gabinius.

"Leave the protection of Marcellus to me," he said. "You keep your appointment with the man that you normally meet with and tell him what you have heard. Tell him that you do not yet know who will be carrying it but will let them know tomorrow morning or whenever you find out. Say that you will give me an excuse that you are feeling ill, or going to the market or whatever, and so leave the house at any time of the day. Then tomorrow you can tell them who it is. I shall make sure that no harm comes to Marcellus." Gabinius got up and said.

"We cannot apprehend anyone, or we will give the game away, but I bet you that the moment that the ship sails, your father will be set free. We shall be on the look out for him. Now away you go."

Rachel thanked him for his kindness and help and went on her way.

* * * * *

Marcellus showed up at the house to say goodbye to the family and to pick up the veil.

He was a handsome young man in his very early twenties. He was tall, sturdily built, with a mop of dark brown curly hair, heavy eyebrows and a short, well clipped beard and moustache which gave great strength to his square, solid face. When he laughed, which he did with mirthful sincerity, a good set of teeth was pleasantly displayed in concert with a pair of large, vivacious, dark brown eyes that narrowed and sparkled merrily. There was a certain strength in his wide ridged straight nose and thinned lipped mouth, which was readily apparent in his smile.

All things considered, his physiognomy honestly reflected his good disposition and cheerful nature. He was happy that he had done his best in the term of service that he had undertaken and was looking forward to going home to his family with great anticipation.

Susannah had considered asking Aemelia to write a little note to Procula briefly explaining the reason for the scroll having stayed behind. But she desisted in case the veil by some misfortune should fall into the wrong hands, incriminating Procula, and exposing her as a Christian which she now suspected her of being.

Much to Gabinius' regret, as he waved goodbye to Marcellus at the wharf, Cornelius was still not back in Caesarea. The veil was on its way to Rome, leaving behind many disgruntled people and some very joyous ones.

At the sumptuous harbour, the crowds cheered wildly as King Herod and his entourage made their way ceremoniously to the wharf where the Roman warship assigned to him was berthed. The wharf was decorated with olive wreaths and flowers. Horns and flutes blared in joyful harmony, as the Jewish dignitaries bid 'bon voyage' to their monarch. Jewish guards lined up on one side of the wharf, and Roman guards on the other.

Centurion Gabinius and other senior Roman officers stood at attention as the monarch passed, smiling at everyone and highly pleased with himself. He pompously boarded with his male entourage and waved to the ladies of the court who had come to see him off. Marcellus, with the folded veil tucked in his tunic under his shining armoured breastplate, side stepped the whole gathering and made his way to a smaller vessel that was berthed behind the ship bearing the royal Jewish insignia. It was sailing as escort to Herod's ship, and was better armed and manned.

Gabinius breathed a sigh of relief as Marcellus under a six-man escort, walked up the gangplank of his ship. He kept an eye on one particular person whom he recognised from somewhere, and who had been trying to get closer to Marcellus as he walked. He could not put his finger on it, but he was sure he knew the man.

Herod's ship pulled away slowly from the wharf to cheers from the crowd, closely followed by the smaller, faster escort ship. Soon, both were out of sight. It was a warm spring morning, and the sun's heat gathered intensity as the morning progressed and the crowds slowly dispersed.

Gabinius made his way home rather than to headquarters. He had to wait and see how the kidnappers would behave after the event. He was still trying to place the face of the man he had seen. Of a sudden, it hit him. He was a Jewish police officer from the Caesarea Sanhedrin. Hudd was his name. He had worked with him on a case quite a while back.

'Of course,' he said to himself with some annoyance at his own ignorance. 'Sanhedrin! It had to be the Sanhedrin. They hate Yeshua so much that they want the veil to destroy it.' All of a sudden he felt elated and hurried his steps home.

'They will release Rachel's father immediately,' he said to himself. 'They would not have harmed him in any case; just wanted to scare her. What a lair of foxes that Sanhedrin is.'

"Rachel! Rachel!" he called out as soon as Fina let him in to the house.

The girl came running, perceiving the urgency in her master's voice.

"I am almost certain," he smiled, "that your father will be released by his abductors today or perhaps tomorrow."

Rachel's eyes filled with tears and clasping her hands with joy, thanked her master. She turned to go. Then stopped. "Is the tribune safely on his way?" she asked.

"Yes," answered Gabinius, with some joy and some regret.

During the cena, which Rachel had prepared with particular love and care, Julius explained how he had arranged Marcellus' escort, and advised him to keep his eyes open even onboard ship. He had also briefed him on what Susannah had asked him to tell Procula, once he had found her.

Rachel reached the meeting place and sat on the bench awaiting the stranger. She waited and waited, but no one showed up. She eventually gave up and started for home in the hope that her father would be there. Getting up from the bench, she saw a man walking hurriedly towards her. As the man approached, she could not believe her eyes.

"Father! Father! she cried, and with her eyes suddenly flooding with tears, went to embrace him.

"My child! my dear, dear child!" cried the father whose name was Sol. They lost themselves in in a loving embrace. She pulled away to look at him.

"Are you all right? Did they hurt you?"

"No, my child, though they didn't feed me very well," he laughed, taking her arm and making for home.

"I shall remedy that as soon as we get home," she smiled and squeezed closer to him.

CHAPTER FIVE

MISHAP AT SEA

Marcellus stood on the upper deck of the escort ship. The large ship with the royal Judean ensign alongside the Roman eagle, was sailing a little ahead and to starboard. Using sail as well as oars, it was travelling at maximum speed over a very calm Mediterranean Sea. His smaller ship being a lighter craft, kept pace easily, however the pace was gruelling where the oarsmen were concerned. It seemed that there was no need to be travelling at that speed, over a prolonged period, since there was no challenge from any enemy ships, and full speed would only be employed briefly and in battle situations. The rowers were being needlessly fatigued. It was assumed that the larger ship which carried the Jewish king, had been ordered to speed up at his whim.

Presently, the big ship's oars were pulled up. The piper's pace -setting 'aulos'(flute) immediately stopped, much to the relief of the rowers who slumped over their oars in a state of exhaustion. A skin of water was passed around, and each man given a chance to drink to the count of ten.

The lighter escort vessel also pulled up its oars and trimmed its sails to maintain its present position in relation to the larger ship which was then being driven by sail alone.

The young tribune stood on deck lost in thought revisiting his experiences in Judea during the last three years. He could boast of having been engaged in a number of skirmishes, but no real pitched battles. He had served most of the time under Centurion Gabinius, who had taken him under his wing and had been like a father to him. A couple of minor wounds were all he could show for battle scars, but he had acquitted himself very

111

ably and learnt much of the art of warfare. Perhaps, he thought, the experience would carry some weight if and when he tried for the Senate.

His musings were suddenly interrupted by the sound of female voices.

"We will be stopping at Cyprus, the captain says."

"I thought we would go by way of Crete, and Syracuse, my lady."

"Evidently the Jewish king does not like long uninterrupted voyages."

Marcellus turned to find himself face to face with a most beautiful young woman perhaps a year or so younger than himself. She was talking with her travelling companion. He was surprised to hear that they would be interrupting their journey prior to reaching Crete, which was the time honoured and only stop on the route to Rome.

Being captivated by the girl's beauty, he went over to the pair and introduced himself.

"Good morning ladies," he greeted with a big smile and a shallow bow. "My name is Marcellus Fulvius and I am on my way home to Rome."

"Good morning to you," said the girl with a lovely smile. "I am Livia Celestinus, and this is my companion and loyal servant, Penelope.

He nodded to her and said.

"I overheard you saying that we would be touching Cyprus at King Herod's request. I suppose he finds his diet rather restricted at sea. I hear he is a capricious eater."

"Indeed, so I have also heard. Ha! Ha!" laughed the girl.

"It will put us out of the way and lengthen our journey by a couple of days at least," stated Penelope confidently.

The conversation continued for some time, acquainting themselves with each other.

The sound of the aulos (flute) caught their attention. The ship began to pick up speed as the oarsmen got their oars working., and easily keeping up with the trireme which had employed its oars again.

Soon lunch time arrived. Livia remained on deck whilst Penelope went below accompanied by Marcellus. They got their provisions from their respective baggages and returned to the upper deck to eat. They sat on the bare deck. Penelope spread a small tablecloth which she had brought and placed their victuals on it. The impromptu maritime picnic commenced. Their trivial and happy chatter added flavour to their otherwise cold, dull, meal.

They were the only passengers on board. The remainder were military personnel and crew. The latter consisted of a total of seventy hands of which fifty were busily employed at the oars. The military personnel, one hundred in number, completed the vessel's complement at a total of one hundred and seventy souls all told.

The ship was equipped with two catapults, and there was a handy supply of smooth stones of appropriate weight stored in a heavy wooden enclosure built into the deck. Bows, arrows and pilii (spears), were stored in a similar manner, but had retractable wooden covers to protect them from the elements. Soldiers wore their gladii whilst on their watch. The off-duty personnel kept their swords with their belongings below deck.

Marcus, the captain of the vessel, spent most of his time at the stern of the ship where he and Festus the helmsman, were somewhat protected by an open tent-like wooden structure. They enjoyed a visual advantage owing to the rising nature of the rear deck as it neared the swan's head; a refinement which also gave the ship a touch of elegance.

The journey as the fifth day came to a close, had been uneventful. The weather held, and a favourable wind made life a little easier for the oarsmen of both vessels. Cyprus was almost in sight, and both passengers and crew were looking forward to a few hours on land whilst the ships were revictualling.

"Land ahoy!" sang the helmsman pointing ahead.

The captain who was on the lower deck talking to Livia and Marcellus, invited them to join him on the upper deck so that they could enjoy the sight which would soon unfold. Penelope also joined them.

The space in the lower deck that the three passengers shared was partitioned off into four cubicles, each with a heavy curtain closing them off. There was just enough room in each cubicle for a narrow bed with a mattress, a small table with a wash bowl and jug. Under it, sat a ceramic pot with a handle and lid. The baggage was kept under the bed. The straw mattresses on the bed were rather thin and uncomfortable. But that was the only space on the ship for passengers and captain. The crew's quarters were also below deck but partitioned off from the passenger area. It took up most of the remaining space on board.

A warship offered very little comfort indeed. It rarely carried passengers as its destination was never a certainty. In this particular case however in its role as escort for the royal ship, its destination was clearly set. Provided no naval engagement became necessary there would be no deviation from the prescribed route.

"You will enjoy your short visit on this island," said Marcus with a smile. "It's quite beautiful."

"How long will you take to revictual?" asked Livia.

The captain peering intently over the railing at the sea below, answered, somewhat distractedly. "You will have four hours to wander around. Make sure you buy enough food for another another seven days. We will not stop again until we get to Phoenix in Crete."

A loud ripping sound suddenly coming from somewhere below, urgently drew their attention.

"We've run over rocks!" Shouted the helmsman as the captain scurried off below to investigate what that he had but a moment earlier suspected.

"Are we going to sink?" asked Penelope with great alarm.

"We'll do our best to keep her afloat," asserted Festus with a smile; trying to downplay the danger.

Marcellus and Livia silently and anxiously awaited further news from below deck.

"Sound the alarm, and send down carpenters with some planks," came the voice of the captain. Three loud blasts from a horn were heard, answered moments later by another three far off blasts from the horn of the Royal ship which however continued on its way.

Two shipwrights rushed down to the hold with their tools and some boards in their hands.

Once the men got to work, Marcus returned. He came up, surveyed the coastline and said to Festus." Steer for that beach over there. He then called out to the piper.

"Play for maximum oar speed." Next, he commanded the complete trimming of the sail.

He then addressed his three concerned passengers.

"I am going to have her steered right onto the beach and also try to keep her from overturning. You will all have to push against something solid that will keep you from being driven forward on impact. You will be better off down below. Listen for a horn. I shall blow on it just before we hit the shore."

The three of them immediately went below and surveyed the area. The beds were nailed to the deck, so they would remain in place, but the rest of the furniture and baggage would have to be moved in front of and pressing against the sturdy partition which divided off the passenger area; otherwise it would fall on top of them. They busied themselves and soon all was in place. Livia and Penelope took their place leaning heavily against the mattress and furniture which they had placed following Marcellus' instructions.

Marcellus took the wrapped veil from his baggage and put it in his tunic. He then quickly buckled on his belt with scabbard and sword. He had barely time to lean on the mattress in front of him, when the horn sounded. A few moments later, following a long scraping sound, the ship came to a sudden halt. They found themselves pressing heavily against the furniture and partition, which held their weights with ease.

"Quickly!" said Marcellus. "Lie down and take a hold of the legs of the bed like this." He showed them how. "The ship may yet topple to one side."

The women did as they were bid, and all waited for a few moments. Gingerly the tribune rose to his feet. The next moment, he was in the air and falling past the women, who found themselves dangling from their beds.

Marcellus fell heavily against the sand, as he fortunately cleared the railings that surrounded their area. He was about to rise, when a wave smashed into him and covered him completely.

He got on his knees with some difficulty. As he stood up, the next wave came. He held his ground firmly gripping the steering oar which had somehow found its way into his space.

"Help us Marcellus!" screamed the women. "We cannot hold on much longer," cried Livia.

Livia was the closest to him. Her feet were dangling about a man's height above Marcellus' head.

"You first, Livia," he said. "When I say jump, let yourself go. I shall catch you."

He kept his eye on the next incoming wave. It would be waste high and would assist in buffering the fall.

"Jump!" he shouted.

Livia let go her hold, and down she went straight into Marcellus' waiting arms. They both tumbled into the surf, and for a moment, disappeared. An amused pair looked at each other as they rose out of the water laughing.

"I'm coming!" shouted Penelope.

"Hang on until I tell you," he shouted back. She waited. He gently moved Livia to one side.

"Now!" signalled Marcellus.

Penelope dropped, but being a little further away than Livia had been, and somewhat heavier, overpowered Marcellus who sank into the surf with her on top. She got up and was about to thank him, when she noticed that he did not rise.

The two women rushed to his assistance. Together they helped him get up just before the next wave hit them. He was breathing with some difficulty and seemed in pain. At this point Livia realised that they could get out of there if they crawled out on their knees. Their baggage and furniture had already been washed out that way ahead of them.

They waited for the next wave to come and go, and off they went.

The helmsman Festus, seeing them crawling out, rushed to assist them.

"They are all well Captain!" he shouted as he helped the women up.

The captain had been hurt in the beaching and was nursing a badly bruised leg further up the beach. He too had been thrown violently when the ship tilted over. In fact, there were many casualties sitting and lying on the beach being attended by the ship's three capsarii (medics) as best they could.

One of them approached Marcellus who had flopped down on the sand in pain.

"You've possibly cracked your rib," he said. He examined him by pressing gently on one of the tribune's ribs. A stab of pain ran through the patient's chest. Again the man pressed the adjoining rib. Same result registered. He tried a third one but there was no painful response.

"You have cracked two ribs," he said. I don't think they are broken, but you will be in considerable pain for many days. There is nothing that can be done for you other than lightly bandaging your chest, which sometimes helps. I shall do that for you now. He began to take Marcellus tunic off. As he did, Marcellus reached for the veil which he had moved to one side of his chest whilst the man was examining him and gave it to Livia to hold.

"Please hold this for me," he told her. "It's very important."

Penelope was most concerned. She kept apologising. Marcellus tried to console her, but she was very upset with herself. To distract her, Livia asked her to go and have the sailors bring their luggage which had been retrieved by them from the surf and placed nearby.

The ship's stern continued to be pounded by the surf; it being high tide. It was expected to run dry as the tide receded. Help began to arrive. The news of the beaching of the galley having soon spread, the Roman authorities jumped into action. Presently, many hands were helping to unload and pull the ship further up the beach where the next tide would not encumber the repairing to the torn hull. News was sent by military courier to Paphos where the royal ship was headed.

The three passengers were taken away in a cart with all their luggage to the governor's house, where they would await passage on the next military ship bound for Rome. Or, if they preferred, to wait until their ship was made sea worthy again. The captain, crew and soldiers were to be housed in tents on the beach where they could work on the ship.

Marcellus' pain was aggravated by the jostling of the cart, and he breathed a sigh of relief when they entered the gates of the governor's house. There, they were made welcome by his wife. She was a good looking thirty-eight-year-old of Greek extraction and answered to the name of Athena. She had deep, dark, penetrating but kindly eyes, which smiled with unabashed sincerity as she welcomed the shipwrecked trio into her well-appointed house.

Each of the unfortunate trio was allotted a separate room. All three rooms, lavishly furnished, overlooked picturesque views of the sea and garden.

Marcellus was not permitted to do anything but rest and eat. Penelope fussed around him like a mother hen; much to the amusement of her dear lady, who being gifted with a good sense of humour, found her attentions to the young handsome tribune quite amusing. An occasional touch of envy however, could not be discounted on the lady's part.

Livia's admiration for Marcellus grew as the days passed. She found him handsome; most reliable; congenial; well bred; and like herself, in possession of a good sense of humour. A strong feeling that he also admired her even though as yet they had found very little time to be together, grew stronger in her heart as they became better acquainted with each other on their daily strolls in the garden of the house. At such times, Penelope would tactfully find some pretext to leave her beloved mistress alone with the young man.

Marcellus' convalescence was going well. By the third day he was able to breath with less pain and managed to get some sleep at night. The evening of the fourth day Captain Marcus appeared in the garden as the two 'lovebirds' (as Athena was now calling them,) sat beside each other conversing amiably. Penelope sat a little ways apart, enjoying the beauty of the garden and keeping a watchful but approving eye on her lady.

"Good evening to you all," greeted Marcus, approaching Marcellus and Livia. He walked with some confidence but with the aid of a staff. He too was much recovered, but his leg still bothered him. "How are those ribs?" he asked, addressing the tribune. He gave Livia a shallow bow and waved hello to Penelope.

"I am better, thank you. It only hurts when I move my arms."

The captain smiled.

"Do you think you will be ready to continue with your journey tomorrow morning?"

Marcellus looked at Livia as if asking her opinion. She did not offer any comment but simply returned his gaze.

"Would it be possible to have a thicker mattress on my bed?" he asked the captain. "I shall pay for it of course."

"Certainly," answered Marcus. "Then, you will join us tomorrow morning?"

"Marcellus looked at Livia once again." She smiled and nodded. Yes, she too would go.

"The three of us will be there tomorrow morning," assured Marcellus, who looking at the captain's leg, remarked. "You yourself, may find the trip uncomfortable. I hope you have a good lieutenant who can take on some of your duties."

The captain answered in the affirmative, and saluting the three, left them.

The repaired vessel sailed late the following morning with the passenger trio on board. Their next stop would be Phoenix in Crete. Marcellus was optimistic that his injured ribs would have completely recovered by the time they got there.

Festus the helmsman, who took on a few of the captain's duties, explained to Marcellus how unchartered rocks near the surface often escaping the scrutiny of mariners, posed a constant danger to shipping. Marcus, he told them, had reported the location of those hidden rocks to the harbour authorities in Paphos.

"We trust that their exact position will be incorporated into the next issue of maps pertaining to this area," said Marcus, addressing his three passengers who were sitting on the deck nearby.

The weather held out, making for smooth sailing. Marcellus and Livia found it very difficult to share time together privately. Privacy was one luxury that a military ship did not afford.

They were therefore looking forward with impatience to their arrival at Phoenix where they could perhaps spend a few hours together. Livia was apprehensive with regard to leaving Penelope on board so that she could give her lover her full attention. She knew that her servant would also be pining for some relief from the monotony of life on board ship and just as eager as she to find her land legs. In any event, the slave would feel it her duty to supervise her mistress' activities as per her instructions from Livia's parents, to whom she would have to ultimately answer.

"You can all go ashore and enjoy the town for three hours," said Marcus, addressing his three passengers, as the crew passed down ropes to the men on the pier for the berthing of the ship. "The beautiful town of Phoenix awaits you," he continued with enthusiasm. "We will sail again in three hours time, so please don't stray too far."

The trio left the ship with some relief finding their land legs very quickly.

Marcellus helped Livia and then Penelope down the gang plank, and promising to be back on time, they took leave of the captain who bade them a good day with a twinkle in his eye.

Their first task was to find a good food shop and eat a hot meal which was an impossibility on board ship.

They were soon enjoying their food accompanied by some good wine; putting them in a very pleasant mood and giving their little escapade a great start. Penelope announced that she would be shopping for their food supplies to replenish those already consumed and left the pair to browse the bazaars on their own promising to meet them in a couple of hours, at the food shop where they had lunched.

Phoenix, with its international flavour soon captured the imagination of our starry-eyed couple, who after a cursory round of the animated bazaars and shops, found their way up steep, winding, and narrow cobbled streets to the hill that overlooked the town and busy port.

There was a cool sea breeze blowing, making the heat of the day bearable. On reaching the park-like summit of the hill, the happy couple found themselves in an enchanting garden setting. Their eyes simultaneously fell on a roughly constructed pergola prodigiously covered in purple wisteria, and which they unhesitatingly approached. It offered them a shady nook emitting an intoxicating perfume. An inviting stone bench conveniently placed under the pergola caught their attention and they sat down. In contrast to the busy streets they had encountered in the town below them, they found themselves alone, in a magical, peaceful setting, and rejoiced at their luck.

"Oh, what a heavenly spot," sighed Livia; inhaling the heady aroma of the wisteria and looking lovingly at Marcellus. "I could sit here with you for the rest of my life."

"I was enjoying similar thoughts," agreed Marcellus, taking her hand and searching her enchanting brown eyes.

"Every night since I met you, I have dreamt of this moment; sitting here with you; the most beautiful woman I have ever set eyes on."

She smiled and reddened a little at the compliment. He drew closer. Their eyes locked together, then closed as their lips met, drifting them out of this world and into their own private paradise for the next few pleasurable moments.

"I am in love with you," he said; his big dark eyes opening again.

"I have fallen in love with you also," she whispered as she pouted her luscious red lips in expectancy of another kiss.

He quickly satisfied her desire, and putting his arms around her slim waist, allowed her to rest her head on his shoulder. She, with a delicious feeling of contentment, reposed in his arms, dreamily admiring that incomparable mountain-top view, whilst he gently and lovingly, stroked her silky light brown hair. Her palla had slipped in the embrace, leaving her hair provocatively exposed.

"Will you be my wife?" he whispered, as if trying not to disturb the sacrosanct serenity that absorbed them. There was no immediate reply. After a few moments of silence which tantalised him, she looked up to meet his eyes once more, and said.

"I shall treasure this moment for the rest of my life."

"You have not answered my question," he said with a touch of concern.

"Yes!" she whispered back. "Of course I shall marry you, my love."

Those words were followed by another long passionate kiss and embrace, sending them floating joyfully back into their newly discovered and deliciously private world.

"They are kissing! Ha! Ha!"

Three little children; one mischievous five-year-old boy and two younger girls, suddenly materialised in the front of the absorbed couple. With mocking eyes, they snickered and pointed at them with great mirth and satisfaction.

The now betrothed pair returned to earth, eyeing with some annoyance the little brats that had destroyed the serenity of those beloved moments. An irate nanny ran towards them with great urgency to retrieve and reprimand her cheeky, intrepid wards.

"Please forgive the children," she pleaded with an embarrassed look.

"Remind me," said Marcellus with a big smile, looking at Livia, but pointing at the children, "when we are married, never to have little rascals like these."

The nanny gave the lovers a sympathetic smile and ushered the little 'rascals' away'.

Their precious and memorable moment destroyed, the disconcerted lovers bid a reluctant 'au revois' to their magical surroundings, vowing to revisit some day, and made their way down to the town.

As they walked hand in hand, Livia, now feeling herself a part of Marcellus' life, dared to ask him about the contents of the package with which he had entrusted her when his injured ribs were being treated and which she had subsequently returned to him.

Marcellus in turn, feeling that she had a right to ask, explained the mission he had been entrusted with and as much as he knew of the powers of the veil.

"My goodness," she said. "That is an extraordinary tale. If your folks don't know where Pontius Pilate resides, perhaps mine do."

"Yes," he said. "That increases the odds of our finding him."

"I would love to see that veil," she said. "You will show it to me, won't you?"

"Of course, my love," he replied with a happy smile.

They made their way back to the food shop, where Penelope with a basket full of food supplies, was anxiously waiting for them.

"You had me worried, she admonished them with motherly concern. "You have been away longer than I expected."

"We have happy news for you. We will tell you later," said Livia with a big smile.

A few days later, Marcellus, whose ribs were recovering well, cautiously showed the veil to Livia and Penelope. The latter, who was just as stunned as her lady by the face they beheld, was able to relate many things concerning Yeshua whom she was sure the image represented.

Marcellus and Livia listened with growing interest to Penelope's stories which she dispensed in small anecdotes during the remainder of the voyage. She was as yet not officially a Christian, as she had not been baptised. However, she had heard many stories of Yeshua from one of her fellow servants who was from Galilee and had listened to him a number of times. Penelope was now a believer.

"I feel sure that if my friend Salome were to see this image," she said pointing to the bag where it was kept, "she would identify it as being the Lord Yeshua."

The ship finally entered the port of Antium, bringing an end to a tedious and often perilous passage which was the lot of every seafarer of that first century. Antium was the port often used by military vessels, in preference to the larger port of Puteoli or Ostia, which was perhaps the most congested port in all the Roman Empire, catering to all the commercial vessels bearing cargoes bound for Rome. The ship soon found berth on one of the wharves, and Captain Marcus saw his three passengers off with a broad smile and wishes for a happy future.

Livia was home. Antium was her home town, and she quickly commandeered a clean cart pulled by a single horse to take them to her father's house. She felt sure that Marcellus would be a welcome guest for at least a few days.

"You will like my parents," Livia told Marcellus with a lovely smile. Penelope agreed with a nod of the head and a smile of her own.

The house stood at the opposite end of town. It took them a while to get there.

"My father," said Livia, is an avid hunter. "He chose the site for our house bordering the countryside, so that he could simply ride out to his hunt without having to go through the town with his dogs. I am sure he will invite you to hunt with him."

This was great news for Marcellus, who being a skilful archer also shared a love for the hunt. He was keen to meet the man whom he hoped would be his father-in-law in the not too distant future.

At last they arrived at a large house surrounded by a high wall, and approaching the gate, Marcellus rang a bell that hung on the outside.

An old gatekeeper walked in their direction as quickly as his worn legs could carry him. A cry of delight escaped his lips as he recognised Livia. He promptly opened the gate and exchanged a loving hug with her.

"Ah! my lady dove," he exclaimed, looking at her with adoring eyes. "You have come back more beautiful than when you left."

"I have missed you Alphonsus," she said with a smile. "You do not look a day older."

They made their way up to the house whilst Alphonsus secured the gate again.

At the main door a maid appeared and joyfully throwing her hands up in the air, screamed.

"Lady Livia is here!"

A moment later a clatter of footsteps announced the family, who rushed to embrace and welcome their beloved Livia home.

Marcellus rejoiced at the enthusiastic welcome with which his beloved was received. He took it as proof of the good temperament which he felt, defined her character.

Penelope was cordially welcomed and she soon, giving Marcellus a fond smile, disappeared to her quarters.

The young tribune was warmly received by a grateful family, who were impressed by Livia's account of the dedication and assistance that he had given her during the course of that difficult and dangerous journey.

Livia's father Egnatius was a portly man in his early forties. He had dark brown hair, and light brown eyes accentuated by heavy, straight bushy eyebrows that almost joined each other. He had a well-formed Roman nose, a sensuous thin-lipped mouth and a heavy-set jaw. He studied Marcellus' comportment during the sumptuous cena which followed soon after their arrival, and which occasioned a forum for a parental assessment of the young man whom they suspected of having shown more than a passing interest in their daughter during that long and arduous voyage.

"My daughter tells me that you are fond of hunting," said Egnatius, with a smile. "What game have you hunted in Judea?"

Marcellus looked at the man, and with a smile replied. "Mostly rabbits, but occasionally deer when we could find them. We had no dogs to flush them out of the bush. Sometimes we would stumble on a wild boar, but that was most unusual. There are of course other wild predators such as mountain lions and jackals, but I do not hunt what I cannot eat."

"Wild boars present the biggest challenges as you know. I lost a good friend who died of injuries received from one of those rascals. But their meat is excellent."

"We can buy it at the market with a lot less trouble," said Livia's mother Fortunata with a touch of sarcasm and a shrug of her shapely shoulders. She, like Livia, was a beautiful woman. She was a little heavier than her daughter but endowed with most of the well-proportioned features that the latter had inherited. Her eyes were a dark brown; the oval of her face was pleasantly elongated allowing for a straight and well-proportioned nose, long in actuality, but light in appearance; her mouth was small, full lipped and sensuous.

Marcellus observed that Egnatius was well pleased with his wife's beauty. There was, even after so many years of marriage, a revealing look of admiration in his eyes whenever he looked at her across the table. The young tribune took pleasure in contemplating what his beloved Livia would look like twenty years or so down the road. He too was much pleased.

"What are you going to do now when you get back home?" enquired Egnatius with a smile.

"I really don't know," replied Marcellus. "My mother wants me to try for the Senate and be a senator like my father. He, has not expressed any wish on his part. I suppose he would rather I make up my own mind. I suspect though, that he would want me to join the family business so that he can dedicate himself solely to the Senate and the administration of our properties."

"What is your family business?" asked Fortunata, peeling a fig which she had just taken from the silver bowl in front of her.

"We own vineyards in Umbria. My father has to travel there a number of times a year which is understandably tiring for him as he grows older. I have an older brother who helps my father, with our ship chandling business, but he does not want to leave Ostia. He has a lovely house by the water on the outskirts, and his wife is from there.

"The wine business is a good business," remarked Egnatius raising his cup to drink. "It is also a healthy occupation as it keeps all concerned working out in the open with lots of sun to enjoy. The weather in wine country has necessarily to provide for a lot of sun, as well as soft soaking rain at the appropriate time."

"Yes," agreed Marcellus taking a good sip of wine from the cup in his hand. "This is excellent wine," he said. "You know your wines."

The cena over, the family retired to the peristyle where they entertained themselves all evening. Livia talked about her six month stay in Caesarea with her aunt and uncle, and Marcellus was asked to talk about his experiences in the Legion. That, greatly impressed Egnatius who had never served in the military, much to his regret.

Livia's sister Aelia, had just turned sixteen. Her looks were pleasant but unremarkable compared with her elder sister. She was however an exceptionally talented musician. She sang and played the harp with great feeling, drawing much admiration from all present. Sabino the baby of the house was twelve years old and quite a handsome boy. He, also joined in the entertainment trying go accompany his sister with his flute.

The only absented member of the family was Livia's brother, Avitus. He was away on business. He was a year younger than Livia and was his father's right arm in the family business so to speak.

"He does most of the travelling for me," said Egnatius. "He is very good at buying things that sell well in Rome and the surrounding area. We, as a result import many things, including grain from Egypt and other commodities from Hispania, Gaul, and Greece."

Marcellus had been at Egnatius house for five days. He hunted with his host who was very impressed with his marksmanship and congenial nature and they soon became good friends.

Sitting in the peristyle the evening of the sixth day, Marcellus announced to the family that he would be leaving the following day, and that he wished to talk to Egnatius before leaving.

Livia knew that Marcellus was going to ask her father for her hand in marriage and was very excited, but she kept it to herself.

Carrying their wine cups in their hands, Egnatius led Marcellus into his study.

"Make yourself comfortable," said the master of the house pointing to a chair.

Marcellus sat down and took a sip of his wine. Egnatius sat opposite his guest and quickly swallowing a mouthful of his wine, motioned with his hand for him to start the conversation.

"First," said Marcellus, "I would like to ask a favour of you."

Again, Egnatius motioned to proceed.

"I am trying to contact a certain person, and I shall need as much help as I can get to find him."

"Who is this person?"

"His name is Pontius Pilate. He was the Procurator of Judea for almost eleven years. He has now returned; possibly to

Rome, but I do not know. He could be living right here in Antium, or any other town for that matter." Marcellus looked at his host expectantly. The latter stared into space for a few moments.

"No," he said, shaking his head slowly. "But I have one particular friend who knows a great many people. I shall ask him. Perhaps he can help." Egnatius drank some more of his wine.

"Thank you. I appreciate that...Now," said Marcellus. "I have something of great importance to ask of you." There was a touch of nervousness in his voice. He studied the other's face, and bravely said.

"I wish to ask you for Livia's hand in marriage."

Two pairs of eyes locked together for a few pregnant moments. One pair with hope. The other pair with regret.

The father quickly and mentally summed up the situation. The scales tilted in Marcellus' favour. Egnatius had taken a liking to the young man. He knew that his family was of the best, and his future bright and secure. He was also quite handsome, and his prospect of acquiring some very good-looking grandchildren pleased him.

"Livia!" He called out.

She materialised in front of them almost as soon as the last syllable had escaped her father's lips.

"Yes, father?" she asked with a beautiful smile; a tear glistening in her eye.

Egnatius thought he would have a little fun at the expense of the expectant pair.

"This man says he wants to marry you.... What am I to tell him?" he asked with as straight a face as he could muster.

Livia literally jumped on Marcellus throwing her arms around his neck.

"Yes!" She cried. "Yes!" And pulling away from Marcellus, hugged and kissed her father.

"What is all the commotion?" Fortunata's voice preceded her entrance into the study, followed by the whole family, and servants.

"You can have her!" bellowed Egnatius over all the noise and activity.

It took the happy Marcellus a few moments before he could release himself from the arms of the women, to embrace and thank his future father-in-law. Both men were ecstatic. They were also greatly amused to see the women of the family clucking like a bunch of hens, already making plans for a wedding that was well into the future.

Marcellus left as expected the following day with the family's blessings; leaving behind a sad Livia. He promised to return as soon as possible to assist with the wedding arrangements.

The secret of the veil remained solely with Livia and Penelope; both having promised to keep its existence to themselves. Marcellus carried it on his chest under his tunic once again.

CHAPTER SIX

ROME

Marcellus arrived at home in Rome to a rousing welcome. It was mid afternoon and his whole family was there. His father, in the garden talking with the gardener, was the first to see him as he approached the gate and rang the bell. He went quickly and joyfully to greet his son followed by the gardener-gatekeeper.

The gate was promptly opened. A happy Marcellus embraced his overjoyed father and smiled a hello to the gardener.

"Welcome home my son," said Porcius Fulvius with a loving smile.

"Good to be home again," greeted Marcellus. "You are looking well Father. How is Mother?

"She is well, my son, and will be overjoyed to see you... come." Porcius threw an arm over his son's shoulder and led him towards the house.

Ignatia, Marcellus' mother suddenly appearing at the main entrance, rushed to embrace her son. She called for her daughter Rufina, and Marcius her younger son, to join her. All three fell on a happy, beaming Marcellus, greeting him with loving embraces and kisses.

"Oh! What a wonderful surprise," cried Ignatia; tears of joy filling her eyes. "We have missed you so much."

Young, fourteen-year-old Marcius took one of Marcellus' bags from him, and all walked into the house. Rufina hung on to her brother's arm with a smile of admiration lighting up her beautiful young face.

"You missed my eighteenth birthday by only two days," she pouted as he smilingly kissed her brow. "Oh, that is a shame," he said. "I shall make it up to you."

The family cena that evening was quite a celebration. The young ex-tribune entertained his admiring family for hours bringing them all up to date with his military exploits and lastly with the news of his betrothal to Livia. This last piece of news gave rise to many questions which were answered during the course of the evening as they sat conversing in their striking peristyle.

Ignatia and Rufina wanted to know everything about Livia and her family.

"We shall have to visit them soon," said Ignatia. Throwing a questioning look at her husband.

"When does the Senate adjourn, Porcius?" she asked.

The senator, busy talking to Marcellus, turned to face his wife with a distracted look in his eyes. "I am not quite sure dear, I shall try to find out tomorrow." He turned again to his son. Their conversation continued as they discussed the need for finding Pontius Pilate's whereabouts.

"There was some talk of his having returned from Judea," said Porcius. "However, nothing more has been heard of him for some time. I shall make enquiries concerning him tomorrow. I feel sure that we can track him down; probably through his father-in-law who will certainly know where his daughter is." Taking a sip of his wine, he gave his son a reassuring smile.

The strains of a harp interrupted the father and son conversation. Rufina's nimble, well trained fingers confidently plucking the strings of the instrument, interpreted with great feeling, a tantalizingly joyful melody that filled the lovely peristyle where the family sat, capturing everyone's attention. Her beautiful light brown, long lashed eyes had a vacant look about them, as her soul soared with the music.

Elegantly poised and gently leaning forward as she played, she unconsciously displayed to great advantage, her lithe youthful figure. Her graceful, agile hands occasionally abandoned the strings to quickly brush back her long brown hair which inevitably slipped forward onto the strings. Her straight and well delineated nose led the eye to a small sensuous mouth; its full red lips curving gently in the hint of a smile, as her well trimmed, straight eyebrows, rose and dipped in concurrence with the expression that the phrasing of the music conveyed.

In short, she presented a beautiful picture which could not but enhance her delectable performance.

Hearty applause greeted the end of the song; especially from Marcellus, who was stunned by the proficiency that his sister had acquired in playing the instrument during his absence. Getting up from his cushion, he went over to her and kissed and hugged her with great emotion.

"My goodness," he exclaimed, "you have been working hard at your music. I have never heard a better rendering of that tune by anyone."

Rufina smiled gratefully, and Ignatia was quick to confirm her daughter's dedication. She turned to look at young Marcius.

"You, young man, will have to try a lot harder on that aulus of yours if you are ever going to accompany your sister."

Marcius made no reply. He simply looked at his brother and smiled.

"Will you let me have a look at your gladius Marcellus?" he asked with eagerness in his voice.

The ex-tribune got up, went to his room, and was soon back with his sword, which he handed to his brother.

"Careful now, it's quite sharp," he warned. His mother watched with a little concern.

The week that followed was a very pleasant one for Marcellus who was smothered with attention by his loving family. He rode every morning with his father, spent the evenings with his friends; both male and female, and had many hours of intimate conversation with his dedicated sister in whom he had always confided. Having been let into the secret of the veil, Rufina was most keen to see it.

"I swear to keep it to myself," she said. "But you must show it to me. What an incredible thing it must be."

Late one evening, when the house was at rest, Rufina tiptoed quietly to Marcellus' room and knocked lightly on the door. He was still awake and hastened to open for her.

"I have come to see the veil," she whispered. "Will you show it to me?"

He went over to his travelling bag, opened it, and took out the veil which was wrapped in a piece of linen and tied with some string. She, taking the lamp from the table beside his bed, held it up to assist him in untying the string which had been knotted rather hastily and was giving him some trouble unravelling it.

Finally, the knots were undone. He withdrew the veil, and opening it, laid it open on the bed. She stepped back precipitately; startled at the realistic image in front of her. He took the lamp from her unsteady hand.

"Oh!" she gasped. "It's unbelievable. What a realistic face." She bent over it, examining it with great care. "I agree with you. It is certainly not painted," she whispered, feeling the silky fabric. "How could this have been accomplished?"

"It baffles everyone," said Marcellus. "For those who believe in miracles, and I for one do; it is said to be a miraculous veil."

"How is that?" asked Rufina, with a look of surprise in her pretty light brown eyes.

"My superior, Centurion Gabinius in Judea," explained Marcellus looking intently into his sister's eyes, "had his son miraculously cured by this veil. The boy had a fall which left him totally paralysed. He had a broken spine and was at the point of death. The physician had given up on him. The veil was draped over the boy's head, and he recovered instantly."

She straightened and took a step back, a look of scepticism in her eyes.

"If someone else had told me that story," she responded. "I would not have believed it. But coming from you... I believe it."

He took her hand in his. "Remember dear sister that you have promised not to tell anyone." She kissed his cheek. "I shall keep your secret. But what are you going to do with it?"

"I undertook to deliver it to its rightful owner. I shall be leaving tomorrow for Pyrgi. There, I am to meet someone who will direct me to the owner's house. It is in a small village not far from that city.

Rufina felt like asking her brother who the owner was but desisted. She gave him a kiss and wishing him a good night went back to her room.

Marcellus was in the act of folding the veil to put it back in the linen wrap. He felt a great tingling through his arms, followed by a feeling of sadness that he had never experienced before. He pulled away, rubbed his arms, and waited a few moments. The tingling stopped. Once again he took the veil in his hands, and continued to fold it...The tingling returned.

He persevered however despite the feeling. He re-wrapped the veil in the linen cloth and put it back in his bag which contained other useful things that he normally carried when on horseback. It was actually a double bag, which straddled the horse in front of him and sat on the flat saddle. One side contained a small bronze shield, and still had room for his scabbard and gladius which he at time stored there but normally wore. A few pieces of clean cloth and some salt in a little crucible would also be housed there. The other part of the bag would carry a small water skin and some food.

The following morning, a handsomely attired Marcellus; the veil folded on his chest underneath his tunic, appeared in the dining room to have a leisurely breakfast with the family.

"My goodness!" chorused Ignatia and Rufina. They both gotup and embraced him.

"Where are you bound for looking so dapper?" asked his mother with a teasing look in her eyes. Rufina said nothing. She knew where and why he was going.

"I have to deliver a package to a lady of note who leaves near Pyrgi...Actually Procula. Pontius Pilate's wife."

Ignatia nodded as if impressed. Though she had no idea who Pilate was.

"You will probably have to stay the night somewhere," warned Porcius, wiping his mouth. "It's a fair distance, and your horse will thank you for it. Are you taking Artemis?"

"Yes Father. I want to see if he is as feisty as ever."

"He still goes like the wind. No one can touch him when it comes to speed," laughed Porcius.

Breakfast over; Marcellus bid farewell to all. He kissed his mother and sister; ruffled his brother's hair lovingly; and made his way to the stables with his father. Celsius, the stable hand prepared Artemis for him. Porcius waved at his son as he rode out of the gate.

"Enjoy your ride," he shouted. Marcellus dug his heels into his mount's side and rode away at a canter.

He expected to reach Pyrgi in four hours and questioned the need to put up for the night as his father had suggested. The vibrant and crowded city of Rome however, made for slower progress than he had anticipated. He was forced to dismount and lead his horse on various occasions due to the density of the crowds on crossing marketplaces and travelling some of the narrower streets. Heavily laden wheelbarrows and carts constantly crossed his path and made it hazardous for horse and rider.

It was midday by the time he pulled into an inn for lunch and have his horse rested and fed.

After a leisurely meal he continued on his way, making good headway once he had cleared the city and rode towards the coast. The day was hot, but as he slowly trotted down from the hill country towards the sparkling blue Mediterranean Sea, the briny breeze gave him some respite and made his ride more comfortable.

Finally, Pyrgi came into sight. The colourful little town spread lazily along the sea shore for quite a distance. An avenue of trees leading to a wide stone arched entrance welcomed the traveller. Riding into the town, he soon found himself in a large square with many tents at its centre, forming a busy and well attended marketplace. Though crowded, there was ample room to ride around its perimeter which was lined with bazaars and shops fronting pretty multicoloured buildings one or two storeys high; their windows and balcony's adorned with iron railings and flower pots.

Marcellus rode around looking for the sail-maker's shop where he expected to be given direction to Pontius Pilate's residence. The owner was a friend of a friend of his father's.

After a couple of unsuccessful rounds of the square, he dismounted and asked one of the bazaar owners for directions. It was not in the square he was told, but in a street nearer the beach on the outskirts of the town. After a while he found the shop. The owner proved most congenial and not only gave him good directions to Pontius Pilate's house, but also invited him to have some refreshments with him.

"I am Petronius," announced the man with a big smile. "And who have I the honour of meeting?" He stretched out his hand for Marcellus to press.

Marcellus, giving his name, took the man's hand and smilingly pressed it.

Petronius took charge of his visitor's horse and walked it to the stable in the back yard. He put it beside his own horse, gave it a drink of water and placed a basket of oats in front of it on the stable floor.

"What a beautiful horse. Is he an Arabian?" asked the man with admiration in his eyes.

"Yes," answered Marcellus, pulling his saddlebag off the horse. "My father owned two of them, but he gave me this black one for my birthday three years ago just before I left to join the Legion."

They entered the house and Marcellus was shown into a very neat and well-appointed room. The host, inviting him to sit, disappeared into an adjoining alcove.

"Would you like wine or juice?" called out Petronius.

"Wine will do beautifully. Thank you," answered the guest.

A few moments passed, and the smiling host reappeared bearing a tray with some enticing victuals, a jug of wine and two cups.

"I have to fend for myself. I live alone," said the man with a smile.

"You're a bachelor?" ventured Marcellus, with a questioning look.

"No. I'm a widower," answered Petronius, who was in his early forties.

A friendly conversation ensued in which among other things, the host informed his guest of Pontius Pilate's love for sailing.

"I made a couple of sails for him," explained Petronius. He took a sip of his wine and continued. "He has a very nice little boat which he handles all by himself. He is a very private person. Never says much but pays well and seems pleased with my work. We get along just fine."

"I have never met him," said Marcellus. "I have a small parcel for his wife which was given me in Judea to deliver into her hands."

A pleasant hour went by very quickly for the pair of new friends. The well rested visitor got up and made ready to leave. Petronius accompanied him out and into the stable.

Marcellus, mounting his horse once more, bid his new friend farewell.

He was soon on his way to the address given him. Petronius had explained that Pilate's house stood on a promontory just outside of Pyrgi. He could not miss it as long as he held the shore line in view.

The road that led to Pilate's house was a quiet road with the sea on his right as he rode. He was enjoying his ride but felt like giving Artemis a bit if a gallop. He could see Pilate's house on the top of the cliff. It was a breathtaking sight. The sea though relatively calm, swelled up as it approached the promontory and even from that distance he could see the foam, as the waves pouring over offshore rocks, crashed with astounding force against the cliff face sending big clouds of spray high above the water.

He steered Artemis towards the beach. On reaching the sand, he became suddenly aware of two horses cutting in behind him. Looking back, he saw two masked riders coming at him with drawn swords. He dug his heels into his horse. It instantly responded, and a close chase began. Galloping along, Marcellus assessed his situation. As usual when he travelled, he wore his Gladius, and the veil rested on his chest inside his tunic.

Reaching into his bag, he pulled out the shield. He would need it against two attackers. Using his military know how, he rapidly formulated a plan of action. He would make an abrupt stop, and turning, charge back at his enemies catching them off guard.

Ahead of him were some rocks which formed a type of gateway or broken arch. He decided to make the turn, immediately on passing them.

As he rode through the archway, he felt something fall over him. It was a net, and it pulled him off his horse and onto the sandy beach with a heavy jolt. He struggled with it, trying to cut it with his gladius. Then someone jump on him. He felt a sudden sharp pain in the head, and everything went black.

It was late afternoon when Marcellus opened his eyes. His head was extremely sore. He touched it and found that he was bleeding. Some of the blood had already dried and encrusted around the wound. He was naked. Looking around still in a haze, he spotted his torn inner garment lying on the sand a few paces away. He reached for it. With great difficulty he struggled into it and got on his feet. His arm was very sore. The rocks around him had sheltered him from the view of passersby on the beach.

He walked to the shore and splashed some water on his face. That woke him up a little, and he began to consider his next move.

After some thought, he decided to continue on and try to get some help at Pilate's house. Pilate, he hoped would at least alert the soldiers who patrolled the area, and perhaps apprehend the robbers. He staggered on uncertainly, burdened by continuous dizziness which made every step a challenge.

Marcellus was still very uncertain on his feet as he rang the bell at Pilate's gate.

The gatekeeper approached, and seeing him half naked, asked rather dryly what he wanted.

"I am the son of Senator Porcius Fulvius. I have been attacked by robbers. I need help," said Marcellus, and collapsed.

"We will follow your directions." Those words uttered by a pleasant female voice, brought Marcellus back into the land of the living. He opened his eyes and beheld a very beautiful woman perhaps in her late twenties, very attractively attired, who was talking to someone who had just left the room. Presently, she turned, and finding him awake, approached his bed.

"Ah! You are conscious again," she smiled with relief.

The invalid smiled back.

"I am Procula. My husband is Pontius Pilate; former procurator of Judea. You are safe now."

Marcellus smiled again and nodded.

"You are the son of Senator Porcius Fulvius the gateman said." Her hands pressed the side of her head in alarm.

"My, my!" she said. "You are lucky to be alive. The physician had to suture your head. He directed us to talk to you and keep you awake for a good while, and to call him again if you talked nonsense or your sight was impaired in anyway."

"I thank you for your kind help," said Marcellus. "I was on my way to bring you a veil that you left behind in Judea. A woman servant of my superior officer and previously a servant of yours named Susannah, wanted you to have it. It performed an extraordinary miracle on Centurion Gabinius' son. It has unique powers." Marcellus stopped. He realised that Procula was crying.

"Oh, my goodness," she whispered bringing her face closer to her guest. "You must keep this to yourself. We shall talk privately later. My husband must not know." She tentatively looked around… "Or anyone else for that matter. Please say that you were attacked near here and just happened to come for help and to report the incident." She looked pleadingly at Marcellus.

"Of course," he smiled. "It will be our secret."

"How is the invalid?"

Those words heralded the entrance of Pontius Pilate.

"I feel better. Thank you," responded Marcellus.

"I have alerted the local patrol to spread the word and track down your horse. I assume you were travelling on horseback. It will likely expose your assailants," said Pontius with a determined look. "Presumably there were more than one. They seldom operate on their own." He stretched out his hand for Marcellus to press. The latter took it and pressing it with a grateful smile, introduced himself.

"I am Marcellus Fulvius, and I am most indebted to you and your charming wife for looking after me so well."

"It is our pleasure…. Tell me. Was your horse a valuable one?"

"Yes. I am afraid so. It's an Arabian. Very black and bearing our family brand."

"There! Right there, is the reason for them attacking you. They will be found fear not. A horse like that is difficult to sell without attracting attention," assured the host nodding his head with certainty.

Pilate was a tall slim man, in his early forties. He was not handsome, but neither was he ugly. His long ponderous face and bushy dark eyebrows gave him a certain distinction. Marcellus could not make up his mind whether the man's mouth; large and thin lipped; and smiling in concert with his eyebrows; expressed mirth or cynicism. He had grey/blue, enquiring eyes and a long slender Roman nose. His dark brown hair, thin and closely cropped, was combed forward on his large and somewhat wrinkled brow. His ears were close to the head, and not overly large for the length of his face. He was splendidly dressed in a dark blue toga with a silver fringe which appeared and disappeared as he moved.

"We must let the patient rest," said Procula, who had been silent since her husband entered the room.

They both turned to go. Then Pilate stopped and looking back at Marcellus, said.

"I should dispatch a rider to your father's house. Is your return overdue? Would they be concerned about you?"

"Yes. I was supposed to return at latest the day after I had left." said the invalid. "How long have I been here?"

"One day," said Procula, approaching the bed again.

"That is very kind of you, but hopefully, I shall be able to leave very soon, since I feel much recovered. So there is no need for you to take the trouble."

"You may have further dizzy spells," said the hostess with concern in her kind eyes. "For the moment, just rest. Tomorrow you can get up if you feel well enough, and we will see if you can walk around steadily."

Husband and wife left the room. Marcellus felt his bandaged head and lay back to rest. His head still ached but to a lesser degree. The pain in his arm remained but was much improved. He was thankful that it was not broken. He soon fell asleep.

A few hours later, there was a knock at his room door.

"Come in," answered Marcellus sitting up in bed.

Pontius walked into the room with a satisfied look on his face. "They have found your horse and apprehended two robbers."

"That is great news," responded the guest. "But there were three that I could tell. The third one threw a net over me. He was hiding in the rocks waiting for me to be chased past him."

The following day, after a splendid seafood lunch, Marcellus sat in the shade of a pergola on the terrace of Pontius' house enjoying the view of the sea immediately below him. He had been dizzy-free all morning and was optimistic that he could be on his way soon to question the two robbers with regard to the veil.

Both Procula and Pilate were sitting with him. The latter was somewhat surprised at hearing that as a tribune, Marcellus had been serving in Judea, and privately wondered at the coincidence of their meeting at this time. However he made no remark; though he felt a pang of jealousy, knowing that Procula was much younger than he, and that this handsome young man, might have a crush on her even though she was somewhat older than him.

He dismissed the thought. He trusted his wife who had always dealt with him in a loving and devoted way.

"I shall leave you both for a little while," said the host. "I have to see to a small repair on my boat." Turning to Marcellus, he said. "Please do not leave until I return. We shall ride together to interrogate the robbers. I may be of some help to you in that regard."

Marcellus nodded in compliance, and Pilate went off to his task.

"I am glad that Pontius is inadvertently allowing us a little time to talk," said Procula as soon as her husband was out of sight.

Her guest nodded and smiled but said nothing.

"What I tell you now," she said with great earnestness in her voice. "You must promise me never to divulge. It could cost me my life." She looked him in the eye as she spoke.

"You have my promise."

"The veil that you were bringing me, has the image of my God and Saviour. The Lord Yeshua. I am a Christian." She clasped her elegant hands as she said those words, and a look of reverence directed skywards enveloped her eyes.

"He has I suspect, performed a number of miracles through the veil. One of which I told you about," volunteered Marcellus. "I myself experienced a strange tingling in my arms when I last touched it on packing it into my travelling bag. Perhaps it was a warning of what was to befall me. I simply must find it again and bring it back to you. I have also come to believe in the power of Yeshua, even though I am not a Christian."

"As you probably know, Caligula is persecuting the Christians and putting them to death."

"Yes. So I hear," he answered.

"My husband, as you may have heard in Judea, was the man who sentenced Yeshua to death on the cross; even though he thought him innocent." Tears glistened in her lovely dark eyes, recalling that dreadful, fateful day.

Marcellus with a look of surprise, waited for her to continue. He had heard something of the Romans crucifying some Messiah of the Jews, but he had not given the matter much thought at the time. It hardly concerned him then.

"The Jews forced him to do it," she continued. "They hated the man even though all he did was good. He cured countless of sick people. Even Romans."

She drew a little closer to him and looked around anxiously. "Pilate suffers from terrible nightmares as a result of that judgement which only he as Roman Procurator was authorised to pronounce. That is why I need the veil back. Perhaps Yeshua, who forgives every penitent no matter how bad the sin, has forgiven him, and the veil can free him of that terrible scourge." Again her eyes filled with tears which breaking loose, ran down her lovely face.

"I shall do my best to find it and bring it back to you," promised Marcellus squeezing her hand tenderly.

"Whenever you need to bring me any message, give it to the gatekeeper," she advised. "He is a Christian and I trust him implicitly. He will pass it on to me privately. Though you are welcome to visit us any time you wish; Pontius rather likes you."

Pontius appeared soon after at the terrace. He strode over to them with a confident step; a jovial smile on his long intelligent face. His mind had temporarily blotted out the nocturnal horrors which tortured his soul. He waged a daily battle attempting to gain some respite.

"Are you up to riding out with me to see those robbers?" he asked with a smile.

"I think so," replied his guest with confidence and getting to his feet.

"With a bit of luck, we shall be back in time for our cena," said Pilate scratching his ample and sun burnt forehead.

He threw a glance and a smile at Procula, who smiled back and wished the pair God speed.

"You have a most charming wife," said Marcellus as the two of them rode away towards Pyrgi. "I am so happy to have met her."

Pilate looked at his companion with a suspicious look in his eye. But said nothing.

"I shall soon be married also," said Marcellus with enthusiasm. "I am now betrothed to a beautiful girl whom I deeply love."

"I congratulate you my young friend," smiled Pontius breathing a sigh of relief as his vague and unfounded suspicions about his wife dissipated into thin air. "Good, loyal women are hard to find these days," he said, as if to confirm his faith in Procula.

"I met her on board ship during my voyage from Judea," said Marcellus.

The conversation continued as the horses trotted next to each other. Pilate asked Marcellus many questions regarding his tour of duty in Judea. He recalled Centurion Gabinius quite well, though he had as Marcellus deduced, not heard of young Julius' cure. The ex-tribune made no mention of it, or anything to do with the veil.

"Now, to get these rascals to sing about that other one," said Pontius as the pair rode through the gates of the Legion's barracks where the robbers were held for further questioning.

A centurion who recognised Pontius met them in the quadrangle where there were a number of Legionaries being put through their various drills.

"Good day sir," said the soldier, saluting Pilate. He smiled and nodded to Marcellus as Pontius introduced him as an ex-tribune and the subject of their visit.

"We have them chained up in the dungeon," said the centurion. "Please follow me."

The pair of visitors followed the soldier as he led the way. Soon they were joined by the jailor.

They passed a number of well occupied cells. Each cell was illuminated by a torch fitted into an iron ring on the opposite corridor wall. They stopped at a small cell that held two men.

"Here they are," said the jailor. "What do you want done with them?"

"Do you have an empty cell or a place where we can talk to them separately?" whispered Pilate, partly covering his mouth.

"Yes sir," answered the jailor. He opened the cell door, unlocked the leg chain from an iron ring on the wall, and taking the man by the arm pulled him out of the cell; another chain around his neck dragging behind him. He was a thickset man in his mid forties, with a broken nose and mean looking eyes. The iron collar had made his neck bleed and there was some dry blood on his naked chest. Marcellus felt a little sorry for the unfortunate creature.

The jailor soon found an empty cell, and opening it took the man in, and once again locked his chain onto a ring in the stone wall. The man flopped onto the floor and gave his captors a contemptuous look.

Pontius, looking down his long nose at the prisoner was the first to speak.

"This is the man you attacked," he said with severity nodding in the direction of Marcellus. "He is going to ask you some questions which you better answer truthfully."

The prisoner gave Marcellus a challenging look. He regretted not having killed him when he had had the chance.

"I want to know," said Marcellus with authority, "who that third man who threw the net over me is, and where he is now."

Marcellus reasoned that since the veil had not been found on the two thieves being questioned, it would necessarily have been taken by the third man. He did not want to draw attention to it however in the presence of Pilate.

"Well?" persisted Marcellus seeing that no response was forthcoming.

"I don't know where he went," answered the prisoner with a shrug of his shoulders. "He had gone to buy food for us when the soldiers took us."

"We have means of making you talk," threatened the centurion.

"That's the truth," said the man with apparent conviction.

Neither Pontius or Marcellus were convinced of the man's sincerity, but as there was another to be interrogated, they made it appear that they were satisfied with the information given.

The jailor took back the man and soon returned with the other, having dealt with him in a similar way.

"Now!" said Pontius. His grey/blue eyes looking severely at the man. "Your mate tells us that the man who threw the net over my friend's head has disappeared and neither of you know where he's gone. You tell me what happened."

The man was of medium height, around thirty years old, slimly built, with pudgy nose and a very small thin-lipped mouth. He held it half open as he reviewed his inquisitors. He appeared afraid.

"He got away, because he had gone to buy food. We were trying to sell the horse when the soldiers took us."

"Where do you think he is hiding now?"

"How should I know?" answered the man with little conviction in his voice.

"We shall have to prod your mind to make you guess a little better," said the centurion once again giving the man a fierce look.

"He may have gone to his girl friend's place. I don't know."

"What does he look like?" asked Pontius. "Does he have any distinguishing marks on him?"

The man looked at the floor, then suddenly looking up again, his eyes and Marcellus' met.

"Why should I be punished for that rat's sake? They are brothers. The younger one whom you are looking for is Suliman. He is twenty years old. Tall, thin, and talks with a lisp. He also scratches his neck all the time. It's a habit with him. I overheard them talking about keeping a good portion of my share after they got the money for the horse. Why should I shield them and make things worse for myself?

"Where does he live? And how can we find his girl friend?"

The thief gave them her address but was sketchy about Suliman's. He then asked to be put in a different cell. Marcellus looked at the jailor with raised eyebrows."

"I'll put him with someone else," he said.

The enlightened pair collected Marcellus' horse and left the barracks. Artemis, was led by his happy master who however continued to ride Pontius' horse. They trotted off to the ex-procurator's striking house to discuss the next move in their search for the fugitive Suliman.

Pontius' legal mind was well employed as they rode back.

'Why is this young fellow so keen in finding Suliman?' He asked himself. 'He has that beautiful horse back again. The loss of his clothes or arms would hardly bother him. They can all be easily replaced. What was he carrying that was so important or valuable that he is so set on getting it back?'

The more he thought about it, the less he could imagine what it was. Presently, having arrived at his house, he gave up.

The cena was a cordial affair. The three friends enjoyed their food and each other's company. Procula took an enthusiastic part in the men's discussion as to how to deal with Suliman. The addresses given them were both in Pyrgi, and so that made it a local problem.

Pontius' curiosity was finally satisfied when Marcellus with an undetected wink at Procula, told them that he had been dispossessed of a very dear relic which had been entrusted to him, and which he simply had to try and recover.

Next morning, Marcellus left Pilate's home with the couple's blessings and a very handsome gladius and scabbard that

Pontius had given him as a gift. He began his quest for the mysterious Suliman.

It would hardly surprise my faithful reader to learn that the addresses that Marcellus sought, were in the most disreputable part of town. The last thing that our hero wanted was to be conspicuous in either his clothing or the horse he rode. He decided to call on his friend the sailmaker once again to borrow his horse and the oldest clothes that he possessed.

Petronius was overjoyed to see Marcellus, and after being brought up to date with all that had occurred; with the exception of any reference to the veil, he attended to his friend's needs with great enthusiasm.

A truly common looking Marcellus rode a very ordinary looking horse into the street that he had been searching for. He carefully scrutinised the characteristics of each doorway he passed. Finally, he recognised the sign of a duck, painted crudely and almost faded, on a decrepit arch over a scruffy brown door. He dismounted, and holding on to the reins of his horse, knocked at the door. After a few moments, the door was opened by an attractive young woman of about eighteen, with very untidy hair. She noisily chewed on a piece of an apple she held in her hand. The girl looked at the stranger, took another bite of the apple, and with little interest in her voice, asked.

"Yea. What d'ya want?"

"I'm looking for Suliman," said Marcellus with a coarse intonation.

"He ain't here. Who wants him?"

"My name is Cato, and I've heard that he has a veil with a man's face painted on it. I'd like to buy it."

The girl looked at him with some interest but made no comment.

"I am not going to be in town much longer," said Marcellus, "so if he's interested, tell him to meet me at the wine shop around the corner in about two hours. I will pay him good money for it. Ask him to bring it with him, I don't want to lose any time."

He turned, mounted his horse and wishing her a good day, rode off. He stopped at the end of the street, and dismounting, pulled his horse into an alleyway. He could see the girl's house from there. Presently, she came out and walked past the alley where he was hiding. He followed her at a distance. The street was quite noisy and well travelled, which enabled him to keep an eye on her progress undetected. In actual fact she never turned around.

After traversing a couple of streets, she knocked at a door and waited. A tall thin man opened the door and let her in. Marcellus leant up against a wall holding on to his horse's reins and waited. A while later, just as our hero was beginning to tire, the girl came out accompanied by the man. He said something to her which Marcellus could not hear and went back inside scratching his neck.

Once the girl had gone, Marcellus approached the house, tied his horse nearby and knocked at the door. The man opened it. The ex-tribune was on him like lightning. He gave the unsuspecting wretch a great blow on the chin, sending him sprawling backwards into the house. Marcellus kicked the door shut, and throwing himself on top of the bandit, held a dagger that Petronius had given him at the rascals' throat.

It did not take long for Marcellus to reclaim the veil. Suliman lay on his bed, wrists and ankles tied to the bed's legs. He had been quite easily persuaded to give up the veil which his girl friend had just brought him.

Marcellus left the rogue in his bed prison, and closing the house door behind him, mounted his waiting horse and took off for Petronius' house.

Two hours had passed since the veil had been retrieved. Marcellus, riding Artemis, arrived at the gate of Pontius' house and asked the gateman to announce his visit to his master and mistress.

He was cordially received by Procula who came into the garden to meet him.

"You look like the cat that swallowed the canary," she said with a smile.

"I found the rascal and left him tied hand and foot to the legs of his bed," he said.

Procula laughed imagining the scene.

"Pontius is sailing," she said. "He will be away until cena time. Come on in." She led the way.

"I got the veil for you," said Marcellus as the pair reached the peristyle. Procula received the words with immense joy. He pulled it out from his tunic and gave it to her.

"How can I ever thank you? You are my hero," she said, giving him a warm hug. "Too bad we cannot have a celebration. But who knows what the future will bring?"

"Seeing that Pontius is not here," said Marcellus with a smile, "I shall ride back home. If I can get Artemis to cooperate, I can be home before midnight. Please tell Pilate that I retrieved my treasure and made straight for home. Thank you both once again for your warm hospitality."

She accompanied him to the garden.

"Thank you," she said with a parting smile. "May Yeshua go with you and remain with you always. Come and see us again and bring your wife with you. You will always be welcome in this house."

She waved to him as he rode out the gate.

CHAPTER SEVEN

TORMENTS

It was the middle of the night. Pontius Pilate paced up and down his room in great fear. He dare not go back to bed. The dreaded nightmare would accost him again. He felt tired, and a cold perspiration put his body completely out of sorts. Still, he resisted. 'Perhaps,' he said to himself, 'if I lie down and keep awake, I shall avoid the horror.'

Procula whose bedroom was next door, could hear the constant pacing. In earlier days, her husband's nightmares had been much less frequent; perhaps once a month. But recently they had become almost a weekly occurrence. She was very concerned that the frequency would increase and drive him mad. She got up and went to him.

"Pontius!" she whispered throwing her arm around him. "Go back to bed. Come, I shall lie with you. The bad dreams may not disturb you if I am there."

He looked at her with a faraway look in his frightened eyes. "Do you think they will stop if you are with me?"

"Perhaps, my dear," she said, and led him to the bed. He allowed her to lay him down, and she lay beside him.

"I feel cold," he said. She put a light blanket over him and embraced him as they lay.

Presently he fell asleep. She prayed. "Yeshua, please forgive him. In your immense love forgive the unforgivable. He would never have sentenced you if he had had his way. The Jews were to blame; and they accepted it. He found you innocent. Please Lord, show your divine mercy to him, and free him from these torments."

For a while they both slept. Then suddenly, he sat up, his eyes vacantly staring in horror.

"No! No! No! You must not. No! You will all pay for this."

Procula woke up. Looked with alarm at her husband, and with tears in her eyes shook him and begged him to snap out of the dream. Slowly she coaxed him into lying back again. After a few moments he fell asleep. She followed shortly after; she was too tired to resist.

Morning found the pair fast asleep as if nothing had occurred.

* * * * *

Marcellus arrived home to a very concerned family. His mother in particular was quite upset. She had felt with a mother's intuition that something bad had occurred. The rest of the family suspected that quite possibly Pontius had invited him to spend a couple of days as their guest. But they too had begun to feel uneasy about his further delay.

"My son," cried his mother embracing him with tears in her eyes. "Are you well? I am so relieved to have you back. We have all been very worried about you." Wiping her eyes, she pulled away from him so as to allow his sister and brother to hug him.

"I was on the point of sending Felicius to Pilate's house to enquire after you," said his father.

"Yes, mother," began Marcellus, engaging his mother's eyes and with the semblance of a smile. I have a story to relate to you all; and as you suspected, it did not go well with me for a while.

Marcellus was ushered into the peristyle where he was immediately given some refreshments. As he drank and snacked, he narrated the story they were all dying to hear. He made however no mention of the veil as such but described it as the package which he had been entrusted with.

"But surely," said the father, "you would know what was in that package that you have been carrying since you left Caesarea?"

"Yes. I knew what was in it, but I had sworn to keep it a secret."

"We shall have to stifle our curiosity then," said the father. "Though," he continued, " they attacked you to rob you of Artemis. They knew nothing of the package that you were entrusted with."

"Quite correct Father."

"Let me look at your wounded head," pleaded Ignatia, with a pained look in her eyes.

Marcellus removed his shawl which he had purposely left on and bared his head for his mother. She was shocked at the sight of the ugly encrusted wound healing in the middle of a bald patch. She shuddered as the others all took a look. He pulled his shawl over his head again.

"They could have killed you son," she said, sadly shaking her head.

Later that afternoon during a walk in the garden with his sister, Marcellus filled in the parts of the story that had been left out of his narration to the rest of the family.

"I hope the veil will cure Procula's husband from his terrible nightmares," said Rufina. " I suppose it will remain with the Pilates permanently. Though if we should ever need it, we can always borrow it from them. They can hardly refuse you."

"Oh no. She would never refuse me. But I wonder if it will help her husband. Remember what I told you. He was the man who condemned Yeshua to death. But we cannot understand God's ways."

"How can we learn more about the Christians?" Rufina's eyes sparkled eagerly.

"I shall have to find out. How? I don't know. They are being persecuted by Caligula at the present moment. Procula told me. It's quite frightening."

"Still," ventured Rufina. "If Yeshua is the Son of God as you say they believe, and that when one dies one goes to a paradise, I suppose it is worth it. Our gods promise us nothing, and they certainly do not perform miracles." She bent down and picking a lovely yellow flower, inhaled its fragrance, momentarily closing her beautiful eyes in appreciation.

"I shall be leaving again soon," said Marcellus. "Father is sending me up to Umbria to acquaint me with the vineyards. I shall have to stay there until I have learnt all about wine making. How else can I run that business? I shall have to live there when I marry Livia."

Rufina took a hold of her brother's arm and looking up at him with expectancy said.

"I shall try to get Father to let me spend time with you and Livia. I feel sure that she and I will become great friends."

"Yes, I know you will like her. She has a great sense of humour and a very pleasant personality; apart from the fact that like you, she is very beautiful."

* * * * *

Four months had passed since Marcellus' 'tete a tete' with Rufina in the garden. He was now back home from Umbria, having imbued all that old Sartorius, the manager of the vineyards had taught him about the winemaking business. He looked forward to the family visiting Antium to meet Livia's family prior to the wedding.

Accordingly, Porcius had prepared a comfortable cart to be drawn by two work horses. Young Marcius would be at the reins, whilst Marcellus and himself would ride as escorts on their Arabians. Porcius had served as a tribune in the Legion in his younger days. He, also knew how to defend himself. A great necessity when travelling was such a risky business.

The Legion patrolled the roads regularly, but one could never be sure of not being attacked by robbers.

One sunny morning, the family set out on their journey to Antium. The trip would take them seven hours or so. They planned to be at Livia's home by late afternoon if all went well. The cart carried their food and water for the day. They really did not need to make any lengthy stops along the way. It proved however to be a well trafficked route which though more secure, slowed them down. Many villages had to be passed, and a number of them had local festivities and other encumbrances which hindered their progress. By the same token, they were entertained in many ways by those same nuances, which made for a most interesting and amusing journey. Finally the sea came into view, giving that Roman family a most enchanting sense of freedom and contrasting sharply with their land bound congested habitat.

"Oh, how lovely," cried Ignatia on seeing the sparkling blue sea.

Porcius inhaled pleasurably as the briny smell reached his nostrils. Marcius relished the thought of swimming and enjoying the sandy beaches suddenly appearing in front of them. Marcellus however was a little distressed at the thought that he would be spending most of his time in Umbria away from the sea.

'I would love to have a boat to sail in as does Pontius,' he mused. But he knew his father needed him in Umbria, and there, he would have to reside. 'Perhaps there is a lake near the vineyards.' He consoled himself with the thought.

Marcellus led the way to Livia's house and hoped she and her family could accommodate them all without prior notice. They did not plan on staying long. Perhaps for a couple of days only, depending on how Livia's family could cope.

The gatekeeper, recognising Marcellus, opened for them and rushed off to announce their unexpected arrival. The residing family soon came out of the house to greet the visitors in the front garden.

Livia ran into Marcellus' arms. Her beautiful face overflowing with joy.

Marcellus embraced her lovingly as the two families jubilantly watched the happy couple.

He, taking his betrothed by the hand, brought her to meet his family. She was received by them with great warmth. She in turn taking hold of Marcellus' hand again, led the group to meet her family.

Marcellus introduced his father to Livia's father. The mothers embraced warmly making their own acquaintances, and soon all were chatting amicably; the visitors being shown into the house.

"I hope we are not inconveniencing you with our unannounced arrival " said Ignatia with a questioning look in her eyes.

"Not in the least," replied Fortunata, squeezing her new friend's arm lovingly. "We have been ready for you for quite a while. It's so lovely to have you with us at last."

"Wonderful to be here in your beautiful house." smiled Ignatia, looking around approvingly.

Rufina had joined her brother, Livia, and Aelia, and all four were conversing excitedly as they led the way into the peristyle. Young Marcius, having met Sabino, (the baby of the family) who was almost his own age, disappeared to the latter's room to be shown some of his favourite toys.

Porcius and Egnatius, out on the terrace that overlooked the large back garden and sea, were fast becoming acquainted. Presently a servant appeared with a tray of enticing victuals and some wine. It was a beautiful sunny day, and soon, everyone was out on the terrace enjoying their very pleasant surroundings and new friends, who would soon become their relatives.

The days that followed were memorable days. Particularly for the Porcius family who had had few opportunities of spending time by the sea. Rarely does life offer happy moments like the ones that those two fortunate families were enjoying, and they made the most of it. The size of the house allowed for comfort, and interesting room arrangements were being made. Rufina found herself sharing a room with Aelia; Marcius was sharing Sabino's room. The other four bedrooms were assigned to the two older couples. Marcellus and Livia naturally had their own separate rooms.

That first evening together, the family sat in the peristyle which in that particular house, opened up onto the terrace and the stunning manicured garden. An oblong pool replete with lily pads and goldfish, ran below the entire length of the terrace wall, which was carved in semi relief depicting a line of dancing maidens. It was interrupted at the centre and ends by carved podiums accommodating exotic plants and flowers. The pool was flanked by two stone staircases with stone balustrades; a continuation of those fronting the terrace.

The evening's entertainment was provided by Aelia, Rufina, and a young slave girl that danced beautifully. The parents and the two espoused were engrossed in the planning of the wedding arrangements, which was foremost in their minds. Also, of some concern was the future lives of the young couple who would be living away from both families. They would continue to discuss these same topics for the next few days. For Marcellus and Livia, their prospective new life would be an adventure which promised married bliss and hopefully, success in their endeavours as vintners.

Walking together in the sumptuous garden the following day, Livia had occasion to ask Marcelus about the veil.

"I am most curious to know how you found Procula, and what she is like?" asked Livia with eagerness.

"That is quite a story my love," said Marcellus, and immediately began to relate it to her. She underwent a number of different reactions as the story unfolded.

"You could have died from that wound in your head," she bewailed. "Show me. I cannot see it with all that hair."

Marcellus parted his hair and tilting his head, allowed her to see the scab.

"Oh my!" she said with an air of protestation and a slight shudder. "Perhaps the veil kept you from being killed by that blow."

"Who's to know," he answered with a shrug.

"If we ever need the veil to cure us from anything, we shall have to borrow it from Procula," she said with finality.

"I suppose so," he agreed. "She is very concerned with Pontius, who is suffering from horrible nightmares and they seem to be occurring more often as time goes by. She wants to have him put the veil on, but she is afraid he might be very angry or go mad if he sees the face of Yeshua. He feels very guilty and repentant for having unjustly condemned him to death," said Marcellus lightly shaking his head.

Taking her hand and kissing it tenderly, he walked her back to the terrace to join the others.

* * * * *

Porcius and his family, were back in Rome. Two months had passed since their enjoyable visit to Egnatius' house, and they were all looking forward to their next visit during which the wedding of Marcellus and Livia would be celebrated. A visit to the vineyards was now being contemplated by father and son, so as to formulate a working schedule for Marcellus. The management of three vineyards was a challenging matter. Especially, as Porcius had discovered over time, that one of the three superintendents was rather difficult to deal with, and perhaps not too trustworthy. Marcellus had had an inkling of the man's nature and was prepared to deal with it when he had furthered his experience in the business.

"Sartorius is getting old," said Porcius sitting in the peristyle one day with Marcellus.

"We could lose him any day. Especially if his bones continue to worsen. The man finds it difficult to walk. He gave up pruning a couple years ago. I had to get him two youngsters to take over his part of the work." Marcellus, listening attentively to what his father was saying, nodded in agreement.

"He has a son-in-law who is quite adept at everything around the vineyard," said Marcellus. "I met him. He seems to be quite a pleasant fellow. If he is capable of accepting responsibility, which I think he is, he may be able to take over whenever Sartorius is finished with work."

Porcius got up and walked to the window overlooking the garden. He pensively stared ahead seemingly concerned with something.

"We will have to have a small cottage built for the old fellow," he said. Still gazing out of the window. "You will need the house for yourself and may even have to add to it in due time. He will want to stay on the property. It is his life, and he has served me well," asserted Porcius, taking a sip of wine from the cup he was holding, and fondly pondering.

His memory took him back to when he, as a young man slightly older than Marcellus, took charge of his father's vineyards. Sartorius was in his prime then, and taught him everything he knew about the wine business. Porcius had much to thank his faithful servant for.

"I hope you have as much luck with his son-in-law," said Porcius, "as I have had with him."

The following morning, father and son set out on their exceptional horses with Umbria as their destination. The date for the wedding had now been set and was only a month down the road. Since they were north bound, and their home was in the southern end of Rome, they had to struggle through crowds and obstacles, just as Marcellus had done on his trip to Pyrgi.

After five hours of riding, they were both quite saddle weary, and as evening fell, they rode into a favourite hostel on their route, well away from Rome.

The owner greeted Porcius warmly. He had provided hospitality for his patron for many years and they knew each other quite well.

"This is my son, Marcellus," said Porcius with a smile; placing his hand solidly on his son's shoulder.

"He bears a great resemblance to you except he's better looking," joked the inn keeper whose name was Septimus.

"That is only because he is younger," protested Porcius laughing merrily. "I hope you have something good for the cena. I could eat a horse."

"What a coincidence," joked Septimus, winking at Marcellus, "that is all I have for you...horse."

They all laughed as they walked into the inn's dining room and sat down at the table singled out for them by the amiable host.

"Send us over some of that rancid wine of yours," said Porcius with a wave of the hand and a big smile.

Marcellus rejoiced to see his father in such a good mood after the long and tiring ride, and he was looking forward to the excellent meal which he suspected his host would provide despite all the joking.

The meal had not been disappointing. Septimus' wife who ran the kitchen and did most of the cooking herself, created a variety of dishes which along with some excellent wine, delighted father and son and made for a very pleasant evening.

Porcius, in a state of complete relaxation, and having imbued a fair quantity of wine, bid all present a good night and went off to his comfortable room to get some sleep. Marcellus, who had met Septimus for the first time that evening, sat a little longer listening to local news as related by his host. One particular piece of news which caught Marcellus' attention was the exodus of Christians from Rome to the outlying areas, trying to escape the persecution that the emperor Caligula waged against them.

"People that I had never seen around here before," explained the innkeeper. "Of course they will not tell you that they are Christians, but by the way they talk and behave, I can tell. Though mind you, I keep it to myself."

"How can you tell from their behaviour?" asked the young guest a little perplexed.

"They behave very well actually," said Septimus. "They do not use profane language, and they are friendly and considerate. Sometimes I overhear them mentioning their God Yeshua as they talk almost in whispers among themselves. I frankly don't know why they're being persecuted. They seem quite harmless to me. Nor do they get drunk or give me any trouble." He shook his head, "I don't understand it."

"Well, I shall turn in now," said Marcellus with a big yawn. "Please keep a close eye on our horses, we don't want them stolen in the middle of the night."

"Have no fear, I have two stable boys that sleep in the stable all night. They will sound the alarm if anyone tries to get in there."

"That is reassuring. Thank you, and goodnight," said Marcellus, walking off to his designated room next to his father's.

One by one the oil lamps in the many rooms of the inn, were extinguished. The guests were asleep. The doors had all been bolted, and the stillness of night reigned over the countryside. The moon shone in her fullness giving every object it touched a soft powdery silver hue. The leaves on the trees swaying lazily by a gentle warm summer breeze cast weak shadows that danced among the moon beams on the sun-baked soil.

The top of the white high wall that surrounded the inn, glistened against a purple backdrop of indefinable distance. Two torches on the wall inside the locked gate, lit up the gate's heavy double door and shone their light through the semi-circular wrought iron transom, projecting an intricate shadow pattern on the road below. A cat moved about stealthily on its nightly hunt for mice. The watch dog, a young Alsatian, was asleep by the gate.

Suddenly, a loud bold knocking at the gate broke the pristine silence of the night, waking the sleeping Alsatian and all the residents of the hostel.

Séptimos, dressing hurriedly, hastened across the courtyard to chain the barking dog and open the little inspection window on the door.

"Who the…"

"Open in the name of Caesar!" shouted a soldier, cutting off the inn-keeper in mid speech.

Septimus hastened to remove the iron bars and unlock the doors. A moment later, three soldiers burst into the courtyard. One of them waved a piece of parchment at him and eagerly eyed the building.

"I have an order here to arrest a number of Christians who have fled from Rome and are staying here under your roof," said the sergeant. "Have everyone assemble here in the courtyard right away!"

"Now just a moment," said the innkeeper, with some resentment in his voice. "I cannot disturb my guests in the middle of the night, just because you cannot wait until a decent hour of the morning to do your business."

The sergeant was thrown a little aback.

"I have many guests who are upright Romans," protested an irate Septimus. "They are entitled to their sleep as they have to travel tomorrow. You are disturbing them."

"I am on the Emperor's business," said the soldier, in a more apologetic tone.

By this time, some of the guests had hurried to their windows to see what the commotion was about. Among them Porcius and Marcellus, whose windows overlooked the court yard.

"What is all the commotion?" enquired Porcius in a loud voice.

"These soldiers," answered Septimus, "have come to apprehend some Christians who are evidently suspected of being here."

Some of those at the windows suddenly disappeared into their rooms.

"Wait there!" said Porcius, his finger pointing authoritatively at the soldiers. I shall be right down.

"And who is that? asked the sergeant angrily. "Who tells me what to do?

"That, my friend, is Senator Porcius Fulvius," warned Septimus. "You better keep a civil tongue in your head."

The senator appeared in the courtyard and approached the sergeant.

Marcellus, in the midst of dressing saw his door opening slowly. He reached for his gladius which was nearby. Suddenly as if blown in by a puff of wind, a little female figure silently slipped into his room quickly but gently closing the door behind her.

She looked at him in surprise, her large blue eyes on the sword in his hand.

Marcellus threw it on the bed, and going down on one knee, asked her why she had come to his room. She was perhaps five years old, he thought. She was a pretty little thing in her night gown and slippers. Her long golden hair hung loosely down her back, and on her finger she wore a gold ring.

She pouted and said with some alarm in her voice.

"My Mamma told me to run and hide from the soldiers who were coming to take us away and kill us."

Marcellus was struck dumb. This little girl's parents must be the Christians that the soldiers had been sent to apprehend.

'What am I going to do with her?' he asked himself. 'I cannot let them take her.'

"Here," he said as the thought occurred to him and beckoning to her. "Get under my bed, and don't come out until I come back and call you."

She gave him a slight smile and went under the bed. He draped some of the bedclothes over the side of the bed to better conceal her, and leaving the room went to the courtyard to find his father.

The sergeant, somewhat humbled by the admonition given them by the Senator, called out the names of the people whom they were seeking. The other guests, having put on some clothes, were curiously awaiting the Christians' appearance.

The first to appear, was an older couple in their early sixties. They walked slowly, their faces reflecting the fear that engulfed them. Each carried a bag.

"You won't need these where you are going," snapped the sergeant, tearing the bags from their hands. The old woman stumbled but regained her balance.

"We are old and need our things," protested the woman with tears in her eyes.

Porcius was disgusted with the soldier's inhumanity. 'After all,' he said to himself, 'these people are good Roman citizens, not troublemakers. They have probably worked hard and paid their taxes all their lives, and now, all of a sudden, because they think different to the emperor, they are being mistreated and taken to their deaths.' He could not keep quiet.

"Why are you treating these people so badly? They have been good citizens of Rome all their lives. Enough that they will be put to death. Would you treat your family the same way if they became Christians? One cannot control people's thoughts you know." He picked up the bags and handed them back to the grateful couple and turning to the sergeant he said.

"Your duty is to arrest these unfortunate people and hand them over to the authorities, it does not give you the right to mistreat them in this manner."

The soldier was cursing his luck in having bumped into the meddling senator but dared not confront him in any way. He became even more upset as he was asked to give the name of his commanding officer, though not threatened in any way.

Marcellus was eager to talk to his father about the little fugitive under his bed, but so far had had no chance of doing that.

The next batch of Christians to appear were in actual fact the parents of the little girl, though Marcellus could only guess. They were a young couple in their mid twenties, very well dressed, but with sad countenances. Their clothes and the travel bags they carried, spoke of affluence.

They reported their names, (which Marcellus mentally noted) and were silently directed by the sergeant who seemed to be running out of words for the time being, to join the other two who simply stood there staring at the ground.

There was a further delay, and yet another man appeared and joined the others. He was middle aged, tall, fine featured, and wore a well trimmed beard. He carried a sturdy staff. A second man joined him. He was younger, possibly nineteen years old. He carried a bag over his shoulder, and had a lost look about him as if not comprehending the situation that he found himself in.

The soldier accompanying the sergeant rudely snatched the staff out of the tall newcomer's hand. "In case you are thinking of using it," he said with a laugh.

"It is not our way to hurt others," said the man. He nodded in assent as his name and that of his companion were called out.

The sergeant looked at his six prisoners and said. I have seven names here. He gave the young couple a quizzical look, through in his hard, grey eyes. Where is your daughter Marcia?

The young woman broke into tears.

"Well?" asked the sergeant.

Marcellus quietly left the group and made his way quickly into the house and up to his room. He did not go in, but waited outside in the corridor, having no idea as to what he might do to save the little girl. However, he was determined to try.

"We lost her a month ago. She is dead," lied the mother bursting into tears once more. Her husband put a consoling arm around her. He knew that if his daughter was not discovered wherever she had hidden, they would never see her again; but at least she would live.

"I don't believe you. Our reports are usually accurate," growled the sergeant.

At this point, Porcius who had noticed his son slip away, wondered why he had left without speaking to him. He prepared to follow his son into the house.

"I shall leave it to you now sergeant, I have seen enough. Try to make these people's last journey a little less unpleasant."

The sergeant gave him a shallow bow, and off went Porcius in search of Marcellus.

"Search all the upstairs rooms," ordered the sergeant. "I'll take care of the ground floor. Find the girl. We have to get going." The girl's parents, filled with horror, prayed to Yeshua with all their heart that she might not be found. Indeed, the whole group was silently praying for the same thing.

Porcius reached Marcellus as the sound of the soldier's heavy footsteps entering the house reached their ears.

"The girl is in my room father," whispered Marcellus hurrying into his room.

Porcius realised that his son meant to shield the girl, and not knowing how he would do that, resolved to use rank if necessary, to intimidate the soldier who now appeared at the top of the stairs.

The man burst into the first room. After a few moments he came out and made his way into the next one. Porcius stood in front of his own door with the door ajar. He noticed also that Marcellus had opened his door and was standing in the doorway. The man came out of the second room looking rather frustrated. He looked at Marcellus.

"No luck?" asked the latter with a disinterested look on his face.

"Not yet," answered the soldier peering over Marcellus shoulder. Then of a sudden he brushed past him into the room and made for the window.

"We must keep an eye on those people down there." He leaned out of the window and shouted. "Brutus!" An answer came back. "Yea."

"Keep a close eye on those people, till the sergeant gets back to them." He counted them aloud, and turning, looked around the room.

"Nice gladius," he said looking at the sword on the bed.

"I was a tribune in the Legion until recently," answered Marcellus.

At this point, Porcius came into the room, simultaneously with the sergeant's voice bellowing.

"Have'nt you found her yet?"

The soldier went back to the window. Marcellus gasped in horror as the girl's foot slipped out from under the bed. The soldier turned, Marcellus reached for his gladius.

Porcius spoke tartly. "When are you two going to let us sleep? You still have two rooms to check." Marcellus took advantage of the distraction, and gently pushed the little foot back under the bed with his foot.

At the senator's words the distracted soldier left the room. He only peered into the latter's room in passing, and after checking the last room, ran down the stairs again to join his sergeant who having searched the garden, stables, and lower part of the building, had at last given up on the child. He was now ushering the captives out of the courtyard and onto the waiting barred wagon.

"If she is not dead, she soon will be," said the sergeant (still unconvinced), to the girl's heartbroken parents.

The wagon of death rolled away, leaving a very sad bunch of guests back at the inn.

Slowly, they all found their way back to their rooms. Soon the house was still once more; though whether anyone slept was another question.

Having again locked and secured the gate, Septimus made his way back into the house, and after a little delay went up to the senator's room and knocked on the door lightly. There was no answer. He then knocked at Marcellus' door.

Moments later, Marcellus opened the door and seeing Septimus, asked him in.

There on the bed sat Porcius, trying to console little Marcia who was quietly crying for her parents.

"A bad business," said the Senator at the sight of his friend. "We live in a nasty world."

"I had a strong feeling that you were both involved in this little scheme," said the inn-keeper in a hushed tone. "Her parents gave me these things for her." He produced two little dresses and a few other items of clothing. Also, a pair of pretty sandals, and a small bag with money. He laid them on the bed. The child eyed them with pleasure.

"How did they manage that?" asked Marcellus with a happy smile.

"Whilst the sergeant and his assistant were busy looking through the house," continued the innkeeper, "other lodgers came out protesting the intrusion of the soldiers into their rooms, inadvertently distracting the soldier in the courtyard. Her mother was quick to give me these items which I stuffed under each arm and covered with my shawl." He gave father and son a sympathetic smile.

"I am very happy that you have done such a good deed," said Septimus. "Tomorrow morning we shall discuss this matter further my friends.

"Thank you for your help," said Porcius with a fond smile.

"What are friends for?" whispered Septimus and noiselessly slipped out the door.

Marcellus took the child, laid her on his bed, and covered her with a blanket. He lay down on the floor beside her on some cushions that he and his father had in their rooms. Porcius kissed the child and went off to his room to catch some sleep. Marcellus consoled the little thing and held her hand until she fell asleep.

The morning light woke Marcellus who had been restless all night. The new and sudden responsibility that he felt for Marcia had kept interrupting his sleep. However, he knew the day would bring many surprises in the form of unexpected but necessary planning, and he began some hasty ablutions before she awoke.

He need not have hurried. Marcia slept on as children are prone to do after a hectic experience. She later woke up calling for her mamma; her words cutting deep into Marcellus' heart who felt quite helpless as the persistent call for 'mamma' or 'daddy' continued for quite a while. Porcius, hearing the child, joined them, and little by little they managed to appease her. It was fortunate that the room next door to Marcellus' having been the old Christian couple's room, was unoccupied.

"No one must know she is here," said Marcellus, "until we decide what to do."

There was a knock at the door.

Marcellus opened to receive Septimus, who held a tray with some victuals for Marcia. She eyed them hungrily. Soon the girl was tucking away as the three men talked about her future.

"Our plans are about to change," said Porcius. "I think we better get back to Rome. This little thing needs the love and care of a mother, and that means my wife or daughter."

Both men nodded in assent. The child looking at them with her lovely big blue eyes, listened to every word that was being said. She smiled at hearing 'wife and daughter.'

The decision to return to Rome, had been made, even though the risk of running into the soldiers was a distinct possibility. The prison cart would be moving very slowly, and they would have to pass it at some point since their destination was one and the same.

Accordingly, father, son, and ward, set out on their fast Arabian horses. Portius rode alone. Marcellus carried Marcia in front of him. She was enjoying the ride. It distracted her little mind from the tragedy that had befallen her.

After a couple of hours, Porcius rode on ahead, hoping to warn his son if he caught up with the death wagon.

Nearing a village on their route, the senator spotted the wagon in the distance and rode back to warn his son.

"We must circumvent the village," suggested Marcellus. "Once we are ahead of them, they will never catch up with us."

Father and son trotted off to survey the terrain around the village. They needed to gallop through unimpeded so that by the time they cleared it and were back on the main road again, they would be out of sight of the morbid retinue.

The surrounding countryside was hilly. Not the best scenario for a quick get-a-way. One side of the village however was more promising than the other.

"Failing any unforeseen obstacles, we should be able to at least, trot through on this side," said Porcius pointing ahead, "even if we cannot gallop."

The decision made, they pulled off the road and began to trot their horses along the right side of the village. The hilly nature of the terrain gave them visual protection. They were almost out of the village boundaries when a large flock of sheep obstructed their way.

It was a frustrating experience. The shepherd was doing his best to clear a path for them, but there they were locked in the middle of the path and time just going to waste. Marcellus could imagine the wagon almost abreast with them. Chances were that if this situation continued much longer, they would break into the main highway at the same time as the wagon.

At last they rode clear leaving the sheep behind them. The shepherd shook his head apologetically; the fold had simply been too large for one man to handle.

It was noon, the sun was beating mercilessly down on them. Marcellus ensured that his little ward was well shielded from it, though the heat made her very thirsty, and she called out for a drink with regularity. They also had to rest their pampered Arabians. Even though water was not a big issue for them, they would however have to be rubbed down, and that would delay them again.

Then Marcellus had an idea.

"Let us find some shade up here," he said with resignation. "We can tend to the horses, eat our lunch, and keep an eye on the road. The wagon will be visible from here. We will have to follow them to the next village and then try this same trick again. Hopefully, next time we will have better luck."

Three hours later, following Marcellus's 'plan, they found themselves circumventing another village, with better results than the previous time. They soon reached the main road. Porcius dismounted, and climbing up some rocks which gave him a good view of the village, surveyed the road behind them. It was clear. Obviously, the wagon was still trying to traverse the village. He mounted his horse again, and signalling Marcellus to join him, put his mount into a canter. Marcellus followed, and on reaching his father they both galloped off at last, feeling that they would never see the wagon again.

It was a truly weary pair of horsemen, and one soundly sleeping child that finally rode through the gate at Porcius' house. It was past cena time. The travellers were absolutely famished, but celebrating in spirit their triumphant and charitable venture.

To those who do not take the trouble to find God, the little adventure which evolved around the child Marcia, would have been assigned by common consensus simply to luck. But to those who prayed that night in the courtyard of Septimus' hostel, it was an act of God performed by his divine Son Yeshua to whom the prayers of those believers, similarly unjustly condemned to death, were addressed. A heartfelt thanks-giving would surely have followed if they had only known.

Ignatia ran into her husband's arms as he walked into the atrium. She froze on seeing Marcellus carrying his new charge. Leaving Porcius, she went to him, her arms spread widely as she embraced both him and Marcia who continued to sleep.

"Who is this dear little creature?" she asked; her eyes opening wide with wonder.

"This is Marcia," said Marcellus with a big smile. Placing a tender kiss on the child's forehead, he gave her to his mother.

"What happened? You are back much too soon. Not that I am complaining. It's great to have you home so soon."

"Stop your chatter woman," said Porcius good naturedly, "and get us something to eat."

She ran off almost colliding with Rufina and Marcius who came running to welcome their father and brother home. They both fell on the pair of tired voyageurs with hugs and kisses.

Ignatia gave the cook her order and returned to the peristyle where they all gathered. Rufina and Marcius stared in wonder at the little golden-haired doll in their mother's arms.

"What happened?" asked Rufina,

Before anyone could answer, Marcia awoke. She looked at all the new faces around her.

"Mamma! Mamma! she cried bursting into tears. Not finding her or her daddy, she looked around and seeing Marcellus again, spread her little arms out to him, tears running down her red cheeks. He quickly took her, hugged her, and kissed her forehead; fighting back tears, which clouded the eyes of the female members of his family.

"Hush little one," said Marcellus lovingly. "We will take care of you until your mamma and daddy come."

The child again continued to call for her unfortunate parents, and again it took a good while to calm her down. Marcellus ate his cena with the child on his lap, as Porcius told the tragic story which kept Ignatia and Rufina tearful for some time.

"Now I understand," said Ignatia, looking lovingly at her son. "You have done a great and unselfish thing. I am so proud of you." She got up and kissed her son and then the little one, who looked at her in awe.

CHAPTER EIGHT

THE WEDDING

The wedding of Marcellus and Livia was only three weeks away. Porcius had decided that their aborted journey to the vineyards at Umbria had wiped out their chances of making that trip again prior to the wedding. It was left in abeyance for the time being until Marcellus was married. Then it would be undertaken again. It would give the family a chance to visit Umbria and the newly weds after they had had a little time to themselves.

Marcellus felt a need to talk to Livia with regard to the adopting of Marcia. The little creature had become very attached to him, and he to her.

"I'm going to Antium," announced Marcellus one morning at breakfast.

"Now? Before the wedding?" asked his mother with surprise in her voice.

"Yes," he replied, "I have to tell Livia about Marcia. After all she is going to be her mother."

Little Marcia was not at table with them; Rufina was playing with her in the garden.

"I think it is only fair," remarked his father, busy pouring oil on his bread.

Marcellus got up and went into the garden. Marcia came running as soon as she saw him.

He picked her up, gave her rosy cheek a kiss and told her that he would be going away for a few days.

"I shall bring you a nice present when I return," he told her.

She complained with tears in her eyes, and as usual it took him and Rufina a while to placate her.

She waved to him along with the rest of the family, as he rode out the gate on an unremarkable horse. He was not going to be concerned with having it stolen again and being attacked in the process.

"Once bitten, twice shy," he said to himself as he urged the beast into a canter.

This time his trip was uneventful, and he reached Antium in the estimated time, having enjoyed the sea view during the latter part of the journey.

Livia was overjoyed but surprised at seeing him.

"Oh, how wonderful to see you my love," she said kissing him ardently. "Is everything well with your family? What brings you here so close to the wedding?

Marcellus was about to answer all her questions, when Egnatius appeared followed by Fortunata. Livia's questions were left unanswered as the family fell lovingly on Marcellus welcoming him. Aelia and Sabinus joined the reception; all talking at the same time.

Egnatius clapped his hands loudly. "Enough noise!" he said with a big smile. "Now, let us sit in the peristyle and hear what this young man has to tell us."

Livia's questions were duly answered by Marcellus. The conversation continued in a light vein for a while. Then the real reason for his visit was unfolded as the tragic story of Marcia was told.

Again there were tears shed, and overtures of sympathy made by the whole family.

"What are you going to do with the child?" asked Livia, with a curious look on her face.

"I would like to keep her, and bring her up with our children," said Marcellus with a smile.

"That is a big responsibility," said Livia, looking at her mother.

Egnatius got up and said." This is a matter for Livia and Marcellus," we are not involved. He motioned for all to leave. They obeyed.

The lovers were left alone to discuss the first real problem that had presented itself since they met. However, it was of vital importance and had to be solved.

"Do you not approve of my bringing up this child?" asked Marcellus with surprise and a feeling of disappointment.

"I am not sure if I want to share the love of my children with a stranger," she said with a downcast look, and slowly rubbing her hands in contemplation. He waited a further reason.

"It isn't fair," she said with a sad pout, reminding him of a spoilt child.

"I don't see how this can interfere with our love for our children," he protested. "She is a loveable little creature and will be easy to love. Right now she is very badly in need of it."

"Yes, I understand that. But how can I love her as my own, when she is not mine."

"That, only time can tell. But you would be doing a very worthwhile thing by taking her to you. You will be her mother, and she will love and respect you as such. I feel sure. She has already taken to me as if I were her father."

Livia made no response. She was thinking. Thinking hard.

'If he already loves the child, what chance have our own children. He will favour her always at the expense of our own.' She felt totally confused and wished that her parents had stayed to help her out.

"I wish you could see her," he continued. "She has beautiful long golden hair, and big blue eyes. She would capture your heart instantly. The journey would have been too much for her, or I would have brought her. I can take you to her if you wish, and you can spend time with my family as well. Rufina is longing to see you again." He got up and sitting beside her took her hand and kissed it.

She kissed him on the lips, but the passion was gone. They both felt it, as a cloud of doubt and uncertainty enshrouded their young hearts.

"We must be very sure of our decisions my love," he said with a sinking heart.

"I need time to think about this," she whispered; thinking that she needed to talk to her mother.

"Let's leave the matter rest for the night," he said. "We will talk further tomorrow. I must not press or rush you. It is a big decision for you and I understand."

Marcellus left her and went to talk to Egnatius.

"We have made no decisions. Livia needs time to think," he told his still hopeful future father-in-law.

They spent the evening in small talk. All knowing that the wedding could collapse any moment.

The new day brought new hope to Marcellus. After breakfast, he and Livia walked in the garden, enjoying its coolness before the heat of the day made it more difficult to walk there.

"Can you not give the child away to some nice couple who might want it?" asked Livia.

"I could not live in peace not knowing if she was being mistreated, or unloved." The question upset him. 'Would she ever be able to love this child as her own?' he asked himself. He was beginning to perceive an answer, but it was one he did not like.

"It seems you love this child more than you love me," she protested with a little anger in her voice.

"That is not fair, my love. The two types of love are not the same. And yet they can both exist together if the right attitude is taken. I love you, and I have come to love her. If and when we have our own children, I shall love them also, and I shall be fair to all of them."

"You have a greater capacity for love then than I have," she said with great sadness in her voice. Marcellus suddenly felt a great loss. He had set his hopes so high. He had not for a moment doubted that she would even hesitate to accept little Marcia as he had done.

'She is a gift from God to me,' he told himself. 'I would rather die than abandon her. Her little heart has already been broken enough.'

He painfully looked into Livia's eyes.

"I suppose you have given me your answer," he said feeling a big lump in his throat.

She said nothing further.

"Is everything over for us then?" he asked. Still with hope in his heart.

She looked into his eyes with regret.

"Yes," she replied, with tears brimming in her eyes.

He left her in the garden and went into the house to look for her father.

Egnatius was in his office. He had a very unhappy look on his kind face.

"I came to tell you," said Marcellus, his voice breaking, that Livia has decided not to marry me.

The father got up and embraced Marcellus warmly. "I am distressed to hear that my son," he said with a frog in his throat. "Just as your father will be. We had such great plans for you both." He shook his head sadly, "Fate is a powerful thing."

"I prefer to say that God is very powerful," said Marcellus parting from the embrace. He asked Egnatius to be allowed to say goodbye to Fortunata and the rest of the family.

It was a very sad parting. The two families were ideally suited to each other. A great loss was felt by all. Livia remained in the garden until Marcellus was gone; her heart in shreds.

* * * * *

Marcellus arrived back at his home a broken man. His whole future which had seemed so solidly set had come crashing down with stupefying rapidity. Livia who had ruled his dreams was now no better than a ghost in his life. He was not sure if he still loved her.

'I certainly bear her no ill will,' he confessed to himself.

'My feelings for her have suddenly become numb however. How is it possible for a little thing like Marcia to upset such big plans and still be loved as much as ever. Even more, than ever. Nothing makes sense.' He continued to argue with himself.

'It must make sense to God, or else he would not have put her into my life in such a powerful way. Yeshua,' he prayed, 'I have to learn much more about you. But how?'

Marcellus' family took the news of the cancellation of the wedding with as great a shock and resulting sadness as Livia's family. The only difference was that little Marcia had won their hearts.

"If only Livia had met Marcia and spent time with her," was Ignatia's constant remark. It grew to be her favourite saying whenever the subject of the cancelled wedding was discussed.

* * * * *

Two months passed, before Marcellus, was able to think of his new future.

Porcius arranged for them to repeat the trip to Umbria, but this time they would take Marcia, and Rufina who had become very attached to her. She would stay there to virtually act as the girl's mother for the immediate future.

Marcia would not hear of being anywhere without Marcellus.

Ignatia was not looking forward to this new venture, as she would find herself alone with only young Marcius. She would miss Rufina terribly. She was not a happy woman though she understood the situation and made no protestations to her husband.

The little party left Senator Porcius' house early one morning. The senator rode his cream Arabian stallion, Marcellus was on Artemis, and Marcia rode in a comfortably outfitted cart with Rufina at the reins. The cart was loaded with boxes containing most of their clothes as they would be staying permanently in Umbria. They planned to stop for the night at

Septimus' hostel as on the previous occasion and hoped that little Marcia would not remember much about the tragedy which befell her parents there.

It was past the 'cena' time when the senator and his family arrived at Septimus' inn.

The man himself happened to be at the gate when they arrived.

"Oh, what a wonderful surprise," said the inn-keeper with a big smile, and immediately went to embrace Porcius who had dismounted. Marcellus also dismounted and embraced Septimus.

"This my daughter Rufina," said Porcius proudly pointing to her. "She is the apple of my eye."

Septimus gave her a shallow bow and smiled. Turning to his friend he said.

"She is very beautiful. I suspect she resembles her beautiful mother. It would have been a disaster if she had resembled her father," he laughingly joked. Porcius and Marcellous joined him in the laughter.

That was why Porcius was so fond of the man, he had a great sense of humour, was caring, and honest to the core. A good man indeed, he thought.

Rufina's concern that Marcia might be traumatized by the memory of her last visit to the hostel was soon put to rest. The child had given no indication during their trip that day, that she had any recollection of the tragedy that had befallen her parents at the inn.

Rufina had been careful to feed her a cold supper as they travelled. She was put to bed directly on their arrival at the inn, and being tired from her day on the road, fell asleep almost immediately. Septimus' wife learning that Rufina was baby sitting the girl in her room, sent her a well prepared hot cena.

"Have you had more incidents with regard to the apprehension of Christians?" asked Marcellus of his host as they sat in the dining room during the cena.

"Only one," replied Septimus, "and that was a complete fiasco. The victim vehemently denied being a Christian. That is something Christians never do. It was later found that an erroneous name had been given to the soldiers. So nothing came of it."

"I am glad to hear that," said Porcius." Things have gotten out of hand in Rome."

Septimus drew closer to his old friend and whispered. "They say that Caligula is quite mad. He has even bestowed a title on his favourite horse."

Porcius smiled and nodded his head in assent.

They continued to talk of many things that affected their lives. The evening was going very enjoyably. Several cups of wine had been consumed by the congenial host and his two worthy friends. Of a sudden a commotion was heard which increased in intensity as it approached the dining room where the friends were sitting.

A man burst into the room, demanding his bill of fare. Septimus arose and went to meet the man with a questioning look on his friendly face.

"What is the..."

The inn-keeper did not finish his question.

"You dog! You reprobate! You pig!" Those unholy words were followed by a woman in her night gown with a robe wrapped hurriedly around her.

"Go to her and stay there for all I care. And may Cerebus devour you both." She stopped at the dining room door and seeing Porcius and Marcellus, turned around and went back to her room.

Septimus took the man's money, and seeing him out, returned to the table with the hint of a smile.

"These are the trials and tribulations of the hosteller," he said, sitting down again and taking a good swig of his wine.

They all laughed and finished their drinks. The irate wife had put an end to the peace and tranquility of the evening. Porcius and Marcellus retired to their rooms in the hope of a good night's sleep.

The following morning saw them on the road again. There were still two nights to be spent in hostels before arriving at their destination.

Evening found them trotting into another inn, not nearly comparable to Septimus' but the inn-keeper was courteous and efficient in his service, and they enjoyed a good meal at the cena. This time Marcia had her cena with the family, since the place was new to her and there was no danger of her reminiscing with traumatic repercussions.

The third night went much the same as the second, and the fourth evening found them arriving at their destination.

Greatly and pleasantly surprised at seeing the family appear at the farm house, Sartorius was beside himself with excitement. Nothing unusual ever happened at Menorum (that was the name of their village). This was a memorable event in his life, and he was overjoyed at seeing Porcius and Marcellus again.

"By Jupiter! What a wonderful surprise," he blurted out as hat in hand he met his bosses; his bald head reflecting the light of the torch by the gate.

"We are most pleased to see you," said Porcius in a magnanimous tone of voice, and giving the old man a genuinely happy smile. He dismounted and offered his old servant his hand which Sartorius took and heartily pressed.

Marcellus followed his father's example, and after introducing Sartorius to Rufina and Marcia, followed the old man into the house.

"Aurelia! Lavinia! Antonius!" called out the old superintendent with gusto; his arms spreading and raising himself up on his toes, all in one fluid motion.

There was a moment of silence. Then came the avalanche as the three individuals named, reacting with vigorous animation and much chatter, emerged from their respective situations and materialised into a dishevelled and unprepared presence at the entrance hallway.

They froze at the awesome sight that confronted them. "

'Who were these elegantly dressed people?' they wondered. Sartorius lost no time in enlightening them, albeit in a commanding and impatient way.

"Bow to your masters, and get busy unloading the cart," he commanded with bravado. "You! Aurelia. Into the kitchen. Prepare a good cena as fast as you can. The travellers are hungry. They have spent many hours on the road."

The new arrivals gazed in wonder and some amusement at the explosion of activity which was taking place in front of their eyes. The little army of two, represented by both sexes, strained, pulled and dragged the baggage off the cart and into the hallway, as Sartorius, keen to move his esteemed visitors to safety, ushered them into the living room. There, he sat them down on the many cushions available, and offered them refreshments that he himself; the only idle one of the foursome, would prepare.

Since the preparation of refreshments which Sartorius was capable of, was restricted to the pouring of some wine from a barrel into the designated and well-worn earthenware jug, poor Aurelia was further encumbered with the production of the actual refreshments. She quickly and artfully prepared a platter of sausage meats, olives, grilled red peppers, cold chicken slices, fresh bread and some milk for the child.

These, she arranged with her expert and tireless hands on a large bronze platter and handed it to the waiting patriarch of the household with the solemn admonition. "Don't drop it."

She resumed her preparation of the cena as she had been ungraciously commanded.

The said 'cena' having been eaten and greatly enjoyed by the tired travellers, they now patiently awaited the resolution of the of the next domestic crisis. Their accommodations.

Sartorius, whose head had not stopped thinking since his master's arrival, was now orchestrating with the diligence and resolve of a rear admiral, the conversion of three of the five bedrooms of the house, from their habitual, unabashed rural bedlam, to clean, uncluttered, and comfortable chambers of repose.

At this juncture of my story, please permit me my dear reader, to direct you to the living room of that excellent farmhouse and unfold for your attention a very peaceful scenario whilst the battle for an acceptable standard of hospitality raged endlessly all around.

Porcius, snoring with senatorial authority, his respectability eclipsed by the mundane urgency of human nature, finds himself propped up on cushions; his portly frame held in place by two converging walls. Marcellus in a feeble imitation of his father's unmelodious exhortations, lies partly on a string of cushions, and partly on the bare wood floor. Close by on a bed of cushions, with little Marcia's head resting serenely on her bosom, lies Rufina, occasionally made aware of the cacophony of noises emerging from her two male roommates.

As counterpoint to the peaceful scenario in the living room, the situation in the rest of the household now at a critical stage, had been forced to make an urgent appeal for reinforcements. Aurelia, having eventually reached her house in a state of near exhaustion, sent off Octavius, her husband, and her oldest son, Antoninus, to join the battle in the beleaguered farmhouse.

Progress was finally being made, and the challenging and exhausting work was nearing completion. The hallway of the house, now totally blocked by the combination of incoming baggage and outgoing dilapidated old furniture, clothing, bedding, bird cages, empty wine amphorae, threadbare drapes and many other messier items were now in the throws of being cleaned up, as the work slowly came to a temporary stand still.

The house was at long last, uniformly at rest. The two tired volunteers had returned to their homes, and the trio that remained, had retired to the comfort of their rooms and summarily collapsed onto their beds with rural abandon.

The cocks greeted the morning with their usual enthusiasm and no inkling of the struggles of their owners the previous evening. In a macho driven effort to out-crow each other, they filled the air with their exuberant and annoying sounds much to the ire of the unrested staff, who returned their greetings with many curses and projectiles, mainly in the form of shoes; successfully silencing the feathered disturbers of the peace. The crowing was soon however replaced by the cackling of the hens and braying of the three resident donkeys.

Thoroughly disgusted with the whole situation, and remembering the chaos left in the hallway, Sartorius, once dressed, martialled his troops once again and all were soon on the move. The congestion in the hallway was duly tackled whilst awaiting the arrival of Aurelia, who had, as it was popularly and correctly supposed... slept in.

The visitors were all awake, having been similarly roused by the cocks crowing and the subsequent cacophony of noises.

"I'm starving," said Marcellus, picking himself up from the bare floor and rubbing his aching sides.

"What's that?" grunted Porcius; who had slipped from his sitting position, wedged into a corner of the room all night. He could feel his chin pressing most uncomfortably against his clavicles. He struggled to prop himself up again. Little Marcia, rushing to embrace him, caused him to slide back once more. He bore the well-meant assault however, with grandfatherly resignation.

"Good morning to all," greeted a better rested Rufina. She sat, stretched her arms, and awaited her turn for a hug from Marcia who was now busily employed in a tickling match with Marcellus. She had been entrapped by him following her embrace.

Sartorius, none the worse for wear, presented himself in the living room with the welcome news that the rooms would be ready by the coming evening, and apologised most profusely for the inconvenience caused his beloved patrons.

"We appreciate your efforts," said Porcius with a smile. "What else could you have done without prior notice?"

"Still, I greatly regret that you did not have comfortable rooms to rest in," lamented the old man, throwing an apologetic glance at all his guests.

Rufina got up and asked to be shown the rooms. Sartorius smiled and called out to Lavinia who was busy in the kitchen preparing breakfast in Aurelia's absence. She left everything and joined the party in the living room where she was asked to show Rufina the upstairs rooms.

"Surely Father," she said to Sartorius, raising her strong well shaped arms and appealing with a touch of sarcasm in her large dark eyes. "That, is something *you* could do. I have to get breakfast ready for these good people, or they are going to faint with hunger...Aurelia has not yet arrived."

The old man looked at his daughter, and realising that she was right, he asked Rufina to follow him and led the way upstairs.

Rufina was astounded at the bareness of the rooms. There were no mattresses, no drapes and no carpets (all having been disposed of during the nocturnal battle). The furniture looked as if it would not survive much longer, and the cupboards for the clothes were most inadequate for her standards. No ablution stands were in sight. That, really troubled her.

As a result of Rufina's inspection of the rooms, and the day still being quite young, she, Marcia, and with Lavinia at the reins, made for the village immediately after breakfast in a spruced-up cart pulled by two donkeys.

Four hours later, that same cart fully laden with furniture and accessories and with the three same females walking beside it, was pulled by the tired donkeys into the farmhouse courtyard to a rousing welcome by the waiting male inhabitants of the house.

Presently, another cart, pulled by two mules and loaded with further necessities, appeared in the courtyard. All male hands were now called into service regardless of social standing. The many pieces of newly purchased furniture were taken upstairs to their respective rooms as designated by Rufina, who stood at the top of the landing confidently seeing each piece to its final destination.

By nightfall, the farmhouse had been transformed into a pleasant country home. All the beds were new, and the hitherto non-existent ablution stands with their corresponding jugs, basins, mirrors and towel racks were now a reality in each and every newly carpeted and curtained room.

Porcius was well pleased at the efficient manner in which his daughter had handled the situation. As usual, anything to do with house furnishings he left to the women. They, he would always say, had a better feel for such things.

Once the refurbishing of the farmhouse had been completed, Portius and Marcellus got down to the business of assessing all three vineyards. The astute senator wanted to catch the other two vineyards by surprise but was himself quite surprised to hear that both managers had already contacted Sartorius to enquire if the masters had arrived, and approximately when they might expect a visit from them.

"Here in Menorum," assured the old superintendent with certainty, "it is impossible to keep anything secret." He then proceeded to give father and son a slow, but very worthwhile tour of the vineyard. Every amphora of wine was accounted for, and the roster of workers was detailed with great care. The year was clearly marked on each amphora.

Both Porcius and Marcellus were amazed to see how Sartorius, who could read, but could not write anything other than his name, was quite adept at writing numbers and had a good grasp of simple arithmetic. His crude accounting was flawless, and for the every day descriptions pertaining to wine making, he had a series of parchments which had been scribed for him by someone in the village. They consisted of headings and short descriptions. Against these headings and descriptions, he would write the pertinent figures.

As for the quality of the wine, it spoke for itself. Father and son were well pleased with Sartorius' vineyard as the three of them made their way to their second vineyard to compare it with the first.

Their arrival was heralded by a large shaggy mongrel dog, who recognising Sartorius, quickly ceased his barking and approached him to be stroked; his tail wagging happily.

His master soon appeared with a big welcoming smile on his face. The man's name was Oratius.

He was fairly tall and thin, and as Marcellus guessed, in his very early thirties. His dark face presented well proportioned features with the exception of his chin, or lack of it. It receded noticeably, weakening somewhat a solid but well shaped nose and firm mouth. With friendly, smiling, deep brown eyes, he greeted the trio cordially and bid them sit down under a pergola covered with vine leaves, providing a deliciously cool shade. The visitors made themselves comfortable around a large table that stood under it and where most of the summer meals were eaten.

Refreshments soon came their way, served by Oratius' buxom and handsome wife Hortensia.

'She is probably in her late twenties,' thought Marcellus, eyeing her with some admiration.

A little later, Oratius regaled his patrons with a well directed and interesting tour of the winery, allowing them to sample a number of different grades and vintages. Most of which were well received by the visiting trio.

As the inspectors left Oratius and the vineyard under his stewardship, father and son were quite satisfied with what they had been shown. Their accounting which followed the style and format that Sartorius had established was also quite satisfactory. The only difference was that Hortensia, Oratius' wife, looked after the accounting. She, like Sartorius, could read, but could only write figures.

The cena at Marcellus' house, (for so it must now be called,) was a happy event. Porcius however, missed Ignatia's presence at the table and began to feel home sick. He promised himself that he would hurry through the inspections, and after briefing Marcellus, would leave him to carry on with his life in the country in the company of his sister.

However, he wondered what chance Rufina would have of finding a good husband there of her own class. But they had talked about that before their trip, and she had been adamant about following her brother and Marcia whom she also had grown to love.

The trio resumed their tour of inspection the following morning. They headed out to their third vineyard which was further away than that managed by Oratius. The terrain became more undulating and quite picturesque. They passed and soon left Menorum behind. Continuing on for about another half hour the vineyard came into sight. A village which Sartorius pointed to could be seen in the distance higher up on a hill.

"That, is Salistra," said the old man. "I had a girl friend there before I met my wife. She was quite a girl. I used to ride my father's mule from Menorum just to see her."

They all laughed at the twinkle in Sartorius' eye, and his good memory.

Reaching their destination, the trio rode into the empty courtyard and dismounted. A large golden dog ran out of the house and came charging at them. Marcellus instinctively drew his gladius in readiness. But suddenly the dog stopped, and recognising Sartorius came over to greet him, his tail wagging happily as the old man amiably stroked him.

"There's a good boy Leo," chanted Sartorius. The dog relaxed and proceeded to sniff Porcius and Marcellus; presumably recording their scent for future reference.

Porcius stroked the creature gingerly. Marcellus replaced his gladius in its scabbard.

A woman suddenly appeared. She was in her early forties and somewhat on the plump side. She pressed Sartorius' extended hands warmly. and with a charming smile, in her kind green/grey eyes, made a shy, shallow bow in the direction of father and son.

"I am happy and honoured to see you both again. I trust you had a good journey."

Porcius stepped towards her, and proffered his hands, which she took and pressed warmly.

Marcellus followed his father's example. His eyes appreciating Marina's good looks.

"Alas, my husband is not at home," she said with regret in her voice. "He had business to attend to in Salistra, but hopefully will be back soon. Please come in and have some refreshments whilst you wait."

She led them into the hallway, followed a long comfortably wide corridor, and finally out into the back garden. There, as was the custom in all those farm houses, they were invited to sit down around a long table in the shade of a wooden trellis covered by a living vine which being heavily populated with its wide and attractive leaves provided a very welcome shade. The back wall of the house, painted in an ocher hue, was covered with bougainvilleas that having crept up its wall had had to be trimmed to expose the upstairs bedroom windows, whose shallow iron railed balconies were decorated with potted plants and flowers. The effect was breathtaking, not to mention the delicious aroma exuded by that colourful tableau.

Porcius could not help but compliment the lady of the house on the beauty of her garden, which though not very big, was totally surrounded by a high wall which provided a contrasting backdrop to many species of plants, small trees and flowering climbers.

The efficient Marina regaled her distinguished visitors with mouth watering delicacies of her own creation which not only refreshed them, but revived their admiration at her culinary expertise. The wine was also quite to the visitors' satisfaction.

"I would like to have a cook like her at home," commented Porcius, biting into a delicious morsel with great gusto.

"I should send Aurelia over here to learn from Marina," said Sartorius. "Though mind you," he continued with a tilt of his bald head. "Aurelia is a pretty good cook but does not normally prepare these fancier things for the likes of us."

A couple of hours passed, before Leo's barking, announced the approach of a horse and rider whom he ran out of the courtyard to meet; his bushy tail wagging madly.

Pompinus dismounted, and seeing three horses tied up under the shade of the large eucalyptus tree, vaguely wondered as to who were the unexpected visitors. A closer look soon discovered the two Arabian horses, and he realised with great mental rapidity, that his patrons had arrived and were waiting for him. He made haste to meet them.

As his legs carried him into the presence of his masters, the picture of the two beautiful Arabians taunted his devious mind, and he grudgingly considered with some envy in his heart, the difference in status between himself and his patrons.

He put on the best face he could muster and was soon engaged in the business of directing the visitors on a tour of the vineyard.

Porcius and Marcellus were satisfied by the vineyard itself. The vines were looking quite healthy and were obviously well cared for, and the quality of the wine was good. However, the accounting was somewhat confusing and did not follow the format that Sartorius used. The fact that Pompinus could read and write and yet his figures did not seem to add up, made the trio suspect that there might be some underhanded business being carried out.

"Your production is somewhat below that of my other two vineyards," said Portius, giving Pompinus an enquiring look and fully expecting an explanation.

"We have drainage problems, which cause water to stagnate around some of the vines. The hilly nature of the land plays tricks with their irrigation," said the man, looking at Sartorius as if for concurrence. The latter made no effort to respond.

"Have you tried digging shallow channels to control the water flow?" asked Marcellus.

"I've tried everything. It has all been a waste of time."

The meeting with Pompinus came to an end a little later. The trio, politely and somewhat regrettably declining Marina's invitation for the cena, took leave of her and her husband and started for home.

Rufina welcomed them back. Marcia had been put to bed a while earlier, protesting that she wanted to stay up and see Marcellus and Umpa: for so she called Porcius, who was greatly amused by his new name.

"I do not trust this fellow Pompinus," remarked Marcellus during the late cena that had been left for them by Aurelia, and which Lavinia had warmed up. The latter was then serving it with the aid of Rufina who presently sat down to join the men.

"What do you think of his excuse for being under production?" asked Portius searching Sartorius' eyes.

The old vintner took a sip of his wine.

"I think he's exaggerating the problem of the stagnating water. Sure, he may have an irrigation problem, but with all that undulating land he could have the water run off from the collection points. Hardly enough to make a big difference in production."

"He has the largest of the three vineyards has he not?" asked Marcellus savouring a piece of sausage.

Sartorius, took another swig of his wine, and smacking his lips, said.

"By far."

Rex, the household Alsatian made his appearance begging a morsel with his large eyes.

The old man threw him a bone with some ham still on it. The dog squatted down happily to eat it.

The unsettling conversation continued well into the evening, and by the time they parted to their respective beds, they had unanimously agreed that Pompinus was robbing his masters of a substantial piece of their profits. Marcellus promised to keep a very close eye on the suspected thief in the future. He would, he said, remain at the man's house during the next harvest if necessary, and personally count every measure that was poured into the earthenware vats. A careful accounting would be taken of every amphora in stock, and so from then on, any attempt by Pompinus to steal from the owners would be easily uncovered.

* * * * *

Whilst Porcius, Marcellus, and Sartorius were enjoying their cena, and discussing their problems with regard to Pompinus' suspected dishonesty, the latter was also having his cena, and venting his frustrations on his unfortunate wife.

"Why were you so nice to them? They have only come to destroy our livelihood."

"They are the owners. If we do not please them, they may put someone else in your place," said Marina; not just in self defence, but because she felt it was only good business; apart from the fact that she was very elated at the compliments she had received from Porcius.

No one ever complimented her on anything. She was just taken for granted by her husband and everyone else.

"You are a fool, woman," said Pompinus with hatred in his voice. "Maybe they impressed you with their fancy manners and rich clothes? Well, you're never going to have any rich clothes like them. Doesn't that not bother you?"

"I would like to have some nicer clothes, but if I cannot, then I am content with what I have. They are different from us. We can never be like them," she protested.

"Everyone has a right to be like them. I'll show you that I am as good as them. Just a few more harvests, and I'll have enough money to buy a vineyard of my own." He took hold of the wine cup in front of him and greedily drained it.

Marina, leaving her cena half finished, went into the kitchen to be alone. She did not know what her husband was doing or planning to do. He never told her anything other than throw angry words at her.

An hour later, she was being summoned to serve two friends of Pompinus, who had as usual dropped in to drink his wine and incite him on to his reckless ambitions.

Marina felt lonely. Her daughter Diana whom she dearly loved, had married and gone to live in Genua, where her husband worked as a government official with the port authorities. Her son, the youngest of her two children, had joined the Roman Legion and was presently serving somewhere in Gaul. She was no fool however, and wondered how her husband, who only had a superintendent's salary, could even think of buying his own vineyard.

* * * * *

Porcius having concluded his business in Umbria, prepared to return home. He had promised himself that he would do so at the very first opportunity. Three days after the meeting with Pompinus, he was all set to go, riding his beloved and much envied Arabian.

Marcellus was a little concerned about his father travelling on his own on that horse. He remembered his experience on the way to Pyrgi and felt that a similar misfortune could befall him. Porcius however stated with confidence that he had made that particular journey on that same horse a number of times, and that he had never had any problems.

The whole household was in the courtyard to wish the senator God speed.

He confidently rode out of the gate waving back lovingly.

Marcellus braced himself for the life that had been destined for him, and which he would deal with to the best of his ability.

* * * * *

A month had passed since Porcius' departure. Rufina was playing with Marcia in the garden, when Lavinia brought the news that a stranger was in the courtyard enquiring for Marcellus. Leaving Marcia with Lavinia, she hurried to meet the visitor.

Rushing through the hallway, she almost bumped into the young stranger, who had to side- step to avoid her.

"Oh! I apologize," she blurted out with blushing cheeks.

"No apology necessary," replied the man, "I should have waited in the courtyard."

"It's perfectly alright. I was moving too fast." she admitted, with a lovely smile at the tall handsome stranger.

"I am given to understand that you are enquiring after by brother."

"Yes," he affirmed, removing his shawl, and exposing a good head of curly dark brown hair that Rufina was quick to notice and admire.

"My name is Tullius Ledicius," smiled the stranger. "I was asked to seek Marcellus Fulvius, whom I take it is your brother?"

"Please come in. We can sit in the garden and wait for him. He has been in the vineyard all day. I expect him back shortly."

They walked through the hallway and breezy corridor into the garden. Marcia left Lavinia and ran to Rufina who sat her down beside her and opposite Tullius. Lavinia was introduced to the stranger and at Rufina's request, went to prepare some refreshments.

She soon returned, and placing the tray on the table in front of Rufina, smiled at the guest and left her to entertain him. She had to help Aurelia with the cena, which was due in less than an hour.

Marcia, seemed to take to the stranger, who made her laugh by gently pulling her pretty little nose and pretending to throw it away. She laughed with some uncertainty. He, with an amused look, said.

"There! You look so funny without a nose." He looked at Rufina for concurrence. She, feeling quite comfortable with the amiable stranger, played along, and soon an uncertain Marcia was glaring into the lily pond to examine her reflection in the water and verify that she could see her nose as surely as she could feel it.

"I am Rufina," said the beautiful hostess with an enchanting smile. "Please forgive me for not introducing myself before. It was quite unintentional I assure you."

'Why am I explaining myself to this stranger?' she asked herself.

"A lovely name," he asserted with a charming smile. "Quite as lovely as its owner."

His smile was returned with as much pleasure as his compliment had occasioned.

Sartorius appeared at the other end of the garden. He was coming home for the cena. He had been tending to the vineyard all day and looked tired. His worsening limp was quite noticeable as he approached the big table where Rufina and the stranger were seated. Little Marcia ran to embrace him.

He held her away.

"No! I am all sweaty and sticky. Save my hug for later," he said with a laugh and a smile. Marcia asked him for Marcellus.

"He will be here in a few minutes," he told her; his eyes on the visitor.

Sartorius was introduced to Tullius, and promptly excusing himself, went off to his ablutions.

"Here is Cellus" cried Marcia, running off to the end of the garden to greet him. Marcellus picked her up, hugged her, and carried her with him to meet Rufina's guest.

"This is Tullius Ledicius," said Rufina gesturing elegantly at him with her slender hand. "He has come looking for you."

Tullius got up and extended his hand for Marcellus to press.

"Pleased to make your acquaintance Tullius," said Marcellus taking the man's hand and giving him a warm smile. "What can I do for you? Please sit down."

Rufina asked Marcia to find Lavinia and ask her to bring some more refreshments. The girl ran off to do as she had been asked.

Marcellus, looking at Tullius, invited him to state his business.

"I have business in this part of the country, and I was asked by Procula, who knew I was coming this way, to drop in and see you. She felt that what I have to say would greatly interest you."

Rufina looked very surprised at this piece of news. She knew who Procula was but was anxious to learn what she would want with her brother.

"I wonder how she found out that I was here? How is she by the way?" asked Marcellus.

"She is well but concerned about her husband's condition."

"Is it getting worse?"

"It seems so I'm afraid," said Tullius, gravely. "We continue to pray for his recovery without his knowing of course, but so far to no avail. She is still reluctant to try the veil's power. She is not sure that it would work for him."

"I'm sorry to hear that," said Marcellus nodding his head in sympathy.

Rufina listened with great interest. 'Who is this man who prays for people?' Her answer was at hand.

"Procula knows," continued Tullius, "that you believe in the source and power of the veil, and that you had expressed a wish to learn more of the man whose image is on it. The man's holy name is Yeshua, the Son of God; in whom she and I believe. You see," he smiled with a sparkle in his deep brown eyes. "We are Christians and I am a priest of that faith. However, I make my living as a physician."

Rufina shuddered as she remembered the poor people who had been rounded up so cruelly at the hostel on her father and brother's last trip. She pulled Marcia closer to her and hugged her, as the girl's unfortunate parents came to mind.

"Yes," said Marcellus, "I am most interested in learning all that you can teach me about Yeshua." He turned to Rufina and searched her eyes.

"Yes," she said. "I am also greatly interested." She was filled with admiration at Tullius' status both in the religious and secular sense.

Tullius had been a guest at the farmhouse for close to two weeks. He taught Marcellus and Rufina many things that Yeshua had done and said.

One evening, as he sat with them at the table under the pergola enjoying the evening breeze, he announced that he was looking for a place in Umbria, where he would like to settle.

"I shall be settling down around here," said Tullius, motioning with his hand and looking at his new friends with enthusiasm in his eyes. "Probably in Salistra, which is the largest of the surrounding villages, and where I shall hopefully base my practice whilst I spread the 'Good News' of Yeshua. We are far enough from Rome, that I do not anticipate any danger as far as persecutions are concerned. Hopefully," he continued, lowering his voice. "Caligula will not last long in power, and the next emperor may see the Christians in a different light... For this we must pray." He took a sip of his watered wine and asked.

"Have you made up your minds yet, whether you wish me to baptise you before I leave?"

His eyes, shifted eagerly from one sibling to the other.

"Yes," answered Rufina. Followed by her brother, who nodded his head in ascent.

"Good!" said Tullius with satisfaction. "It will probably be a while before I get a chance to visit you again. I have a lot of ground to cover for now. The Gospel has to be spread to all who will listen."

"You be very careful to keep your faith a secret," advised Rufina with some concern.

"I shall do my best," he smiled, "otherwise my career may be a short one."

"Will you let us know where we can reach you as soon as you are settled?" asked Marcellus, before his sister could make the same request which was on the tip of her tongue.

"Most assuredly so," replied the priest with a nod.

Tullius rode off to Salistra the following day, with the warm wishes of Marcellus and Rufina who now began their new lives as baptised Christians. Of this great occurrence, the rest of the household including little Marcia remained ignorant for the time being.

CHAPTER NINE

FISHING FOR MEN

It was Tullius' second month in Salistra. He had found a small house to rent and had placed a sign in his front window which had brought him a number of patients. However he was as yet not earning enough to make a living. He had to continually dip into his savings to make ends meet.

He had been able to interest a few in the Good News, though as yet he had not performed a single baptism. Preaching publicly in the street, which would doubtlessly have yielded much better results was out of the question. He had to preach the Gospels in a clandestine manner because of their proximity to Rome. The risk was high.

His little congregation, consisting of fifteen souls were very secretive about their prospective religion and met separately or in pairs for their instruction in Tullius' house. He also gave lessons in writing and arithmetic. That, supplemented his income and acted as a decoy to safeguard his missionary work.

In his loneliness, he often thought of Rufina for whom he felt more than just a passing interest. Her beauty and warmth had struck a note in his heart and was testing his resolve to serve Yeshua in a celibate manner. Apart from his personal feelings, he felt an obligation to visit her and Marcellus, with the intention of performing a 'Breaking of the Bread' service for them. 'They were,' he told himself, with a sense of personal inadequacy, 'the only two Christians in the area.'

One morning he rode off to Menorum. It was a sunny morning promising a hot day. The sun's rays falling merrily on each enduring dew drop, animated the grassy slopes by the side of the road, and greeted the multitude of multicoloured wild flowers which opened up to receive its invigorating beams.

His thoughts kept him company as his appreciative eyes enjoyed the colourful and serene landscape through which he travelled. He met many people along the road, making him deplore for the umpteenth time, the way that the Christian religion was being persecuted.

'How I would love to stop anywhere along this beautiful route,' he mused, 'and call out to these good people. Come! Listen to the wonderful news I have for you. I know that I could capture their hearts with the stories of Yeshua. These people are thirsting for a faith that will give them hope. Their useless and unreliable gods will dwindle to nothing when I tell them of Yeshua, and how he died for them and rose from the dead to save their immortal souls.'

"Help! Help me!" A pleading voice coming from behind a small rise by the side of the road and on the edge of a copse, pulled him out of his reverie.

Dismounting, he led his horse in the voice's direction. He left his animal beside a tree and climbed over the rise to investigate. There, on the ground lay a man in his fifties. His head and left arm were bleeding badly, and he seemed unable to get up. His tunic was drenched in blood.

The priest carefully examined the man. Going back to his horse, he took some cloths from his baggage and returning to his impromptu patient, wrapped a piece tightly above the arm wound to stop the bleeding. With another larger piece he wrapped the man's head as best he could to temporarily absorb the blood.

"I am a physician," he said. "I must suture your wounds as soon as possible. You are losing much blood." He took the man's arms and placed him in a sitting position.

"Are you dizzy?"

"Yes," answered the man.

"I have to get you up on my horse. Can you stand?"

"I shall try."

With Tullius' help the man managed to stand. The physician put the man's arm over his shoulder and holding him by the waist, walked him slowly and with difficulty to the waiting horse.

Just then two peasants approached. Both were men. The priest got them to help him sit the wounded man on the horse. They supported the swooning man whilst Tullius jumped up behind him and held him firmly. Thanking the peasants for their help, the physician and his patient continued on the road to Menorum at a fast walk.

Tullius rang the bell loudly at the open gate of Marcellus' farm house and rode into the courtyard. Rex, the Alsatian, came running out to investigate in the noisiest of fashions, alerting the household as to the new arrivals.

"Alright Rex. Don't you remember me?" sang out Tullius smiling at the dog.

Lavinia came out on hearing Rex's barking and seeing Tullius with the wounded man, ran back into the house for help.

Presently, Rufina and Sartorius appeared.

"Greetings to you all," said Tullius, with a particular smile for Rufina. "Please give me a hand with this poor man who has been brutally attacked on the road.

Many hands were applied to the task, and soon the man was bedded in the vacant bedroom. The wounds were promptly cleaned and skilfully sutured by the experienced hands of Tullius, who sat by the bed waiting for the patient who had passed out during the suturing, to regain his consciousness.

"I have brought you some refreshments," announced Rufina walking happily into the room.

"That is most thoughtful of you," said the physician appreciatively, admiring her alluring light brown eyes, which spoke of love as they met his.

"It's so good to see you again," she smiled, putting the little tray on a nearby table.

He got up, and examining the tray, picked a few grapes from a bunch. He put one in his mouth and motioned for her to sit in his chair. He, sat on the bed at his patient's feet.

"I have missed you so much," said Rufina with a lovely pout. "Why did you stay away so long?"

"I have often thought of you. It gets pretty lonely over there in Salistra," he said looking deeply once more into her expressive eyes.

"Where am I?"

They both turned to look at the patient who had suddenly awoken from his coma.

"Welcome to the land of the living my unknown friend," laughed Tullius, getting to his feet." I think you will feel better now that you have stopped bleeding."

The man looked wonderingly at the pair beside him.

"Can he eat?" asked Rufina with some concern.

"If you can get Aurelia to get him some good wholesome soup," said the physician. "I think he will enjoy it. He has to get his strength back." He pressed the patient's hand.

"My name is Tullius," he said, "and I am a physician. You are at my good friend Marcellus Fulvius' farmhouse. Who do I have the honour of addressing?"

"My name is Sabinus Celorius. I am the governor of this Province. I am most indebted to you my friend," said the patient with a serious look on his face.

Sabinus went on to explain the attack on his life, and the subsequent robbery of his money, horse and sword.

"I never imagined," he continued, "that they would attack an official. The rogues were probably following me. They knew who I was and most likely intended to kill me. It was very foolish of me to venture out unescorted in civilian clothes, and with only my gladius. Their faces were covered. They caught me completely unawares as I was cutting through the little copse that runs parallel to the road. It was such a beautiful morning; riding among the trees was most enjoyable. In hind sight, I should have stayed on the road of course."

He shook his head and regretted it immediately. He felt a stab of pain and grimaced.

"From now on I must travel with an escort," he continued, "even when I go riding for pleasure. How annoying... A man in my position has many enemies."

A sudden thought occurred to him; his eyes widened, and his bushy eyebrows lifted. "My horse must still be wandering around the countryside."

The soup arrived. Sabinus lost no time savouring it. A dizzy spell however made him stop and hand the bowl back to Tullius who fed him a spoonful at a time.

"The dizziness should go soon," said the physician, giving his patient the last spoonful.

"I shall keep you on soup until it goes away. It could take a few days."

"My family must know what has happened," said the patient. "Could you send word to them?"

"I shall ask Marcellus," promised Tillius.

"If he can get someone to ride out to the Legion's barracks in Salistra with the news," said the governor, pressing his badly throbbing, bandaged arm," they will dispatch a courier to my wife in Ariminum. I have been away from home for almost three weeks. I should have been home by now and she is probably concerned." He closed his eyes. His head ached badly.

Antonius was entrusted with the mission to the Legion's barracks. He promptly acquiesced.

It took Sabinus five days to recover from his dizzy spells. The military courier who had brought him a fresh set of clothes, was asked to check back in two days with a military escort. Tullius had advised his patient to stay an extra couple of days, just to be sure that the recovery was complete.

A very grateful Sabinus rode out of Marcellus' courtyard with an escort of three soldiers, having promised Tullius a generous remuneration for his troubles, and his very sincere thanks to the Marcellus family for their hospitality.

During the time that the governor had been recovering, Rufina and Tullius had spent some very pleasant hours in each other's company. An amorous relationship had been established between them, much to Marcellus' approval. He and Tullius had become good friends and discovered that they had much in common.

Rufina, had been instructing Lavinia, Aurelia, and Sartorius, in the faith for the last couple of months as best she could. They had accepted Yeshua with enthusiasm and were looking forward to further instruction, and baptism at Tullius' hand.

No sooner had Sabinus gone than arrangements were made for the solemn service that would make them Christians. Antonius, was not yet ready to accept the faith, but the family was praying for him.

Marcia was kept ignorant on matters of the faith until she was old enough to be trusted in keeping it secret.

The Baptismal service took place the night following Sabinus' departure. Marcia was asleep.

"Congratulations to you all," said Tullius with a big smile, putting down the jug of water which he had used to baptise them. "Now I have a congregation of five."

That same night, after the service, the three friends sat in the family room enjoying some refreshments.

"I shall be leaving tomorrow," announced Tullius with much regret to those present. "I have work to do in Salistra. A number of people are about ready to accept Yeshua, and all they need is a little encouragement to get them over their fear. This terrible persecution in Rome is making my work very difficult. Rumours keep coming this way, and people are afraid."

"We must all continue to pray that they get rid of Caligula soon," said Marcellus.

"There is no guarantee that the next emperor will be any better," said Rufina sadly shaking her head in disgust. "They need to keep the people entertained, and we Christians are paying the price."

"I shall have to go to Rome again soon," announced Tullius.

"Why?" asked a concerned Rufina. Her eyes displaying a sudden sadness.

"Linus, my superior, must know what I am achieving; which at the moment is pretty meagre I fear."

"But you cannot be blamed for people's fears," said Marcellus.

"Linus is a very understanding and kind man. He will not berate me. But he may be able to offer good suggestions, since he is well experienced and in the thick of it."

"Oh dear," complained Rufina, we shall lose you again for another few months.

"God's work is constant," explained the priest. "Those of us who undertake to actively serve him accept these sudden changes in life style. Our time is not our own any more. It is whatever the Lord decides."

Marcellus got up and bidding both good night, left them. He knew they needed some time to themselves, and he had other matters of his own to consider.

Once Marcellus had gone, Tullius moved a little closer to Rufina.

"I shall come and visit you for a few days before I leave for Rome," promised Tullius.

"How long will you spend in Salistra?" she asked.

He took her hand in his, and with tenderness in his voice, said. "As long as I need to win at least ten more souls for Yeshua. Hopefully another couple of months."

She squeezed his hand lovingly but said nothing. There was much turbulence going on in their heads. Mental battles were being fought. Rufina was the most confused of the two. She could not understand his hesitation in declaring his love for her. She knew that she had fallen in love with him, and strongly suspected his love for her.

He got up, and bowing, took her hand and kissed it tenderly. With a sad smile he bid her good night. She sat there for a long time, musing over his reluctance which she could not fathom.

Tullius left the following day. Riding back to Salistra with a heavy heart he pondered over the complications in his life.

'I am a man called by Yeshua to proclaim and spread His Word,' he told himself. 'My life must be lived with Him at the centre. He must have preference over all and everything. How can I ask Rufina to be my wife? My life is one of uncertainty. I cannot offer her any stability, even though I can soon offer security when my practice picks up. But she does not need security, she is wealthier than I shall ever be. No! Money plays no part in this.' He nodded, returning the greeting of a passerby. His musings continued.

'She loves me; of this I feel sure, as I indeed love her. If I were a normal man without duty to Yeshua, all would be so simple.' He looked around admiring the vineyards. The rays of the morning sun bathed the vines, endowing them with a transparent and vibrant look. They swayed contentedly in the light warm breeze.

'Her faith in Yeshua is strong,' he continued. 'Possibly as strong as mine. She would perhaps understand and accept the mode of life that I am committed to live. A life of such loneliness. When I am with her, she cheers me up and I feel encouraged. If we were to marry and have children, how often would I see them? And how much attention would I be able to give them? I have no guarantee that I would not be relocated. It would be very unsettling for them. If this persecution continues we could soon be running for our lives. At such times, my family's welfare must be sacrificed for the good of my flock.'

His horse began to climb up the hill that led into Salistra. More peasants passed by and he saluted them with a smile and a wave of the hand.

'I must think this thing through, very, very carefully. Let's see what I can achieve here. It may help me make up my mind.'

He rode into the picturesque village square with its many lemon trees aglow in the morning sun and made his way to his house

* * * * *

Marcellus walked through his vineyard with Sartorius. The grapes were almost ripe for picking. The harvest would soon be upon them, and the matter of keeping an eye on Pompinus had to be resolved.

"I hate the thought of having to live with that fellow for the duration of the harvest. What could we possibly do to ensure that he does not steal from me?" asked Marcellus with little expectancy of a practical answer.

"It's a difficult problem," said the old man, removing his cap and scratching his bald head. "Perhaps," he suggested with some hope, "if we placed a spy or two among their pickers, they could keep an eye on things and let us know what he's up to."

Marcellus thought for a moment. 'Sartorius could be right. It would not even cost me much. If they could find how the wine is being taken, and where, I could then catch Pompinus red handed and fire him.'

"By Jupiter!" exclaimed Marcellus, slapping the old man lightly on the shoulder. "That is a good plan."

Sartorius was pleased at his master's enthusiastic approval.

"We would go occasionally and unexpectedly, until we find out what is happening to the wine," said Marcellus with relief.

As they walked back to the farmhouse a little later for their cena, the satisfied pair discussed who would be chosen from the pickers to act as spies. It was agreed that there would have to be two, in case one met with an accident or became ill.

"I think it wiser," said Marcellus, "to recruit them separately. One should not know that the other is performing the same service for us. What do you think?"

After a few moments of silence, and stopping to rest his aching legs, Sartorius nodded his head in agreement.

Most of the pickers were perennial workers and were known to Sartorius who had been hiring them for years. They usually divided themselves into teams, and each group was assigned by him as head superintendent to work in one of the three Fulvius vineyards. Two men whom the old man knew he could trust were interviewed separately and recruited as spies. Pompinus was not popular among the pickers so it was with some relish that they undertook the task.

* * * * *

Procula was in the midst of trying to pacify her husband during one of his terrible nightmares which were now almost a nightly occurrence. She lay beside him as he twisted and turned in his sleep making it impossible for either of them to find rest.

She was still apprehensive about showing Pilate the veil. She feared it might trigger off an attack of insanity from which he would never recover.

'He seems to be quiet for the moment,' she said to herself. Taking a deep breath, she got out of bed and went over to the little trunk where the veil was stored and knelt in front of it. After some hesitation, she opened the trunk and pulled it out.

'I wonder,' she mused hopefully, 'what would happen if I put the veil over him while he sleeps?'

Procula, now a Christian, and finding herself on her knees, fervently prayed once more for Yeshua to forgive Pontius whom she loved. She knew he was sorry. She had overheard him say so many times whilst talking in his sleep.

She arose and with the open veil in her hands, approached the bed. Carefully and reverently, she draped it over him and lay beside him continuing with her silent prayers of supplication. She waited hopefully. The nightmare did not materialise. Presently, she unintentionally fell asleep.

The night passed most peacefully. She awoke before him as usual, (she, like most of her sex was a light sleeper,) and realised to her horror that she had fallen asleep. With a thankful heart she removed the veil, folded it quickly, and placing it back in the trunk, returned to bed.

Pilate, awoke a little later; his eyes wide with excitement. He gently shook Procula's shoulder.

"Good morning!" he cried with a big smile.

"My nightmare did not come back last night," he said.

"Yes," she smiled back and kissed him lightly. "I am aware of that. I also slept my dear."

"Maybe it's gone for good?" he said, looking listlessly around with hope in his eyes.

"We shall have to wait and see," she smiled.

* * * * *

The vendimmia (harvest time) had arrived. It was the second week of September. The pickers set up the tents provided by the vineyard. These would house them until all the grapes were gathered and pressed into juice. Usually a matter of five or six weeks.

Spirits were high, and though some very heavy labour lay ahead, the general mood was enthusiastic and jovial. There was something magical about the gathering of those colourful and delicious little globes. It seemed to give the pickers an inexplicable reverence and sense of propriety that kept them coming as if on some religious pilgrimage year after year.

They were proud people who took a personal interest in their work, as if enchanted by their sun-soaked, colourful surroundings. They became engrossed in their labour and sustained a constant joviality, socializing with their fellow pickers; their tongues keeping pace with their fast, experienced hands.

Every now and then, someone with a gifted voice would break into song, eliciting the choral response which invariably followed. The tempo of those songs was geared to the steady rhythm of the hands at work. Full of joy and hope, the music captured the essence of the vendimmia and exuberantly proclaimed as if of their own creation (which might well have been the case), the carefree disposition and abandon of the happy, invigorating tones of the "tarantella" of later days.

Marcellus, who had never attended a grape harvest was soon captured by the magic of the annual event. He thanked God for having given him ownership of those vineyards, and prayed that he might be a good steward to all those people who came to help him fulfil his life in such a wonderful way.

With Rufina and Marcia at his side, he happily walked among the pickers, occasionally stopping briefly to talk and encourage them. Little Marcia soon became their pet and they kept her entertained all day long. She was soon joining in the singing, and having a most enjoyable and instructive time.

Sartorius circulated constantly among the workers directing and keeping a vigilant eye on everyone. Marcellus, also caught up in the picking frenzy, helped out wherever he could. After the first couple of days in his own vineyard, he rode out by himself to see how Octavius was coping with his, and then checked into Pompinus' one. He made no attempt to contact either of his spies as he knew that they were probably busy investigating, and in any event, it was too early to report any misdemeanour on the part of their boss.

Sartorius and Lavinia, taught Rufina much with regard to the catering of food to the tent camp where the pickers ate. Aurelia who had hired extra help for the four or five weeks of the vendimmia, was extremely busy in the farm house kitchen. Antonius with the help of some of the workers, transported the food daily to the tent camp in the vacant field adjoining the farmhouse garden. There, several large tables and many benches had been set up for the pickers' use. They ate mostly outside as the weather was generally dry and a pleasant breeze was almost always present.

The evenings were short for all concerned. Everyone was up at the crack of dawn and the work was tiring.

One evening, Marcellus and Rufina, sat at the table in the garden all by themselves discussing the events of the day. Rex, the Alsatian, lay at their feet under the table. Marcia had been asleep for a couple of hours.

"I wonder how Tullius is doing," murmured Rufina somewhat listlessly as if musing aloud.

"He is probably working hard to make those conversions that he told us about," said Marcellus.

"He would enjoy seeing what is going on here," she said, brushing back her hair which had been blown into disarray by a light puff of wind. "I wonder if there are any Christians among the pickers?"

"That would be most difficult and dangerous to find out. I am not aware of any signals that they might be in the habit of giving."

"Perhaps there should be some sign by which we could communicate. Who knows? There may be one already and we do not know it," she suggested. "Maybe Tullius knows?"

Brother and sister, were about to turn in for the night, when Rex growled and stood up. A young man suddenly appeared in front of them. He bowed to Rufina and addressed her brother.

"Master Marcellus," he began. "My brother Fabianus asked me to ride out and tell you that he has discovered something that you would be interested in knowing.

"Did he tell you what it is?" asked Marcellus.

"Yes." answered the boy. "He says that there is an abandoned barn on the property, and every day after the treading, Pompinus takes a number of large jars filled with the day's juice to that barn in his cart.

Marcellus thanked the boy and gave him a gift of money which was reluctantly accepted, and off went the messenger.

"Aha!" cried Marcellus. "So that is how he robs me. Wait until I tell Sartorius tomorrow."

"Oh my," groaned Rufina, who for a nineteen-year-old was endowed with wisdom beyond her years. "Who needs trouble now that everyone is working so contentedly. I marvel at their good humour and how well they all seem to get along. There have been no fights or any kind of disorder.

"Oh my," she repeated sadly, and getting up, she kissed her brother on the cheek and began to walk away. Rex followed her. Suddenly she stopped, turned around and said.

"Would it not be better to wait until the end of the vendimmia? When the pickers are gone, and things return to normal? You can better deal with him then I think."

"Perhaps you are right," agreed Marcellus. "Let's hear from Sartorius in the morning."

Getting up, he followed his sister into the house.

* * * * *

Whilst Marcellus had been sitting with Rufina that same evening, Pompinus had been enjoying some wine with his usual two friends, sitting around the table in his garden.

Marina had been sent to bed when they arrived. She would not be needed. He would take care of them himself, her husband had told her.

"I have some interesting news for you Pompinus," said one of his friends who went by the name of Calvus.

The latter, took a hold of a jug sitting on the table and poured himself a very full cup of wine.

"Do tell," said Pompinus with a curious look in his eyes.

"There is a physician called Tullius in Salistra, who I am told is a Christian and is trying to convert some people in the village."

"Great!" blurted out Pompinus. "Why should that interest me?"

"Wait till he finishes," said Nonus; wiping some sweat from his fat, miserable looking face.

"Go on," said the vintner, nodding and motioning with his hand for Calvus to continue.

"What would you say if I told you that the physician is a very good friend of your dear boss?"

"I would believe you," said Pompinus dryly. Pouting disinterestedly with a shrug of his shoulders.

Calvus got up, and coming around the table, put his arm meaningfully over his friend's shoulder. He looked at him straight in the eye said,

"Maybe your boss is a Christian too."

Pompinus' eyes took on a faraway look. "Mmmm... Wouldn't that be something?"

"Ha! Ha! Now, you get it. Ha! Ha! Now, you get it," repeated Calvus with gusto.

"Hahaha!" they all laughed. "Hahaha!"

* * * * *

The vendimmia finally came to an end. The wine in all three vineyards was now stored in large earthenware jars, awaiting the proper time to be transferred to amphorae, where they would be tagged with the vintage year and left to continue their slow fermentation until the mature date when they would be sold.

The Fulvius vineyards produced red wines exclusively, though Marcellus was considering adding white wines to his repertoire. It had been a good year. The grapes had enjoyed a well-balanced proportion of sun and rain, and all concerned were well pleased with the prospects of profitable sales a few years down the road.

That, is what made the vintner's trade a difficult one to embark on in any way other than purchasing a reputable vineyard. The first few years' yields would not be remunerative in any significant way to the pioneering vintner, since young wines, though saleable, would hardly establish a much-needed reputation for the owners. Only mature and knowledgeably tended wines would by their quality, guarantee the degree of excellence and consistency that the discriminating consumer would expect.

Marcellus was most fortunate in that regard. His father's vineyards had been operative for over twenty years. Thanks to the know-how and dedication of Sartorius, the Fulvius family could now boast of producing some of the country's finest wines.

"How are we going to put a stop to Pompinus' pilfering?" asked a very concerned Marcellus.

Once more the little group gathered around the garden table, listened with great interest to the words that the head of the house had spoken. No one was looking forward to the unpleasantness that would accompany any action taken against a man like Pompinus. He had destroyed the good relations and confidence that had existed between owner and managers.

Sartorius took an unusually big gulp of his wine and looked intently at his master.

"We have to expose him for what he is," he replied with a flick of his wrist and a tilt of his bald head.

A pregnant silence followed. Their sadness was readily apparent. The vendimmia had gone so well. Everyone had done their best. The spirit of the enterprise had been something that Marcellus and Rufina might well remember with nostalgia in future years. It was their first experience of the kind. Their interacting with the peasantry of that beautiful countryside in such a disinterested and pleasant way, despite the fact that their interests were very much at stake, embedded itself with permanence in their hearts.

"Suppose we ignore it all and continue as usual?" suggested Rufina with hopeful resignation.

"I wish that were possible," sighed Marcellus. "His poor wife Marina will be the unfortunate victim, and that, I do greatly regret."

Sartorius, however was not in the least perturbed by the consequences of such an action. He knew the code that every manager was bound to, and whoever transgressed that, deserved to be punished. In his view, it was not fair to the other manager and himself. Both were content with their good wages and occasional generous bonuses.

"It's your decision Master," he said with sincerity, gulping down another mouthful of wine.

"We cannot ignore it," said Marcellus; realising it was his duty to chastise the thief; the others expected it of him.

He got up from the table and taking his wine cup with him, walked away from his sister and Sartorius absorbed in his thoughts.

'If my father were here,' he said to himself, 'I am pretty sure that he would have opted for disciplining Pompinus. But how does one punish the man and let him continue? There is only one way to deal with him, and that is to dismiss him. I could even report him to authorities...No. I don't think I want to go that far.'

He swallowed a good mouthful of wine and returned to his seat at the table.

"Tomorrow morning," he said, striking the table with his fist as if to put an end to his mental anguish, "we shall go and see Pompinus."

Marina met Marcellus and Sartorius in the courtyard of her house the following morning.

"Welcome to you both," she greeted with a sincere and lovely smile.

"Good morning to you Marina, glad to see you looking so well," said a smiling Marcellus.

"Is Pompinus at home?" asked Sartorius with a sober look on his old face, which Marina was quick to interpret as the harbinger of trouble.

"No," she replied he is in the village. "He did not say what he was going there for, so I have no idea when he will return. Sometimes he is away all day."

"Can I help you in any way? Would you like some refreshments?"

"No thank you," said Marcellus with the hint of a smile. "I shall be riding around the vineyard to inspect the vines and see that everything is to my satisfaction. We shall see you again on our return. If Pompinus arrives in the meantime, please ask him to ride out and find us."

"Yes, of course. I shall send him to you," promised Marina with a sinking heart. She realised that there must be something serious afoot, and her husband as usual had kept her ignorant of it. Whatever it was.

Marcellus lost no time in finding the old barn. They dismounted, tied their horses to a nearby tree, and walked up to the door. It was locked. Sartorius pounded on the door, but no answer came.

"That's very strange. It's been locked from the inside. I can see an iron bar across the wooden door," said Sartorius as he strained to see through a separation in the boards.

Marcellus unsheathed his gladius and slid it through the boards.

"Wait!" cried Sartorius. "You will ruin the blade of your sword. Come, let us look around the back and see what we can find."

Marcellus put his gladius back in the scabbard. Both men walked around the barn, carefully scrutinising every board. The side of the barn yielded nothing of value to them, but as they reached the centre rear of the barn, Sartorius spotted a piece of branch about the length of a hand with some thin rope wrapped around it. Being tight to the barn face and well above a man's head it could easily have gone unnoticed.

"Aha!" cried Sartorius as his eyes fell upon the object. "I'll bet this'll open the barn door."

He took a hold of the branch and pulled it down slowly until a good length of the rope appeared. Then, spotting a couple of hooks attached to a board very close to the ground, he continued to pull until the branch reached the hooks, and he secured the two.

"I think we will find the door open now," assured the old man, whilst Marcellus stood there admiring the ingenuity of the locking device.

They went around to the front again and easily pushed the door open. The iron bar was now leaning to one side against another larger hook on the door post. The rope passed through a couple of pulleys and out the back of the barn.

"Very clever," said Marcellus. "We shall have to watch this fellow, he is probably full of tricks in other respects."

"Aha!" cried Sartorius once again. "Take a look at this, Master." He pointed at two large earthenware jars buried in the ground. Only a short collar and the mouths protruded.

The latter were plugged with hardened clay contained in a heavy cloth. This was a common way of allowing the fermentation process to breath through the dry clay of the plug.

"He has a good number of amphorae from other years," remarked Marcellus, realising that the thief had been carrying on a side business for quite a while. "He would only now be ready to begin to sell the more aged wines."

Marcellus walked over to a stack of amphorae and examined the dates on them.

"Perhaps," he said turning to Sartorius, "he has not robbed me yet. His oldest wine is only six years old. See here!" He pointed to the dated amphorae.

"Unless he has been selling young wine every year," remarked Sartorious. "He has no reputation to defend, and yours is already made. The old vintner gesticulated with his arms. "I'll bet that is what he's been doing. The older wines will be a real boon for him soon."

"I see you have discovered my little secret."

The investigating pair turned to find Pompinus staring at them.

"Why have I not been told of this," said Marcellus, recovering himself quickly and pointing at the buried jars and the stack of amphorae.

"These are my experimental wines. I am merely amusing myself and you would have been told later when they were mature enough to be tasted," explained Pompinus in a nonchalant manner followed by a laugh. "I have to find things to keep me busy during the winter."

"I don't think you need such a large amount of wine to experiment with," said Marcellus pointing at the large jugs in the ground. "In any event, you should have told my father what you were up to. No wonder your production was below the other two vineyards. From now on I forbid you to continue to use this barn. This not your wine and you have no right to have done this without my father's permission."

Sartorius kept silent. He prayed however that his master would not dismiss the thief. He was afraid that Pompinus was evil minded enough to cause considerable damage to the vineyard prior to his going. If he was going to be dismissed, he should be caught by surprise and sent off the premises immediately under supervision.

"I shall write to my father," said Marcellus, "and find out how he wishes to deal with you."

He gave Pompinus a stern look. "You are paid well as are my other managers." Pointing at Sartorius who nodded in compliance.

"I am very disappointed in your untrustworthy behaviour."

"I meant nothing by it," complained Pompinus. "I have told you why I did this. Frankly, I did not think you would mind." He threw up his hands in a gesture of resignation.

"Very well. I shall not come back to the barn. You are welcome to take stock of what I have here, but these wines must be kept separate from the other wines. They are different."

"We will let the matter be for now," said Marcellus. "I shall await my father's decision."

Marcellus and Sartorius left the defiant Pompinus, and after bidding goodbye to a very flustered Marina, rode back home to their vineyard.

"I was praying that you would not dismiss him today Master," said Sartorius as they rode along. I think he is a vengeful man, and he might damage the vines or poison the wines if he knew that he was being dismissed. At least now he is uncertain and will do no harm for the time being."

"Yes, that is what I was also thinking," said Marcellus. "When we dismiss him, we must do so without notice and escort him off the premises. Perhaps even involve the authorities in the matter."

* * * * *

A month passed. The matter of Pompinus had not yet been resolved when Tullius visited Marcellus and Rufina on his way to Rome. He had won and baptised fourteen more souls for Yeshua, and felt that it was time to report to his superior Linus, from whom he also wished to seek advice concerning his love for Rufina. His medical practice had grown considerably as well.

Rufina was beside herself with excitement at seeing Tullius again. They embraced lovingly, quickly enkindling the brief and enduring love affair that they had shared on their last encounter.

Marcellus gave them as much time together as possible. He took charge of Marcia who was normally entertained by Rufina in her motherly role. In her turn Marcia was delighted that Marcellus was paying more than usual attention to her, for she loved him deeply. She was now nearing the age of six and being a very intelligent little girl, asked many probing questions.

"Cellus," she said, (for so she called Marcellus.) one afternoon as they sat in the farm's living room. "Fina told me that my Mamma and Daddy are in heaven. Why did they go without me?"

Marcellus was stunned by the question so innocently asked, but so difficult to answer. He hesitated for a few moments trying to give the little thing some explanation that would console her; since the matter, he imagined, must have been weighing heavily on her mind. He sat her on his knee and caressing her silky golden hair, said.

"What I am going to tell you, you must always keep secret." She looked at him and nodded.

"Yes," she said. "Please tell me."

"They did not want to go and leave you. They were forced to go. Bad people came and took them away. That is why your mamma told you to run and hide. Remember, you came to my room?" She nodded again; a little pout on her lips.

"Why did those people want to take my Mamma and Daddy away? Did they do something bad?"

"No, my love. Your parents were very good. They loved the Lord Yeshua, who is our God. The people who took them away hated Him."

"But to go to heaven, one has to die first." Her eyes searched his. "That is what Fina told me."

"Yes. She told you the truth."

"So my Mamma and my Daddy died?" she said.

He hugged her gently. Tears appeared in her eyes.

"Yes," he said soberly.

"How did they die?"

"I don't know how they died my love, but they did not want to die and leave you." He groped for more words.... She quickly asked.

"Were they killed by those bad people?"

"Yes," he said. "They loved you very much. Now, Fina and I also love you very much. You are a present that they gave us. And when you are old and go to heaven too, you will be with them again. We will all be together there for ever with Yeshua who loves us very much."

He wiped her tears which were running down her pretty red cheeks and kissed her.

"I love you and Fina too," she gently sobbed; nestling in his arms.

CHAPTER TEN

INTRIGUE

A bright sunny morning greeted Tullius as he walked into the Eternal City carrying a large piece of baggage on his broad shoulders. He had left his horse at a farm on the outskirts of the city. He felt it would be a real problem trying to manoeuvre a horse through crowds that would constantly impede his progress.

He made his way to the bakery that his Christian contact and friend owned and operated. Rome as usual was buzzing with activity. It seemed to him that it grew by the day. The crowds were denser than he remembered from his last visit only a few months earlier. At times he had to worm his way through narrow streets blocked by vendors' carts surrounded by eager buyers. Roman soldiers tried to keep order and the streets clear, but it was a losing battle.

The occasional open spaces in the form of squares, offered some relief; but they too were crowded with tourists grouping around many of the attractions. Impressive monuments, musicians, rhetoricians, snake charmers and other diversions, all vied for their attention. A temple dedicated to one of the many Roman gods would often grace a square or minor forum; their visiting devotees inevitably aggravating the existing congestion.

By the time Tullius reached the street where the bakery was situated, he was hot and tired. It had taken him a good part of the morning to cross just a portion of the city. A couple of teen agers, running from someone chasing them, suddenly bumped into him. He managed by sheer dexterity to avoid stepping into the cloaca that flowed down a channel in the centre of the cobbled street and openly carried the local raw sewage in its watery wake.

To his chagrin, the bakery was also crowded, and he was obliged to cool his heels outside the shop for a while before he could find an opportunity to enter and catch the baker's ear.

"Greetings Demetrius," said Tullius, finally reaching and embracing his friend.

"Wonderful to see you again," returned the other with a toothy smile.

"Go into the house, I shall join you in a little while. Cecilia will give you some refreshments...You look weary."

The priest went around the counter and into the back of the shop where the living quarters were.

"Tullius! what a joy to see you again," greeted the baker's wife embracing him warmly.

Cecilia was a most congenial woman. Her more than fifty years did not fall heavily on her narrow but shapely shoulders. She was quite tall (actually a little taller than her husband) and constantly displayed a cheerful attitude in her unremarkable but pleasant face.

"My dear Cecilia," smiled Tullius, "You are looking very well. I hope your health fares as well as your looks."

"I have missed your compliments my young flatterer. Yes. My health is good. My problems I leave to the good Lord who willingly takes them and solves them for me; even if it takes Him a little longer sometimes."

"Wonderful!" said Tullius, sitting down as she had motioned him to do. He observed his immediate surroundings with an appreciative look.

The room was comfortable, though not large. The carpet which completely covered the floor was decorated with tastefully designed, brightly coloured, swirling shapes, which livened up the space and reflected the facile character of the mistress of the house.

By contrast, the many cushions carefully positioned on the carpet, were in neutral colours of varying shades and showed well against the low, black lacquered tables interspersed around the room. An ornamental marble vase, obviously chosen with great care and at some considerable expense, displayed a colourful and carefully arranged bouquet of freshly cut flowers. It sat proudly on a long, low, red lacquered sideboard, and was unquestionably the focal point of the room.

Elegantly decorated, tall bronzed stands, each holding a ceramic oil lamp, took their place at each corner of the room. The early afternoon sun entering through two elegantly draped windows cheerfully directed its bright warm rays onto the multicoloured carpet animating its hues with a most pleasing effect. Obviously, much care had been taken not just in the furnishing of the room, but also in its arrangement.

For a baker's wife, Cecilia had tastes beyond her station.

"This room gives one a truly happy feeling," said Tullius with sincerity. "You have very good taste Cecilia."

"There you go again, you flatterer. It's a wonder that with your honeyed words you have not yet found a nice girl to marry."

The priest smiled at his hostess and told her about Rufina whilst she busied herself preparing refreshments for him.

"What are you waiting for then?" she asked, placing two small jugs, of wine and water, on the table in front of him. She continued to converse with him as she went back and forth to the kitchen.

"When one is a priest," ventured Tullius in a low tone of voice, "it is not an easy decision to make."

Suddenly Demetrius' head peered around the door post.

"I shall be with you soon my friend," he said and disappeared again.

True to his word, the baker joined his wife and friend a half an hour later and all settled down to an enjoyable evening of conversation.

Though not apparent from the street, Demetrius' property was quite large. The bakery, contrary to the normal bakery layout was at the very back of the building, with the living section dividing it from the shop.

"I refuse," pointed out Cecilia with uncharacteristic sternness, "to have people with muddy feet carrying flour bags and all sorts of things through my house. This way, they deliver round the back and go directly into the bakery. Later when the bread is baked and ready, we carry it through the corridor," she said, flicking her head in its direction.

Tullius spent the night with his friends. They had a very comfortable and well-appointed spare bedroom which he had used before on previous visits. For him it was a home away from home. He had no family to speak of. His only sister lived in Hispania where her husband, a centurion, happened to be posted.

Next morning after enjoying a very restful night, Tullius parted from his friends and ventured out to find his superior's whereabouts.

Linus' place of residence, if it could be called that, (It often changed depending on the circumstances,) had been disclosed to Tullius by Demetrius, who being very active in the Church saw a good deal of the saintly man.

Tullius rang the bell at the gate of a large house some distance from Demetrius' bakery.

It was early afternoon. The gate keeper came quickly to enquire the visitor's business.

"I've had a difficult day so far, don't tax my patience," said the priest. That was the code Tullius was to give the gatekeeper. "Hasten to tell your mistress that her hairdresser is here," he concluded.

Nodding, the gate keeper walked swiftly to the house and entering announced the visitor, who had given the correct code. The hairdresser impersonation was just an excuse meant for loose ears.

Galena, the mistress of the house, asked the gatekeeper to show him in and rushed off to find Linus who was at his prayers in his room.

Tullius entered the atrium to find Linus and Galena waiting to receive him.

Greetings and niceties were duly exchanged, and presently, Tullius found himself in his superior's room giving an account of his work with which (as you my dear reader knows) he was not in the least satisfied.

"You are too hard on yourself Tullius," said Linus with a shake of the head. "These are very difficult times for us Christians. Many prospective followers of our divine Lord are afraid of losing their lives because of the faith. But then again, there are many that will not hesitate to be baptised. Their faith is stronger."

"How difficult it is for us here," protested Tullius. "I am told that in other parts of the Empire, Christians are not persecuted. They even build places of assembly quite openly, which they call churches."

"We must each work where Yeshua needs us," said the older priest placing his hands together as if in prayer. "Remember my good friend that this life is but a trial for the other. Our Lord knows that we are on the front lines of this fight for the salvation of souls. He has put you and me here in Rome, because He knows that we are strong and can handle the dangerous work that we have been called to do. Have courage my son and patience with the 'fishing of men,' the nets will be filled in due time... God's time."

Tullius thanked Linus for his advice and encouragement and then brought up the other matter which was also close to his heart.

"On that score," said Linus, with a smile. "I must caution you to proceed slowly...Very slowly. As you were reminding me a few moments ago, if you had been appointed to carry the faith to other regions such as Cyrene, or Alexandria for instance, where people like Simon or John Mark are being permitted to put down strong roots, I would not hesitate to advise you to follow your heart. Provided of course that your future wife is as strong in the faith as you. However in our very precarious circumstances, I must ask you to proceed with the utmost caution."

Linus got up from his cushion and drained the cup of watered wine from which he had been sipping.

"And now we must part once more," he said with a paternal smile.

Tullius got to his feet, his eyes fixed on his superior's face.

"I thank you for your advice Linus. You have given me much to think about. I shall do my utmost to bring as many souls to Yeshua as circumstances will permit. Please pray for me, as I shall for you."

Tullius bowed his head to receive a blessing from Linus, who then embraced him warmly and accompanied him to the door where Galena was waiting to bid him farewell.

* * * * *

News arrived from Porcius regarding the punishment to be meted out to Pompinus.

Rufina received the scroll from the courier, and immediately went in search of her brother, who was out in the vineyard with Sartorius.

"Take me with you!" called out Marcia from the garden where she had been playing by herself.

"Come on then," cried Rufina maintaining her hurried pace.

Marcia easily caught up and ran beside her.

"What are you taking to Cellus?" asked the girl, eyeing the scroll with much curiosity.

"A scroll from my father," said Rufina holding it out.

"Is Umpa coming?"

"I don't know. You ask too many questions. Have patience and we will soon find out."

"Marcellus! Marcellus!" shouted Rufina, as Marcia disappeared among the vines.

Barking could be heard at a distance and soon Rex found Marcia. The little girl hugged the dog happily. "Where is Cellus and Sartorius?" she asked. "Take me to them."

The big dog looked at her and ran on ahead; stopping and turning every now and then to make sure she was following.

Rufina was still calling out for her brother when Marcia, following Rex, found him.

"What are you doing here all by yourself?" asked Marcellus. Then hearing his sister's voice, he addressed the dog.

"Go Rex," he said, "Go bring Rufina."

Shortly after, the clever dog returned; his quarry not far behind.

"Hi Marcellus," laughed Rufina. "I am going to have to give you a banner on a staff to carry so that I can tell where you are. I have a scroll from father...here." She handed him the scroll which he opened with a sense of urgency and began to read it to himself.

"Are father and mother well?" asked Rufina with anticipation. Marcia's eyes were glued to Marcellus' face.

"Father is not well," said Marcellus. "He wanted to come, but says he is not up to it. Mother is fine, and so is Marcius."

He rolled up the scroll again and began to walk back to the house followed by the fair pair and Rex. Sartorius who had been with Marcellus, had gone off to the barn for some tools.

"Sartorius can finish the job by himself now," said Marcellus. "It only requires one person to complete what we were doing."

Marcia who walked holding Marcellus' hand, kept looking up at him; expecting him to say more about the scroll which had taken him some time to read. To her disappointment, he divulged nothing further.

"You can read it for yourself when we get back, Rufina," said Marcellus at last, but still keeping the scroll as they walked. Marcia was somewhat concerned by the grown-up's silence, but she was too well mannered to ask what the disturbing news might be.

As usual, the contents of the scroll were discussed after Marcia had been put to bed. The two siblings accompanied by

Sartorius sat around the garden table enjoying the cool of the evening.

Rufina had read the scroll earlier. Sartorius was reading it for the first time. Both waited for him to finish.

"I am sorry to read that the Master is not well," he said with a sad shake of the head and handing Marcellus the scroll.

"As you both read," said Marcellus, "he wants us to call the authorities and have Pompinus arrested. Then we are to give his wife some money and find her a place to stay. Perhaps she can remain at the vineyard as cook for the new manager, he suggests, until her husband gets out of prison; if ever."

"He obviously feels sorry for Marina as indeed we do," said Rufina with some sadness in her kind eyes. "No matter what we do, her life is going to get much harder."

Marcellus poured himself a cup of wine. "I don't know that we should call the authorities and have him arrested," he said. Much to the surprise of the other two.

"How else are we going to get rid of him?" asked Sartorius, his eyes widening and reaching for the jug of wine. Rufina said nothing. She was deep in thought.

"If you and I stay there until he has taken all his stuff and gone," said Marcellus, "we don't have to have him arrested. He will see our goodwill in not punishing his wife along with him and will go peacefully."

"That's a good idea," remarked Rufina, clapping her hands and smiling at her brother.

Sartorius was not so sure that it would work and said so with some moderation in the tone of his voice. He was disagreeing with both his superiors and felt uncomfortable.

"Why do you think my idea will not work?" asked Marcellus giving his old manager a questioning look.

Sartorius took off his hat and twisting it around thoughtfully in his hands, answered.

"Pompinus is not the type of man you think him to be. He will not appreciate your good intentions towards his wife. He is ambitious and will be revengeful. I don't know what he can do once he has been expelled from the vineyard but try some act of mischief he will. If I may be so bold, he is best put out of the way as your father advises."

Marcellus thought for a moment, and looking at his sister, said:

"We will try my way first. If it doesn't not work out we can always call the authorities."

The following morning, Marcellus and Sartorius packed some clothes to see them through a week approximately and started off for Pompinus' vineyard.

Pompinus was about to mount his horse on his way to Salistra when the determined pair rode into the courtyard of his house.

"I was just about to leave. I have some urgent business in the village," said Pompinus dropping his horse's reins and approaching the visitors with the hint of a smile on his smug face.

"You have much more urgent business here, I assure you," said Marcellus with authority.

"Well, in that case I had better stay." He went back to his horse and taking the reins, tied them to a nearby post. The visitors dismounted, and following Pompinus' example, secured their horses. They took their baggage with them and followed him into the house.

Marina met them in the hallway with a bright smile and welcoming words. Pompinus told her to leave them to themselves, and walking into the living room he slumped down on one of the cushions, motioning for the visitors to sit.

Presently, Marina appeared again. She carried a tray with some wine and a few victuals that she had quickly put together, along with three cups. She placed them on a table near them and was about to leave when Pompinus rudely admonished her.

"We have business to discuss here. Don't come back unless I call you. You hear?"

Marcellus was astonished at the way the irate man had spoken to his wife.

"You don't have to be so hard on your good wife," he admonished in turn. "She only meant well."

Pompinus flicked his hand as if to dismiss the whole matter.

Marina, in a most uncharacteristic manner, lurked in the hallway, ready to listen to all that was transpiring in her family room.

'For once,' she said to herself, 'I am going to know what's going on.'

"Now!" exclaimed Pompinus, with a challenging look in his cruel eyes. "What is this urgent business that I have to deal with?"

Marcellus realised that Sartorius had more accurately assessed the character of this man than he and braced himself for a good fight.

"I shall be brief and to the point," began Marcellus. "My father advises me to report you to the authorities for theft and have you arrested and tried."

"I have not stolen from you."

"Yes, you have, and we can prove it."

Marcellus reached into his baggage and pulled out an unopened pitcher of wine. Which had the mark of the Fulvius vineyards on it.

"Here is the proof. We have more of these pitchers and a couple of amphorae in our possession."

Pompinus was caught by surprise. He kept silent as his head wrestled with the conundrum that he now faced.

"So go ahead," he bluffed. "Call in the law. See where that will get you."

Marcellus looked at the thief with severity and pointed a threatening finger at him.

"Because I do not want to hurt Marina who will be a victim of your dishonesty, I have decided that rather than call in the law as my father would have me do, I am simply going to have you leave with all your belongings and that's that." Marcellus poured himself a cup of wine and taking a sip to wet his throat, continued.

"Find yourself some other vineyard to rob," he said, "as far from here as possible. I do not care to see your face again. You have doubtlessly robbed me of enough money to keep you in comfort until you find another place to manage."

Pompinus poured himself some wine, and turning to Sartorius, said.

"I want to talk to your Master alone."

Marcellus protested the request, but Pompinus was adamant.

"It's alright Master, I will go chat with Marina in the meantime." He got up and walked out of the room, leaving a very perplexed Marcellus.

Sartorius almost bumped into Marina as he entered the hallway. She took a hold of his arm and motioned to him with her head to stay beside her and listen in.

"Very well," said Marcellus. "What is it that you want to tell me out of Sartorius' hearing?"

"You are not going to do anything to me. Neither out of your father's plan or yours."

Marcellus was now beginning to be really concerned, though he did his best not to show it.

"You seem very sure of yourself," he said with some sarcasm in his voice.

"That is because I am... Christian."

A terrible shiver suddenly ran down Marcellus' spine. He could never have imagined that his faith would be known to this evil man. He could not deny Yeshua. His faith would mean nothing if he did, and it meant everything to him.

"That is a terrible accusation. I suppose you can prove it?"

"Oh yes. I can," teased Pompinus, "That good friend of yours in Salistra; the physician. He is a Christian priest. I have people who will swear to it. So why would you not be a Christian too?"

"You have to prove it," said Marcellus with reluctance and a guilty feeling.

"Of course. See how simple it is...Are you a Christian?"

A long silence ensued. Marcellus had never felt more helpless. His mind was racing. He did not even try to pray for help. He really expected none. This was a personal decision. It was not just his own life that was threatened; his sister's life and all those in his vineyard were at stake, even little Marcia's. Tullius would have to be warned, as he would surely be denounced and could be arrested at any time. It all depended on his handling of Pompinus.

He knew that the authorities would also keep a sharp eye on his activities once this man had denounced him. But he would have to be caught red handed during the 'Body and the Blood' service or attending some preaching. He and his family would be marked people as were all the Christians of Rome. Still he was feeling very cowardly at not owning up to be an ardent follower of Yeshua. He prayed for Yeshua's forgiveness. It was not for himself, but for his family that he was stalling. If it were just himself and the authorities, he would have owned up, but he felt that this depraved and evil man did not deserve to be treated with integrity.

"As I just told you, you will have to prove that I am a Christian. I will remind you however that you are dealing with the son of a senator. In the meantime, you can start packing. I want you out of here immediately. Sartorius and I will stay to see you gone. We have someone to take over the moment you leave."

"You can avoid a lot of problems for yourself and your priest friend if we can come to an arrangement!" said Pompinus. "I simply want some of the things you have. We can become partners so to speak, but on the quiet. When I have enough money to buy myself a small vineyard, I shall cancel our little agreement and you can continue again as you are now."

"Your audacity is beyond limit," snapped Marcellus angrily. "How dare you propose such a thing? "Then, thinking again of the danger that confronted Tullius on his return. He said.

"My friend, whom you say is a priest, is an excellent human being, a good physician, and a law-abiding citizen. How can you even consider causing him harm just for the sake of being destructive? You can pack your things and go right now and thank your stars that I do not call in the authorities and have you taken to prison for the rest of your life."

The two siblings sat around the garden table two days later.

"I think you did splendidly well, considering the problems you were faced with," said Rufina. "Now we have to try and reach Tullius as soon as possible. But where exactly is he?"

"He should be back soon I hope," replied Marcellus. "He has been away for almost two weeks.

"What are we going to tell father?" she asked.

"We have to think up a good story for him," said Marcellus. "He is not easily fooled."

* * * * *

Pompinus, had left the vineyard the day following his dismissal by Marcellus. He drove off in a cart with a very confused and saddened Marina sitting beside him. The cart carrying all his belongings was pulled by a single horse. His dog followed. Their destination was a friend's house in Salistra where he would seek refuge until he found a place to live.

Marcellus remained at the reclaimed vineyard whilst Sartorius rode back for Antonius and Lavinia, who would be the new managers. The following day with the pair's appearance, Marcellus returned to his vineyard, leaving Sartorius to brief his son-in-law on his new responsibilities. There was much tension in the air, since no one knew what the outcome of this unfortunate and unsettling upheaval would be.

Finding himself alone with Rufina and Marcia, Marcellus was most apprehensive about their security. He knew he had to hire some help to fill the void that Antonius and Lavinia had left. This he would have to do with the utmost urgency. Sartorius would not be back for a few days, and in any event, his son-in-law also needed to hire some help. Lavinia could not be left alone in the farmhouse all day whilst her husband was tending the vineyard. No one knew what mischief Pompinus would be brewing up over the next weeks or even months.

* * * * *

An irate Pompinus arrived at his friend Calvus' house and rapped at his door. Moments later Albina his wife opened. She looked at Pompinus, gave him a half-hearted smile, and looking past him at Marina who sat listlessly in the cart, called out in a high-pitched voice.

"Calvus! Your friend Pompinus from the vineyard is here."

Marina shuddered at the odd way in which the woman greeted her husband. Surely, she considered him a stranger. Her heart sank, as she realised that their visit, if only temporary, would be an unwelcome intrusion into their privacy. A troubling thought came to mind as she mused, awaiting the appearance of Calvus, whom she disliked.

'Where did Pompinus go all those times that he said he was going to Salistra? It obviously was not here,' she said to herself with suspicion and anger.

"Good day to you Pompinus my friend," greeted Calvus on seeing him. He edged past his wife who turned and walked back into the house.

Pompinus smiled.

"I have to ask a favour of you."

"Sure, my friend. What do you want me to do?"

The visitor turned and nodded towards his wife and the loaded cart.

"We need a place to stay until I find a house to rent. It should not take long."

Calvus looked at Marina and the horse and cart.

"Wish I could help you my good friend, but the house is too small to accommodate any one else. We only have one bedroom and a very small family room as you have seen. I don't even

236

have a place to put your horse or cart. What happened to you? Did that Christian fellow throw you out?"

"No. I just thought I would take my wife and furniture for a little ride in the country," scowled Pompinus sarcastically.

"I'll help you find a place. I know of a couple of houses that are for rent, and you can probably move in right away. One of them even has a stable at the back."

Pompinus stroked his scraggly beard and looked at his friend with some disdain.

Marina rubbed her hands; relieved that they would not have to stay with that horrible couple.

"I'll be back in a while," shouted Calvus to his wife. He shut the house door and motioned to Pompinus to follow.

The latter, quite disappointed at his now 'former friend,' followed the man glumly and without a word. They walked for a while, eventually stopping in front of a house with a blue door and shutters. Pompinus looked at Calvus. The latter smiled at his friend and knocked at the neighbour's door. A young woman answered his knock.

"Yes?" she smiled, her eyes scanning the visitors.

"My friend here," said Calvus, gesturing towards Pompinus, "is looking for a house to rent."

"I have the key. I can show them the house," she said, looking at Marina.

"Alright," said Pompinus, "let me see it."

The girl went back into her house and soon returned with the key.

She looked enquiringly again at Marina who in turn sought her husband's eyes.

Ignoring Marina completely, Pompinus followed the girl into the house. A couple of tears escaped the kind wife's eyes as she waited patiently for her rude and uncaring husband to come out. Calvus was about to go with them, but seeing Marina's sad face, changed his mind and waited with her. However not a word passed between them.

After a little while, Pompinus reappeared followed by the girl.

"I shall go find the owner for you," she said, "he lives nearby."

She went back into her house and promptly reappeared with a palla over her head. She gave Marina a sympathetic smile and rushed off in search of the owner.

There was very little in the way of conversation as the trio awaited the owner's arrival. Eventually, after a good while, the man arrived conversing amicably with the girl.

"Julia here, tells me that you are interested in renting my house," said the man addressing Calvus. "My name is Florianus."

"No. Not me," said Calvus. "Him." He pointed at Pompinus.

"How much do you want a month?" asked the latter.

The two men began to haggle over the price. After much discussion, they arrived at an agreement. Pompinus was given the key, and soon, Marina, followed by the cart's contents were taken into the house. Calvus assisted his friend with enthusiasm. He felt relieved that he had not had to put him up at his own house. He knew his wife would not make them feel welcome; she had often expressed her dislike for Pompinus and his rude and boisterous ways. Pompinus however was not going to continue his friendship much longer with the man.

He felt hurt by Calvus' lack of hospitality and promised himself that he would never have anything further to do with him.

Marina was quite shocked. The work of moving all the contents of the cart had been accomplished, and her ungrateful husband simply told Calvus that he could go. He did not even thank him for his help in seeing them settled.

Calvus in his turn took his leave with a sad countenance. All of a sudden he felt sorry for Marina, who unlike his nagging wife, put up with such rudeness and humiliation at the hands of a man like Pompinus. He smiled at her sympathetically as he left.

* * * * *

Marcellus was still trying to find a way to explain to his father, why he had not brought the full force of the law to bear on Pompinus. The sound of a horse's hooves entering the courtyard, pulled Rufina out of a day dream. She left her room in a hurry and rushed to the courtyard hoping it was Tullius who had finally arrived.

To her chagrin, it was a stranger who pulled up in front of the house asking for Marcellus.

"He is not here at the moment, but I am his sister. You may give me the message."

The man handed her a scroll.

"From the house of Porcius Fulvius," he said.

"Just a moment," smiled Rufina. She rushed into the house, and returning a few moments later gave the man a few coins.

"This is for your troubles," she told him. The man thanked her and turning his horse around, rode out of the courtyard.

As might be expected, Marcellus was in the vineyard during the day.

"Marcia!" called out Rufina. The girl came running.

"Take Rex and go into the vineyard and find Cellus."

Marcia called Rex, who promptly woke up from his sleep in the courtyard and went to his young mistress. They were about to leave when Marcellus appeared. He looked tired and was perspiring profusely as he walked into the hallway.

"A scroll has arrived from father," said Rufina with anticipation, handing it to her brother.

Marcellus hastened to open it. As he read, his face became very saddened. "It's from mother," he said; his voice breaking. Rufina and Marcia gave him an alarmed look.

"Father is dead!" he said with a broken voice.

Rufina let out a pitiful cry. Tears poured down her lovely face. Marcia embraced her substitute mother's waist; tears also filling her bright blue eyes. Marcellus struggled with his deep emotions. The lump in his throat threatened to choke him.

It was a very sad evening in the house of Marcellus. Many prayers were offered for the salvation of the noble soul of Porcius, even though the now Christian household knew and regretted the fact that the beloved and Christo-sympathetic deceased had died a pagan. The fact that their parents and siblings were pagans was the greatest regret of both Marcellus' and Rufina's lives; they being so strong in their faith,

"I must go to Rome right away and bring back Mamma and Marcius," announced Marcellus.

"Yes," agreed his sister who felt great concern for her mother. "How lonely Mamma must be feeling,"

The following morning saw Marcellus waving goodbye to his rural family and riding away to his urban family.

The weather was mild, and he made good progress.

As each night fell, Marcellus sought accommodation at his favoured hostels along the route. The first and second nights were quite uneventful. His horse was well taken care of and he enjoyed a good cena at each location. The third night, as he pulled into Septimus' hostel another horseman rode in just ahead of him. They both dismounted in the courtyard, and as the man turned, Marcellus recognised Tullius.

"Good heavens!" exclaimed Marcellus. "Fancy finding you here."

"What a wonderful surprise," beamed the priest with a big smile.

"Are you on your way back from Rome?" asked Marcellus embracing his friend.

"Yes. And if I may ask, what brings you here?"

The two friends soon brought each other up to date with all the news, taking all evening to relate and discuss it. Tullius did his best to console his friend on the loss of his father. Septimus, was also very saddened by the news. He gave the two young men an excellent cena at his own expense in honour of Porcius, and made their stay as usual, a very pleasant one. The priest was made aware of his precarious situation back in Salistra.

Tullius, volunteered to accompany Marcellus back to Rome and assist him in whatever way he could. His offer was gratefully accepted by the latter, and they left the inn the following morning together, bound for the Fulvius residence.

They arrived late in the evening to a very sad and emotional welcome from Ignatia, who was taking the death of her husband with very little resignation and looked quite ill. Marcius was not at home. He had been working with his older brother Felicius in Ostia for many months learning the ship chandling business. He and Felicius had attended their father's funeral and after a very short visit with their bereaved mother, both had returned to Ostia.

"Mother," said Marcellus that evening during the cena. "You must come to Umbria and live with Rufina and me. You cannot stay here on your own, it will be a lonely existence for you."

Ignatia looked at her son with much sadness in her eyes.

"I miss your father so much," she wailed, as tears which had already been abundantly shed, dampened her cheeks once more.

"Precisely for that reason," insisted Marcellus. He stroked his mother's hand tenderly.

"You must come with us," he said, looking sympathetically into her sad eyes.

"Little Marcia would love to spend time with you, and so would you with her. It would make you feel so much better. Father would not want you to be sulking all the time."

"The house will have to be sold," she said. "Oh, dear!" and broke into tears again.

"I will do that before we go," promised Marcellus, "It won't take long to sell. In any event, my friend Tobias the Jew, will find a buyer and will get us the best possible money for it even if we've already left for the vineyard. He has often said how much he admires the house."

"What about my money?" asked Ignatia. "How are you going to get that to Umbria? It is a risky business to carry so much money on one's person." Her hand flew to her brow.

"I have heard," said Tullius, who had been sitting very quietly eating his fish, "that there is a way to send money with very reliable people who travel alongside the Legion patrols. It is a slow process, but the money would arrive safely. You would pick it up at the patrol barracks in Menorum.

"There you see," said Marcellus. "All will work out well for you."

Despite the assurances that Marcellus had given his flustered mother. He had one particularly difficult duty to perform which out weighed the concerns regarding the selling of the house. The servants would have to be dismissed. The slaves, all three of them, would have to be given their freedom, as he, being a Christian, could not condone slavery.

"What do I do with three ex-slaves," he wondered. "I cannot just throw them out as free persons and let them fend for themselves. They have always been protected and directed."

He conferred with Tullius on the matter.

"Your mother must help us with this," advised the priest. "It will give her something to think about other than her grief."

Marcellus wished in vain that Rufina were there. She would surely have some good suggestions to aid them with that problem.

Ignatia was duly consulted. The two young men were surprised to learn that she had, amidst her grief and suspecting the inevitable, found new positions for the servants among her many friends. The slaves of course were another matter. She would have to take them with her. There was no question of her selling them. They were a part of her family and well loved.

On being consulted on the subject, the grieving mistress of the house displayed a resourcefulness for which she had not been credited by either her son or Tullius. After all, she had been responsible for the running of that large house and directing of the family's social life since her marriage to the good senator whom she had always loved and admired.

"My servants and slaves have been a great concern to me since your father's death," she asserted with great confidence, addressing herself to her son during at the cena a week after Marcellus' arrival.

She turned and smiled at the servant who was serving at the table. The maid returned the smile with love and regret in her eyes. She had already been engaged by a friend of Ignatia and knew that her mistress had done the best she could for her and the other servants. She was very sad however at losing her master whom she had greatly admired and respected, and also the way her well ordered life had suddenly crumbled.

"I have managed to find all of my servants good homes to work in. However, my three slaves are giving me some concern." She looked at her son with appealing eyes and suggested:

"We could leave Evandros and Jocasta here to oversee things and supervise the selling of the furniture and other things. Mind you I cannot trust them to be together unsupervised. I have suspected for some time that they are in love. Unfortunately, Leia, her mother, cannot be left here with them. I need her with me.

Marcellus leaning forward grasped his mother's hand across the table, he looked around to ensure that there were no servants in the room.

"Mother. You must listen to what I am about to tell you, because it is the kindest way that you can deal with these bonded servants that have served you so faithfully for so many years."

Ignatia met her son's eyes with interest. Marcellus took a quiet deep breath.

Tullius who sat beside Marcellus, listened with great interest, guessing what his friend would advise.

"Mother," began Marcellus. His deep Christian convictions colouring with the utmost intensity his forthcoming proposal. "First, I am going to ask you to free your three slaves."

A great silence followed. Ignatia's beautiful eyes widened in horror. Then, catching her breath again, she gasped.

"Give them their freedom?"

"Yes! That is precisely what I am saying," affirmed her son with a smile.

Ignatia could not believe her ears. 'Why would I want or need to free my slaves?' she asked herself. 'What would Porcius say if he were alive? I would never dream of selling them of course but to give them their freedom?'

"Son," she said. "We shall take them with us but why free them?"

His mother's reaction came as no surprise to Marcellus.

"My second suggestion, is that you will see Evandros and Jocusta married before we go. What happiness you would give them. Later when the house and contents are all sold, they can join us at the vineyard. There, as free persons, they can, and I am sure they will, continue to serve us as they have always done with dedication and love. And, much gratitude to boot."

The mistress of the house's eyes were fixed on her son's. This suggestion was alien to her whole way of thinking in so far as her slaves were concerned.

What could have got into her son that he was advising such measures? She knew he had a kind heart. Even from his early childhood, he had always been exceptionally considerate to his little playmates at the risk of his own toys; allowing some of them to take advantage of him. And what about his rescuing little Marcia? She pulled herself out of her puzzling reverie.

"What you are proposing my son, is very difficult for me to understand. You must give me time to think. Who would have thought...?" She stopped, her mind wondering again.

Marcellus threw a quick glance at Tullius, who smiled back knowingly. He went around the table, and standing behind his mother, leant over, kissed her head, and said.

"Take your time Mother, I know it is an unusual suggestion, but I am confident that your kind heart will see the merit of my words. Think of how much happiness you can bring to these three souls, who will I am sure continue to serve you faithfully as free persons for the rest of your life."

She got up, hugged Marcellus, and smiling at Tullius, who knew better than to interfere in the mother and son conversation, walked away to the garden, where finding her favourite bench sat to consider what had been told her...and to reminisce a little.

Breakfast was being served to Ignatia as Marcellus and Tullius made their appearance in the garden. On warm sunny days it was the habit of the mistress of the house to breakfast under the stunning pergola. It was richly covered in wisteria which hung in bunches over a sumptuous stone table. Colourful cushions sat on the stone benches around the table. After kissing his mother, Marcellus sat down on the one next to her. Tullius with a happy smile, nodded good morning as he took his place opposite them.

As soon as the maid had left to procure the breakfast for the two men, Ignatia, hands pressed together on her lap and looking vacantly past Tullius who read determination in her eyes. Said.

"I have given the matter of the slaves much thought and have come to the conclusion that the marriage of Evandros and Jocasta which you advocate, should be carried out immediately. It will require little ceremony, I am really in no mood for a wedding. You can report it to the proper authorities along with our consent. A contubernium will be recorded, and then we can be off to Umbria with the knowledge that their behaviour will not bring any dishonour to our good family name. I think your father would have approved of our decision. I know that it will make them and Leia very happy."

Marcellus was not happy with this solution offered by his mother. The slaves would be married as slaves and not as free persons. Ignatia however was adamant. She, in her astute way, reasoned that if she left them as slaves, and promised on their wedding day that she would free them when they arrived at the vineyards, then they would have every incentive to do their best in caring for the house, and the disposal of her furniture and goods in her absence.

Ignatia looked around. Seeing that the maid was not in sight, she whispered.

"I have a surprise for them. I shall promise on their wedding day, to give them their freedom, when they eventually join us again in the vineyard."

Marcellus and Tullius, realised what a clever person Ignatia was. They both had to admit that from a logical point of view, and with her there existed no other point of view, she had got the better of them. They would have to pray that in the future, the young couple would be given the faith, and then marry within the Church.

"I must congratulate you on a very clever solution, Mother," said Marcellus giving her a hug and kiss on the cheek

The maid suddenly appeared carrying a large tray with their breakfast.

* * * * *

Four weeks later the house had been sold. Evandros and Jocasta were now husband and wife by Roman law. All that remained to be done was to sell the furniture and other paraphernalia pertaining to the house.

Marcellus visited the newly weds just prior to their departure, as usual accompanied by his friend Tullius, in whom he totally confided. The couple had just come back into the house. Ignatia was busy bidding goodbye to the remaining servants.

"We are now ready to leave," said Marcellus. "I wish you both a happy and enjoyable time together. He winked at Evandros, whose face suddenly fell. The master looked at Jocusta who showed no signs of joy either.

"What is the matter with you both?" asked Marcellus with concern. Tullius as usual held his peace.

"You would not understand and might not approve either," said the groom.

"You know me well enough by now to confide in me. I would not harm you for the world."

Jocusta looked at Tullius with uncertainty in her eyes and said:

"Can we rely on this gentleman?"

"By all means," confirmed Marcellus. He is like a brother to me."

Tullius nodded and thinly smiled.

"Have you heard of the Christians?" she asked with an uncertain look on her lovely young face. She was only seventeen.

Marcellus took a step back almost bumping into Tullius who was quite as dumbfounded.

The newly weds drew together and fearfully embraced; their eyes wide open with apprehension.

A look of utter joy covered the faces of both friends, extracting a sigh of relief from the two slaves.

"Welcome in the Lord's name," blurted out Tullius spreading his arms and embracing Evandros, as Marcellus embraced Jocasta with great zeal.

"God be praised!" sang the slaves overflowing with joy.

Then came the gloom into their young faces once more.

"We are not married said Evandros with a sudden sadness visible in his eyes.

"Ha!" said a cheerful Marcellus. "But you will be in a moment."

The bewildered couple looked from one face to the other.

"Evandros," said Tullius looking around to see that no one was coming. "Please take Jocasta's hands."

The man did as he was bid; a look of wonderment in his eyes.

"Evandros. Do you take Jocasta to be your wife?"

"Yes. I do," he answered, his eyes on Jocasta

"Jocasta. Will you be Evandros' wife?"

"Yes," she replied.

"In my capacity as a follower of Yeshua and a priest of the Christian Church." He looked at the two surprised faces watching him. "And with my good friend Marcellus as a witness, I pronounce you man and wife, in the name of the Father, the Son, and the Holy Ghost."

There was an explosion of joy shared by the four protagonists of that very important event. They were all propelled back into reality, by the voice of Ignatia announcing her approach, followed by Leia who could not immediately be informed of the happy nuptial that she had missed being part of, but would later be told; she also being of the faith.

Marcellus had made arrangements for a good portion of their money to be sent by a special courier who travelled with the Legion patrol. As indeed, Tullius had advised.

The cart that Marcellus had prepared for the comfortable transportation of his mother and Leia, was now ready and waiting. Bidding the remaining staff their farewell, Ignatia and her faithful slave climbed in. Leia took the reins, and out they rolled bound for Umbria.

Marcellus rode Artemis. Tullius rode Porcius' Arabian; his own horse being of little value in comparison was hitched to the cart. A fair amount of money divided between the three travelled with them. Marcellus, armed with a gladius, led the trio out of Rome. They had opted to travel alongside the Legion patrol which would see them even if slowly, most of the way to Septimus' hostel where they would spend the night.

Septimus greeted Marcellus and company with his usual warmth and amiability. He was particularly attentive to Ignatia's wishes, and she soon comprehended the love and admiration the man had for her late husband.

"He became a very good friend of your father's," said Ingenia to her son as they prepared to turn in for the night. "I suppose it grew over the years since your father stopped here everytime he visited the vineyards. Poor Porcius spoke very highly of him, and now I can see why."

The next morning, Septimus arranged for them to be accompanied by several travellers who happened to be going in their direction. Among the group there were two well armed men. That, gave Ignatia who was still somewhat concerned, some peace of mind. There was also a mother with two young children who had been travelling on foot. They were invited to ride in the cart, which they gratefully accepted.

Their second day on the road came to a happy end as they rode into the next hostel on their route. It had taken them longer than anticipated. Some people who had joined them on the road, travelled on foot, and all had been obliged to move at their pace.

The last morning of Marcellus' journey, saw the group of the previous day break up, as all save one man were headed in different directions. Another man armed with a gladius, joined them at a gallop moments after having left the inn. He had been staying there for the previous two days, he said, and was heading home to Salistra.

Ignatia and Leia, travelled more comfortably, now that the mother and daughter no longer rode with them. The cart slowly rumbled over the stone road leading to Menorum and Salistra. The countryside acted as a soothing balm for Ignatia. She, being accustomed to the close life of the city, had lived in deprivation of the beauty which gradually unfolded before her eyes. She was also enjoying Leia's company. The latter had become quite adept at the reins over the course of the journey; something new to the amiable and well-educated slave. She greatly anticipated her promised freedom; more as a matter of personal pride than anything else.

It was a warm sunny day. There was hardly a puff of wind. The gently rolling hills entertained the travellers with a constantly changing panorama as the cart dipped and rose at every stretch of the undulating road. It being autumn, the fields were golden with hay and much activity could be observed as the peasants toiled to cut it down and build their haystacks.

Wild multicoloured flowers softened the hard edges of the stone road. They grew merrily around the feet of the majestic poplars that lined some stretches of it, like dark green sentinels protecting the beauty of their surroundings. An occasional stone bridge broke the monotony of the route. The sight and sound of the burbling water below them sent a quiver of joy through the heart of the travellers as they rode over them in silent appreciation. Peace and tranquility reigned.

Shortly after passing over one such bridge, the party came upon a Legion patrol. All stopped to hear what the soldiers might communicate to them with regard to the road ahead.

A few moments were spent in amiable conversation, and presently the patrol rode away at their habitually slow pace. As usual, the mounted members of the patrol being handicapped by people accompanying them on foot.

Marcellus' party continued on their way relaxing somewhat after their conversation with the patrol sergeant. As they rounded a turning in the road a short while later however, the unexpected occurred. They were suddenly confronted by two bandits who, without notice, charged at them with drawn swords.

'Oh, for a shield,' thought Marcellus as he pulled off his shawl and quickly wrapped it around his left arm. He shouted for the other two men who were with him to follow his example. He pulled out his gladius in readiness for the skirmish which was about to take place. Urging his horse forward, he cleared the cart where his mother and Leia sat at the reins, both mesmerised by the sudden change of events and horrified by the danger which suddenly precipitated itself on them.

Tullius, who was unarmed as might well be expected, turned his Arabian around and galloped back to find the patrol which he knew would not be far away.

Marcellus parried the first thrust from the leading bandit, and quickly turned to meet the second strike. His Arabian horse Negrus, showed its worth as it seemingly glided through the turn in such a way that he put his beloved rider in a very favourable striking position. The bandit was only halfway through his turn when Marcellus had the opportunity of ending the contest. He took full advantage of the situation, but not wishing to kill the man, struck him hard on his sword arm. To his surprise, not only did the man's sword drop, but his arm dangled uselessly, as he fell from his horse.

Looking back, he could see that one of his party was on the ground. The other was busily flaying away at the second bandit with whom he seemed to be well matched. Marcellus hastened to his aid.

Suddenly Tullius accompanied by four Legionaries appeared at full gallop. The fighting bandit quickly abandoned the fray and turning tail, galloped away. Two of the soldiers, increasing their speed gave chase. The sergeant and another patrolman, stopped. The former rode up to the cart.

Marcellus' eyes searched the cart with concern. His mother was not visible. He approached it with great apprehension and anxiety. Ignatia was lying inside in Leia's arms, quite unconscious.

"Mother!" he cried. She did not stir. He climbed in and to the slave's surprise, gently slapped her face.

The mounted patrol sergeant beside the cart, waited to see if she was all right.

Finally, she stirred, and with wide open eyes enquired as to what had happened.

They all laughed in relief as Marcellus explained and assured her that all was well.

Tullius, in the meantime had his hands full tending to the soon to be a, 'one-armed' bandit. The man was losing a huge amount of blood. With the help of the patrolman, he started a fire by the side of the road to enable him to cauterise the stump of the bandit's arm.

The skilful physician completed the severing of the bandit's arm, with the aid of a very sharp knife (one of the medical tools,) that he carried in his baggage. He then took advantage of the man's unconscious state to properly cauterise all the blood vessels in the exposed stump. The patient was then left in the hands of the patrol with the proviso that he be handled gently as he could die from surgical shock. He then turned his attention to the fallen comrade who though not nearly as severely wounded as the bandit, was also losing a considerable amount of blood and needed suturing.

As they travelled, Tullius, sitting in the moving cart beside his patient, sutured the deep cut in the man's shoulder. Marcellus and the other man who went by the name of Lucianus, rode beside the cart and took charge of the two loose horses. Ignatia sat looking straight ahead so as not to witness the painful surgery that Tullius was busily performing.

Suddenly the two patrolmen who had chased the bandit reappeared. One of them, leading a horse with a man lying upside down on it, his hands and feet tied under its belly. The man appeared dead. The soldier, silently but meaningfully, ran a finger across his throat as he passed.

It was late evening when Marcellus and his party arrived at the farmhouse. Rufina came to greet them and ran to her mother. A sad scene ensued as mother and daughter mourned there and then for Porcius. The others were ushered into the house by Marcellus who was quickly assisted by Sartorius and Lavinia, who happened to be visiting her father.

Rex was never known to be so quiet. He simply stood there as if stupefied by the proceedings. Presently, he went into the kitchen to see if perhaps by some chance, Aurelia had left him a bone

The wounded man was laid on Marcellus' bed as every other bed had been spoken for other than the one in the guest bedroom, which was immediately designated to Ignatia. She, finding herself totally exhausted after the unsettling journey, opted for going to bed at the expense of the cena, taking her slave with her.

As soon as she saw her mother in bed, Rufina, inviting Leia to the cena, went down to the living room where the tired party had settled on the profusion of cushions that covered the carpeted floor. Tullius, Marcellus, and Lucianus, were enjoying some wine prior to a makeshift cena that in the absence of Aurelia, Lavinia would have to cook.

Rufina was overjoyed that her brother and Tullius were back safely.

"Mother told me," she said, with pride in her eyes and addressing her brother, "that you fought with great courage and dexterity,"

"How could she tell you that?" laughed Marcellus. "She passed out and didn't see a thing."

He took a gulp of his wine and turned to Tullius. "I was more worried to see her lying unconscious in the cart," he said, "than I was about my opponent." All laughed at those words from Marcellus.

"You acquitted yourself like a true Legionary," said Lucianus with a smile and a nod of the head. "I myself spent the last twenty-five years as an infantryman in the Legion. I am not so good on a horse though."

"From what I could see," said Marcellus, "you kept that rascal well occupied. I too was in the infantry. I did three years as a tribune. But I have ridden horses since I was a youngster, and my horse moved incredibly well in that little battle. I was not aware of that, until I felt him glide through what turned out to be a crucial turn, performed in half the time of that of the bandit's horse...That was the bandit's undoing."

"Those Arabians of yours are quite remarkable. I envy you that," said Lucianus soberly.

Presently the cena was served and duly enjoyed by all. Lavinia showed herself to be a better cook than she had previously been given credit for. Marcellus thanked her with enthusiasm and a big smile. She retired to the kitchen where she and Leia who had come downstairs, enjoyed their supper in the company of Sartorius. The slave related with great gusto and eloquence, the details of their dangerous but exciting journey.

Shortly after the cena, Lucianus, thanking Marcellus profusely for his hospitality, and inviting him to pay him a visit in the very near future, took his leave from all and rode off to his farm near Salistra.

Marcellus and Tullius went up to check on the wounded man. Sergius, (for that was his name), woke up to the sound of their voices, and using his uninjured elbow, painfully sat up in bed. Marcellus offered him something to eat which he welcomed. Tullius, after checking the wound, rebandaged it with a satisfied look on his face, and went off to ask Rufina to see that a light supper was sent up to the room.

"You are most kind," smiled Sergius. "I feel I'm imposing rather badly on you and your family."

"You are very welcome here," assured Marcellus with a smile. "Tullius will tell us when you are strong enough to ride. Your horse is being taken care of in the stables. Someone will exercise him daily. How far from home are you?"

"I live in Vialignus," said Sergius. "That's about a two-hour ride from here."

"That's not too far. Perhaps within two or three days you will be ready to make the trip. But for now, you must rest. You cannot risk having the wound festering. Tullius will keep an eye on you until then."

Marcellus was most concerned about Tullius' safety now that he was back in the vicinity of Salistra, where he was in danger of being denounced and apprehended for his faith. But he need not have been so worried. His physician friend had a few tricks up his sleeve which he proposed to put into action.

Sergius had left a couple of days before, and since all the rooms were occupied now that Ignatia was living there, Marcellus had a bed set up in his room for Tullius. Leia slept in Ignatia's room on a pile of cushions, until better accommodations came her way.

"I really need to add at least two more bedrooms to the house," said Marcellus one evening as the family sat in their living room.

"Marcia will soon be needing a room of her own too," pointed out Rufina, stroking the girl's hair and giving her a big smile.

"I shall have a builder come this week and give us an idea of the best way to go about it," said Marcellus; trying to envisage what part of the house would best allow for the projected expansion.

"You will be rid of me by the end of the week," said Tullius, his eyes scanning the company.

"I have to get to my house as soon as possible and see how my people are doing. I have been away long enough."

"You will be walking into a trap," warned Marcellus. "How are you going to continue tending to your little flock?"

"The good Lord will guide me. I shall sneak into the house of someone reliable until I can get into mine unobserved. Once I can get in, I have a few ideas that I would like to put into practice. The only problem is that I cannot continue with my work either as physician, or teacher. Money will be my biggest problem I'm afraid."

"You can always count on us," said Marcellus with a nod of the head, earning a smile of gratitude from his sister.

Later that evening, Tullius asked Rufina to walk with him in the garden behind the house. She hastened to pick up her palla and join him. He, also pulled his shawl over his head, just in case anyone was snooping around.

"We are going for a short stroll," shouted back Rufina, as the pair walked away. The others remained seated around the garden table.

"I need to talk to you about something that I think you already suspect," began Tullius as soon as they were out of earshot.

Rufina looked at him with love in her beautiful eyes. Her lips parted in expectation of what he was about to say.

He took her hand in his, and leading her a little further out of sight of her family, stopped.

"You know that I love you," he said in somewhat of a whisper.

Her lips spread in a lovely smile, her eyes fixed on his.

"Yes," she answered. "I love you too." She stood on her tip toes and pouting her lips, pressed them hungrily on to his.

His head suddenly swam with joy and confusion. All his sober considerations dissipated as he took her in his arms and kissed her with great passion. He held her tightly for a few moments and then gently released her. The reality of the situation invaded his being again.

"Please forgive me. It cannot be," he said in a low mournful voice that cracked as he spoke.

Rufina's heart sank. Tears brimmed in her eyes. She looked appealingly at her reluctant lover.

"You told me once, that priests were allowed to marry." she cried. "Did you lie to me?"

She stepped away from him. The moon breaking through a cloud cast its beams on the troubled scene lighting up Rufina's face and accentuating her striking features.

Tullius was beside himself with admiration and regret.

"I would never lie to you my love," he said, with all the gentleness that he could muster.

"This is tragic," she sobbed. He drew her to him.

"Did the bishop prohibit you from marrying me?"

"No. Not exactly. He only reiterated to me what my mind had already told me."

She kept silent, throwing around in her disturbed head all the negative reasons that she knew he was also wrestling with.

"You are a highly intelligent person," he continued, taking her hands in his. "You can imagine the dangers ahead; not just for Marcia, but for any other children that we may have. I could not in good conscience endanger my family and not be able to protect you properly. My first duty as a priest is to my flock. Dear Lord," he prayed aloud, "I would have to sacrifice you my dear, all for their sake if the need arose." To console her, he tentatively said.

"Linus told me, that if we lived in Cyrene or Egypt, he would have no hesitation in permitting us to marry. There is peace there. They are even building places of assembly known as churches where people attend the 'Breaking of the Bread' service every Dies Solis. The persecutions are taking place only in and around Rome and to a lesser extent in Judea. But unfortunately, we are part of the Roman Church and I have to obey Linus' orders."

CHAPTER ELEVEN

MASQUERADE

Keeping in mind the warning that Marcellus had given him, Tullius who was presently sharing Marcellus' bedroom, went the following morning into the kitchen and asked Aurelia for a jug of hot water. He took it up to the room unobserved by anyone. Each member of the household was busy with their own chores; even Rex, who ran around trying to keep some straying hens from going out the courtyard gate.

The priest took out a number of interesting things from his baggage and laid them out on a table. He sat down, and with the aid of the washstand mirror, cut as much of his short, neat, beard and moustache as he could. He went back to the washstand, replaced the mirror, and with the aid of the hot water, some olive oil, and a very sharp knife, proceeded to shave his face clean. Drying his face, he went back to the table and opened a number of small vials and jars. He began to apply their creamy contents carefully to his face. With the aid of some brushes varying in degrees of softness, he created false wrinkles on his face and brow. When all was finished, he took a light grey hairpiece from his baggage and with some difficulty, put it over his own hair.

Taking the oldest cushion he could find in the room, he removed some of its wool stuffing. He slipped it on to his back under his tunic and held it in place with his belt. A few more adjustments followed, and he was ready to proceed with his masquerade.

Tullius required a staff, but there was none at hand. He decided to go to the garden where he thought he had seen a piece of branch lying there that would suit his purpose.

As luck would have it, Ignatia who happened to be coming out of her room, saw him just as he reached the bottom of the stairs. She waited for a moment and saw him walk through the corridor leading to the back. Hastily descending, she went into the kitchen to ask Aurelia about the old man who had come from upstairs and had gone to the garden.

"I don't know of any old man in the house my lady," said the cook shaking her head.

"Please go see what he wants, and why he was upstairs. Maybe he is a thief," said Ignatia with some concern in her voice.

Aurelia did as she was bid and hastened into the garden with a rolling pin in her hand.

"Ah! There you are." shouted Aurelia, as she spotted the 'aged' Tullius searching for the staff.

Tullius was momentarily taken aback. But when he realised that he had been spotted and reported, he began to play his theatrical part as a practice run for his coming adventure in Salistra later that day.

He moderated his voice to suit his pretended age, and soon convinced Aurelia that he was a somewhat demented old man who happened to have unwittingly wandered into the farm house by mistake.

The cook feeling sorry for the poor man, asked him into the kitchen intending to give him some of the soup that she had made for the cena. She wondered how Rex had not announced his presence, but promptly dismissed the thought and prepared to serve the intruder his soup.

Ignatia, sitting in the kitchen, looked at him with suspicion as he appeared in the doorway.

"What were you doing upstairs old man?" she asked with a stern look.

Tullius realised that she was looking at him not because his make-up was inadequate, but because she suspected him of robbery. He did not answer Ignatia's' question, but going into the kitchen, he sat in readiness for his soup.

Ignatia got up.

"See if I can find my daughter," she said, indignantly walking out of the kitchen.

Tullius, drank the tasty soup with his wooden spoon accompanied by the occasional slurp, which he deemed appropriate for an old man. He impatiently awaited the final test: The appearance of his beloved and now saddened Rufina.

'At least,' he thought. 'I shall make her laugh for a few moments. Last evening was very hard on us. We both need a laugh.'

The delicious soup reposed happily in Tullius' grateful stomach. 'Good soup is welcome at any time,' he mused, as the sound of light, familiar heels, clicked to a rapid rhythm through the corridor. Moments later, Rufina's beautiful face confronted him.

"Good morning," she said with a quizzical look in her lovely eyes. "I hear you're lost."

"It seems that waaay," said Tullius, using his old man's voice again, and shaking his head.

"Do you remember your name?" she asked with pity in her eyes.

"It could be...Tullius. But I...am not...suuuure," he said, trying hard to keep a straight face.

"Aurelia! Did you feed him?" she asked.

"She gave me some lovely soup," said Tullius in his own voice, and getting up stood his full height.

Rufina turned to him, still not believing the old man to be her lover. Then, the fact that he had called himself Tullius, dawned on her.

"Tullius. Is it really you?"

"Yes," he avowed. "But I cannot take my disguise off."

Rufina burst into a hearty laugh, joined by the man himself, and Aurelia, who laughed most heartily, and clapped her stout hands finding the clever performance particularly comical. The sudden eruption of laughter brought Ignatia and Marcia to the kitchen; much to the confusion of the former, who stood with her adopted granddaughter at the kitchen door totally bewildered.

That evening following the cena, which Tullius attended fully disguised having also fooled Marcellus and the other members of the household, the physician priest left. With him went everyone's prayers. He walked away in the direction of Salistra leaning on his staff, and carrying only a small bag.

* * * * *

Antonius, lost no time in procuring an Alsatian puppy to train as a guard dog for his vineyard. With Marcellus' permission, he also hired a gardener who would double up as gatekeeper and another assistant who would help him with the everyday chores in the vineyard.

Both men were tall and ruggedly built and would provide security when needed. Especially as it was suspected that Pompinus could cause trouble.

Antonius himself was quite a powerfully built man. He was only average in height, but had broad shoulders and a thick neck. His rugged, weathered features, strong rough hands, and piercing black eyes would convince even the most unobservant of persons that he belonged on the land, and conversely, the land had a natural claim on him. He had waited many years for an opportunity to manage a vineyard like his father-in-law, and now at the age of thirty-one, he had finally been given that opportunity. He had a good marriage with Lavinia whom he had known from childhood. As yet they had no children.

She too was a product of the land. She was younger than her husband by three years; very feminine in her demeanour, with an attractive but sturdy figure of medium height. Her features were well proportioned, though on the heavy side. Her straight nose somewhat thick at the ridge, played well with her full lipped mouth and solid, but pleasantly contoured chin. A cheerful disposition, sparked by a pair of vivacious grey/blue eyes and blonde hair, completed the picture, and made her the charming and helpful person that she was.

As my faithful reader will remember, she proved to be a better cook than had been apparent whilst serving at Marcellus' farm house. There, she had been in the shadow of the masterful Aurelia. Now that she was her own boss so to speak, she promised herself that she would out-do that great and perhaps overly lauded maverick of the kitchen.

Sartorius visited Octavius to inform him of the sacking of Pompinus and cautioned him to keep very alert for any overtures that the latter might make. He then returned to keep Marcellus company and to look after his young boss' interests with added vigour, now that his father was gone, and trouble might be brewing in the not too distant future. He regretted the young master's decision in not having had Pompinus arrested and prayed for time to prove him wrong.

* * * * *

Tullius' little masquerade had yielded good results. He arrived at his house on foot as he had proposed. Slumping forward, he passed it by slowly, cautiously, looking out for anyone who might be keeping watch on it. There was not a soul in sight. He walked to the end of the street and turning around, repeated the surveillance procedure.

Once certain that no one was looking, he pulled out his key, opened the door, and quickly entered. A careful examination of the rooms confirmed that no one had been there since he left.

He opened the shutters and let in some daylight. Having hastily lit a fire in the kitchen hearth, he took some food from his bag, and proceeded to cook himself a meal. He kept his disguise on as he might still have a need for it.

Shortly after he had finished eating there was a knock at the door. Pulling the shawl over his head, he inspected his face in a small mirror that hung in the hallway. Remembering to stoop, he opened the door. A middle-aged woman whom he recognized, stood staring at him.

"Good afternoon. What do you want?" he asked in his 'old man's' voice.

"I'm sorry to disturb you," she said. "I was expecting Tullius to open the door. Is he at home?"

"Tullius?" he asked, with a questioning look in his eyes.

"Yes," she said with conviction.

"Oh! The young man who lived here before?"

"Yes," said the woman with a surprised look in her eyes. "I did not know that the house was rented to someone else now."

"Indeed. I am the new tenant, and at your service."

The woman left. She was one of his flock, but she had not recognised him. He felt very elated at the success of his disguise. He would reveal himself to her at a later date.

'I have not told my landlord that I have taken over the rent,' he suddenly thought.

'I must do that right away.'

He left the house soon after and went in search of the owner whom he knew to be an old man who spent his life in a wheel chair. He had suffered an injury to his spine when he was a teenager and lost the use of his legs. Fortunately, his parents owned a number of houses in Salistra which he had inherited. The man who owned the butcher shop in the village, a cousin of his, collected the rents for him every month.

"As long as my rent comes in every month, and the house is not mistreated, I don't care who lives there," he said throwing an unconcerned look at his new tenant.

Tullius left the man with some peace of mind. He had realised however, that being an old man was a tedious thing to be masquerading as. The make-up took a good bit of time to do, and he could not relax at home fearing someone would come to the door and catch him without it. He needed to disguise as a younger man. His hair would stay as it was, and perhaps dye it and keep it that way. He would refashion his nose and eyebrows and grow a longer beard that he could quickly trim or shave any time if the need arose.

The clever physician was developing a type of skin made from animal skin, that he would be able to put over his nose and perhaps even cheeks. He resolved to experiment. That way he could assume different personalities in very short order.

Before he changed from his old man impersonation however, he decided to visit a friend whose wife was a reliable member of his flock. The man was a prominent personality in the village. In fact he had recently become the Mayor.

The latter received him with the cordiality of a new politician and invited 'the old man' to sit with him in his garden and enjoy some refreshments whilst they talked.

"How can I help you?" asked the mayor. They sat on a wooden bench facing a little pool replete with brightly coloured fish that swam lazily among water lilies.

"You can begin," said Tullius with a grin, "by telling me that you've missed me."

"Missed you, sir?" he asked with somewhat of a mocking smile. "I have never had the pleasure of meeting you."

"Really," joked Tullius. "My dear Atelius. Must I have to baptise your wife again?"

The mayor looked hard at the priest but was quite dumbfounded.

"I am Tullius in disguise," said the priest in his own voice. "I cannot take the disguise off at the moment, but so that there remains no doubt in your mind, I shall tell you a few things that only you and I are aware of."

Tullius finally convinced his friend who he was. They both shared a hearty laugh. Later, during their cena in the company of Cornelia, Atelius' wife, the two men put up a convincing performance at the poor bewildered lady's expense, until out of pity for her the imposter was unmasked, much to her glee.

"From now on," said Tullius, "I shall be adopting many disguises, so as to make it more difficult for those who hate us to find me, and also more secure for the people I am responsible for. Some people in the village have threatened to denounce me, if they have not already done so. I must tread very carefully for everyone's sake.

"Perhaps, soon, you may have no need for masquerading," said Atelius with sincerity.

"Please do not say anything of my disguises to your Christian friends," said the priest addressing Cornelia. "I mean to let them all know, but individually as the opportunity presents itself. I do not know who my enemy is as yet." He got up to leave.

"I shall keep you posted as to where we can meet for the next 'Breaking of the Bread' service. If you hear of any one else who would be interested in talking to me about Yeshua, please send word to Herminus. He will find me."

Tullius left the mayor's house and made his way home.

* * * * *

Two months had passed since the sacking of Pompinus. He had tried to find a vineyard to manage but thus far had had no luck. Since he had enough money to carry him for a good while yet, he decided to begin his hate campaign against Marcellus.

From his other friend Nonus, he learnt that Tullius the physician and Christian priest had disappeared and that the house which he used to rent had changed hands many times. At the moment the house was evidently occupied by a red headed physician who walked with a limp.

Pompinus dismissed the matter of the priest, and concentrated his efforts on spying on Marcellus, whom he felt that sooner or later would give himself away. Having permanently broken off with Calvus, he attempted to recruit Nonus to help him.

Nonus was a mason and enjoyed almost continual employment. He was therefore most reluctant to spend his spare time helping his friend spy on his previous boss which in his opinion would be a waste of time.

"That fellow is too smart to give himself away," said Nonus in an effort to dissuade the obsessed Pompinus.

"I am smart too. I'll put him away you'll see."

"I wish you luck of course, but I don't know how often I can help you out," said Nonus with a tilt of the head. "My work keeps me busy every day, and I need time with my family."

"I can pay you a little," coaxed Pompinus, who needed a witness should he catch his enemy in a compromising situation.

"No. I don't want any money," said Nonus. "I'll go with you when you feel that there is something about to happen that will incriminate him, but mostly, you'll be wasting your time."

Nonus slapped his friend's shoulder and wishing him a good day went home.

That same evening, Pompinus rode over to Marcellus' farmhouse. He left his horse tied up some distance away from the house and going on foot to the side of the house, climbed over a low stone wall and into the vineyard. Of a sudden Rex could be heard barking in the courtyard.

'Confound the dog,' said Pompinus to himself. 'I shall have to watch my step. They probably let him loose at night just as I used to do with my dog.'

He could hear the voice of Sartorius talking to the dog, then silence again.

'They're probably at the back,' he said to himself.

The spy walked well away from the house and made sure that he was down wind before he attempted to double back to the garden where be could spy on them from behind the wall. Rex would have trouble sniffing his presence as long as the wind did not change.

He could see Marcellus, Rufina, and another woman sitting at the table, Sartorius was standing and saying something that Pompinus could not make out. He was too far from them as yet. Trying to get closer would be very risky. He contented himself with simply observing them.

An hour later, a very disappointed spy climbed over the wall again, and found his way back to his horse accompanied by more barking from an excited Rex who had either heard his footsteps, or perhaps picked up his scent.

Sartorius went back into the courtyard as Rex once again began to bark.

"What's the matter with you tonight?" he said. "You're so restless. Come to the back."

He took the dog's chain off and let him loose. Rex ran into the garden, and after sniffing around for a while, crept under the table; settling down with his head resting on Rufina's foot. She stooped and patted him fondly on the head.

The conversation which had been interrupted by the dog's barking, continued.

"He has now a total of forty converts," said Marcellus. "He is having a busy time catering to them all. I met him in Salistra at the mayor's house quite by accident when I visited Cornelia to enquire about him. He has red hair now. You should see him. He is practicing his physician's trade again. He really needed the money to keep going."

"When is he going to come and visit us?" asked Rufina with some anxiousness.

"Very soon he says."

"I'd like to see what he looks like with his red hair," laughed Rufina. "Though knowing him he will probably surprise us with another of his disguises."

"Rex will sniff him out," smiled Sartorius.

Ignatia had not as yet been informed that she lived in the midst of a Christian family. Even Aurelia the cook was a Christian. Their nightly prayers were always said in the living room after Ignatia had gone to bed. She usually retired quite early blaming the country air for her drowsiness. Leia took advantage of her mistress early bedtime to join the others for night prayers whenever she could manage it. The morning prayers were said privately.

They were all looking forward to Tullius' visit so that he could perform the 'Breaking of the Bread' service which they had not had a chance of attending for months. Also, his sermons explaining some of the Gospels, was something that they yearned for with great anticipation.

Marcellus was praying that his mother would receive the gift of faith once it was explained in it's true light by someone gifted to do so. He was excited at the prospect that Tullius might convert her from her lifetime of paganism into the light of Yeshua. He regretted the loss of his father without having had a chance of being converted to the faith.

One morning, Marcellus woke up to Rex's incessant and urgent barking. He peered out of his window that looked on to the courtyard and to his surprise saw Evandros and Jocasta sitting patiently in a cart, awaiting to be rescued from the ferocious dog (as they perceived Rex).

"I shall be right down," he shouted at them, struggling to get his tunic on.

Sartorius however also having heard the barking, went to the rescue of the visitors.

"He is quite harmless," he assured them, "even though he appears so ferocious."

Pointing towards the house, he ordered Rex to go inside. The dog obeyed.

The two arrivals jumped off the cart, and took the extended hands that Sartorius offered them in greeting.

"I am Sartorius," said the old man with a smile.

"This is my wife Jocasta, and I am Evandros. We are servants of the...

"We have been expecting you," interrupted Sartorius.Welcome," he said, and eyeing the luggage in the cart. "Leave everything there, until we can deal with it." He was thinking that he might have to leave his room to this young couple and go stay with his daughter for the time being, since she had a room which he occupied on his occasional visits to her vineyard. At this juncture Marcellus arrived, followed by Leia, who ran to embrace her daughter.

The entire household was now up, and all converged on the courtyard to welcome the newcomers.

Marcellus was happy to see Evandros in particular, for he had plans for him. With Sartorius growing more incapable by the day, he hoped the young man would take his place in the near future. The young Greek was very handy, had a good head on his shoulders, and had proven himself to be a hard worker. Jocasta was also quite capable in her own way. The young couple would be a real asset to the vineyard.

* * * * *

Marina was feeling very poorly. She had been ailing ever since her life had fallen apart with the expulsion of her husband from the vineyard. If she was surviving the life shattering ordeal, it was only because Julia, the girl next door who had befriended her, cheered her up when she fell into her depressed moods. Pompinus gave his wife no love whatsoever. He simply demanded everything from her and did not give one mite for her feelings.

Julia was a Christian. She realised what a miserable life poor Marina lived and did her best to entertain her and bring some joy into her life. The girl was eighteen years old. She was pretty in the sense that though her features were not in any way remarkable, there was a general aura of congeniality in her face that made it most attractive. In contrast, Marina possessed true beauty in her regular features. Two dimples that formed in her cheeks when she smiled, and which unfortunately had become a rarity of late, endowed her face with a unique personality.

"You are running a fever," said Julia, feeling Marina's brow.

"Strange," said Marina, "I am feeling cold all over."

The women were in Pompinus' house. He was in the back garden.

"I think we should call a physician," said Julia. "See! ...You're shaking."

Marina slumped against the wall in her living room. "I feel very poorly," she complained.

Julia went out into the back garden and informed Pompinus of his wife's condition. The latter followed the girl back into the house complaining as he went.

"What's the matter with you?" he gruffly asked, looking at his wife who was now lying flat on the floor; her head propped up on two stacked cushions

"I don't know..." said Marina. "I feel terrible."

"I think you should allow me to bring a physician to examine her," volunteered Julia.

Pompinus thought for a few moments.

"Yea. Get one over here."

"Please put some blankets over her whilst I'm gone. See how she trembles," advised the girl, as with a concerned look on her face, she left.

A knock at the door gave Tullius a start even though it was only early afternoon. Every knock at his door gave the priest a start. He always expected trouble from some quarter or other.

He checked his face in the mirror and gingerly opened the door.

"Ah! Julia, it is you," he smiled with relief.

"Please come with me," said the girl with an anxious look on her face, "a friend of mine is very sick and needs a physician I'm sure."

Pompinus opened the door in answer to the physician's knock and led the way into the living room where Marina was lying on the floor cushions. She was still shaking, even though she was covered in blankets.

Tillius who had given his name as Servus as he entered the house, knelt down beside his patient and whilst feeling her brow and wrist, asked her a number of questions.

"I need to boil some herbs," said Tullius, "can you help me Julia?"

The physician got up and taking his bag with him limped into the kitchen followed by Julia.

271

Pompinus observed the physician with interest. The man looked queer with that red hair.

'He must be a Northerner. No one around here has hair like that,' he mused. 'And he's lame.'

Presently, Tullius and Julia returned to the living room. Pompinus sat his wife up against the wall, allowing Julia to administer the herbal soup to her shivering friend, one spoonful at a time

Tullius waited for Julia to finish feeding Marina and announced that he was leaving.

"What do I owe you? ...My name is Pompinus,"

Tullius' ears perked up. 'Was this not the man that Marcellus had discharged?' he asked himself.

"You can pay me tomorrow. Let's see how your wife reacts to the herbs I have given her. I am optimistic that she will be feeling quite recovered by then."

Tullius bade them all a good day and made for the door. His mind was however occupied with Pompinus, and he forgot to limp on the first three steps he took as he walked to the door. Pompinus was quick to notice. The physician, correcting his error, resumed his limp once again.

To everyone's relief, Marina was well again the following day.

Shortly after midday, Tullius returned to Pompinus' house. The man himself opened the door.

"Come in," he said with a smirky smile.

"How is your good wife today?" asked Tullius with a smile.

Marina suddenly appeared and thanked him profusely for his help. Pompinus took the opportunity to question the physician.

"Tell me Servus," he began, "does your leg bother you much?"

Tullius was taken aback by the suddenness of the question and smelt a rat. He remembered having forgotten to limp the day before and tried to patch things up.

"It bothers me much of the time. But every now and then it rights itself; but unfortunately, very briefly. It happens of a sudden and as I said, regresses very quickly."

"Did you break it?" asked Pompinus, with pretended seriousness.

"No. Nothing like that. It has been with me since I was a child. However it gets worse as I grow older."

"Too bad," said Pompinus shaking his head. "How much do I owe you?"

"One denarius will do. Thank you." said the physician. "I am glad to see your wife well again."

Pompinus gave Tullius the coin.

"I am at your service whenever you need me," said the physician, and turning, limped away.

Pompinus poured himself a large cup of wine and sat down to think about Servus and his limp. He was not convinced by the physician's explanation. He admitted to himself that he had nothing against the man, but if he could use him as a pawn in the game against Marcellus, that would be great. He had been spying on Marcellus for a couple of months, but nothing productive had come of it. He continued to wrack his evil brains for a solution to his constant problem.

Suddenly the thought came to him.

'The feast of Bacchus is almost here. If he is a Christian, he will not come to the feast. I remember Sartorius and Octavius both came last year before this man arrived. I shall be ready for him if he doesn't show up to offer his wine to the god.'

* * * * *

Rufina was busy coaching Marcia. The girl was displaying particular talent as a harpist, and her adoptive mother was thrilled at the proficiency her ward had attained in just a few months of instruction. They were in the living room of the farm house in the early afternoon. Ignatia sat nearby with Leia at her side, enjoying the performance.

"You, also learnt very quickly," she said looking at her daughter. "Your tutor was quite amazed at how easily you took to the instrument."

"I am glad that she learnt to play so well," said Marcia putting down her harp and smiling at Ignatia. "Now she can teach me all that she learnt and soon we can play together."

"That will certainly be a treat!" came a masculine voice, as a handsome red-haired man entered the room.

All four women stared in amazement at the intruder.

Then Rufina, remembering what Marcellus had told them, realised it was Tullius, and getting up hastened to embrace him. Marcia, Ignatia and Leia were puzzled at the apparition.

"It's so good to see you Tullius, I have missed you so much. Marcellus is going to be thrilled to see you too. He is out in the vineyard with Sartorius and Evandros."

Tullius disengaged himself from Rufina and went over to greet Ignatia who stood awaiting her chance to greet the friendly physician. He took her hands warmly and told her how glad he was to see her looking so well. Marcia left her harp on the floor and going over, gave him an enthusiastic hug. Tullius took out a little bag from his tunic and gave it to the girl. She opened the present.

"Oh! Thank you," she cried. "I love these."

She showed Rufina the candied fruit, and smiling happily put one in her mouth. Then, remembering that she should have first offered the fruit to the others, she smirked and said:

"Would anyone like one?"

Rufina and Ignatia smiled and shook their heads.

"No thank you. You eat them," said Rufina. Marcia sat down next to her harp to enjoy her treat.

"Why did you colour your hair?" asked Ignatia. "Are you fond of disguising yourself?"

"No. Mamma," said Rufina dryly. "Tullius has to keep his identity secret. There are many people persecuting him, and he has to hide from them."

Tullius could not allow Ignatia to suspect that he was some sort of criminal. He knew that even if she did not convert, she would never give him away. He went and sat beside her.

"No, my dear lady," he said. "I do not relish having to masquerade all the time. But I happen to be a Christian, and that carries a death sentence with it as you have probably heard."

Ignatia was visibly shocked. She might as well have heard that he was a bandit. Here was this man, accepted and even loved by her family, and in the twinkling of an eye, they could all be taken off somewhere and murdered, just as little Marcia's parents had been. Dumbfounded, she looked at the priest.

Rufina seeing the expression in her mother's face was quick to react.

"We are all Christians, Mamma; except Marcia, and she will hopefully be one very soon. She is now close to seven years old and will understand the reason why her parents went so bravely to their deaths."

"Oh my!" cried Ignatia, her hands pressing her cheeks, and searching for words to express her distress.

"Please listen to what Tullius has to say," coaxed her daughter taking her mother's hand and sitting down beside her.

Marcia who had been attentively listening to the grown-ups talking, stopped munching on her candied fruit and placed her hands on her lap in anticipation of what Tullius was to preach.

Tulius pulled the shawl off his shoulders and placed it on a cushion beside him. He looked deeply into Ignatia's eyes, and with love in his voice began his sermon. Leia sat up and prepared to listen.

"What I am about to tell you Ignatia, is a most beautiful and endearing story. It is a true story. One of great love. A divine love, proven by a unique sacrifice to save all mankind from their sins and give them an eternal life of happiness."

Tullius continued his captivating narration, introducing Yeshua into Ignatia's consciousness. As he spoke, he prayed to the Holy Spirit to guide his tongue so as to inspire in his listener the faith that was so vital for her conversion.

Marcia listened intently, fascinated by what she was hearing. It seemed to bring her more and more into communion with her beloved parents as the sermon continued. Little by little her open childish mind absorbed the gift of faith that was being offered her by the Holy Spirit.

Ignatia, on her part was still wrestling with her old beliefs and ways of life as the narration continued. However there was a softening of heart occurring which at least gave her reason to reassess her children's acceptance of this new religion.

"We are dealing here," continued the ardent and inspired priest, "with a God who took on human flesh, and then gave his life for your salvation and mine. He could have stayed up in his heaven looking down on us and leaving us to our own troubles, like the gods that you have worshipped all your life. They do their own self-centred wills' caring little for humans. Often, they are even promiscuous, and give you no direction for a virtuous and sinless life."

Ignatia began to realize that a God who lived and died only recently, and who had performed so many miracles including rising from the dead, was by far more believable than her own gods that had really never done anything for her or anybody else. Certainly, none of them had ever promised them an eternity of happiness.

Tullius finally stopped. Aurelia had quietly, whilst the sermon was in progress, brought in a tray with a jug of fresh lemonade and some cups and left it on a table beside them. She now stood listening at the door with Jocasta who had just joined her. Tullius reached for a cup, and pouring some lemonade into it, took a good gulp to freshen his throat.

"Well?" he asked; his eyes on Ignatia's considerably appeased face.

She returned his look for a moment and turning to her daughter, quietly said.

"It is certainly a very inspiring story. I can see now why you find it so captivating and attractive. I shall have to give it further thought. I am very confused right now. Your father and I have always followed our beliefs, in Zeus, Hera, Diana and the others. They were good stories too. But this life of Yeshua and his extraordinary power, certainly makes all those other gods..."

She stopped abruptly.

"You spoke," she said turning to Tullius, of Yeshua's Father in heaven, as being Yahweh, the God of the Jews. "They claim him to be a living God also. Is that not so?"

"Yes," said Tullius. "He did not appear in person to his people at that time, but he performed incredible and highly believable miracles for them through Moses whom he had empowered to do his Will; particularly, freeing them from slavery in Egypt. He also appointed prophets to correct the Jews in their transgressions of his law and to announce important coming events such as the coming of Yeshua; their Messiah.

"I have to think about all you have said. After all, if I come to believe in Yeshua, I too will be in danger of death." She got up, and nodding for Leia to follow, walked away to her room to ponder further on the revelation that had been given her.

"We must pray earnestly for her," said Tullius.

"When can I become a Christian...?"

All simultaneously turned to look at an expectant pair of large blue eyes. Marcia's request snapped them out of their thoughts concerning Ignatia, and they now attended to the eager girl's words.

"Let's wait for grandma Ignatia," said Rufina. "If Yeshua answers our prayers soon, Tullius will baptise you both at the same time and we shall have a celebration.

The matter of Ignatia's reluctance to convert to Christianity, continued to weigh heavily on Marcellus' shoulders. As he pondered on her obstinacy, another important matter came to mind, which he had totally lost track of. The freeing of the three slaves. His mother had made a promise and it had been delayed long enough.

With the aforementioned in mind, he knocked at his mother's door one morning. It was opened by Leia, who wished him a good morning with a sunny smile on her pleasant face.

"Good morning Leia," he greeted, "I wish to speak to my mother."

The slave smiled, again, made a short bow and left the room. Ignatia was sitting by the window admiring the surrounding countryside. She turned at the sound of her son's voice and prepared to receive him with a big smile.

"It is so beautiful out there," she said, her face lit up by the morning sun coming through the window. "It is like a different world from Rome. There is nothing to restrict the view. Everything looks so clean and still. I can hear the goats' bells up on that hill over there," she said, pointing to it.

Marcellus rejoiced that his mother was in an appreciative mood. He gave her a kiss on the cheek and said:

"I have come to remind you that we have not yet set our slaves free. They are surely eager for their promised freedom. They of course have said nothing, but we must proceed right away. I am going up to Salistra today," he continued, "and it is a good opportunity to take the writ ordaining their freedom with me. I shall give it to Atelius and he will ensure that it will be officially processed. May I have your permission to go ahead? We can have a little celebration tonight."

"Yes," said Ignatia, with some regret. "I suppose now is as good a time as ever. I did promise. Though I still don't see the need for it," she complained, "It will only cost us money, as we shall have to pay them now."

"They will not require much money but look at the joy that you will put into their lives. It must be a terrible thing to be owned by someone. Not to be master of one's own life. A great calamity usually caused by wars." He paused and walked to the window. He looked out and pointed. "Everything out there is free. God made man to be free and equal. When as Yeshua promised we go to heaven with him, each man will be judged on his own merits. He makes no distinction between rich or poor, clever or stupid, educated or uneducated. In all cases however, he will favour and reward the good, and punish the bad." He walked back to Ignatia, took her hand, and looking deep into her eyes, he said.

"You mother will be doing something really good. Your reward in heaven will be great. The only thing that is missing, is that you believe in and love Yeshua who will give you an eternal life of happiness."

"Go ahead my son," she said walking back to the window. and looked out on to the beautiful panorama.

"I remember your father mentioning every now and then," she continued, "that he felt pity for their situation, but never got around to freeing them. I suppose it was because he treated them the same way as he did his freemen, and they were all made to feel part of the family."

"Father also felt a great sympathy for the Christians," said Marcellus. "I believe that if he had lived, he would eventually have become one. It us our great regret that God chose to take him before he had a chance to accept his Son Yeshua. Rufina and I pray for his soul constantly, that Yeshua may have mercy on his soul and allow him into heaven."

Silence followed those words of Marcellus. He went to the window, gave his mother a hug, and promising to bring her the writ to sign, left her to her thoughts.

A little later that same day, a satisfied and happy Marcellus rode off to Salistra, with the signed writ in his tunic pocket, and made his way to the mayor's house. He anticipated with great pleasure the celebration which they would have that evening at the vineyard, and the happy faces of his slaves, when they came to the realisation that they were slaves no longer.

CHAPTER TWELVE

THE FEAST OF BACCHUS

The Mayor of Salistra welcomed Tullius once again. The priest immediately disclosed his identity to his friend as they met. He had had his visit to Marcellus' farmhouse cut short by some urgent news from Julia who had personally walked all the way to the farmhouse just to find and warn him. She had heard from Marina that her husband suspected him of being an imposter, and that might well brew trouble for him.

Tullius was disguised once again, this time he was clean shaven and bald. He had got rid of all the red hair and beard, and concentrated only in changing his nose, and darkening his eyebrows. He painted on a few wrinkles and so changed his whole aspect.

"I would never have recognised you in your new disguise if you hadn't told me," said Atelius, with a smile and putting an arm around his friend. "How can I assist you?"

"Will you allow me to stay here for just a few of days? I cannot return to my house until I see what develops. If anything. In any event I must find a different place to live."

"I may be able to find you a place if given a couple of days," said the mayor as they walked into the garden. "In the meantime, you are most welcome here."

"No. I thank you," smiled Tullius, "but we must never seem connected in any way. It would endanger Cornelia and who knows even yourself. I must find a place on my own. Hopefully within a couple of days. My practice as a physician will suffer once more, since I can only administer to the members of my flock."

Presently, Cornelia, wearing a lovely smile, but a puzzled look in her amiable eyes, joined them.

"Hello Cornelia," greeted the priest. "It's me, Tullius."

"Oh my, you will succeed in driving us crazy," she laughed, holding out her hands which he amiably pressed.

They went on to talk about many things. Among them, the oncoming festivities in honour of Bacchus which were traditional to the area. The peasants from the surrounding villages, took the feast quite seriously.

"Atelius will be very busy," said Cornelia with some concern. "I shall be absent of course as usual. Last year I feigned sickness. This year I am considering visiting an aunt who lives not far from here in Suplicium. These pagan feasts will be the end of us Christians," she said drawing closer to Tullius' ear.

"Yes," agreed Atelius; kicking a stone that lay in his path and looking at his wife.

"One has to be very creative in lying for you my dear," he said. She smiled at him.

"There are times when I wish I had not been elected mayor," he continued. "Every year it becomes more difficult. When is this insane persecution of your faith going to stop?" Cornelia shrugged her shoulders and sat down on one of the garden benches, throwing an enquiring glance at priest.

"We pray for that constantly my good friend," said Tullius, joining his hostess on the bench. "It seems that thus far it is what our God has willed for us to bear and we must be patient. I for one, will remain in my new lodgings during the feasting...Once I find it."

Cornelia thought for a moment... "You could accompany us to my aunt's place," she suggested, her eyes on Tullius. Then, turning to her husband, she said. "You would have some company on your way back. What do you say to that my dear?"

"Yes, that would be excellent," said the mayor smiling at Tullius. "Then, when we return, you could stay here out of sight and keep me company until the festivities are over.

* * * * *

The villagers of Salistra were busy putting up the decorations for the upcoming feast. A number of adjoining villages including Menorum, were taking part in the festivities and so many tents were being set up around the village as people began to arrive. The local market place was beginning to bulge at the seams. The demand for food and drink in particular, increased ten-fold. Flower stalls, and the parade of colourful costumes added much liveliness to the annual celebration. Music soon resonated around the village, as impromptu dancing groups quickly formed, each performing in their particular characteristic way.

The mayor and Cornelia, sitting in a cart pulled by a single horse with Tullius riding alongside, quietly sneaked out of the village early in the morning two days prior to the start of the Bacchanalia. They would return hopefully the following day allowing Atelius to make a last moment inspection of the decorations and approve the various activities which were his responsibility to oversee.

True to their expectations, the two friends were back in Salistra shortly after noon the following day. No one seemed to have missed them. No embarrassing questions were asked in connection with Cornelia's disappearance.

The feast of Bacchus was really not that popular a feast in the rest of Italy. In fact, in the past, it had been banned in a number of places including Rome; having been considered somewhat of an occult feast. However, as I wish to point out to my faithful reader, in that particular part of Umbria where our story takes place, and where wine was their livelihood, it was traditionally celebrated with great zeal. Being the type of feast that it was; where wine would flow abundantly, things sometimes got out of hand, requiring the intervention of the law.

Precisely at noon, the mayor stood on the balcony of his house which fronted the square. The crowd below impatiently awaited his signal to start the festivities.

Atelius raised his hands; each holding a cluster of grapes, and with the words:

"We honour you Bacchus!" He threw the grapes high into the air as the crowd cheered.

The people parted to open a path the length of the square. A life size statue of the god Bacchus bedecked with flowers and carried in a cart pulled by two gaily decorated donkeys, was wheeled into the centre of the square. Children promptly surrounded it dancing and screaming enthusiastically at the top of their thin piercing voices.

A second cart with two barrels of wine lying on their sides, followed. That cart was surrounded by happy peasants, who holding their cups at the ready, eagerly waited to have them filled. Musicians, dancers and singers, soon appeared, creating space for themselves as they wove their way around the statue, jumping and pirouetting as the space permitted, to the sound of pipes, tambourines, and clapping of hands.

The mayor remained at the balcony smiling and waving to the people for some time. Finally, concluding that his presence was being ignored and he would not be missed, he retreated into the house to join Tullius who sat sipping watered wine which was in no way connected with the honouring of Bacchus.

"I'll join you in a drink, and then I have to go mingle with the crowd," said Atelius. "There are people I must talk to and keep happy."

The feast was well under way. The afternoon was spending itself and evening was looming. The popular Atelius, continued to circulate amicably among the enthusiastic crowd.

The time for the presentation of the offerings to the god was drawing near. The vintners were beginning to group with their offerings of wine from various nearby vineyards. Each vintner had a small barrel of wine in front of him awaiting the signal from the mayor to approach the statue and place the barrel beside the cart.

Pompinus was in the crowd, keeping close to his fellow vintners. The previous year, he, Sartorius and Octavius, had each brought a barrel. This year however, he noticed that neither Sartorius, or Octavius were present.

'Ha! I knew it. I knew it,' he said to himself. 'He *is* a Christian, and he does not allow his managers to bring wine to honour Bacchus...I have him now.'

Pompinus was ecstatic. He immediately began to devise a plan for destroying Marcellus.

Atelius gave the signal for the vintners to individually approach the statue. The crowd cheered loudly every time a donor placed his barrel beside the cart. Everyone was having a good time. Many were beginning to show signs of inebriation, but most of the people were simply having fun. No one really missed the wine offering from the Fulvius vineyards, since there were a good many other vineyards that had participated in the offertory venue.

Pompinus, finding his friend Nonus, made known to him his evil plan.

"By Jove!" said Nonus. "You're probably right. Why would he not send wine over? Three barrels is nothing to him. Yea. You're probably right."

The two shady friends pushed their way through the crowded square and found the mayor.

Pompinus took a hold of Atelius' arm.

"We need to talk to you for a few moments Mayor," said Pompinus. Nonus pressed closer to his friend.

"What can I do for you my friend?" asked the mayor innocently.

"I want you to come with us and bring some soldiers with you."

Atelius was quite perplexed. "I cannot go anywhere right now. My duty is here. What are you asking of me?

Pompinus became upset. "There is a Christian whom I want arrested."

The mayor was shocked. "A Christian? You want me to leave my duty here to arrest a Christian? How do you know he is a Christian? Did he tell you?"

"No, but I can prove it."

"Listen my friend," said the Atelius attempting to keep calm. "When the festivities are over, come and see me and I shall listen to your story. In the meantime, go and enjoy the feast."

"He owns three vineyards and he hasn't offered a single barrel this year. How would you explain that?" insisted an irate Pompinus.

"Yea!" agreed Nonus. "My friend has a point there."

"Please, do as I say," said Atelius tiring of the pair. "If he owns three vineyards, he is unlikely to disappear. He will still be there two days from now. I cannot look after your complaint at this moment." The mayor turned and walked away from the two irate men.

"You decided to stop in for some refreshment at last," said Tullius with a beaming smile, as Atelius walked into the peristyle with a perplexed look on his face.

"What's the matter, you seem upset?" asked Tullius getting up from his cushion.

The mayor explained the behaviour of the two men in the square, and seeing the expression on Tullius' face, he frowned deeply.

"It's Marcellus they're after," said the priest with much concern in his voice.

"Marcellus?"

"Yes. That man is Pompinus," pointed out Tullius. "He was the manager of one of his vineyards, and Marcellus fired him for some heavy stealing over a number of years. His father Porcius wanted to have him arrested. But the son felt sorry for the rascal's wife, and so he merely fired him. The thief now wants to take revenge exposing him as a Christian. In fact, as I remember, he already threatened him and wanted to force a deal with him prior to his being fired."

Atelius explained that he had asked the man to come and see him in two days time. He suggested that Marcellus should be warned.

"If these two rats insist," said the mayor, I shall have no alternative but to put the matter into the military's hands. I shall surely be asked to accompany them when they go to his farmhouse.

"I'll ride over immediately and warn him," said Tullius, "I'll be back tomorrow and let you know if anything has developed."

So saying, Tullius took leave of his good friend and taking his horse out of Atelius' stable, rode off to find Marcellus.

The sound of his horse's hooves mingled with Rex's welcoming bark as Tullius rode into Marcellus' courtyard. Aurelia peeked out of the high kitchen window.

"Rufina!" she called out, hastening to put a lid on a pot that was boiling over.

Moments later, Rufina appeared, busily adjusting her shawl which had fallen over her shoulders.

"Rufina!" cried out Tullius. "It's only me."

Rufina looked at the clean-shaven stranger.

"Tullius, when will you stop tormenting me? When am I going to look at you and say. This is my Tullius?"

"Perhaps never my love. I have something serious to report to Marcellus. Where is he?"

"He is here!" Those words from Marcellus as he appeared at the farm house door.

Tullius dismounted and hastened to embrace his friends.

"What serious thing have you to tell me?" asked Marcellus fearing the worst.

"That depraved person that you dismissed from your vineyard is demanding you be investigated as to your being a Christian. Atelius is most upset. They approached him, and though he shirked them off for the next day or so, he still has to follow up on their demands. There are two of them, but Pompinus is the instigator".

Tullius stayed the night at Marcellus' house, but first thing in the morning he was on his way again. He had performed the "Breaking of the Bread" service for the whole household with the exception of Marcia and Ignatia, who attended but did not partake. Aurelia stayed late to be able to attend.

He had promised Rufina, that if Marcellus was arrested, he would be nearby and would keep her posted.

Tullius rode away again without having baptised Ignatia or Marcia. The mother was not ready to convert yet, though she was seriously thinking about it...The priest was very hopeful.

On his arrival back in Salistra, Tullius, enquired at two different locations to see if they would rent him a house. There was one that was right on the square which would have suited him well, but without his being able to carry out his profession as a physician, he would not be able to hold it for long. He stopped to think for a moment. It occurred to him that the same man who was causing Marcellus a problem, was affecting him the same way. If that rascal could be got rid off, life would be much easier on him and on Marcellus. But how?

He returned to the mayor's house, where he settled once again for the night.

Tullías awoke next morning, to the sounds of voices in the atrium. He tiptoed out of his room off the peristyle and walked cautiously to where he could hear what was being said.

"I am sure he will admit to it. They always do."

"We will have to wait and see," came the voice of Atelius.

There was the sound of receding footsteps, followed by the front door closing, and presently, a maid scampered past him and disappeared into the kitchen.

The priest returned to his room and dressing quickly. He rushed down to the stable, took out his horse, and waving a greeting to the stable boy, rode off to catch up with the retinue whose destination he knew.

Tullius kept well behind the group as it made its way to Marcellus' vineyard.

On their reaching the farmhouse courtyard, Rex came out and stood snarling at the horsemen. His snarl changed into a bark as he announced the unwelcome visitors.

Marcellus walked out into the courtyard alone. He went up to Atelius and acting as if he had never seen him before, said:

"I am Marcellus. What can I do for you gentlemen?" He gave the others a quizzical look.

"We wish to ask you a few questions," said the centurion in charge of the investigation.

"Go ahead," said a serious Marcellus.

The centurion motioned with his hand at Pompinus and Nonus.

"These men here, are accusing you of not having offered your vineyards' wine to the god Bacchus at the sacred festival, with the intention of insulting him.

"Is one obliged to do that?" asked Marcellus, spreading his hands.

The centurion looked unsure. He looked at the mayor. Atelius raised his hand as if saying I don't know.

"It seems that your complaint is invalid." said the centurion looking at Pompinus.

Pompinus was fuming, it had not occurred to him that the offering to Bacchus was a voluntary act. There was really no obligation attached to it.

"I know he didn't make the offering because he is a Christian," insisted Pompinus with great hatred in his voice. "Ask him. Go on. Ask him if he is a Christian."

The mayor was about to call the whole thing off. He was in the midst of turning his horse around, when the Centurion asked. "Are you a Christian?"

The silence was deafening. Marcellus took a deep breath and looking up to heaven said.

"Yes! By the grace of my God Yeshua, I am."

An evil smile spread across Pompinus' lips. "I told you so," he said.

"Take him," ordered the centurion.

"There is no need. I shall come willingly," said Marcellus walking towards them.

"One moment please!" The voice of Ignatia resounded through the courtyard.

They all stood still listening for what the woman who had suddenly appeared might say.

"I am Ignatia," she said with authority. "Wife of the late Senator Porcius Fulvius. I am this young man's mother and the owner of three vineyards in this district. Centurion. I want you to arrest that man who goes by the name of Pompinus." She pointed him out. "Yes, the one that has just accused my son."

She walked up the centurion who was still in the saddle.

"That man," she said, with great conviction, "has been stealing from my family for years whilst managing one of my vineyards. I have ample proof of his crime, and I want him arrested, tried, and sentenced."

The soldier turned his horse towards Pompinus, and unsheathing his gladius, told him to dismount. Another soldier went over and tied his hands behind his back.

Nonus was aghast and scared, though no one even noticed him. Tullius had heard everything from his hidden location behind the vineyard wall. He was most distressed that the centurion should have asked the question that would automatically condemn his friend to death.

Rufina came rushing out of the house, and running to her brother, embraced him lovingly.

Ignatia was also permitted to embrace her son. And then came Marcia crying Cellus! Cellus! She hugged and kissed him ardently; her little heart breaking. It took all Rufina's strength to tear her away from him.

The centurion was visibly moved and regretted greatly having asked the deadly question. There was no going back however. He shook his head and saluted Ignatia as he rode away.

The retinue left with Marcellus and Pompinus walking beside the horses. Marcellus was unbound, but Pomoinus was not only bound, but had a long rope around his neck, which one of the riders held on to firmly.

When all had gone, Tullius came into the farmhouse to try to console the family. It proved to be a very sad night for all. No one slept a wink, including Marcia, who was reliving her parent's tragedy all over again. She adored Marcellus who had become her father.

Tullius kept a particularly sharp eye on the girl. They all tried their best to console her. No one however, would go so far as to say that all would be well with Marcellus. A later shock might affect her even more they feared.

Sartorius was virtually back in charge of affairs as far as the vineyard was concerned. Fortunately, he had Evandros to help him. The young ex-slave was learning fast and proving himself to be a hard and enthusiastic worker.

Tullius promised Ignatia and Rufina that he would diligently report back all news concerning Marcellus. There was some consolation in the fact that the mayor was a good friend and would try to influence the military in Marcellus' favour.

Atelius awaited anxiously the arrival of Tullius. He was quite sickened by what he had witnessed at Marcellus's house, and his wife still being away at her aunt's, he needed someone to talk to.

The priest arrived just before noon the following day and was warmly invited to lunch.

"I am totally distressed," said Atelius as they ate, "It is beyond me that a louse such as that, can, with just four words, ruin an excellent man's life."

"That is the terrible risk that all we Christians run." said Tullius. "Or, anyone connected with us." He chomped on his lamb chop and looked searchingly at his friend.

"If they took Cornelia away from me, I don't think I could bear it," sighed Atelius, taking a gulp of his wine.

"Where are they holding Marcellus?" asked the physician. It suddenly came to him that the danger to himself personally had passed, now that Pompinus was in prison awaiting trial.

'I can return to my house and be myself again,' he said to himself.

"They have him in the local prison at the Legion Barracks just down the road," said the mayor. "I have one of my maids take down food for him every day. He will not be mistreated. The centurion likes him. At least that is a consolation. He is in the only above ground cell. The thief is in the dungeon at the other end of the building."

"Can I get to see him?" asked Tullius.

"You can try. Simply say you are the family physician checking up on him at his family's request."

The following day, Tullius found his way to the prison. The centurion, though never having seen him before, permitted him to see Marcellus.

"Here is your physician," said the soldier looking at Marcellus. "Your family have sent him to make sure that you are alright."

He opened the cell door and let Tullius in. Then closing it, he locked the pair inside and asked Tullius to shout out when he was ready to leave.

"Good to see you," said Marcellus as the two friends embraced.

"You are looking well. Atelius tells me he sends you food every day. That's really nice of him. He is very concerned and feels quite helpless."

"Yes, he is a good soul," said Marcellus with a nod of the head.

The two friends talked about a number of things that needed to be discussed. When they were done, Marcellus called the centurion.

The man came quickly. He let Tullius out and locked the door again.

"You can come any time you like," he smiled.

The physician thanked him, and waving to Marcellus, walked away.

"Too bad, you can't walk away too," said the jailor, with an apologetic look on his face, when he and Marcellus were alone.

"You, fixed that for me," said Marcellus, shaking his head at the man.

"Yea, and I'm sorry. If I had known before that that rat was a robber, I would never have heeded him. You have a nice family. Your father was a senator?" He shook his head.

"Life can be tough at times."

"What are you planning to do with me?" asked Marcellus.

"You will remain here until the governor of the Province arrives, and then you and the other two prisoners will be judged and sentenced," explained the jailor.

"If I am sentenced to death; for that is what the Emperor wants. I wish to be beheaded."

"Aren't you rushing things a bit?"

"I have served three years in the infantry as a tribune. Surely that should qualify me for a beheading? It is my right as a Roman if I appeal to the Emperor; and I intend to."

The centurion was much surprised and impressed at Marcellus military record.

"Why did you not run for the Senate like your father? You finished your 'Cursus Honorem' did you not?"

"Yes, but I liked the idea of learning the wine business, and I love the countryside. How long do you think before the governor arrives?"

"Don't hold me to it, but he should be here within the next three weeks. He comes only once a year as a rule. You are lucky that he is due soon, otherwise we would either have to take you up to him at Ariminum. Or else to Rome."

Marcellus did not say anything to the centurion, but he recalled having had the governor treated and nursed at his house after his having been assaulted on the road. Tullius had saved his life.

The two men talked for a while longer. It was the beginning of an odd friendship.

* * * * *

Tullius called on Julia and told her what had happened to Pompinus. He asked her to tell Marina in case her husband's friend had not informed her. He offered his help in resettling her, as she might well be destitute seeing that she was now on her own.

'Being the man he is,' he said to himself knowing Pompinus,' he may not have told her where he keeps his money.'

Two days later, Julia came to his house to tell him that Marina had found some of her husband's money, but she was sure there was more somewhere. The girl had also told him that Marina was very receptive to the good news of the Lord, and that he should visit her himself in the near future to complete her conversion.

Tullius felt very relieved of late. Unfortunately, it was at his best friend's expense. Pompinus was no longer a threat. But he was still much troubled. Marcellus could pay with his life.

In the three weeks that followed and prior to the expected arrival of the governor, Tullius visited both Marcellus and Rufina regularly. The tension in the family was considerable, and prayers were being offered by the whole of Tullius' little flock for Marcellus' release.

The governor's arrival stirred up much excitement in the village. That too, was a perennial occasion as was the Bacchanalia, though certainly not as festive or happy.

Riding ahead of a large military escort, consisting of one full 'turma' of thirty-two cavalrymen and commanded by a young tribune, the governor rode into the village square. The permanent garrison at Salistra in comparison, merely amounted to sixty soldiers or so, even though under a centurion's command.

The military regulars lined a scantily populated path in the square leading up to the mayor's house. The crowd of onlookers, behaving quite calmly, filled in the gaps between the fully uniformed Legionaries.

Atelius, was waiting at the door of his attractive house, wearing his chain of office and a big smile, as the governor rode up to greet him.

Other years, the governor, whose name as my esteemed reader may recall, was Sabinus Celorius had arrived with a small escort of three or four soldiers. This year however, in view of the assault he experienced on his last visit to Salistra, he had brought a much larger contingent. Because of the added personnel, he concluded that his accommodation at the local barracks would be cramped and inadequate for his accustomed life style.

On previous visits, the mayor had offered him accommodations at his home, which he had politely refused. Generally speaking, he was reluctant to accept favours from anyone, since it might in the future, restrain him in the execution of the law.

On this occasion however, he accepted the invitation; much to the surprise of Atelius, who was yet to undergo many more surprises in the coming days.

"Welcome to our humble home," greeted the mayor, directing the governor to a very well-appointed guest room right next door to the room that Tullius had occupied during his stay a few weeks earlier.

"You are most kind," said Sabinus with a nod of the head and surveying his comfortable surroundings. Not to mention his expectancy of a few good home cooked 'cenas'.

"I am afraid that the accommodations at the barracks would be rather strained seeing as I have brought a rather heavy escort with me."

"After your experience of last year," said the mayor with a smile, "who can blame you?"

Suddenly he remembered Marcellus telling him how Tullius had saved the man's life, whilst convalescing at his farmhouse.

'By Jupiter,' said Atelius to himself, "is the governor going to get a shock when he finds Marcellus in jail. And even more when he learns of what he is accused of. This is going to be an interesting week,' he said to himself in utter disbelief. 'I must speak to Tullius before I give this mess further thought.'

The cena at the mayor's house was well under way when Tullius walked into the dining room on the heels of the servant who announced his arrival.

"Oh!" said Tullius, realising that the mayor had a cena guest. "I do apologise for the intrusion."

"Not at all my friend," sang the mayor, getting up and embracing the physician. He was well aware of the fact that Tullius knew the governor, but nevertheless, he thought it best to attempt to formally introduce him.

"Permit me me to introduce to you the governor of the Province... Sabinus Celorius."

"Whom I am most fortunate to know," interrupted the physician with a big smile and nodding to Sabinus.

Sabinus got up and warmly embraced Tullius much to Cornelia's surprise, who having recently returned from the visit to her aunt, thanked God for finding her friend the priest out of disguise.

"Have you eaten Tullius?" she asked as her husband and Sabinus resumed their seats.

"No," he said, with a big smile, "and I'm starving."

"Please be seated," said Atelius pointing to a cushion beside his wife's. Tullius pressed Cornelia's hands in the manner of greeting and sat down.

"You are looking very well," said the physician addressing the governor.

"I feel very well, thanks to you," said Sabinus with a smile that lit up his habitually sober face.

"I merely did my duty as a physician, and luckily for you I succeeded," said Tullius with a laugh.

"I hate modesty," said Sabinus. "You are a very good physician, and a very warm-hearted man. You can be as embarrassed as you like, but that is what I think."

Cornelia and Atelius burst into applause, and laughingly chided their friend for his humility.

The governor proceeded to tell Cornelia and her husband the terrible ordeal that he had undergone the previous year, and how Tullius and his good friend Marcellus had between them saved his life. Atelius listened with amazement as to how this upcoming drama was going to unfold. Cornelia was simply fascinated. She had not been told the story before.

"You are going to be quite shocked," said Cornelia, addressing the governor with sudden sadness in her eyes. "When you meet Marcellus."

Atelius shuddered. Tullius cringed.

"Is he infirm?" asked Sabinus, with great concern in his baggy eyes.

Cornelia caught the warning in her husband's eyes, but it was too late.

"He is in prison," she said with a fallen countenance.

Sabinus was perplexed by the expression on her face, and the news she gave him. His brow knitted into furrows.

"In prison?" he exclaimed in wonderment; his eyes widening. "What could he possibly have been accused of?"

The governor looked at each of his table companions with searching eyes.

Silence reigned for a few moments. Then, almost in a whisper, Tullius said.

"Of being a Christian."

Sabinus sat in his room. It overlooked the village square. He got up and went to the window. The square was empty and quiet. The lemon trees that bordered it, caught by the light of the torches on the posts around the square, shimmered in the light breeze that gently caressed their leaves; their double shadows falling in different directions, as the moonlight vied for prominence over the light of the torches.

He soon became enraptured with the power of that rural serenity which he pleasurably experienced but a few times each year; when his duties took him into the country and away from the busy city that was home to him.

'When I retire from public office,' he mused, absorbed in his pleasant reverie, 'I think I shall come to live in a place like this, where I will not need to be constantly on my guard as to what I say, or be suspicious of people whom I have to deal with. I shall be as candid and understanding as these people are; unambitious; living and enjoying each day as it comes; eating well; enjoying the fresh air; the beauty of the countryside; and making new friends.

Suddenly the thought of his friend in jail, burst with a jarring dissonance on his tranquil mind.

'That noble creature Marcellus.' he said to himself. 'In prison? On the accusation of a thief? That's ridiculous!... How am I going to save him? The law is clear on the matter. Until these confounded emperors cease to consider themselves gods, there is no hope for the Christians. They are considered harmful, simply because they are harmless.'

Sabinus walked away from the window. The fairy-tale feeling had evaporated. He sat on his comfortable bed with his head in his hands, following his now more disturbing thoughts.

'How can they consider themselves gods? They all die. Some of them have been mad. This one we have now. Caligula; he is quite mad. But one cannot even insinuate it to one's colleagues. No one can be trusted. I owe this man and his friend the physician my life, I must find a way to help him.'

The following morning Sabinus visited the prison. The centurion whose name was Augustus, met him as he entered, and after saluting him smartly, gave him a scroll with a list of the inmates' names and crimes.

The governor immediately spotted Marcellus' name and asked to be taken to him.

"I shall start with him," said Sabinus as they walked down the dimly lit corridor that ended at Marcellus' cell.

"This one is an unfortunate case," pointed out Augustus shaking his head. "A most unfortunate case," he repeated as if to himself.

"Marcellus!" called out the centurion. "The governor is here to see you."

The prisoner, who was asleep, quickly woke up and sat on his bed just as Augustus reached the cell.

"Please let me in," said Sabinus.

The jailor did as he was asked, and then stood by the door awaiting further instructions.

Marcellus kept silent and still.

"You may lock the door if you wish, and leave me with the prisoner," said Sabinus.

Augustus did as he was bid and left the two men to themselves.

"I am most distressed," said Sabinus, embracing Marcellus warmly; Augustus having gone. "Your friend Tullius, the physician, whom I met at the mayor's house told me the whole tragic story. I noticed that the centurion is also unhappy about your situation."

"Yes," said Marcellus, "he greatly regrets having publicly asked me at my accuser's instigation if I was a Christian. We Christians will not deny our living God Yeshua."

"Needless to say," said Sabinus, "I shall do all in my power and more, to have you set free. But in the case of Christians, the present law allows for no alternative but death as you already know.

The two men talked for a while longer. Finally, Sabinus got up and as he made ready to call the jailor, he said.

"For now, I shall use the only tactic that I have at my disposal.... Procrastination." He walked to the cell door and turning, said. "I may have to bring you up to Ariminum if Rome tries to get a hold of you. But if I delay reporting the matter, because of my forgetfulness of course, no one is really going to be concerned about your terrible crime." He smiled at Marcellus and called out for the centurion.

Marcellus felt more at peace after having talked with the governor. He knew that Sabinus would try every legal trick at his disposal to set him free. He knelt down and thanked Yeshua for his good fortune, even if it was only temporary. At least he would continue to be treated well and receive food and visits from his friends. He hoped Rufina would be allowed to visit him.

His predicament gave him much time for thought, and the miraculous veil that he had been so involved with once, found its way into his wandering mind. He did not see how it could help him in his present predicament, but wondered how Procula was keeping, and if she had been able to cure her husband's nightmares with it.

'Will I ever see them again?' he mused.

* * * * *

The day of the trials arrived. The governor sat in a small hall in the Legion barracks. The mayor and two other local dignitaries attended. All sat glumly awaiting the first prisoner to be called in.

The centurion announced the first prisoner, and the crime that he was accused of.

The hapless man sat on a wooden bench with hands tied in front of him. Two Legionnaires guarded the only door into the room. The offender was promptly dealt with and taken back to his cell.

"Next!" cried Sabinus.

"Next!" repeated the guard at the door addressing his mates who waited in the corridor with the two remaining prisoners.

Pompinus was the second prisoner to be brought in. On being asked, he confirmed his name.

"You have been accused," said the governor, his eyes scrutinising the accused, "of regularly stealing from your employer Fulvius' vineyards. How do you plead? Guilty or not guilty."

Pompinus did not answer. The governor repeated the question. Still there was no answer.

Sabinus gave the man a long enquiring look, and receiving no response said.

"Your employers have in their keeping as evidence, and I have seen them; containers of wine bearing the name of their vineyards that you have been selling for a number of years without their knowledge or authorisation.

Do you deny that?

Finally, Pompinus answered, "No."

"Very well," said Sabinus throwing a stern look at the man. "I sentence you to twenty years in the mines."

Sabinus, though the law would not support it, actually sentenced Pompinus not so much for having stolen, but for maliciously ruining the life of a just and innocent man.

"Who's next?" he cried, as the thief was led away.

Marcellus passed his convicted accuser in the corridor. The two men exchanged resentful looks.

"You should have gone for my deal," hissed Pompinus, sneering at his enemy. "We would both have been better off."

Marcellus was brought into the room and sat on the bench; his hands tied in front of him.

He, also confirmed his name on being asked.

The governor looked at him with pretended seriousness.

"You have admitted to being a Christian. Have you not?" asked Sabinus. The tone of his voice expressing great severity.

"Yes," answered the prisoner.

"I could sentence you to death right now. But we are not prepared for executions here in Salistra," said Sabinus. Turning to the mayor and his associates, he asked. "Have you ever had an execution here?"

The mayor looked at his colleagues. They shook their heads.

"No," said the Atelius with silent relief.

Sabinus gave Marcellus another harsh look.

"You have been found guilty of the crime of being a Christian. You will be sentenced and executed at a later date in Ariminum. In the meantime, having learnt that you are the son of a senator, and that you honourably held the rank of tribune in the Legion for three years, I will place you under house arrest until the time of your sentencing. You are to remain at your farmhouse and within the limits of your property here in Umbria. On your honour you will not travel anywhere without my prior permission.

Since Marcellus was the last of the three prisoners to be judged, the moment he was sent back to his cell, Sabinus pronounced the proceedings ended. All parties, taking their leave of one another, went their separate ways.

During the cena at the mayor's house that night, Tullius, Atelius, and Cornelia, thanked Sabinus for the postponement of Marcellus' sentence, and sending him home even if with strict restrictions.

"Whilst there is life," said Sabinus with a nod, "there is hope."

They all understood that the governor would do his utmost to delay the deadly sentence.

Two mornings later and having spent a few enjoyable days with Atelius and Cornelia, whom he now counted among his friends, the portly governor, once more in the saddle, led the 'turma' out of the village square and on his way to Ariminum, where sooner or later Marcellus would have to follow; short of a miracle.

CHAPTER THIRTEEN

A CHANGE

Tullius looked with disappointment in his eyes at the unexpected young Christian visitor who sat across from him in his living room. He gave grave consideration to the news that the latter had just divulged to him. The news will surprise you my good and faithful reader, as it surprised our hero.

Linus had found an urgent need for Tullius' services and had sent a young priest to tend to his flock in Salistra, Menorum, and vicinity. It was not to be a permanent appointment for Tullius, but it was however a rather unusual one, and one that would perhaps keep him busy for quite some time.

At least, that is what Alphonsus, the new priest had been asked to relay to him, without giving him much more information as to the nature of his assignment.

Alphonsus, was a potter. He would have to find a suitable location where he could build his kiln and set up shop to sell his pieces. That would allow him to make a living and 'fish for men' at the same time.

With the young priest's needs in mind, Tullius immediately introduced him to Atelius, who was best positioned to help him find and set up his shop.

The mayor and Cornelia were most distressed at the prospective loss of their friend but promised non-the-less to do their best for the new priest.

Despite the fact that Tullius had envisaged a like scenario, he had never for a moment expected to see it materialise so soon. He had been in Menorum for four years and had begun to feel that it was home to him; especially as Rufina was relatively nearby. Though he persisted in his celibate life, it was very important to him to be able to spend time with her on his regular monthly visits to Marcellus' farmhouse.

Marcellus continued under house arrest. Sergius, the governor had not visited Menorum for the last two years, as there had been no serious crimes to judge since the sentencing of Pompinus. Smaller crimes or infractions, were dealt with by Atelius and two other elected officials. The guilty culprits would be publicly whipped and sent home with certain restrictions to their liberty, or made to pay fines and perform acts of restitution to the offended parties.

The governor's behaviour was much appreciated by Tullius and Marcellus in particular, who soon learnt from the friendly Centurion Augustus his former jailor, (who acted as his supervisor on behalf of the law,) that all the Legionaries who had been at Marcellus' internment and trial, had been posted elsewhere. As a result, the convicting of Marcellus was all but forgotten around the area.

Tullius rode into the courtyard of Marcellus' farm with a very heavy heart. As usual, Rex was there to greet him expecting some loving pats. Aurelia announced his arrival jubilantly from the kitchen. Barely had he dismounted than Rufina, dashing out of the house, ran into his arms.

"My love," she smiled with unrestrained joy in her heart, "why did you stay away so long? I have missed you so."

"I have had much to do," he replied, trying to sustain a smile. He took down his baggage from the horse, patted Rex' who wagged his tail happily, and taking her hand led her into the house.

"I don't expect to see Marcellus at this time of day," said Tullius, "but where is Marcia?"

"She is also in the vineyard with him and Sartorius, who is constantly teaching her things about the vines. I rarely see her before cena time."

They walked through the corridor. Tullius stopped to be hugged by Aurelia and Jocasta, who awaited him at the kitchen door. "

"I have a good hearty soup for your cena," said Aurelia with a warm smile. "You look thinner. You must be praying too much and fasting too often I suspect."

"I am at your mercy for the next few days I'm afraid," he laughed, and followed Rufina to the table in the garden where the trellis, heavily covered in vines, provided a delicious shade at that early hour of the afternoon.

They sat next to each other. She quickly gave him an ardent kiss which he affectionately returned. He took her face in his hands, and engaging her captivating eyes, he said with apparent regret and pain.

"I have to leave you my love, for an indefinite amount of time I'm afraid."

Her eyes suddenly brimmed with tears which soon spilled over and rolled down her lovely face. He wiped them with his shawl. She, taking his hand, kissed it and muttered.

"Linus, I suppose, needs you somewhere else. Just as we have always feared."

Aurelia who was taking some refreshments to them, stopped in her tracks as she was about to enter the garden. She realised by their serious countenances and intimate gestures that there was something of consequence afoot and quickly returned to the kitchen.

'They'll call if they need anything,' she said to herself with a shake of the head.

"Yes," continued Tullius. "Linus sent a young priest to take over my flock. He needs me to do other work for him, and it will entail being constantly on the move. Alphonsus, the new priest tells me that he needs a man with my experience and knowledge of disguises. The work, he says is of the greatest importance."

"That means that you will be constantly in danger, my love." She burst into tears again.

He was in the midst of drying her eyes with his shawl once more, when Marcia came running into the garden followed at a short distance by a limping Sartorius.

Tullius got up and spread his arms to receive her. She ran into them with a cry of joy. He swung her around and gently put her down again, giving her red cheek a kiss.

"You have grown again!" he taunted. "Soon I will not be able to spin you around anymore."

"Where is your grandmother?" he asked. "I have not seen her yet. Please go find her I must talk to you both."

Marcia's bright blue eyes registered a happy smile as she undertook her errand.

Sartorius shook hands with Tullius, said a few kind words, and excusing himself, went off to his ablutions.

Rufina was quite distraught. She had never believed that Tullius would be sent away from Salistra. Though she knew that it was probably a very necessary mission for her beloved friend, she could not help harbouring a certain resentful feeling towards Linus. All her hopes and prayers that somehow Tullius would change his mind and marry her, were now dashed. She had to admit that his reticence to commit himself to her had been justified. If he was going to be moving around all the time, how could he drag a family with him. It just did not make sense. With great sadness she resigned herself to her fate.

'It is God's will!' she told herself with sternness. 'It must and will be done.' She wiped here eyes with her palla.

'Yeshua, give me strength to bear it for your sake,' she prayed and walked off by herself to the pond, where amidst her continuing tears, she sat vacantly contemplating the water lilies.

Tullius watched Rufina walk away with a terrible sense of loss. He might never see her again after this visit he thought.

Presently, Marcia appeared with Ignatia in tow.

Tullius got up and went to embrace her with warmth in his heart. She in turn embraced him with apparent warmth, though with some reticence which for some unaccountable reason, inhibited her confused soul.

"I shall be leaving you all soon for quite some time." said Tullius, withdrawing from her embrace. Marcia listened with tears in her eyes. She had grown quite fond of Tullius.

Addressing Ignatia, the priest said with hope in his heart.

"I really do not know how long this new mission will take me to accomplish, so I would love to baptise you and Marcia before I leave. That is if you are ready for that sacrament.

"I'm ready," cried out Marcia, with enthusiasm. She wiped her eyes with the back of her hand and managed a smile.

"I wish," said Ignatia, "that I could say the same, but unfortunately I cannot as yet."

Tullius was saddened by the response and as Rufina rejoined the group around the table, he prayed that the new priest would eventually succeed where he had failed.

"Very well young lady," he said as he took Marcia's hand. "Tomorrow, if Marcellus gives me his permission, I shall baptise you. He is your father here on earth as I am sure that Rufina has told you. Your real daddy is in heaven with our beloved Lord Yeshua. As is your mom."

Marcellus and Evandros suddenly made their appearance in the garden simultaneously with Sartorius who came out of the house fresh from his ablutions.

Tullius went to greet them and the three friends embraced heartily.

"It's about time you remembered us," said Marcellus. "We have missed you my friend."

Marcellus sat down for a few moments, but promptly got up again and dashed off to his ablutions, followed by Evandros.

"I shall be with you all in a few moments," he called back.

The conversation was rather restricted. All awaited the return of Marcellus, when all the news would be unfolded.

Ignatia, felt some relief at Tullius' leaving; perhaps for good. She thought that possibly her beautiful daughter, would meet some young well-to-do vintner, who would fall in love with her and give her the stable type of life that she, her mother, personally wished for her. Rufina was now twenty-three years old, and her mother was concerned about her daughter wasting her life waiting for this man, who made no commitment and lived a life of uncertainty.

Rufina, in turn, thought of the terrible loneliness that would engulf her at the loss of her beloved Tullius, and privately promised herself that no one would ever take his place. She was also quite distressed at her mother's decision not to adopt the faith.

'Perhaps in the future the new priest would be able to win her for Yeshua,' she mused.

Marcia, was saddened by her grandmother's refusal to be baptised, but she was now nine years old and could make up her own mind. She would then be a Christian like her sainted parents, and that, she thought, would greatly please them if they only knew.

The following morning, Marcia's Baptism was performed by a happy Tullius, and a celebration followed, bringing much joy to the girl's heart. Marcellus promised her a pony of her own which he would teach her to ride. Rufina gave her a beautiful bracelet, and Ignatia did her part by presenting her an heirloom pair of gold earrings.

A week later, Tullius made ready to leave for Rome. Marcellus would gladly have given his friend one of his Arabians, but knowing the trouble that they could brew, he desisted. Instead he made him accept a gift of money which he said, was to further the Lord's work, which Tullius could not refuse.

Having at last taken sad leave of all the others at the farmhouse, he walked out of the courtyard accompanied by Rufina and away from the house where they would be alone. Rex of course did not count, but he walked alongside the pair regardless.

"Some day God willing, I shall come back to you," he said taking her in his arms. "Things may be different then. This persecution cannot last for ever." He lovingly stroked her long silky hair.

"Look after the little one. Make sure she grows in the love of Yeshua."

He kissed her tenderly. "I shall always love you," he said. "Pray for me, as I shall constantly pray for you." He looked deeply into her watery eyes.

"If someone captures your love when I am gone, and offers you a better future, know that your happiness is my greatest concern. Do what your heart tells you. I shall never reproach you for that."

She kissed him ardently. "I am yours forever. Don't even think of things being any other way. I shall always love you. Come back to me whenever you can. I shall be waiting right here."

They embraced one last time.

"May the Lord keep you," he said with a forced smile.

"The Lord go with you and keep you safe." She braved a smile; her eyes wet with tears.

Tullius mounted, urged the horse forward, and slowly rode away. She watched and waved until he was out of sight. Rex led her back to the farm house; a cloud of sadness accompanying them.

* * * * *

Linus sat in his room in the house of one of his flock. He was moved around almost on a monthly basis. His people felt that if he lodged temporarily with different families, he would be less likely to be exposed to the surveillance of the Roman authorities; if indeed that was the case. Invariably, he would be housed with the more affluent members of his flock. The wealthy members having more influence in civil and commercial matters were better respected and less likely to be suspected of being Christians, or harbouring them.

The saintly man found that arrangement easier for keeping in contact with his flock, and in the performing of the 'Breaking of the Bread' service. He reasoned that his living in a large well protected house, would keep prying eyes outside its walls, and would allow for small groups of visitors to be received on the occasional evening without arousing suspicion.

As he sat looking out of his window at the well groomed and colourful garden, his thoughts were greatly disturbed by a recurring situation which existed, and as usual he was powerless to prevent. The children of Christians who had been put to death, were being sold into slavery at the slave market in Rome.

What could possibly be done to save some of those innocents from such a horrible fate. Even if it could only be carried out once, it would save a number of young lives. They were subject to unmentionable atrocities with little hope of salvation, temporal or spiritual. He held his head in his hands in utter mental anguish.

'How many had already been subjected to that life of horrors?' he thought.

'I simply must find a way,' he told himself with solemn determination. Then, of a sudden, as if through the inspiration of the Holy Spirit, to Whom he constantly prayed, and feeling His awesome presence, a possible solution presented itself.

It would require the skill, creativity, and dedication of some very talented person, to carry out so difficult a mission. He suspected it could be done. But who and where was that person?

After some pondering on the people available to him, Tullius came to mind.

'Yes! He might be the man I need,' he said to himself. 'Judging by what I have heard of him, he is a master at disguise, and a very creative thinker. Yes! I must summon him right away.'

Linus fell on his knees and thanked the Holy Spirit.

Two weeks later, Linus welcomed Tullius with a fatherly embrace, and a sad smile.

"I apologise for taking you away from your parishioners and friends. If the need was not great, I would have left you to enjoy the fruits of your labours, which have been plentiful and well earned. I need you here now though."

The senior priest walked over to a desk where there was a pitcher with orange juice, and poured some into two cups that were at hand.

"Have a cup of orange juice," he said, handing one to Tullius. He sat down on one of the floor cushions. The priest followed his example.

"I have a very difficult mission for you Tullius," began Linus, taking a sip of his juice.

"Your prowess as a masquerade artist has reached my ears, and for that reason, I need you to do things that others cannot do. You will not be 'fishing for men'. You will be rescuing them.

Tullius was surprised that his disguises had been reported to his superior, and he wondered who in his flock had been the informant. He took a sip of juice and gave Linus a questioning look.

"What do you have in mind?"

"There are a variety of projects or missions if you prefer, to be carried out," began Linus, engaging his subordinate's eyes with expectancy. I need a man of your creativity and courage around here." He sipped his juice and continued in a moderate tone.

"Though we Christians are committed to non-violence in our behaviour, it does not mean that we are not going to try and escape from our tribulations whenever we can. Sometimes we can hide or disappear if we receive evidence that we are about to be arrested. Other times, we might want to be rescued and distanced from the mad persecutions in Rome." Linus took yet another sip of his juice. Tullius did likewise.

"Where shall I live? and with what means?" asked the confused priest.

"You will stay with the people you are working among. They will feed you, and give you a bed to sleep in. I shall see to your expenses. I receive money from many of my flock who contribute to the support of the Church. Everyone contributes one way or another. If not with money, with assistance. I shall give you whatever monies you need to live and accomplish your missions."

Tullius realised that this was a special position that Linus had decided to create, and he might be committed to it for the rest of his life. He accepted Yeshua's will with great love and dedication, and silently prayed for success in whatever venture his superior would assign him.

"Very well, Linus. I am at your service," said the resigned priest with a smile.

"Good. My prayers, and indeed the prayers of all the Christians of Rome attend you."

Linus stood up and walked to the window once more. Looking out at the garden, he explained the plight of some nine children of varying ages, from toddlers to a couple of eight-year-olds, who were being held by the auctioneers at their place of business. The place was equipped with cells for their prisoners awaiting the next auction day.

He turned around to face Tullius who remained sitting and attentively listening to Linus' story.

"That auction will take place two days from now. The coming Dies Solis. Do you think you can rescue these children before then?"

Tullius stared past the bishop into the bright blue sky outside the window. Linus waited patiently. A good interval passed. Then, he said.

"If you can supply me with three or four men and three carts, complete with donkeys, and a horse for myself, I have a plan that may work."

"You will have all the help you need," said the older priest with great hope in his eyes. "The children, once released will be given to Christian families well away from Rome with whom they will find much love and be brought up to love the Lord."

"I need to meet immediately with someone who knows the auctioneers' place, and who can give me some idea of the number of guards that I am likely to deal with," said the priest.

Linus promised to attend to everything with promptitude, and off went the priest to call on the first member of his rescue party.

It was the evening of Dies Saturnis. The day before the slave auctions. An old man leaning on a staff, approached the door of the auctioneer's jail and knocked on it boldly. The door was opened a few moments later by a man of medium stature with a mop of dirty black hair, and a weather-beaten face.

He looked at the old man with disdain. "You drunken old fool," he said. "What do you want here?"

"Heh! Heh! Heh!" laughed the old man, taking a small bag from his tunic, and dangling it in front of the man. "How would you fellows in there like to win some of these nice coins that I have in this little bag?"

The jailor made a snatch at the bag, but Tullius, (who was in fact the 'old man' in disguise) was quicker and pulled it back.

"You have to beat this old fellow with your dice first. Heh! Heh! Heh!"

"Have him come in," said a gruff voice from inside the jail."

Tullius leaning heavily on his staff shuffled into the room. A stout man sat at a table with a pitcher of wine and two cups in front of him. He motioned for the old man to sit down opposite him. The other jailor sat on one side of the table between the two.

"So you think you can take our money?" sneered the fat one.

"There is a good chance of that. You will have to play to find out. Where are your dice?" asked Tullius.

"Have a mouthful of our wine," said the man who answered the door.

"No thanks. I never drink when I play." said Tullius.

"Please yourself old man," he scoffed.

The stout one got up, and going to a nearby shelf, took down a small wooden box and returned to the table. His slimmer partner sat waiting impatiently to get started.

"Seeing that you will be paying," said the fat one sitting down heavily on his stool and giving the newcomer a feline smile. "We will use these newer dice." Opening the box, he rolled the dice onto the table. His partner quickly snatched them.

The room being very dimly lit favoured Tullius. His make-up would not be so easily scrutinised, and it would help with the trick which he proposed to carry out when the opportunity presented itself.

The game started. Tullius awaited the opportunity to put his plan into action. The men became very engrossed in the game. Especially the fat one who happened to be winning.

Tullius who had been watching, saw that their wine cups were almost empty. He needed to get the pair away from the table and wine jug for a few moments. He had brought with him a special sleeping powder that he had concocted from a recipe that a world traveller friend had given him a few years before.

The players settled their accounts after each game. Tullius held his little bag in his left hand whilst tossing the dice with his right. Having lost that particular toss, he reached into his bag fora coin to pay once more. He pretended to fumble as his fingers reached into the bag, with the result that he let it fall on the floor; the coins rolling all around the room.

All three were up on their feet in an instant. The two jailers got down on their knees looking for each coin. Tullius took advantage of the opportunity he had created, and quickly taking the pouch of powder from his tunic, emptied it into the pitcher of wine, and swirled it around.

"Now don't you be keeping any of my money. I can't bend down to pick those coins. I am depending on your honesty," bewailed 'the old man' followed by a feigned spell of coughing.

"I think we got'm all," said the slimmer one handing Tullius the bag. "We'll win it back from you soon enough."

They refilled their cups, and the game began again. Shortly after, their cups being half drained, the jailors began to feel weak and drowsy. They became suspicious and looking at

Tullius with a scowl, reached for their daggers. Tullius held his breath. The fat one, dagger in hand reached over the table for the old man, but halfway through the motion his head fell with a heavy thump on the table. The other, who sat beside Tullius, drew his dagger but the priest held his wrist before he could raise his arm to strike. There was very little power in the man's arm, and as he wrestled with Tullius, he slumped back and fell off his stool heavily onto the floor unconscious.

The priest, still acting his 'old man' masquerade went in search of the prisoners. There was a corridor nearby leading to some steps down to the dungeons. The way was lit by torches placed at intervals on the walls. He soon found the children's cell. The key hung on the opposite wall. "Children wake up!" he shouted taking the key and opening the cell door.

The children were soon on their feet.

"Get ready to follow me I am taking you out of here," he said, his eyes scanning the cell.

"What about us?" Shouted an adult male voice further down the corridor.

Tullius told the children to be ready to go, but to quietly stay in their cell until he returned.

There were two other cells. One with men and one with women. The keys were also hanging on the wall opposite each cell. The physician opened the doors and told the people to run for their lives as quickly and quietly as possible.

The cells emptied with amazing rapidity. The elated prisoners giving their thanks as they passed; ran through the corridor; up the stairs; and past the sleeping guards to freedom.

"Now children," said Tullius, follow me quickly and very quietly.

He was about to go when he spotted a little body lying on the floor of the cell. Going over he stooped and felt the child. He was running a fever and made no effort to get up. The physician picked him up, and heading out of the cell, directed the children to follow him.

Waiting outside the building, were a few men with three donkey carts and a horse for Tullius. They made ready to take the children away.

Tullius instructed the children to do as the men said, and soon they were divided among the three carts and covered up; some with hay; some with bags and things. Away they went, all in different directions as had been planned by the priest. He himself took the sick child, a boy of about six years of age with him on his horse and made for the house where he was staying.

The following day, Rome was aghast with the news of the freeing of the slaves. There was to be no auctioning on that particular day, and that, had never happened before. The guards had been arrested, and everyone found the story of the old man most amusing.

Linus was beside himself with joy on hearing of the successful mission.

"Not only children," he told his hostess, "but all the slaves in the place." He could hardly wait to congratulate the clever priest.

The clever priest however, had been busy all night trying to save the life of the little boy he had rescued. Tullius had tried everything he knew to make the boy well; including constant prayer. However as morning dawned, and after having been baptised by the priest, the child slipped away.

"Rejoice, my dear lad," said Tullius as he and his host prepared him for burial.

"You will now be with your martyred parents. You, have also been martyred. But in your case, for your 'future' faith."

The boy was secretly buried that same day in a small out of the way cemetery in a nameless grave.

Linus, welcomed Tullius with open arms.

"The Lord bless you my dear friend," he cried, throwing his arms around the happy priest.

"I cannot wait to hear how you accomplished this amazing feat."

"All your prayers were obviously heard, because everything went without a hitch. Well... almost," explained Tullius, giving his superior a faint smile, saying.

"Please sit down and tell me all about it."

Linus poured some juice into a cup from a jug that was on a table beside him and handed it to his priest. He then repeated the process for himself, and with an expectant look and the enthusiasm of a child, gesticulated with his hand for Tullius to begin.

The priest recounted the whole mission; beginning with the planning, and then the execution, which was aided at the escape stage by various members of Linus' flock.

Linus was so absorbed in the story, that he did not even remember to sip his juice. He sat there, cup in hand, totally spellbound until Tullius had finished.

"I must ask you to keep my identity secret," said the priest, taking a mouthful of juice. "The men who helped me did not see me out of disguise and know nothing of me other than I am a Christian like them. The only ones who know who I am in person, are Sabina and her husband Marcus, with whom I am presently staying. Incidentally, they took care of the burial of the little boy who died.

"That was the sad part of the story," decried Linus, solemnly bowing his head in a short prayer. "But the other children," he exulted. "They will now be adopted by Christian couples who will make them a part of their family and give them parental love and a Christian upbringing...As indeed their unfortunate parents would have done. I am so happy for those innocent little ones." He clapped his hands and smiled with a meaningful tilt of the head.

"I rejoice also for all those other unfortunate souls that got away," continued the senior priest. "Perhaps some of them will receive the Grace of our Blessed Lord, if they were not already members of my flock. They will learn that their rescuer was a Christian, as has already been popularly suspected. They too will be won over to us. They are all God's children and have a right to live in freedom."

Tullius was invited to stay for the cena. However the matter of the rescue of the slaves which was brought up by the family at whose house the Linus temporarily resided, was discussed by the knowing pair as if they too found the news surprising.

"My dear friend," said Linus as he accompanied his priest to the door. "Yeshua will surely reward you for what you have done. It is imperative that you remain incognito. I may need you again for other difficult projects. The Lord go with you. Please continue to minister to my flock for the time being. I shall call you when I need you."

Tullius left his jubilant superior and walked off to his lodgings.

The following morning, as Tullius ventured out into the street where he lived. He was almost swept away by a great crowd of people on their way to the Forum and Senate to celebrate the sudden assassination of Caligula, whom they vehemently denounced as they walked.

The buzz caused by the rescue of the slaves the previous day was all but extinguished by the new frenzy that suddenly threw Rome into a festive mood.

Tullius joined the throng. As they marched, he questioned a number of citizens regarding the auspicious event.

The general consensus seemed to be, that a Republic was inevitable, as no worthy candidate could be found to replace Caligula. This did not displease the people, who for the most part were fed up with the tyrannical rule of the emperors, and felt that the Senate could handle the workings of the empire much more equitably and effectively if left to their own resources without having to please a dictator.

The Forum soon filled with people. All the streets leading to the Senate were clogged. It was almost impossible to move. Every now and then a senator would appear at the Senate's massive doorway and give the crowd some inkling of what was occurring inside. Much was indeed happening among them. They were divided in finding a solution to the sudden situation, which though majorly welcomed, nevertheless had to be resolved for the establishment of the new Government.

As evening fell, it became obvious to everyone waiting that an impasse had been reached, and the matter might not be solved that night.

Of a sudden the crowd in the Forum parted with great difficulty to allow a group of mounted soldiers to pass. The Pretorians, for so they were, forced their way through, shielding a man who was soon recognised as Claudius 'the idiot.' A hush came over the people as they awaited the outcome of this new development. Some thought that Claudius had been arrested and was going to be summarily sentenced to death. Others, better informed on the personality of the so- called 'idiot', speculated on the intentions of the Pretorian Guard. After all, why would they not have quietly assassinated him also if a republic was to be declared. Why bring him to the Senate?

It was with great concern that the citizens of Rome awaited some concrete news.

A half hour before midnight, the monumental doors of the Senate opened wide, and there, illuminated by many torches and to every one's amazement, stood Claudius Germanicus in a pristine white toga with the golden crown of the late Caligula on his head. He spread out his arms and gave the people a big fatherly smile.

The crowd erupted with enthusiastic cheers.

"Hail Caesar! Hail Claudius! Hail Claudius!"

The chant went on for some time. The new emperor was obviously enjoying himself. He kept waving to the crowd and chatting with the senators and military officers that attended him.

After a while, that mostly jubilant crowd began to disperse. The doors of the Senate had closed, and the Emperor and dignitaries were waiting for the streets to be relatively clear so that Claudius could ride his chariot back to the palace accompanied by his Pretorian escort.

Tullius approached the imposing Senate building and sat on the steps. He needed time to think.

'Perhaps,' he said to himself as he watched the crowd dispersing; many with lighted torches in their hands, 'the Christians will no longer be persecuted. This man has a look of honesty and even kindness about him. He did have a speech impediment, but what he said was well structured and sensible. I would hardly call the man an idiot as Rome has been led to believe.'

He moved up a few steps closer to one of the majestic columns and into the light of the many torches that illumined the handsome facade.

It would not surprise me,' he continued thinking, 'if he has been playing the fool just in case the madman whom he is succeeding thought of having him eliminated, since he is certainly one of the family.' Suddenly a wonderful thought occurred to him.

'Marcellus could be a free man now.' His handsome mouth spread out into a smile as he looked around him with obvious joy in his face.

"You seem very happy that Claudius is our new emperor."

The voice; a female voice, pulled him out of his reverie and his eyes focused on a woman who sat on the steps a few paces away from him.

"Yes," he replied. "He appears to care for the welfare of his people."

"That will be a most pleasant change," said the woman, and turning continued to converse on the same subject with three others that were with her.

"Won't you join us?" asked one of the men in the little group.

"Thank you, but I must leave, I have already spent too much time sitting here thinking."

He promptly took leave of the group and made his way to his lodgings; musing over Marcellus' good fortune, and how happy Rufina and the family were going to be if things mapped out as he was hoping.

'Perhaps,' he thought, 'the governor will rescind Marcellus' previous conviction seeing that this is a different administration. I doubt there is a written law requiring the persecution of Christians with its automatic death penalty. It was simply Caligula's hatred and madness that created such a reign of terror for us.'

Tullius arrived home to a happy Marcus and Sabina. They were still up and waiting to hear what he thought of the new emperor who had surprised all of Rome.

* * * * *

The news of Caligula's assassination came as a great relief and filled the house of Marcellus with vibrant hope. Prayers of thanksgiving flowed through the household, and fervent requests to Yeshua for Marcellus' release from his deadly conviction became the first order of things during the next few uncertain but hopeful days.

Centurion Augustus appeared at the farmhouse the very next day after the news of the coronation of the new Emperor Claudius had been received by military courier at the barracks in Salistra. He had become a good friend of the family, and as he dismounted from his horse, Rex welcomed him in his usual rambunctious way.

Marcellus was at home. Glad to have received news of Caligula's death only the day before, he did not have the desire for work that day. He opted to sit at his table in the garden and daydream about his chances of being free once again. On hearing Rex announce a friendly visitor, he hoped against hope that it was Tullius who had arrived. Then he thought:

'Surely that's ridiculous, he couldn't possibly have gotten here so soon.'

"Where are you Marcellus!" The call reverberated around the house as the centurion entered the hallway and stood waiting for his friend to appear.

"Here I am," shouted back Marcellus from the corridor on his way to meet the visitor and recognising Augustus' strong voice.

"I am sick and tired of being your jailor," laughed the centurion embracing his friend.

"Do I really have a chance of being free?" asked Marcellus, with great hope.

"I am not as conversant with the law as your good friend the governor," said Augustus with a smile. "But I venture to guess, that in a change of government, certain laws, especially those which are non-constitutional but are simply the personal whim of each emperor, can be rescinded. If the worst comes to the worst, the matter can always be appealed to Claudius, who has just been crowned and who will certainly be more magnanimous than his predecessor. I suspect that the governor will simply tear up all material evidence concerning your trial. Who's to know? The original accuser will never be back. Those mines that he was sent to, finish off even the toughest of men within ten years."

He walked with Marcellus into the garden where Jocasta, soon made an appearance bearing refreshments for her boss and his very welcome visitor.

"And I," continued Augustus taking off his helmet, "being a military man, have no say in anything. I have but to follow orders and keep things to myself."

"I thank you my friend, for those kind and encouraging words," said Marcellus gesturing to the centurion to sit as they reached the table." I feel privileged to have you as a friend."

"The privilege sir, is all mine," said the congenial soldier with a bow and a playful smile on his rugged, kindly face.

At this point of the conversation, Rufina made her appearance, sending Augustus to his feet in deference to her. He greatly admired Rufina and it was quite apparent to her brother, who prayed that his military friend would not make any advances to her. Tullius was like a brother to him, and he could not bear the prospect of anyone else, even Augustus, falling in love with his beautiful sister.

"Hello, Augustus," she greeted with her usual lovely smile, and sat down beside her brother. He sat down again.

The news from Rome with all its ramifications was discussed at length. It was not until well after an enjoyable and somewhat extended lunch, that the centurion took his leave and rode off to his duties in Salistra.

No sooner had Augustus left than Ignatia came downstairs with Marcia, whom she had been entertaining whilst the grown-ups talked around the garden table. Aurelia had carried their lunch upstairs where they had eaten privately.

Ignatia was also aware of Augustus' admiration for Rufina and felt him uncouth and totally unsuited for her daughter. She tried whenever possible to distance herself from him, even though she was in her own pompous way, grateful for the way that he treated her son.

* * * * *

Governor Sabinus was elated at the news of Caligula's assassination. His thoughts immediately recalled Marcellus and his unfortunate plight.

"Now at last," he said to himself, I can free him from his life of imprisonment and uncertainty.

He lost no time in retrieving all evidence of Marcellus' trial. A courier was dispatched to summon Centurion Augustus to Ariminum at his earliest convenience.

* * * * *

Pontius Pilate received the news of Caligula's assassination with relief. He had a feeling that Claudius, whom he had met once prior to his going to Judea, would certainly be a better emperor. He had struck Pontius as being a mild man, interested in philosophy and art but without touting his knowledge to everyone he met. Pontius remembered having to lead him into discussions rather than waiting for him to initiate them. Claudius had avoided the lime light, preferring to keep to himself and displaying a disinterested attitude towards politics.

'Perhaps,' wondered the ex-Procurator, 'he may remember me, and will call me for advice on anything to do with Judea.'

Procula, who had now settled down to a quiet life by the sea with her little group of rural friends, had no desire to find her husband embroiled in the political intrigues of the Senate or the palace. She did not openly discourage Pilate from his hopes of being once more of service to Rome, but tactfully dissuaded him from such ambitions fearing that the reign of Claudius might be a short one. She had been influenced by the general consensus around the upper circles of the ineptness and gullibility of the new emperor, and she feared he would be done away with by the power mongers in the Senate who favoured the establishment of a Republic.

Pilate's nightmares were now a thing of the past, though as yet he was not aware of the reason for his emancipation. Procula diligently rose before him each morning and removed the veil from his bed cover.

'It's about time,' she said to herself one day, 'that I let him see the veil. His health has improved considerably, especially his mind. I feel he can cope with the shock of confronting the face of my beloved Yeshua. He must not be deceived into thinking that those horrible nightmares have vanished of their own accord.'

That same night, Procula prepared for the great risk that she was about to take. She spent an hour in prayer asking Yeshua to support her actions and to bring things to a happy conclusion for her husband.

Pilate got into bed. She followed. They kissed each other goodnight and soon he was fast asleep. She waited a half hour or so. Just as an unwelcome drowsiness began to overcome her, he sat up in bed. His eyes looked as if they would explode; his mouth was open in horror; and his body trembled. She shook him gently. He looked at her as if in a daze.

"It's all right dear, I shall put a stop to your nightmare," she said.

"Just lie back now and shut your eyes." He reluctantly did as he was bid.

Procula took the veil which she had concealed under her pillow, and held it, still folded, on her side of the bed and waited.

Suddenly, the nightmare returned. Once again he was struggling in horror.

"I am going to put something over you, and it's going to stop your nightmare." she promised.

"You must trust me," she said. His wild eyes searched her's.

"Now lie back."

"Yes!" he cried with some desperation in his voice, sinking back uncertainly onto his pillow.

Procula carefully draped the veil over him.

"Aah! Aah! He exhaled in utter relief.

"Now my beloved husband. You must trust me completely and know that it is through His love for you, that you are healed from your nightmares. She unfolded the veil and held it up nearer the light.

Pilate was horrified. He looked at the face of Yeshua. His hands shot up to cover his eyes.

"Where did you? What did you? Oh! Oh! Take that away! Away I say!" he cried, turning away his face; his voice breaking. "I cannot bear to look at him."

Procula, still holding the veil but letting it drop onto her arm, reached out for her husband's hand. He let her take it. A great, almost inhuman sob, as if resonating from the depth of some unearthly cavern exploded from his mouth. The evil that had been threatening to destroy him seemingly erupted from his tortured soul with volcanic force.

"Yeshua," she said with great tenderness and love, looking deeply into his staring eyes, "has been keeping you nightmare-free all these months, through the power of his love and through his image on the veil," He sobbed as if his heart would break.

"He can never forgive me," he cried. "I killed him. He was innocent...and I knew it. How can he forgive me?"

Procula had much confessing to do that night, in the hope of convincing her husband that Yeshua had forgiven him already. She had to tell him that she was a Christian, and that Yeshua the Christ had died to save all men from their sins, including him.

Pontius was utterly distraught. He remained in his bedroom for the next few days, refusing to go anywhere or see anyone other than his wife. His nightmares had vanished, but his remorse was acute, and the oppression that settled over his soul robbed him of interest in anything around him. He became obsessed with his guilt.

It seemed providential that about that time, Tullius who was not further engaged in clandestine projects, but was marking time tending to his flock, decided to visit Procula. He arrived at their house in Pyrgi a day following the onset of Pilate's depression. The worried wife received him with great delight.

"Surely you are God sent," she told him as they embraced in the atrium of her elegant house.

"It's been a long time," greeted Tullius. "You are looking well; and as beautiful as ever."

"You flatterer," she laughed.

"How is your illustrious husband keeping?"

"He is most disturbed."

She walked over to one of the couches in the atrium and sat down motioning for him to sit beside her. Her lovely eyes became glazed with tears.

"I shall explain all that has occurred since you saw him last."

Procula gave a very thorough account of her husband's condition and how she had handled the application of the veil. Finishing her story, she looked expectantly at the physician-priest.

"You have handled things most commendably," said Tullius with a sympathetic smile.

"His sense of guilt is obviously very severe. He must be made to understand that our Lord has forgiven him."

"I have already told him so," said the unhappy wife. She wiped her eyes and getting up from the couch, motioned for Tullius to follow her.

"Please come and talk to him," she said, leading the way to the peristyle. He followed.

Procula crossed the very colourful and well-appointed courtyard and stepped into a large bedroom where Pontius sat looking out into the manicured garden fronting the sea.

"I have brought you a visitor my love," she announced. "You met him once a few years ago when he healed me of that terrible pain in my stomach. He is not only a physician, but also a Christian priest. I hope he can help you."

Pilate turned, and looking at Tullius, nodded his head in greeting, but said nothing.

"I am very glad," said the priest, "that the veil has cured you of your dreadful nightmares."

Procula remained by the door making no attempt to interrupt the proceedings.

Tullius approached his patient.

"I understand your feeling of guilt in what you did. Your sin in condemning Yeshua, the Son of God to death, was as serious as a sin could be. But guilt is the first step towards sorrow; sorrow leads to repentance; and repentance by the grace of God, leads to forgiveness. If we believe in Yeshua the Christ."

Pilate did not take his eyes off Tillius as the latter spoke. The priest continued in a soothing tone of voice.

"Taking a wider view of your behaviour that dreadful but auspicious day," said Tullius sitting down beside Pontius on the couch. "I personally, would have assigned much more guilt to the Jewish authorities than to you. They, by far, committed the greater sin. You, considered Yeshua innocent. You were caught in an hour of weakness and though you suspected that you were dealing with a unique person, you did not then believe that Yeshua was actually the Son of the God of the Jews. They on the other hand, renounced him, and continue to do so even to this day with the full knowledge of who He is."

Procula approached the couch and standing behind her husband, placed her hands lightly on his shoulders.

"That day," continued Tullius, "was the day of fulfillment of a plan that God had devised, in which he had offered his only Son as a willing sacrifice to save mankind from their sins."

The priest's eyes locked into those of his troubled patient.

"God gave you an important part to play in his omnipotent plan. If Yeshua had not died that day as the divinely directed sacrificial lamb, the world would have been for ever lost in sin with no chance of salvation. So you see you did not cause things to happen. You were merely playing your part in that divine drama. Yeshua is love itself. I believe that he would and actually has, forgiven you because of your sincere repentance."

At last Pontius spoke.

"I am not a Christian. Why would he bother to forgive me?" His eyes searched those of the physician.

"You believe that He is the Son of God. Do you not?"

There was a long pregnant silence. Procula's eyes were raised to heaven, tears filled her eyes once more. Tullius held Pilate's stare, but his mind was with Yeshua. He prayed for an answer that would snatch that unfortunate human being from the clutches of the devil and save his soul.

"I suppose I do...yes! I do believe. But as to his having forgiven me? I don't know."

Procula looked at her beloved husband with some relief, and said.

"A vengeful God would have smothered you when I put the veil with his sacred image over you. But instead, you were cured. Does that not prove that he has forgiven you?"

"Perhaps," said Pilate, still doubting.

Procula taking his hand, had him rise from the couch and finally led him out of his room. The three made their way to the garden and sat in the shade of a most attractive pergola to recuperate from the storm of life that had engulfed the troubled trio.

"I think I shall have Linus come and see you," said Tullius, addressing Pilate.

"Who is the man?" asked Pontius

"Procula explained, starting with the Apostles, and going on to the embryonic hierarchy of the fledgling church."

"I am only a soldier in the battle for the salvation of souls," said Tullius with characteristic humility. "My superior, Linus, is better equipped to deal with difficult cases like you."

"Yes, indeed," said Pilate with a sad nod of the head. "I really am a difficult case."

Tullius had been invited to stay the night at Pontius Pilate's house. He took leave of the kind pair the following morning soon after breakfast and rode back to Rome in search of Linus.

The latter had been moved once more, and it was almost cena time before Tullius finally arrived at Linus' new lodgings.

A young female servant with a very pleasant face opened the door and politely asked the priest regarding his business.

"I am here to see Linus," said Tullius.

"Linus? No one by that name lives here."

Tullius realised that he had no coded password to give her. She however seeing the expression on his somewhat bewildered face, helped him.

"Begging your pardon," she said, "but can you describe the man?"

"Yes. He is of medium height; slightly on the chubby side and; is around fifty-six years of age.

His dark brown eyebrows contrast greatly with his grey hair and beard. I regret that I am unable to give you the required information, it is not always available to me."

She smiled, asked his name, and on receiving it, ushered him into the atrium. She dashed off to announce the visitor.

Presently, Linus appeared in person, and after a fond greeting, led the way to his room off the peristyle at the back of the house. Once again his room looked out onto the garden which greatly pleased the saintly man.

"Good to see you again Tullius," said Linus. He poured a cup of juice and handed it to his subordinate. He poured himself one also, and slumping down on a cushion invited Tullius to sit.

Linus looked at his young friend with a smile and said.

"When I don't hear from my young colleagues, I know that everything is well and under control. But I do wish you wouldn't take so long to visit me. Being an old priest is a lonely affair you know." He laughed and so did Tullius. But the priest knew that Linus was in earnest.

"I shall try and visit you more often if that pleases you. I think most of us do not visit more often, simply because they do not wish to disturb you," said Tullius. "And incidentally, you had better give your future hostesses, a name and description of your priests. I was diligently questioned just now by the girl who answered the door."

Linus was one of three pioneering priests in Rome. He had been ordained by the apostle Peter in Antioch, and had subsequently returned to his home in Rome, to start his mission establishing the Roman Church. He was therefore considered a senior priest, along with two other two priests by the names of Clement and Anacletus, who had been similarly ordained by Apostle's. (The three men were later consecrated as Bishops by St. Peter on his visit to Rome many years later.)

"What brings you today?" asked Linus, lifting the cup to his lips.

"Quite an extraordinary and in fact, unique problem," said the priest.

"I might have expected that from you. You do not normally deal in trivialities."

"This is something quite difficult, and I was unable to totally convince my subject of Yeshua's great love for him. I left the man with a disturbing doubt in his troubled mind. I would like you to come with me and win this man over to Yeshua."

The superior was intrigued that Tullius had accepted defeat in an attempted conversion.

"Who is this person, and where is he?

"His name you will surely be familiar with, his whereabouts are in Pyrgi."

Linus was most intrigued, and even perhaps apprehensive as he awaited the name.

Tullius gave his superior a sinister look.

"Pontius Pilate!" he said.

Linus froze. An unsettling silence followed. He scratched his bothered head and said.

"No wonder you are having difficulties with a situation like that. Indeed, one of a kind. How are we to assure this man that the Lord has forgiven him? You better give me the complete story, for surely it must be a most intriguing one."

Tullius spent the remainder of the evening after the cena, discussing the very thorny problem with his superior.

Two days later, both priests rode out of Rome with Pyrgi as their destination.

Their eventual and uneventful arrival at the residence of Pontius Pilate in the early afternoon, was announced by the gate-keeper, who recognising Tullius and being himself a Christian, sought out his mistress in preference to his master.

Procula soon appeared and was most happy to welcome Tullius and his friend.

The priest introduced his superior to Procula who gave him a lovely smile and extended her hands to him.

"I am honoured to meet you Linus, and we are very grateful for taking the trouble to visit us. As Tullius has I'm sure told you, my husband has been cured miraculously by a veil with Yeshua's image imprinted on it. The veil has worked a number of miraculous cures it seems though I only know of two others. But that is not the present problem."

"May I see the veil?" asked Linus; his eyes sparkling inanticipation.

"Please come," she said, pointing the way.

The veil resided in the little trunk where she habitually kept it. Taking it out, she held it up for her trusted visitors to see.

Tullius had seen the veil before, though he never ceased to marvel at it. Linus however was quite dumbfounded, and though he had never met Yeshua he instinctively knew that this was no hoax. He took it from Procula's hands and ran his fingers over the material.

"This has not been done with earthly hands," he muttered almost to himself.

"No. This is a materialised miracle I have no doubt." He opened it up again, scrutinized it once more and reverently kissed it.

"The Lord be praised for allowing us to see his divine face." He looked at Procula.

"This treasure," he continued, "must stay in the church. When you feel that it is time, please contact me or any other priest, and give it into his safe keeping. This is truly a great relic and must be venerated by as many Christians as possible. Though for now, during these treacherous times, it is best that you be its custodian...may the Lord keep you safe."

Procula put the veil back in the trunk, and proceeded to explain to Linus, her husband's problems of which he was already aware from Tullius' account. He listened without comment. She then took her visitors to meet her husband who was sitting in the garden with his disturbing thoughts.

She introduced Linus, who could not help feeling a strong resentment for the man who had crucified his Lord and Master. Indeed, if it was not because Yeshua had commanded that he love his enemies, Linus would have turned around and left the man in his misery for ever.

Linus looked at Pilate and said with much frigidity.

"Your good wife tells me that you do not believe that my Lord Yeshua will forgive you for having crucified him."

Pilate's intelligent but sorrowful eyes searched Linus's.

"I crucified the Son of God. What god would forgive a sin of that magnitude?" Said Pilate with conviction. "It does not stand to reason."

"Do you believe that Yeshua is the Son of God?" asked Linus.

"Yes. I believe it now. I didn't before. Though I suspected something very unusual about him and his words when I spoke to him privately at his trial."

Both priests held their breath in anticipation of what Pilate would say. Neither of them knew anything of what had been said during that infamous trial. Procula's ears also perked up, she too was ignorant of that dialogue between Yeshua and her husband.

"I asked him questions and he remained silent," continued Pilate. "I told him that I had the power to condemn or release him. He then said something which baffled me greatly at the time. *You would have no power over me, if it had not been given you from above.*"

He shook his head sadly and continued.

"Those strange words did not have much import then. But lately, it has become very clear to me that he was speaking of his father. The God of the Jews... I have killed the Son of God. Of that I have no doubt. How can I possibly be forgiven? I cannot understand how he allowed his image on that veil to cure me of my horrible nightmares. I simply cannot understand it. He should have choked me with it as Procula said any other god would have done. I certainly do not deserve to live." He again melancholically shook his head; his hands dropping to his sides.

"Now," he continued with great solemnity in his voice, his repentant eyes fixed on Linus. "It is my turn to be judged."

Linus was somewhat moved by the sincerity and obvious repentance in the man. He turned, fell on his knees and covering his face with his hands, spent some time deep in prayer. Tullius and Procula also stood and prayed. Pilate sat there in apparent contemplation; though he also, could well have been praying to Yeshua.

Linus got on his feet again. He addressed Pilate with compassion in his voice.

"We are not here to judge. Only God can do that."

"As a man," he continued, "your forgiveness is hard for me to accept, but as a Christian I must. Yeshua died to redeem every person from their sins which would condemn them to the everlasting fires of hell, and so even *you* come under his mantel of salvation. Tullius and I, as his ministers, have to obey." Linus stopped. He went over to Pilate, and standing in front of him asked.

"Do you repent of having crucified Yeshua, the Son of God?"

"I repent with all my heart," said Pilate, falling on his knees; his voice breaking.

"In the name Yeshua, I forgive that, and all your other sins," said Linus. "Even though you are not yet a baptised Christian."

Pilate got up and looking deeply into his confessor's eyes, said.

"I believe Yeshua *has* forgiven me...But how do I forgive myself?"

CHAPTER FOURTEEN

COMPROMISES

Linus and Tullius rode away from Pilate's house in silence, each deep in their own thoughts. In their musings they shared a number of topics. It began with Pontuius Pilate, but slowly, wispily, as if reflecting the cloudiness of the sky under which they were riding, they drifted in Tillius' direction. The younger priest's thoughts were introspective; the elder's retrospective. Tullius was the subject.

A storm was imminent. The heavy leaden clouds still at some distance but driven by a fair wind blowing in from the sea gave notice of a coming storm. Chances were that before the morning spent itself the priestly pair would be engulfed in the rain and soaked to the bone.

They continued on, urging their mounts to a faster canter. Despite their prayers to the contrary, two hours later, the rain began. Slowly at first, but soon they had to seek shelter. There was an inn just up ahead, and presently, they steered their horses into the courtyard. Quickly dismounting, they surrendered the reins to a stable boy who took charge of the horses and rushed them into the stables.

The rain fell in torrents, loudly pelting the closed wooden shutters of the inn. The priests thanked the Lord for His benevolence in putting that hostel so opportunely in their path.

It was lunchtime and they made the most of it. A well-prepared repast presently came their way, and as the storm raged unabated outside, they sat leisurely having a highly pregnant conversation, born of their earlier musings.

Linus, had for some time observed that not withstanding the dedication and ability with which Tullius performed his priestly duties, he was not an entirely happy man. He recalled how the young priest had asked his opinion about the possibility of marriage and felt that his continuing love for Rufina was interfering with his complete happiness in serving the Lord. He resolved to meet this young woman and assess for himself her suitability for marrying his priest; whom he considered his right arm so to speak. With this in mind, he took the opportunity which the storm had occasioned them to have a heart to heart talk with his beloved Tullius.

Linus settled comfortably near the cheerful fireplace in the inn's parlour.

"I have been thinking of taking a little time to myself," he began, "and am wondering if could spend a few days at that lovely vineyard in Umbria that you are always talking about.".

Tullius followed his superior's lead and slumped down onto an adjoining cushion. He felt quite relaxed after his enjoyable lunch. He was greatly surprised by Linus' request, but overjoyed at the same time.

'He must want to meet Rufina,' thought the clever Tullius. 'Perhaps he is going to change his mind and allow us to marry.'

"I feel sure," he said, "that all concerned at the vineyard would be honoured to have you visit them, especially Rufina."

"I would love to meet this young lady who seems to have won a good half of your heart," said Linus with a fatherly smile. "If Octavius will stand in for me whilst I am away, I feel sure we can abscond for a little while. It will be impossible to give them prior notice. Will they be inopportuned do you think.?"

Tullius who was poking at a log in the hearth just for something to do to hide his utter joy at the prospect of Linus meeting his beloved Rufina, turned to face his superior.

"It's a big farmhouse. There is ample room to provide for your comfort. In fact they will spoil you given the least chance. Aurelia, their cook is an artist at her trade and her delicious food will add appreciatively to your waist if you are not on your guard." He laughed, and so did Linus, who tried to visualise Aurelia.

The two priests continued their conversation; made more pleasant by enjoying some watered wine which happened by sheer coincidence to be the product of the Fulvius wineries.

At last, the storm abated, and Linus settling their account with the friendly inn-keeper, ventured out. They reclaimed their horses and continued on their journey to Linus' place of residence.

* * * * *

Rufina was in the kitchen discussing the menu for the cena. It was mid afternoon, and they had fallen behind in their preparation. Jocasta was busy cleaning after the workmen who had started the construction of a new wing to the farmhouse. An addition which would comfortably house all the servants. Marcellus had assigned the supervision of the construction to Sartorius, who was finding it difficult to walk even with the use of his staff.

The sound of horse's hooves in the courtyard captured Rufina's attention. Rex who would have announced the visitors in his inimitable and dependable way, was somewhere in the vineyard with Marcellus and Marcia.

Not bothering to peek out of the high kitchen window, she tidied her hair, straightened her house clothes, and hurried out with some concern, accompanied by the buxom Aurelia, to meet whoever it might be.

Tullius having dismounted, awaited Linus, as Rufina and Aurelia made their appearance.

"Tullius!" my love." screamed Rufina at seeing him, and before he could introduce Linus, she jubilantly rushed into his arms. "The Lord be praised!" she said with great gusto and tears of joy in her lovely eyes, as he with a big smile, gently parted from their embrace.

"My dear, I wish to present to you my superior, Linus, of whom I have spoken to you many times.

Rufina blushed, gave Linus a shallow bow accompanied by a sweet smile, and bade him welcome on behalf of her brother and herself. The last thing she expected was to have Tullius' superior as a guest. The fact that he was there in front of her however, quickly occasioned a surge in her almost abandoned hopes.

Linus dismounted, and stretching his hands out to her, gave her a paternal smile.

"Tullius assured me," he said, gently pressing her hands, "that my unannounced visit would not inconvenience you. I pray it be so."

"I am honoured to have you with us. We will do all we can to make your stay an enjoyable one." said the excited hostess, and with a graceful gesture of her slender hand, showed the way into the house. The men took their baggage, tied their horses' reins to the hitching posts, and followed Rufina into the house. Aurelia having unobtrusively slipped away, was already busy preparing refreshments for the visitors.

Ignatia, who was about to go downstairs, on hearing men's voices stopped on the upstairs landing. Recognising Tullius' voice, she slipped back into her room and asked Leia who was in the midst of mending some garment and as usual keeping her company, to go down to the kitchen and find out from Aurelia who the visitors were?

Aurelia was in the living room serving the new comers watered wine and juice, prior to her bringing them some victuals. Leia waited in the kitchen.

"This is my superior, Linus," said Tullius addressing Aurelia, as she placed the tray she was carrying on a table in front of them.

She bowed and said, "I am very pleased to meet you."

"I am happy to meet you too," said Linus with a smile, and pointing at Tullius he said.

"My good friend here has told me what a great cook you are. He has also warned me to keep an eye on my waistline during my stay."

"With all due respect, you could both do with a bit of fattening," answered the congenial cook. "As I always tell Tullius here," she said nodding to him. "You priests pray too hard and fast too much."

"Ha! Ha!" chuckled Linus. "You may have a point there."

Aurelia then left the room and made her way back to the kitchen. She busied herself with the preparation of the victuals whilst informing Leia as to who the visitors were.

"So that is Tullius' superior," confirmed Ignatia, as Leia sat down again to the sewing her mistress had interrupted. "I wonder why he has come."

Aurelia returned to the living room with a tray of tempting victuals, which she deposited on the table, and expressing the hope that they enjoy the food, went back into the kitchen to prepare the cena which had already suffered enough delays.

The lady of the house passed the time in friendly conversation with the two priests and sharing the delicacies that had been placed in front of them.

As the cena time approached, Marcellus accompanied by Evandros made their appearance, followed closely by Marcia and a happy, muddy, Rex, who immediately went to greet Tullius.

Linus was duly introduced to all by Tullius. Rex was sent away because of his muddy paws. Marcellus welcomed Linus with great enthusiasm and then excusing himself, made for his ablutions followed by Evandros. Marcia replaced her muddy shoes with house slippers and sat beside Tullius.

Rufina had a feeling that her mother, not particularly enthused by the presence of Linus, was staying away on purpose. She excused herself and went upstairs to fetch her and Leia.

Just as all the introductions had been completed, Sartorius and Jocasta made their appearance. They were duly introduced to Linus. The old man joined those in the living room and

Jocasta begging their leave, went to the aid of Aurelia in the kitchen.

Linus, who was certain that he had been introduced to all the members of the household, was once again surprised by the appearance of Ignatia and Leia.

The weather being a little chilly that first evening of Linus' stay, the cena was served in the living room. Linus was well aware that the only one in the household who was not a Christian, was Ignatia. He was particularly careful not to offend her.

Tullius who knew 'the lay of the land' where Ignatia was concerned, conducted the prayer before their meal. Ignatia did not leave however, but sat quietly listening, and kept her thoughts to herself.

As she sat making polite small talk during that first meal in the company of the two priests, Ignatia considered all the implications that their visit signified. With the occasional tear in her eye she reminisced.

It was with good reason she remembered, that her dear deceased Porcius, had lovingly called her my "clever little thing" so many years ago when their marriage was in its infancy, and they would discuss during their cenas some of the thorny problems that he as a young and very green senator had had to tackle. Her good advice was used to advantage on a number of occasions.

Over the years, her family had been led by her example and good advice. Now, even though only forty-four years of age, still beautiful, of great distinction and aristocratic bearing, her ideas and proposals no longer carried any weight. In her own estimate she was no longer taken seriously, and even her scanty religious beliefs which had added interest to her pampered and pleasure-filled life, had lately been disproved and had created a great uncertainty under which she was even now struggling. The only thing that she found of any positive value seeing that all her better plans for Rufina were about to be dashed, was the thought that hopefully soon, she would be enjoying some beautiful grand children who would brighten up her existence.

In the days that followed, Linus was able to learn first hand much about Rufina's faith and character. He began to admire not just her beauty but her good qualities and intelligence. She showed a willingness to conform to a life of waiting and understanding of Tullius' work for the Lord, for whom she also was willing to sacrifice herself.

The knowledge that Rufina was well able to fend for herself and was wealthy enough not to have to depend on Tullius for her income, gave much weight to Linus forming a favourable opinion of their marrying.

By the end of that week, Linus had, after much praying, come to the decision that Tullius would serve the Lord better by being married than by remaining celibate. Rufina had exceeded his expectations, and he felt as confident as a man could, considering the metaphysical aspects of a question which could only be judged by God.

"You have my permission to marry," said Linus to Rufina and Tullius late one evening as the three of them sat alone in the living room. "And may the good Lord bless your marriage and make it fruitful."

Embraces abounded, as the three protagonists of the situation expressed their utter joy in the favourable decision that had finally been made as a result of all their prayers.

The following morning, the house was given the joyful tidings, which were received with great joy by all with the exception of Ignatia, who though far from enthusiastic, had the grace to show a good face in the matter. She embraced her future son-in-law with a little more warmth than usual and surprised herself by silently saying...'It is Yeshua's will.'

Tullius accompanied by Linus rode off to Salistra with the intention of giving Atelius and Cornelia the good news and an invitation to the wedding. Also, and more importantly, to fetch

Alphonsus, the new priest, who would accompany Linus to Rome and remain there until Tullius' return a couple of weeks hence.

Alphonsus, was at a very critical stage in the shaping of the large pot that he was working on at the wheel when Linus and Tullius suddenly appeared in front of him. The surprise that reflected in his eyes was echoed in his hands, which instead of releasing, continued to press the clay; the pot growing taller and thinner to the point where its wall collapsed inwards giving it an unintentional and extraordinary shape. The young potter-priest looked at his pot and threw his hands up in disbelief. Bowing his head and displaying a sheepish smile, he welcomed the visitors who were much amused at the havoc that their sudden presence had reaped, and burst out laughing.

"See what you've done," said Alphonsus, washing his hands in a nearby basin. "But it is worth it for the pleasure of seeing you both again." He dried his hands quickly, and warmly embraced his brother priests.

"You look well my dear boy," said Linus, admiring the glow of youth on the young man's plumpish cheeks. "You must feed yourself well."

"I have a friend who has been teaching me how to cook, and I am learning fast," answered the young priest spreading his arms in concert with his words.

"You have some beautiful pieces here," said Tullius eyeing the pottery displayed on the shelves around them. You obviously don't get interrupted too often as happened just now."

"Ha! Ha! no," laughed Alphonsus. "I am left to myself most of the time. I welcome company when I can get it. Except for the 'Breaking of the Bread' on the Dies Solis service which is never a certainty either in actuality or with regard to the location, and a few weekly excursions to fish for men, I am pretty much left to myself. Occasionally, Cornelia invites me over for the cena, which is always a great treat for me."

Linus' keen mind was at work as he listened to the young priest explain his activities and enquired.

"Is this friend of yours that is teaching you to cook a Christian?"

"Yes. She was baptised by Tullius some time ago." He looked at Tullius. "You remember Julia, don't you?"

"Yes, of course I do, she was responsible for Marina's conversion. "But she is in Menorum. She and Marina own a bakery there I am told."

Linus was most attentive to the conversation.

"What does this Julia look like," he asked, with a smile, knowing full well that it was a leading question. Tullius also had a smile on his face.

"Alphonsus' eyes lit up. "She is twenty years old and very good looking. She has a very cheery disposition and has a great love for our beloved Yeshua."

The old priest allowed his smile to freeze on his face. But in essence it was no longer a smile. Concern invaded his mind once again regarding marriage by his priests. Though he had allowed the marriage of Tullius after much consideration and prayer, he had not realised that he was setting a precedent for the others. Here was another potential marriage in the making if things continued to develop in the way he was already suspecting.

'All I can do is guide them,' he told himself. 'They cannot serve the Lord unhappily. They must put their hearts and souls into what they are doing when they are propagating the faith. Also by their example they can do much good for other less successful marriages. Their love of God will always surpass the love of their women, but both loves together must surely produce great results. I hope for my sake, the Lord Yeshua concurs with my thinking. I am after all, only a man.'

Whilst Alphonsus made himself ready for their departure, Tullius took Linus to meet the mayor and his wife. He explained that whereas Cornelia was an ardent Christian and a pillar in the local Church, her husband, though very sympathetic towards his wife's religion had not as yet as been won over. His viewpoint was similar to that of Ignatia's. They both felt that the submissive element in the Christian religion was a stumbling block in the defence of their families, properties and values. Ignatia for her part felt justified in her convictions after her successful, aggressive, accusation of Pompinus in defence of her son. She also would have been incriminated along with him she felt, if she had been a Christian.

"Yes," said Linus with some regret. "It is their worldliness and lack of spiritual vision, that justifies their thoughts. We must pray for the pagans constantly, until they come to comprehend eternity, and then they will fall at Yeshua's feet in hope of salvation. Their earthly power and goods are too dear to them at the present." He stopped. They had arrived at the mayor's house.

"Shame," said Tullius ringing the bell. "They are such lovely people."

The meeting with Atelius and Cornelia was a very pleasant one. Linus and Tullius were treated with great warmth. Tullius was much loved. The convivial couple made the matter very clear to Linus that he was just like family to them.

On passing through Menorum on their way back to Marcellus house, the priestly trio (for Alphonsus rode with them) stopped at Marina's bakery to invite her and Julia to the wedding.

The visit gave Linus an opportunity to meet and observe Julia, who might well he thought, give him something to think about in the not too distant future. He entered the shop with a feeling of dread. The shop was devoid of customers as it was nearing closing time.

"Tulius!" cried both women in concert, and running out from behind the counter, hastened to embrace him.

Parting from their embrace, Tullius introduced Linus to the two women, and then, Alphonsus, who had stayed in the background, was duly accosted by Marina, and Julia who gave him a particularly enthusiastic smile. The smile however changed into a pout, when he told them that he would be leaving for a while. Linus did not miss this little show of disappointment on the girl's part. He studied her with great but unobtrusive interest.

'Yes,' he said to himself, 'she has a lovely and very honest face. Her eyes reflect compassion even though they seem so jovial in the wonderful light of youth... I am going to be hearing from young Alphonsus soon enough. But they are much too young. They will have to wait.'

Linus' attention then turned to Marina whose mature beauty he also admired. He had been told her story, and he was most pleased that she was fending for herself. He chatted with her for a little while and promised to talk to them again at the wedding. He nodded to his priests, and they all took their leave. They rode away, leaving the two women waving from the shop door.

The arrival of Alphonsus caused a small upheaval in the room arrangements at the farmhouse. Tullius moved in with Marcellus, and a bed was found for the young priest, who was invited by Linus to share his room. Thus, everyone was accommodated. The house had never been more replete.

Rufina's marriage to Tullius received very little publicity. Atelius and Marina had been asked not to make much of it outside of the vineyard, even though they knew that all of Menorum and much of Salistra would be talking about it. Marcellus, felt that the quieter a life he led, the less likely he was to make enemies who would denounce him and his family.

The guests consisted of the people involved in the three vineyards with the addition of Marina, Julia, Atelius, and Cornelia. Centurion Augustus was invited, but realising that many of those present would be Christian, he did not want to create any problems either for them or himself in the future. He made his reasons known to Marcellus who gratefully understood but greatly regretted his friend's absence.

The wedding was indeed a very Christian affair. With three exceptions, all present were baptised Christians. Linus officiated; assisted by Alphonsus. The 'Breaking of the Bread' service followed the wedding vows, and the beautiful bride and handsome bridegroom were well pleased with the wonderful ceremony. It took place in the morning, in the garden which had been decked out with flowers by the overjoyed servants of the house. Aurelia assisted by the equally talented Lavinia, had created succulent dishes which were being much lauded by all present. The best wines from the vineyard's cellars were freely dispensed and enjoyed by all.

Linus found another opportunity to talk to the lovely Julia, which allowed him an excellent appreciation of the girl's character and made his mind a little easier on that score. Marcia also gave the old priest some of her time, and he was much impressed by the intelligence and the budding beauty of the nine-year-old with the gorgeous blue eyes, who later entertained the party with her harp which she played in tandem with her adoptive mother, the happy bride.

Marcellus was overjoyed that Tullius who was like a brother to him already, should now officially be a member of the family. He gave him a very generous present of money to help further the work of the Lord. Linus was very favourably impressed with Marcellus, who had already suffered some persecution for Yeshua's sake. He knew that in the future he could bank on him and the family to assist in the needs of the Church; militant as it always seemed to be.

Two days after the wedding, and having blessed the house, Linus and Alphonsus took their leave of the Fulvius family. The former, would never forget those wonderful days that the Lord had allowed him to enjoy, and the warm-hearted people that he had had the good fortune to meet.

I shall spare my good and intelligent reader the details of that wonderful wedding night of our hero and heroine, since I would hardly dare to trespass on their well-earned privacy. The wedding chamber, which had been profusely over-decorated in rural abandon by the enthusiastic and mildly inebriated female members of the farmhouse staff, ensured the privacy that the two celebrants were fully entitled to on that auspicious night. The only thing that we can assume for certain without invading that privacy, is the extreme joy and satisfaction that Rufina and Tulius would have felt at finding themselves finally, masters of their own minds and bodies; free of all the encumbrances and restrictions, with which they had lived for close to four years.

The guests stayed the night, since travelling was always safer during the day. Once the family had retired to their own bedrooms, the remaining male guests made themselves as comfortable as they could in the living room on its many well filled cushions.

Aurelia invited Lavinia and Marina to stay at her house which was very close by. They were escorted by Antonius who later returned to sleep in the living room. Evandros gave up his bed to Oratius' wife Hortensia, and he also retired to the living room. Julia slept on cushions in Marcia's room, as the two girls though well apart in age, had taken a liking for each other during the festivities.

The exodus of the guests from the farmhouse took place the following morning after breakfast, at which the honoured couple were conspicuously absent. Marcellus stood at the courtyard gate thanking them and seeing them all off on their behalf.

* * * * *

Nine months had elapsed since the wedding. Rufina was in labour. The physician from Menorum was assisting her, as were the women of the Fulvius household.

Marcellus, in the absence of the expected child's father was pacing up and down the corridor between the front door and the garden worrying and praying that the delivery would be a fast and uncomplicated one for his sister, and that the child be normal in every way.

Tullius had been told some months earlier, that Rufina was expecting, but he was left to guess the actual day of the birth of his baby. He really was not expected.

The clatter of a horse's hooves in the courtyard, suddenly aroused Marcellus from his reverie and he made haste to meet the unexpected visitor. To his great surprise, Tullius burst into the corridor even before he reached the main door.

The two friends embraced warmly.

"What a surprise," blurted out Marcellus with relief in his eyes. "Rufina is in labour. I am delighted that you are here. I have been so worried."

"My!" said the expectant father, "I seemed to have guessed the day with some accuracy. I shall go right up to her. Is there a physician here?"

"Yes," said Marcellus, "he has been with her for the past two hours."

Tullius ran up the stairs and walked into the Rufina 's room. The physician gave him an alarmed look as he stepped past him and embraced his overjoyed but beleaguered wife.

Presently, having saluted all the women present, he introduced himself as husband and physician to his surprised colleague and taking him by the arm led him out of the room for a quick consultation.

The visiting physician gave Tullius an account of the frequency of the spasms, and they both agreed that the labour had just begun. All seemed to be well thus far. They returned to the labour room to tell the women that they would be downstairs, and to call when the frequency of the spasms increased.

Rufina, who was greatly encouraged by the presence of her husband, was equally pleased that he had left the women alone, he was not needed as yet she felt.

Marcellus, sat at the table in the garden accompanied by Tullius and the visiting physician. They were soon joined by Sartorius, who excitedly embraced the expectant father.

The cena time was approaching. Aurelia, on her way down to start its preparation, reported that the frequency of the spasms had increased considerably. The two physicians made their way up to the labour room. Ignatia breathed a sigh of relief as they both entered and approached Rufina who was bravely trying to deal with the great pains which accosted her.

The physicians examined her, and Tullius, satisfied that all was in order held his wife's hand gently and spoke words of encouragement in her ear. The visiting physician found a chair and settling down nodded reassuringly to Ignatia, whose face showed some concern.

Sartorius sitting on the bottom step of the stairs, waited for developments. Marcellus, out in the courtyard was tying down Tullius' horse which in all the excitement had been left to wander around at will. Rex with his usual diligence, was lying at the gate ensuring that the loose horse remained in the courtyard.

Aurelia, was on the point of calling all to the 'cena', when a baby's cry was heard. An excited Jocasta ran down the stairs announcing loudly and joyfully the birth of a baby boy. A stampede followed as all those on the ground level ran up to see the little wonder and his mother.

The cena that evening occasioned a great celebration. Tullius, and Rufina who was still trying to recover from her ordeal, had their food sent up to them.

Seven happy days followed. Tullius made ready to depart once more having enjoyed every moment of his memorable stay. Rufina, holding her new little Tullius as they had decided to call the baby in his father's honour, embraced her husband with tears in her eyes, bidding him God speed. The priest kissed his tiny son once more and mounting his horse, raised his arm and giving all a blessing, rode off to his priestly duties which could well keep him away indefinitely.

* * * * *

Linus sat in the garden of the house where he was staying. In his company were two senior priests who, like him, were responsible for a number of priests and had large but secret parishes.

Clement and Anacletus, had been serving in Rome as long as Linus had. Occasionally, those three men met to discuss important and pressing issues that the Church had to deal with.

On this particular occasion, among other pressing issues, the matter of the 'veil' with which they were all acquainted, was being discussed.

"I feel said Linus, that this precious and miraculous relic should be in the safe hands of the Church." He sat back on the garden bench and waited the response of his colleagues.

"I heartily agree," said Clement, "but I question the safety that we here can guarantee?" Anacletus nodded in agreement.

"Yes," said Linus with a shake of the head. "We can hardly keep it safe here."

"It should be in the hands of the Apostles," continued Linus with a hopeful look in his eyes. "But how could they ensure its safety, when they are travelling all the time? Like us, they do not have a permanent and secure place in which to keep it."

"Also," interjected Anacletus, "how do they show it to the faithful? Which is of the utmost importance. It would continue to perform miracles for them, commensurate with their faith.

All three settled down to quiet concentration and prayer.

Linus, was the first to snap out of his reverie.

"Perhaps!" he said, securing the attention of his two holy companions. "We can send it to Bishop Simon in Cyrene, or even to Bishop Mark in Alexandria?" Linus glanced at his colleagues. "They actually have brick and mortar churches there in which I am told they hold services for the 'Breaking of the Bread' each Dies Solis."

The other two priests had heard of the Church in Cyrene being free from Roman persecution and envied Simon's good fortune.

"The Lord is being hard on us," lamented Clement, searching his brother priests' eyes for sympathy.

"That," said Anacletus, "is the only sensible answer to the problem. Remember also," he continued. "Simon helped our divine Lord to carry his cross. He deserves to be favoured."

"Who could be trusted with the delivery of the relic?" asked Clement, spreading his hands in concert with his question.

Linus scratched his head as he considered the possibility of Tullius accepting the challenge.

'Who else was there who could undertake such a responsible and perhaps even dangerous mission?' He could see no other alternative. The other two priests who in time would be consecrated by Peter as bishops, as would Linus, offered no solution, and so the latter said.

"I have a priest who has performed some very difficult duties for me. If he will accept the mission, he would I believe be the most reliable person for the job. He is already acquainted with the veil. He is a physician. A most intelligent and creative man.

Linus went on to relate the rescuing of the Christian children by Tullius, as an affidavit of his proposal.

Tullius arrived in Rome, but his mind was back at the vineyard in Umbria, where his beloved Rufina was adjusting to her new life as a mother. He took consolation in the thought that her mother was there to advise and take care of her. 'Ignatia' he mused, 'had always shown a little coldness where I was concerned.' He suspected the reason for that was that she could not approve of the life of neglect her daughter would be subjected to on marrying him.

'Too bad I could not win her over to Yeshua,' he lamented. 'She would have understood the situation better and would have been more sympathetic towards my position.'

Having arrived at Linus' temporary residence, he cleared his mind of his domestic concerns, and opened it in readiness for the Lord's work whatever it might be.

CHAPTER FIFTEEN

THE MISSION

Linus embraced Tullius with much joy in his heart. He congratulated him on his baby boy, and thanked God that Rufina had been spared a difficult labour.

"Sit down my son, and tell me all about it," said the old priest eagerly.

Tullius, sat down, and related with apparent gratitude for Yeshua's providence, his timely arrival at the vineyard. He went on to elaborate with paternal pride the excitement generated by the new baby.

Linus recalled with satisfaction the enjoyable time he had experienced during his stay at the vineyard on the occasion of Tullius' wedding the previous year.

"Yeshua gives us many blessings for which we must thank him," said Linus.

He got up, poured some juice into a cup and handed it to Tulius. He poured one for himself; returned to his seat; and having swallowed a mouthful, said.

"Now, I have to tell you something that concerns you, and which I have discussed with Clement and Anacletus." He attended to his juice once more, and began:

"We have discussed the 'veil,' and arrived at the conclusion that it should be taken out of Procula's hands where it is relatively safe for the present and sent to Cyrene. There, Bishop Simon has built an actual place of worship, which is being called a church. As opposed to a temple of course."

"Yes," said Tullius with resignation in his eyes. "As we know there is no persecution in Cyrene or indeed anywhere other than here. Unless of course if we consider the animosity of the Jews everywhere, which sometimes turns into violence."

Linus thoughtfully scratched his ample grey beard.

"Unfortunately, we do not know what problems Simon is dealing with or in fact has dealt with. We do not often receive word from there."

"There is also Bishop John Mark in Alexandria. He too, is in the throws of building a church in that city, but we do not know whether he has completed it yet."

"I suppose," said Tullius, that Cyrene would at the present time offer the best option."

"You understand," continued Linus, "that our motive in this undertaking, is to put that miraculous veil at the service of the faithful. To do that it has to be occasionally exposed to view perhaps, as part of a service, but kept secretly and securely hidden the rest of the time. The congregations must also keep the veil's existence secret. It is a treasure."

"Tullius got up, walked over to the open window, and stared out aimlessly at the garden beyond. He sensed that he was going to be asked to undertake the collection and delivery of the veil to Cyrene. Turning around, he looked at Linus.

"Where do I come into this plan?"

"I think," said Linus, "you already know."

"As you expect," said a resigned Tullius, "I shall happily acquiesce."

Linus rose from his cushion and hastened to embrace his priest.

"I knew I could count on you my boy. The Lord and all our prayers will go with you."

Reclaiming their seats, they began to discuss and plan the project which would be no easy undertaking; fraught with many unforeseeable problems. By the 'cena' time, the two priests had planned out the mission to their mutual satisfaction.

"My wife must be told," said Tullius. "She has seen the veil and knows as much about it as I do. I have no concern with regard to her keeping the mission secret from everyone barring Marcellus, whom I would trust with my life."

"Alphonsus, is due here by the end of this month," said Linus. "I shall have him carry the news back with him to Rufina. He too will be asked to keep the matter to himself."

Linus then led the way to the dining room to eat with the rest of the household.

* * * * *

Tullius rode along the main road from Pyrgi to Pontius Pilate's house. Remembering the assault that Marcellus had experienced on the beach that ran alongside that road, he continued on his present course and soon rode up to Pontius' gate.

As usual, the gateman, recognising him, let him in, and with a welcoming smile dashed off to find his mistress.

Presently, Procula made her appearance with a lovely smile on her face. She embraced Tullius, who returned her embrace with warmth and complimented her on her enduring good looks.

"How lovely to see you again Tullius," she greeted. It's been so long since your last visit."

"Yes," he agreed. "It has been quite a while."

He let her take his arm and lead him into the house.

"How is Pontius?" asked the priest.

"He is fine now. He has never had another nightmare and is looking more like a Christian every day, though he has still not forgiven himself."

"I am not surprised to hear that. If he ever succeeds in forgiving himself, he will surely end up a most dedicated Christian."

"He is away at the moment," she said with some regret in her lovely eyes. "He sailed away to a friend's house further down the coast, and I don't expect him back for two or three days. I am sure he would have liked to have seen you."

They arrived at her striking peristyle from where they could hear the waves smashing into the cliff face far below. The occasional cloud of foam appeared in front of them regaling their nostrils with the invigorating, briny smell of the sea. Tullius commented on how very pleasant he found that to be, and she declared with her shapely arms gesturing in concert, how vital that scenario was to her existence and what a sacrifice it would be for her to live anywhere else.

After sharing some refreshments with Procula, and explaining the reason for his visit, Tullius took his leave. The veil was now reposing securely on his chest inside his tunic much as Marcellus had always carried it. Procula had however made a very attractively embroidered pouch for it; certainly more worthy of the treasure it enclosed.

Tullías had explained with the utmost tact the decision that had been made by the three future bishops, and the need for the faithful to venerate the relic and profit from its miraculous powers.

"Perhaps," she had told him, "some day in better times, Yeshua might have it return to Rome."

They agreed that Pilate was to be told only that Linus had asked for it to be given to the Church.

* * * * *

The noisy, crowded wharf; one of a few in the Ostia harbour, made for slow progress as Tullius tried with some annoyance to find the ship that was to take him to Cyrene. He had found some lodgings and after a couple of days of trying, and much to his regret, finally sold his horse at a most unfavourable price at the local horse exchange. He had enquired at the Port Registry Office and had been given the name of a ship bound for Appolonia in Cyrene which was due to sail in two days time.

The ship's name was the *Pretoria*. It was a 'corbita'. A small cargo boat which carried no more than eighteen passengers.

He was overwhelmed by the activity on the wharves, and the number of ships lining the quays or anchored further out in the harbour, and wondered how he was ever to find the ship.

A half an hour later, he finally found it and walked up the plank, hoping that a passage was available. As he stepped on deck, a voice sang out.

"How can I help you?"

You my dear reader, will remember that voice since it belonged to no other than our dear friend Silas, the congenial captain of the *Pretoria*. He now waddled over in his inimitable walk to greet Tullius who was, like many others before him, surprised at the smallness of Silas' head as compared to his thick neck and sturdy physique. And like them he was similarly amused at the extension of the man's mouth as he smiled.

"Good afternoon," smiled Tullius, despite his fatigue after trudging through those crowded wharves for over an hour. "I thought I would never find you,"

"You have obviously never been to Ostia," said Silas producing his face-splitting smile.

"It has to be the busiest and most confusing port in all the Roman Empire."

Tullius pressed the captain's outstretched hand.

"I assume you are the Captain?"

"I have that dubious honour," answered Silas, taking stock of the visitor.

"My name is Tullius, and I am seeking a passage to Cyrene."

"We sail hopefully in two days. At Ostia one is never sure, the loading and unloading is so uncertain." He gestured with his hand for Tullius to follow.

"Allow me to show you around."

The captain took his prospective passenger to see the cabin which he knew to be a rarity.

"This is a very new feature on cargo ships such as mine. Passengers have always slept on deck. But a few years ago, I had this comfortable cabin built and I can now offer two of my passenger's protection from the weather and good beds to sleep in, not to mention privacy."

Tullius was truly impressed by what he saw.

"What would this cabin cost to rent for the passage?"

"To Apollonia, the port of Cyrene, it would cost you forty-five denarii."

"As opposed to what if one travels on deck?" asked the visitor, somewhat stunned by the heavy cost of the cabin.

"Twelve denarii will cover the passage. Water is free. But when we carry wine, which we often do, you have to pay for that."

Tullius looked into Silas' beady, good natured eyes.

"I shall be frank with you. I find the cabin rather expensive especially since I would be allowing one of the beds to go to waste. If my wife were with me, it would be a different matter."

"I understand," said the captain, nodding condescendingly. "It is seldom unoccupied. Especially, this late in the autumn, when it gets quite cold at sea and the weather can be most inclement."

Tullius paid Silas for a regular 'on deck' passage and promised to return the next day to give him a decision with regard to renting the cabin. He was as yet was not sure. It had occurred to him that he could split the cost of the cabin with someone else.

'That of course,' he reasoned, 'would be a risky business unless I knew or could interview the person. But that could only happen at the last moment before the ship sailed, and the captain would hardly wait till then to rent the cabin.'

The *Pretoria* set sail two days later, with Tullius as an ordinary 'on deck' passenger.

* * * * *

The colourful coast of Crete regaled the passengers of the *Pretoria,* as it made its way in fairly calm waters to Phoenix. That busy cosmopolitan town was the last stop before crossing the Mediterranean to Cyrene. Everyone on board was anticipating their arrival. The stop over would allow them to find their land legs again even if only for a few hours and give them the opportunity of obtaining vital provisions for the remainder of the passage.

Three hours later, the little 'corbita' was gently berthed on a wharf. The passengers were allowed to visit the town for the next three hours, during which time Silas would see to the provisioning of his ship and crew with the necessary food and water for the last and longest lap of the journey. It could take up to three weeks, depending on the wind and sea conditions.

Tullius, as did some of the passengers, left his baggage in the captain's cabin whilst they went ashore. He happily walked down the gangplank looking forward to stretching his legs and having a hot meal, which had been an impossibility on board ship.

Phoenix was a busy cosmopolitan town. Many languages could be heard. The native language of course being Greek. It was the common language throughout the Mediterranean and most of the Roman Empire.

The hungry priest soon found a well attended food shop. He bought a bowl of goat stew and a small loaf of bread, and some wine. He settled down nearby in the shade of a large tree under which another three persons were lunching. He ate at leisure, studying as he ate, the people around him.

The locals were distinguishable by their Greek physiognomy and dark hair which most of them left uncovered despite the strong sun at that time of day. There was a particularly animated group opposite where he sat. They too ate under the shade of a tree. They were merchants who noisily carried out their business transactions with much gesturing of hands and shaking of heads. Every now and then one would pass around some piece of jewelry or an artifact for the others to examine.

Tullius watched them with some amusement.

Having finished his lunch, the travelling priest arose and walked away seeking a quieter, higher place with a view, where he could spend a little time watching the city and the beautiful surrounding countryside.

He soon found a path that led up to the mountain behind the town. He cheerfully and leisurely climbed the steep hill, stopping every now and then to admire the picturesque view of the harbour where the little *Pretoria* sat at the wharf amidst a line of larger vessels all waiting to be victualled.

The path he was on was being used rather scantily at that time of day, and so he was enjoying the solitude and thinking of Rufina and the baby as his eyes absorbed the beauty of his surroundings. The path suddenly forked out and he had to make a choice as to what side to follow. There were some caverns further ahead on his left which would obscure his view of the sea. He took the path to his right which offered a clear view. After proceeding a little further, and now being quite high up above sea level, he sat on a rock to rest and admire the gorgeous view.

There before him, twinkling in the early afternoon sun, was that seemingly endless blue sea. Light wispy clouds floated over the distant horizon as if brushed on by an invisible brush. Outside the harbour many sails glided slowly along in the warm moderate breeze. The harbour itself was a picture of activity with ships leaving and arriving, their multicoloured sails billowing voluptuously as their crews scurried to and fro. A large 'tridem', oars going at full speed was headed for open sea. Its sails, which were also unfurled, gave it maximum efficiency as it sped out of the harbour.

Tullius sat enthralled by the panorama for some time, lost in his thoughts. Eventually as the afternoon progressed, it came time for him to find his way back to the ship. He got up, and with some regret, started back down the path. He still had plenty of time he felt to buy his provisions.

Presently he approached the fork in the path again. Suddenly, he felt someone heavy, jump on him and force him to the ground. Two others fell on him and quickly overpowered him. They dragged him into one of the caverns that he had seen on his way up the mountain, and there, they tied his hands behind him, and his ankles together. He was then gagged, with a dirty rag, and searched.

They soon found his money belt, and taking it, ran off, leaving him lying on the cavern floor.

It all happened so quickly that Tullius felt disoriented. One moment it seemed, he had been enjoying the beautiful view of the harbour, and the next, he was lying helplessly inside the cave. He soon realised however that the veil was still on his chest, and though he was now destitute, he thanked Yeshua. For the next hour, he struggled to free his hands to no avail. He had managed to stand, but the floor of the cave was so uneven that he could not risk skipping forward to reach its mouth with his ankles tied. He had tried to find a sharp edge of stone to free his hands but the rock face around him was too smooth to cut into the ropes.

The sound of a horn in the far distance signalled him (he guessed correctly) that the ship was waiting for him and would soon be leaving. He could not hear any voices from passersby, and he suspected that the fork in the path that he had previously followed was the travelled route as opposed to the cavern path. That was why his attackers had waited until he approached the fork to assail him.

Presently the horn signalled once more. Suddenly he heard voices. He threw all his strength into the loud humming sounds of varying notes and pitches that he proceeded to emanate. For a few moments nothing occurred. Then, two men appeared clearly silhouetted against the light at the mouth of the cave. Tillius continued to hum in short spurts. The men entered and seeing him tied up and gagged, quickly set him free.

"Thank you, my good fellows," smiled Tullius. "I was attacked and robbed, and my ship is about to sail without me. I must run."

"We are happy to have helped you. We wish you the best of luck," said one of his rescuers, patting the relieved priest on the back. The latter raced down the hill as fast as he could. The horn sounded once more; a long unbroken blast. Tullius continued his run, praying that he might make the ship in time.

Presently he passed the shop where he had eaten, and then the harbour came in sight. He was almost out of breath as he manoeuvred the last corner around a warehouse.

The *Pretoria*, its white sails billowing, was just visible as it sailed out of the harbour.

Tullius' heart fell as he stood on the wharf waving at the ship that had just disappeared around a rocky point. Only the top of the mast and the 'supparum' sails were visible.

'Now what do I do?' Tullius wondered, leaning heavily against a post on the wharf's edge, trying to catch his breath.

After a few moments of reflection and recovering himself, he made his way to the Port Registry office.

Behind an old wooden counter and surrounded by scrolls and other marine paraphernalia stood a man in his late fifties with a long solemn face and a good crop of grey hair. He was clean shaven, but his side burns were unusually long, as was his nose. He looked at his visitor enquiringly, his bushy eyebrows raised.

"Good day," he nodded. "How can I help you?"

Tullius pulled his shawl off allowing it to hang on his shoulders.

"Good day to you too," he said approaching the desk. "My ship has just sailed without me. I was attacked and robbed of all my money." The clerk's eyebrows shot up once more, and his mouth opened as if to say something. Tullius waited.

"You must be Tullius. Captain Silas was most distraught when you failed to show up. He waited for another half hour for you but could delay no longer." The clerk disappeared behind the counter. Presently, he stood up and placed the priest's baggage on top of it.

"Here," he said with the hint of a smile. "He left this for you with his compliments, and also this." He handed Tullius ten denarii.

"Silas said that some misadventure must have befallen you. Of that he felt certain. He said you were entitled to receive back this money as you had only completed a small part of the journey. He hoped to meet you again sometime."

"I certainly hope so. The captain is an honest and considerate man and I am most grateful for his thoughtfulness."

Tullius pocketed the money and looked at the clerk.

"I am most grateful to you also for your honesty. I cannot afford to give you anything to show you my gratitude, as all I have right now is what you have just given me. But I am a physician, and hopefully, I shall be able to earn my passage money and a gift for you as well in the near future."

"You don't owe me anything. I pride myself on my honesty. I was simply doing my duty."

"May God Bless you then," said Tullius with a smile. "I have made a friend." The priest extended his hand for the clerk to press, along with a silent prayer on the man's behalf.

"You said you are a physician." The clerk pressed our hero's hand.

"Yes."

"Perhaps you may be able to make some quick money. Though the *Pretoria* will not likely be back until after the winter. Autumn is almost gone. Silas will probably winter in Cyrene, unless he is hard pressed for money, in which case he may try one more trip. But he has had a good year, so I doubt it very much. I have no notice of any ship scheduled for Cyrene at the moment.

Most ships will begin to winter within the next two weeks or so. Your'e chances of finding passage to Cyrene will be very slim indeed.

"How am I to do that? I need time to establish a practice."

The clerk whose name was Nisos leant forward on the counter, he looked at Tulius and with an air of mystery, said.

"There is a powerful chief in the mountains near Knossos. His name is Kallinikus. He suffers from a strange disease that no physician has been able to cure. If you can cure him, you will be a wealthy man. He is known to be generous to those who

serve him well. I cannot tell you much about him. I hear good
things and bad things concerning him, but no one really knows
what he is like. You could be endangering your life, so please, if
you do go to him be very cautious."

"How can I find this man?" asked Tullius.

"If you come by here tomorrow, I may be able to tell you. I
have a friend who knows someone who used to work for the
man."

"Where could I stay the night?" asked the priest.

Nisos scratched his chin. His eyes narrowed.

There is a woman named Veleria," he said. "She has a
boarding house just as you walk out of this wharf. Her house
has red shutters and door. She will probably put you up and
feed you for a denarius. Two at the most.

"Thank you. Until tomorrow then," said Tullius, and giving
the clerk a warm smile, left.

Veleria, was a congenial forty-year-old woman. She was
assuredly no beauty but had an attractive medium size figure,
and kind light brown eyes. Her very ordinary features would
cause little excitement in her viewers, but they had a regularity
about them which gave her face an aura of candidness and
honesty. She welcomed Tullius with a warm smile and showed
him to a room on the upper floor overlooking the harbour. It
was clean and equipped with all the necessary furniture. The
tired priest nodded his ascent.

"Have you eaten?" she asked with a concerned look.

"No," answered Tullius. "I am quite famished. I have had a
very trying day."

"Oh, my! The 'cena' will not be for another three hours.
You had better come downstairs and I shall find something to
bind you over till then."

Tullius left the baggage in the room and followed his
hostess.

Veleria served her guest some cheese, bread, olives and
some wine.

"This should dull your hunger until the 'cena'," she told him with a congenial smile.

"You are very kind." He poured himself some wine.

"I don't mean to pry, but can you tell me about your day. My days are always so dull and boring. I like to hear from others."

"I don't mind telling you about it. It was quite different from my normal days to be sure."

Tullius related to Veleria his day's misadventure and indeed more about his trip; other than mentioning the veil.

"Oh, how horrible," she cried with an alarmed look in her eyes. "And they stole all your money. You could have been injured or even killed. That's terrible. Now, what are you going to do? You are so far from home and your loved ones who could help you."

Tullius, helping himself to some more cheese, which he was thoroughly enjoying, related what the clerk had told him.

"That sounds somewhat risky. You do not know this country. There are many bandits in the mountains away from the reach of the law. Can you not find anything to do here in town? Even if it is not what you normally do? You really only need to keep yourself during the winter, and make enough to pay for another passage."

"It is a thought. Thank you, I shall think about it."

That night, Tullius did think about what his landlady had advised him.

'I have no other skills or trade,' he said to himself, 'how am I going to keep myself until the winter is over?'

He could come up with nothing. His thoughts as usual, drifted to his beloved Rufina and new son, and he prayed. Finishing his somewhat shortened night prayers, he whispered.

"Lord, it's all in your divine hands." And shortly after fell asleep.

Tullius was quite surprised the next morning, when on entering the Port Registry office, there were two men waiting for him.

"Good morning," greeted Nisos. "Here are two fellows. One of them will take you to meet Kallinikus, if you have decided on going."

"Yes, I can be back in half an hour with my things."

"This is my friend Euphenes, and this is Keteus, who will take you up to the mountains."

Tillius pressed the men's hands, smiled and took off to fetch his baggage.

Veleria was not happy to see him go. Not only was she going to miss a good lodger, but possibly a good friend. She had been most impressed with the congenial physician.

"I hope to see you again soon Veleria," said Tullius smiling warmly. Shouldering his baggage, he gave her a silent blessing and walked out the door.

* * * * *

The mountains were truly stunning in the literal sense. Tillius experienced the occasional touch of vertigo when the horses rode close to the many sheer precipices and canyons which made up the topography of those wild and beautiful mountains. The beaten paths were rough and dry, as opposed to the surrounding vegetation which was lush and very colourful. Every now and then they would ride through a completely shaded valley, narrow and deep, with a crystal-clear stream running through it. The little farm houses they encountered along the way were surrounded by olive trees and whatever vegetables each farmer happened to grow.

They constantly encountered goatherds tending their goats which somehow prospered in those rocky surroundings, finding much to nibble on among the rocks.

Stopping for their meals in the homes of peasants, they enjoyed among other rural dishes, whole wheat bread, home grown olives and delicious olive oil produced by them in their own backyards. Keteus took care of all expenses. He would be remunerated handsomely by Kallinikus who had always been generous to him, he said.

It took them three days and nights to reach Kallinikus' village. Their nights were spent in warm barns on clean dry hay after a hearty cena. At one particular hamlet, they were served delicious roasted venison which had recently been hunted by the farmer and some friends. The former, with the enthusiasm of a true hunter, regaled the two visitors with the exciting details of the hunt, making for a very pleasant evening.

Tulius had never enjoyed food as much as in those mountains. The pure fresh air had largely contributed to his appetite. It got quite cold at night, and the physician priest, whose wardrobe was very limited, found himself wearing most of his clothes together at one time. Keteus, who travelled well prepared, told his companion that in another month, some of those mountain passes would be snow-covered and very difficult to travel on.

Finally the pair of weary travellers arrived at their destination.

The village where Kallinikus ruled so to speak, was very well situated atop a small mountain which by reason of being mostly snow free in winter, allowed for travel down a winding path through a dense forest to a village in a very fertile and beautiful valley below. Watered by a fast flowing, meandering river, which ran through the centre of the valley, the fortunate villagers enjoyed fresh fish all year round, along with the inevitable sport of fishing that accompanied it.

A horde of children playing in the village square, crowded inquisitively around the two arriving horsemen and noisily escorted them all the way up a shady path through the forest to a sumptuous house at a considerable distance from the square. It was surrounded by a high wall and enclosed by a large double ornamental wrought iron gate.

Two armed men guarded the gate, and as Tullius and his guide approached, they demanded to know what they wanted.

Keteus answered with confidence in his voice, pointing at Tullius.

"I have brought this physician to see if he can help Kallinikus."

"And who are you?" asked one of the guards addressing the guide.

"I am Keteus. I used to work for your boss. He will remember me, though it has been a while."

One of the guards disappeared. The other remained by the gate but made no effort to open.

Presently, the man returned, nodding to his companion who then opened the big gate.

The visitors were led through a large well tended garden and into the house. They entered through a half open double leaved, handsomely carved, wooden door, and found themselves in an impressive hallway. From there, they were ushered into a well-appointed reception room and told to make themselves comfortable. The house was evidently devoid of an atrium. There was simply the hallway, and that particular room. Tullius was aware of a large peristyle beyond another smaller, but intricately wrought, iron gate

"Kallinikus will be with you shortly," said the guard and left.

Soon, a maid appeared with a tray of victuals, a jug of wine and three silver cups. She set it on a low table beside them, and with a smile and shallow bow, left the room.

Keteus poured some wine into two cups and gave one to Tullius, who was busy admiring the impressive furnishings that surrounded them.

The room, which looked out onto the garden had two windows; both heavily shuttered against the heat of the day. These were subsequently opened by another maid, bathing the room with light and exposing some very attractive wrought iron grills.

After a short while, Kallinikus made his appearance. He motioned for his guests to remain seated and flopped down on one of the many beautiful cushions that covered the floor.

"Good to see you again Keteus," greeted the rural chief with a smile. "I trust life has been good to you." He reached over, poured himself some wine, and quickly drained the cup.

Keteus smiling back, replied in the affirmative and proceeded to introduce Tullius.

"This man is a physician from Rome, whom I think may be able to help you. He was on his way to Cyrene but suffered a mishap during his shore leave and missed the departure of his ship. He is in need of money since all was stolen, and I thought of you and wondered if perhaps he could help you with the stomach ailment that constantly afflicts you.

As Keteus and Kallinikus talked of the journey to the village and reminisced over a few other matters leaving Tullius' introduction in mid air, the astute physician was quietly sipping his wine and sizing up his prospective patient.

He beheld a man in his mid sixties, tall in height but thin and somewhat frail. His broad shoulders were hunched and his whole aspect spoke of a once powerful physique emaciated by a disease that had been progressively destroying him over the years. His face was drawn and colourless. His eyes were saddened, most likely by the loss of hope in finding a cure for his debilitating and painful condition. It was difficult to imagine that this decrepit man had held the surrounding countryside in an an iron grip for half a lifetime.

"This is Tullius," said Keteus finally, snapping the physician out of his intense scrutiny of the patient.

Tullius smiled at the man and said.

"I am happy to meet you Kallinikus." He pressed the man's extended hand.

"I shall do my best to alleviate your condition which I can see has been plaguing you for years. I do not know whether I can encourage you to foresee a cure, but I shall use all my skill to attempt just that."

"I haven't had much luck with my physicians. I hope you can do better," growled the disconcerted chief with great doubt in his sad grey eyes.

He suddenly clapped his hands. A maid appeared almost instantly.

"Yes Master," she said, her thin eyebrows raised quizzically.

"Have Prometheus come to me right away."

The girl gave a shallow bow and noiselessly floated away. Kallinikus looked at Keteus and smiled.

"Sixtus will take care of you. Thanks for your thoughtfulness and your trouble. Perhaps we shall see each other again."

Keteus got up, and pressing the chief's extended hand, smiled, thanked him, wished him luck, and nodding to Tullius in farewell, walked out of the room.

"He is a good man," said Kallinikus when Keteus had gone.

Prometheus suddenly appeared.

"You called Master?" he asked, with a shallow bow.

"Look after Keteus for the night and have Sixtus give him three gold aureii (hundred denarii.) He will be leaving tomorrow.

Tullius, stunned at the amount of money that Keteus was to receive just for bringing him to his beleaguered ex-chief, realised that he must have served Kallinikus very faithfully to be so rewarded.

"Very well Master," assured the man, standing there waiting to be dismissed.

"Before you go, see that a room near my bedroom is comfortably prepared for this man. He is a physician and will be looking after me from now on."

The way the chief said, 'from now on,' sounded a trifle disconcerting to Tullius, who could see himself there for the duration.

The servant left them to themselves, and Tulius lost no time in getting down to business.

He soon got to know Kallinikus' medical history, and just what treatments had been given him by other physicians. Some of them, he found to have been rather bizarre, and he was certain that they had done more harm than good.

"Tell me what you eat every week," he asked the chief.

He made a mental note of the diet that the man was following, and the quantity of food he consumed. Tullius was somewhat appalled at the type of food that the man ate and wondered how a frail constitution could deal with that.

Tullius then accompanied him to to his bedroom where he proposed to carry out an examination. On the way to the chief's room, the pair were met by a very handsome woman in her early thirties, whom Kallinikus introduced as his daughter Claudia.

"This is Tullius, my new physician," said the father, "we are going to my room where he wants to examine me."

Claudia smiled sweetly at the handsome physician.

"I shall be nearby in case you need anything," she said.

The examination did not take long.

"Have you ever spat out or vomited blood?" asked Tullius as he felt his patient's stomach.

"Yes, a good number of times. I found there was blood in what I brought up."

Tullius could feel a lump in the stomach area. 'It is an abscess or perhaps a tumour,' he said to himself.

"Is this painful?" he asked gently pressing on the lump.

"Ouch! Yes," assured Kallinikus wincing, and feeling slightly sick to the stomach.

"I suppose you suffer great pain constantly?" asked Tullius. Kallinikos nodded ascent.

"It keeps me up all night and in the morning I'm exhausted. I also feel pain and nausea many times after eating.

The knowledgeable physician then went on to brief his patient on his proposed new diet which was not well received by the latter. His accustomed type of food would suffer a drastic change, and his consumption of wine would be similarly curtailed in favour of milk.

"In addition to that I shall be administering some herbal mixes which I hope will somewhat relieve your pain. I shall be honest with you," continued Tullius engaging his patient's eyes.

"I do not think it is possible to completely cure you. But my treatment will hopefully ease your suffering considerably, so that you can live a fuller life."

Kallinikus listened attentively to Tullius' diagnosis and treatment and hoped that the great sacrifice he was going to make as regards his diet would be worth it. He had an excessive love for his food and drink. No other physician had changed his diet, and he felt apprehensive about Tullius' treatment. He protested, and tried to compromise, but the physician would have none if it. He pointed out quite bluntly, that he would not survive much longer if he continued in his present mode of life. That scared the chief somewhat, and he finally acquiesced to Tullius' plan of action.

Having left Kallinkus to ponder over the proposed changes in his daily habits, Tullius was shown to his room by one of the servants, and he got down to the business of organizing his meagre things, and settling in. He looked around and was well pleased with what he saw.

His bed was most comfortable. There was a large basin on a stand with a water jug inside it, and a glass mirror on the wall at face height immediately over it. The wooden planked floor was stained in a dark brown and covered with three individual carpets; two small ones on either side of the bed, and a large one covering most of the remainder of the room. All three had beautiful designs in various colours. Two small tables stood on each side of the bed, and under one of them sat the indispensable earthenware pot with a handle.

There were ample wall hooks for his clothes, and a small leather covered trunk stood in one corner of the room. Tullius rejoiced to see a table and stool where he could sit and write.

A large colourful tapestry hung on the wall behind his bed and he soon found that his window opened on to a small balcony with a wrought iron railing and some pretty potted plants.

He was on the point of starting his ablutions when there was a knock at the door.

Putting his tunic back on, he hastened to open.

A man about Tullius' height and build stood on the threshold. He had full head of red/brown hair, and a full beard and moustache and could not have been older than twenty-three years of age.

"I am Brutus," he said, with the hint of a smile. "My father tells me that you have come to try and cure him." He did not offer a hand.

"My name is Tullius. I shall do all I can for your father. He suffers badly," said the physician, not knowing what to make of the man who had not offered his hand.

"I am in charge of everything around here. If you need anything, come to me. My father is constantly ill and attends to nothing but himself. Do you need any money?"

"I need to buy herbs and things to prepare my treatment. But that won't amount to much. Maybe your cook can supply me with some of them. As for me, I have no money. I had it all stolen from me in Phoenix. I have yet to discuss my fee with your father. At the moment, I am more concerned with getting him to feel better."

"Very well. I shall leave it to my father to settle things with you. But for anything else come to me." He turned and walked away without a further word.

Tullius closed his door and prepared once again for his ablutions.

'I shall have to watch this fellow,' he said to himself, taking his tunic off again.

It was a little before the cena when Tullius went downstairs to look for the kitchen. A servant who happened to be passing showed him where it was, and he quickly made his way there.

A small chubby woman with a kindly round face and a large knife in her hand, was busy preparing the cena assisted by two other younger women. Tullius walked into the kitchen and asked for the cook.

"I, am the cook," answered the woman looking up at Tullius who towered over her. "My name is Viviana. And who might you be?"

"I'm pleased to meet you, my name is Tullius. I am a physician. I shall be looking after your master. I would like to know if you have a herbal garden here."

The cook stopped cutting the piece of meat and pointed to the window.

"I cannot stop right now, but help yourself," she said and continued with her work. Tullius walked out into the garden and to his joy, soon found a splendid herbal garden. It would enable him to concoct all the recipes that he had created over the years and which he guarded almost as zealously as he did the veil.

For the next hour, the physician took mental stock of the various herbs he would be using.

'With the exception of a couple,' he said to himself with great relief, 'they are all there.'

"Cena will be served in a few moments."

At the sound of the cook's voice, Tullius looked up from the little cluster of camomile he was examining.

"I congratulate you on an excellent herbal garden," he smiled.

"Thank you. It is not often that I receive compliments on my dear little patch."

"We can chat about it when you find the time," said Tullius walking back into the kitchen and then off to find the dining room.

In the peristyle, he met Claudia, who was also on her way to the dining room for the cena.

"Are you going to be able to help my father?" she asked with hope in her eyes.

"Yes of course. But he must cooperate and follow my treatment faithfully. I am not sure yet that he will give up some of the foods that are slowly killing him."

"He is very stubborn and has always had his way. If I can help in any way, please let me know. I hate to see him suffer so."

They walked into the dining room, and Claudia, directing him to his place, sat down beside him. The small family began to arrive, and each sat in their accustomed place.

Brutus sat at the right-hand side of his father. Opposite him sat a man of Brutus' age. He was engrossed in conversation with him and merely threw a cursory look in Tullius' direction.

As the family awaited Kallinikus' arrival, Claudia gave Tullius a quick family history:

Kallinikus was a widower. Her mother had died nine years ago. She, Claudia was herself a widow through a hunting accident which killed her husband under (in her opinion very shady circumstances). She had two children, a boy aged eight and a girl aged six. They were presently staying with their grandparents on the father's side, down in the village.

The man sitting opposite her unmarried brother was, she said, his henchman. His name was Trosinius. Her brother wanted her to marry him, but she hated the man whom she declared with disgust in her lovely light green eyes, was cruel and uncouth.

Tullius listened without interrupting her. He wished to acquaint himself as quickly as he could with the world that he now found himself in and which he felt somewhat uncomfortable about.

At length, the chief arrived, and without a single word or gesture, took his place at the head of the table. All conversation stopped.

Kallinikus looked around him, and then at Tullius.

"This man," he said gesturing at his guest, is my new physician. His name is Tullius, and he will be with us for a while.

Finally, Trosinius nodded his recognition. Brutus gave him a quick look, and Claudia smiled.

The meal was then brought in by two young women, and the cena began.

Tullius observed his patient's behaviour during the meal. Noting his reaction to the things he ate. The man did not over-eat. He was observed to wince every now and then, and as soon as the meal was over he quietly and slowly walked away.

"Where is you father going?" asked the physician turning to Claudia.

"Probably to his room to lie down," she replied with a shrug of her shapely shoulders.

"I must get him to walk after the cena," said Tullius seriously.

"I wish you luck." Was the unexpected reply.

Tullius chatted for a little while with the charming Claudia, and excusing himself, went upstairs to his patient's room. As he approached the door he could hear retching. He knocked and waited. Presently the chief opened the door. His face was white and haggard, and he held himself up by leaning against the door frame, Tullius grasped a hold of his arm and supporting him, walked him back into the room, where he sat him on the bed.

"Are you still nauseous?" asked the physician.

"I think I am over it now," replied the patient; his chin sinking onto his chest.

"Tomorrow," said Tullius with firmness in his voice, you start your new life my friend. I think it will be a very much more comfortable one for you." He got up and squeezed the man's shoulders, and looked deeply into his dim, grey eyes. "Trust me," he said, and walked out of the room.

"Good morning Viviana! "greeted Tullius, walking into the kitchen after breakfast the following morning.

The cook, who was in the middle of her breakfast in the company of her assistants, looked up and smiled a good morning at the friendly intruder.

"Do I have your permission to invade your garden?" said Tullius with a broad smile.

"By all means. It really isn't my garden. It belongs to the house. I just happen to prize it more than all the others seeing that it helps me in so many ways."

"I understand, and I shall treat it with the utmost respect," assured the physician, suddenly producing a pair of scissors and walking off to the kitchen garden.

On his return, laden with the necessary herbs, Tullius noticed a small table just under the window. The women were once again busy chopping up vegetables and beginning their preparations for lunch.

"That table is for your use," said Viviana. "I cannot have you making all those strange concoctions on my kitchen tables."

Tullius was touched by the cook's foresight.

"You are an angel."

"And you are a flatterer," she laughed, pointing at him with her knife.

"It would take a fair pair of wings to carry her around," joked one of the girls with a cheeky laugh. The other one sniggered, and soon all were laughing, even the good-natured Viviana who did not in the least mind laughing at herself.

By lunch time, Tullius was ready to administer his first dose of medicine to the chief. That, would become a daily ritual and continue for some time.

Over the next month, Kallinikus began to feel better. The new diet that Tullius had designed, and Viviana had skilfully made quite palatable, was being received favourably by her employer.

The physician began to settle into his new surroundings and resigned himself to spending the winter there in those beautiful hills. He began to frequent the village, where he had a chance to meet new people and try his hand at fishing in the river. Sometimes Claudia would accompany him and visit her children who were enjoying their stay in the valley with their grandparents. Soon she said, she would take them back up to the house on the hill to be with her and her father. She feared her parents were spoiling the children. Though she knew her father would spoil them just as much, when he got the opportunity. Fearing the children would be an aggravation to him, even though he was always delighted to see them. She limited their visits to the 'big house.'

Tullius became aware as he travelled back and forth to the village, that he was being constantly watched. He could hear the odd branch snap or a head pull back behind a tree, as he traversed the forest path that led to the village. He wondered also where Brutus and his friend spent all their days even to the point of staying away from the big house for days. As the days passed and his visits to the village increased, he grew more familiar with the villagers. He realised that there was an undercurrent of discontent among the people.

One day he shared his suspicions with a man called Lucius, who was the village herbalist, and acted as physician to the villagers in the absence of a real one.

"Is it that noticeable?" asked Lucius.

"It's just a feeling."

"Can I trust you to hold your tongue on the matter?"

"You have my word," said Tullius solemnly.

Lucius stared warily at the door of his shop.

"Your boss' son is terrorizing the people behind his father's back. Everyone is afraid of him and his men. They are foreigners, and don't care who they hurt. I hear he is spreading his tentacles to other villages also."

"Why does someone not tell Kallinikus?"

"It's worth their life to do so. A man and an old woman who threatened to tell his father, disappeared. The old woman was later found in the river. The man has still not been found."

The herbalist drew a little closer to his guest. "Brutus is exacting a tax from everyone over and above what they pay his father. They have also raped some women. The village girls are afraid to leave their houses in the evenings."

"Little wonder I could feel something in the air. It is pretty thick," bewailed Tullius shaking his head.

"What about the authorities? the Legion?"

"They are seldom around, especially in winter. The most you see are two Legionaries every now and then."

Tullius returned to the big house on the hill with great sadness. That beautiful valley full of life and colour was a hell for the people living in it. He could not help the hatred he suddenly felt for Brutus and his gang of murderers. He knew that Kallinikus had always taxed and ruled those people, but at least he respected them and as Claudia had told him, looked after them when they needed help. But his son was a crook and murderer. He shuddered as he considered the dreadful life that the poor people would be subjected to when the chief died.

It was a night of tossing and turning as Tullius fretted over the misfortunes of the villagers. Suddenly the thought struck him.

"I wonder if there are any Christians in the village?"

He had no idea as to how Brutus felt about Christians. The subject had never yet been mentioned at the cena. The man was for ever hating something or other. It appeared to the mild-mannered physician, that there was nothing but hate in Brutus' heart.

'Would Claudia know what her brother was up to?' he asked himself. 'And, would she be brave enough to tell her father? In any event what could the old ailing man do?'

Kallinikus' health began to improve in the second month of treatment. He could keep his food down and the pain had eased considerably. Tullius walked in the garden with him every day after the cena, and his whole constitution appeared to profit from the exercise. Colour returned to his cheeks and Claudia was most encouraged at her father's progress. But the more encouraged Claudia became, the more resentful Brutus felt. He had been waiting for his father's condition to worsen and cause his demise. His father was clearly in the way of his criminal ambitions. He planned on gaining control of two neighbouring valleys ruled by friends of his father's whom he did not care for.

There had been a sworn agreement which had been negotiated many years ago among their chiefs which included his father, and the contract had always been honoured by all. Each chief kept within his boundaries and if any of them were challenged from outside their areas, they were pledged to go to each other's help. Recently their sons had taken over, and they had all agreed to maintain the 'status quo.'

Brutus however planned on changing all of that as soon as his father died. As a result, he began to develop a hate towards Tullius, who was thwarting his ambitious plans. He cursed the day that the clever physician had arrived, and swore to himself that he would put an end to him at the first opportunity.

As a child, he had been thoroughly spoiled by his parents, especially Kallinikus, who taught him to treat everyone in the village as his inferiors. In all fairness to Kallinikus however, he did teach his son to protect and respect those below him; even if he extorted money from them on a monthly basis.

"You must realise my son," he would tell the youngster, "that they depend on us for their livelihood. That is the reason why they have to pay me from their earnings. If they misbehave, you have to judge them, and meet out punishment as you see fit. If they get sick you have to help them get better. So that they can go back to work for you."

As Brutus grew into manhood, he became selfish and greedy, and began to be a constant problem for the girls in the village who soon became afraid of him. The protestations of their parents were played down by Kallinikus, and Brutus was allowed to grow into a real menace for them. The spoilt young man became hungry for power, formed a gang of delinquent youths and began chastising villagers who would not acquiesce to his unreasonable demands. Soon he fell into bad company on his travels to Phoenix where he loved to spend his time and money amidst prostitutes and rogues who hoped to profit from the country boy's ignorance and wealth.

Though he had been taught to read and write, Brutus desired to learn nothing else. He spent his time mock-fighting with his Phoenix friends, and became quite adept at archery which he loved, as it enabled him to hunt in the mountains. He was tall, strong of physique and quite good looking; which attributes became a trap for the unfortunate women that were attracted to him.

It was in Phoenix that he had heard stories about the unpopular and revolutionary Christians, and what an intolerable and dangerous bunch of Jews they were. Those erroneous and libellous stories built a hatred in the young man's heart for the followers of Yeshua.

The Phoenix slave market usually had a few Christian slaves for sale, and he often spent time there eyeing the women that were for sale with great hatred and lust. Fortunately for the poor slaves, he had as yet not enough money to buy one. He doubted his father's slaves were Christians. They were well looked after by his father. Once in his adolescence however, for a period of time, he had abused one of them whom he had fancied. His father had turned a blind eye on the matter and ordered the girl to hold her tongue or he would beat her mercilessly. The unfortunate soul was still serving in the household, and Brutus in his turn, wondered just how many of his father's slaves had been abused and raped by him.

He remembered his now dead mother protesting the way he treated the servants which often led to some very nasty rows; she, generally being the loser. Claudia, then only a girl, bravely defended her mother whom she dearly loved. Brutus, who as the days went by, found himself more and more on the wrong side of his father, became jealous at what his sister got away with where her father was concerned.

The fact was, that Kallinikus was amused at her pluck, and would simply walk away. On growing up however, she became the only person who would stand up to him, putting him to shame whenever he behaved meanly, or merely mistaken in some regard or other.

CHAPTER SIXTEEN

ESCAPE

Tullius walked the forest path down to the village. It was mid morning and the sun's rays filtering through the tall trees brought the place to life, making the leaves sparkle, and colouring the soft floor of the path with many shades of siennas and umbers.

Suddenly he felt the usual presence of someone spying on him, but he ignored it once more.

'There may come a time,' he mused, 'when I shall frustrate this spy's efforts.'

He was thinking of the time when he would leave Kallinikus and his unhappy world and complete his mission with the veil which for the present he kept well hidden in his room. It was only the middle of winter and he was confident that Silas was still wintering in Cyrene or some other port well away from Crete.

Soon, he entered the colourful little village and made his way to the herbalist's shop.

That day he had resolved to find out if his friend Lucius knew anything of Christianity.

Lucius warmly embraced him on entering the shop and invited him to some watered wine, which he knew was his friends preferred refreshment. They sat and chatted for a while about local matters and village gossip. Then Tullius asked the herbalist the question he had been contemplating all that morning.

"Tell me something Lucius," said the physician placing his hand on his friend's shoulder.

"Have you heard of a religion called Christianity?"

"Yes," answered Lucius after some thought. "They are a new sect of Jews."

"Are there any in the village?"

"I don't think so, though one can never be sure."

The priest in Tullius suddenly took over from the physician.

"They are not a new sect of Judaism even though some are Jews. The religion was born in Judea, but it has spread all the way to Rome and beyond, and a great many are Romans, Cyreneans, Syrians, Egyptians even."

"I have heard as everyone knows, that Claudius has thrown them out of Rome and is persecuting them," said the herbalist with confidence.

"Yes, indeed that is very true," agreed Tullius with a smile. "Do you not know any more about them than that?"

"No."

"Would you like me to tell you more about them?"

"I'm always willing to learn," replied Lucius with a smile and a gesture of the hand.

Two hours passed very quickly for Lucius, who was completely enthralled by what the ardent priest related to him.

Tullius got up to leave. He had to be back at the big house for the cena; prior to which he normally gave Kallinikus his medicine. He still did not trust the man to take it by himself.

"You have given me much to think about my good friend," said an enthralled Lucius as they embraced and the priest left.

Claudia was waiting for Tullius in the garden near the door of the house. She was most upset. Taking his arm, she led him back to the gate.

She nodded to the gateman to open again. They walked away from the house, to the sound of angry shouting.

"I am glad I did not bring my children back today, as I had planned to do this morning," she said with tears in her eyes. "My brother and father are having a terrible argument." She wiped her eyes and continued. "My brother has been doing some terrible things, and my father has found out. I don't think you should be burdened with family problems."

"For your father's sake, I wish I could help, but your brother would not put up with my interfering."

"No. He is a hot head and would probably give you a rough time. That is why I waited for you at the house door."

"That was very kind of you Claudia, and I am most grateful for your concern."

Tullius wished he could tell her how the village people were being threatened and bullied by her nasty brother, but it would only make her miserable, and she could do nothing about it anyway.

"I am concerned for your father. As yet, he has a fairly strong heart, but with his serious stomach condition, he could suddenly become very ill. In fact, he could be paralysed as a result of these stresses that are imposed on him by your brother."

"He doesn't care. In fact," she said, with more tears in her eyes and her voice breaking, "sometimes I think he wishes him dead. Then he could be the boss and do things his way."

Tullius did not answer. He felt very strongly that that was in fact the case.

They walked as far as the edge of the little forest, still within sight of the house gate.

"Let us turn back now," said Claudia with a warm smile. "You are a young man, and I do not want to compromise you in any way. The gate guards have been watching us, and so they will be our witnesses."

They turned and began to walk back to the house.

"You have been here for two months," she said with a lovely smile, "and I know nothing of you." She looked at him with expectancy in her admiring eyes. "Surely you must have a family who is missing you badly right now?"

Tullius felt that there was no reason why he should hide his identity from her.

"My full name is Tullius Ledicius, and my family is in Umbria. My wife's family own vineyards there. Her name is Rufina, and we have a son Tullius, who is four months old."

"I knew that a handsome and sensitive man like you had to have someone that deeply cared for him. I too loved my husband very much. When he was killed in that horrible accident, it broke my heart. If it had not been for the love of my children, I think I also would have died. I was ill for many months after."

Some terrible thoughts invaded Tullius' mind. 'Begone Satan!' he said to himself, and prayed that Yeshua would forgive him for judging her brother or even suspecting something that he was not sure about. He had heard of the accident. Viviana had told him. They had all accepted the story that Brutus had given them. But he had detected a sinister something in the way that she had expressed herself.

"What?" asked Tullius, "will you do when your father dies?"

"I live in dread of that, and I am very grateful to you for keeping him alive. I shall likely leave this house, and with the inheritance I receive from him, I shall build a good house in the village and live with my in-laws. They love the children and are fond of me also."

"Yes. That sounds very sensible to me. I shall pray for that," said Tullius unwittingly.

"That is a lovely thing to say... What god will you be praying to for me?"

The priest in Tuliius was awakened once again. He had slipped up, but perhaps Yeshua had caused him to do that. He had not been carrying out the Lord's work lately and felt the guilt in his soul.

"I would love to tell you," smiled Tullius, but you would not understand unless I first explained many things to you."

"I am not a stupid woman," said Claudia with a touch of pride in her voice.

"You are a very intelligent and beautiful woman," said Tullis with a fetching smile. "I have great respect for you and have no intention of offending you. My God to whom I shall be praying for your welfare is at the moment not popular with the emperor. As a result of that, we who believe in Him are being presently persecuted in Rome."

"You are a Christian?"

"Yes. And because I trust you, I can tell you much about Him. There is much that you should know if you really wish to know."

"I have heard my brother say that they are vile people who hate our gods and our emperor, and that they commit all sorts of crimes. But I do not believe him... He often lies."

"I assure you that we bear no one any malice. In fact, our God Yeshua tells us to love our neighbour as ourselves and even to love our enemies for his sake.

Having reached the gate, Claudia gestured with her hand for the guard to open.

The man smiled at her, nodded, and let them in. He knew that she had been keeping the stranger away from the house as the row that was still going on inside was no business of his.

She led him to an attractively carved stone bench surrounded by wisteria which backed against the high garden wall. Its aroma was quite heady and enchanting at that time of the evening.

They sat down to continue with their talk. Suddenly, all the shouting emanating from the house, stopped. Silence reigned.

Presently, Brutus and Trosinius, rode out of the stables at the side of the house and approached the gate shouting for it to be opened. The gateman acquiesced with urgency and away they rode.

Claudia and Tullius cut short their conversation and rushed into the house.

A very unhappy Viviana met them as they entered the peristyle. She complained about her cena going to waste unless everyone hurried into the dining room.

"You can heat it all up later," said Claudia, rushing past her and into her father's room.

The physician waited outside.

"Tullius! come quickly!"

At Claudia's anguished call, Tullius hastened into the room.

Kallinikus was lying on his bed staring up at the ceiling. His breathing was accelerated, and his face was very white. Tullius made a cursory examination and rushed off to the kitchen. He went directly to a small cupboard that the cook had designated for his concoctions and quickly pulled out a small container. Taking a small pot, he put some water in it and proceeded to heat it.

Viviana watched with great interest.

"Is the Master in great pain?" she asked with a concerned look; having now forgotten about the cena.

"No, but he could die any moment if I do not get this into him," he said pointing at the pot.

A few moments later, Tullius was on his way to try and save his employer's life.

An anxious virgil followed, as Tullius and Claudia conscientiously tended to Kallinikus' fluctuating condition.

As the evening came to a close, Viviana brought them some food to pacify their hungry stomachs. She had to leave, but she instructed the two slave girls that assisted her in the kitchen, to stand by in case they were needed. Prometheus insisted on keeping watch by his master, but the other servants of the house, (who were actually slaves, as was Prometheus himself) were dismissed for the night.

Dawn greeted Tullius and Claudia in the form of loud snoring from Kallinikus.

The physician shaking off his drowsiness quickly examined his patient. It was with some relief, that the sleepy physician woke Claudia who had fallen asleep on some of the floor cushions. He gave her the happy news that her father would live.

Prometheus, sitting in the doorway, beamed with joy. He did not look forward to the prospect of having Brutus as his lord and master.

'It was tough enough,' he mused, "dealing with the father. But at least he was never beaten by him, whereas the son often slapped his face and kicked him.'

As Kallinikus recovered, Brutus stayed away from the house. Tullius made excellent progress with the instruction of Claudia in the faith. He thanked Yeshua for giving her the gift of faith, much as He had done for Lucius the herbalist, who had embraced Christianity with great zeal, and was secretly spreading the faith among the villagers much to Tullius' delight. Even if his mission with regard to the veil was temporarily frozen, at least his duty as a priest was being performed.

* * * * *

The winter was almost over. Tullius had become a vital part of many people's lives. Kallinikus depended on his physician for his very survival. Claudia, had fallen in love with him, but realised that he was beyond her reach. The love he bore his wife and child left no room for any other woman in his life.

'If I had only met him a couple of years ago,' she said to herself with great regret. 'I shall be a faithful friend to him. We owe him much.'

Kallinikus had been generous to Tullius. He had so far given his attentive physician sixteen aureii (four hundred denarii). His dependency on Tullius however served as a term of imprisonment for the hapless physician, who saw no end in sight. As winter came to a close, our hero feared that he would be the chief's prisoner until the man's death finally released him.

Very little had been seen of Brutus or his henchman after the horrendous row between him and his father. Claudia suspected the reason, but she was very reluctant to talk about it, and Tullius did not press her.

The Christian congregation in the village was growing quickly. The happy priest had baptised a good number of people including Claudia and Lucius, who had the makings of a good priest if he ever got the opportunity. He took over the organizing of prayer services in secret, visiting each household individually, and pressed Tullius to perform the 'Breaking of the Bread' service, two families at a time, as often as he could.

Rumours however reached the chief, that his son was extorting payments and molesting women in two of the adjoining villages, after having scared them with his criminal acts.

If the rumours were true, dire consequences would surely follow.

The village chiefs in question had been guaranteed by Kallinikus many years earlier that he would not interfere with their domain. Those guarantees between the chiefs were held as sacred. Each chief was to govern their own village, and that was that.

Shortly after the rumours concerning Brutus' violation of his father's agreement with the other village chiefs, two of the latters appeared at the gate of Kallinikus' house, accompanied by their sons and an escort of armed men.

The gate guards were given their names and told to announce their arrival demanding to see Kallinikus.

Tullius was in the middle of preparing the day's medicines when a gateman walked into the peristyle and informed his master of the chiefs' arrival.

Kallinikus, became quite agitated, and in his distress, called for Tullius for whom he had nurtured great respect. The latter hastened to his employer's side taking with him a dose of the medicine he had just prepared?

The guard awaited his boss' permission to admit the visitors.

"Have them come into the reception room, I shall be there presently," said Kallinikus, as Tullius entered the room.

"I feel very jittery," complained the chief. "I am about to have a very difficult meeting with some people whom I have not seen for quite some time. They are friends, but they are going to accuse me rightly of things that I have not been able to control. Can you give me something to calm me down?"

"First, please take this," said Tullius handing him the medicine, "and I shall go and boil a herb that will help you." So saying he hastened to the kitchen and hastily prepared a herbal potion. He asked Viviana to take Kallinikus a cup when it had boiled, and he went into the reception room to greet the visitors.

He informed them that Kallinikus was in the middle of a medical treatment and would be with them presently. Promising them refreshments, he left them to themselves.

On his way back to his patient's room, Tullius bumped into Claudia.

"Would you see to the visitors' refreshments please," he asked of her. "I must tend to your father."

"Yes. But who are they?"

"I shall tell you later, I have to see to your father. He must not get too upset."

Kallinikus had taken his medicine and was sipping his hot and very concentrated dose of lime flower tea.

"I have taken the liberty, said Tullius, "of informing your visitors that you will be a little delayed in meeting with them. Claudia is seeing to their refreshments."

"What would I do without you I wonder," said a somewhat relieved Kallinikus, continuing to sip his tea.

The meeting with his brother chiefs, turned out to be every bit as difficult and distressing as Kallinikus had envisaged. Tullius sat by him, as his employer was told of the criminal acts that his son and his little gang were perpetrating in their villages. They informed Kallinikus, that they would be taking the matter in their own hands and he was not to interfere. An old and long-established agreement had been broken they told him, and he would have to adhere to their collective judgement and resulting punishment allotted to his criminal son.

Tullius and Claudia, found themselves once more, spending nights tending to a very anguished chief, whose nerves were giving the two caregivers new headaches.

One particular night turned into a veritable nightmare. Kallinikus began to shake uncontrollably. Tullius strove feverishly trying to save the man by heaping blankets over him. Suddenly he remembered the veil. Claudia was asleep nearby on some cushions which served as a bed for her or Tullius as they took turns looking after the patient. He felt that there was no need to show the veil to Claudia, or anyone else in the future, as it had become the property of the Church.

The physician stole off to his room, and taking the veil from its hiding place, quickly returned.

Checking Claudia once more, he opened the veil and placed it over the semi-conscious chief.

He waited and prayed to Yeshua. There was no change. The patient was still shaking. He waited a little longer. Still no change.

Finally, after a few more moments, fearing the daughter would wake up, he folded the veil, tucked it into his tunic and took it back to its hiding place.

Two hours later, with his patient still shaking, but very weakly, Tullius woke up Claudia to tell her that her father was quickly deteriorating. They both sat there feeling quite helpless, as Kallinikus, giving a great raspy gasp, departed from this life.

* * * * *

Claudia had been fond of her father, who though tough and at times even cruel with others, including her deceased mother, had always treated her well and had given her whatever she desired. She made all the arrangements for the funeral which was a rather challenging matter since most of the village came to pay their respect, and had to be attended to, with attention and refreshments. She had the help of Sixtus, an old and trusted freeman servant who was well versed with Kallinikus' finances and looked after all money matters for the family. On him she now totally depended.

The village chief's coffin was carried on the shoulders of villagers down the forest path, and through the village square to the cemetery which was just outside the village. Claudia walked beside Tullius directly behind the coffin, which changed hands four or five times as the pall bearers being many, took turns carrying it over the somewhat lengthy route.

The grave had been dug, and the diggers stood by waiting to finish their tasks.

Claudia nodded and bowed her head. Tullius said some silent prayers, as the coffin was being lowered into the hole. Claudia's in-laws were both there with their grandchildren who waved a sad good bye to their grandfather. The children loved their grandfather who had constantly showered them with presents. They cried when Claudia told them that they would not be seeing him again.

It was mid afternoon as the villagers dispersed to their homes. Claudia and Tullius walked sadly back up the hill to the house. The chief's daughter wanted to talk with Sixtus, and acquaint herself with the existing financial situation. She knew that the scroll which contained her father's last testament would not be opened until Brutus was present, along with two villagers acting as witnesses.

Three villagers had been dispatched in various directions to find Brutus whose whereabouts was unknown. Tullius retired to his room and began to pack his things, beginning with the veil, whilst Claudia talked to Sixtus in a small room beside the entrance to the peristyle that was used as an office.

After a while, Claudia went to Tullius' room to find out what he planned to do. She was surprised to see his baggage on the bed and him ready to leave.

"Are you leaving already?" she asked with some alarm in her eyes.

"Yes, if you let me have one of your horses. There is nothing further for me to do here. Your brother will be very happy to see me gone."

"I was hoping you would stay a while and see me settled. As I told you, I have to build a house in the village, and your opinion would greatly help me."

Tullius felt sorry for her, but his mission had been delayed long enough, and besides, staying would only mean confronting her brother whose evil plans would no longer be hindered by Kallinikus' intervention.

"I'm sorry my dear," he said with some tenderness in his voice. "I dare not delay my interrupted mission any longer. I must get to Phoenix and board ship for Cyrene as soon as possible."

Her thin eyebrows dropped. She pouted in protest; her eyes searching Tullius'.

"What am I going to do without you?" she said fighting back tears.

"God will look after you. I shall be praying for that," he said as he embraced her.

"Don't build a house just yet." he told her; parting from the embrace. "Buy one for now. That way you will be able to move in quickly and live in reasonable comfort until you build the one you want. There are a few good houses for sale in the village, all large enough to house you and your whole family."

She looked deep into his eyes. "I am going to miss you so much."

"I shall miss you too Claudia. You have been a good friend, and you have made my stay here a pleasant one. I shall always remember you with fondness." Following a final embrace, he made his way to the stables; his baggage on his shoulders.

She accompanied him.

"Take the black one," she said, "he is a good horse; runs like the wind. His name is 'Negrus.'"

The stable boy saddled the horse, and Tullius promptly mounted the beautiful stallion.

"Oh!" cried Cludia suddenly. "I have not given you any provisions for your journey."

"Don't worry, I shall get some down at the village as I leave."

She was not happy with Tullius's accelerated departure, but she knew her brother could arrive at any time, and she preferred that the two would not meet.

"You do not know the way to Phoenix," she said, with great concern.

"Lucius will be riding with me. He knows a number of routes that we can follow."

Going closer to him, she whispered, "the Lord go with you." And blew him a kiss.

He smiled, tapped the horse gently with his heels and rode over to the gate. At a nod from Claudia, the guards opened for him, and he rode away, waving back at her as he went.

She watched him until he disappeared into the forest.

'May Yeshua go with you my love,' she said to herself.

Lucius was ready, packed and waiting for Tullius' arrival.

"Don't dismount," said the herbalist. "I shall be right with you."

He locked the door and mounted his horse.

"That's quite an animal you have there my friend," smiled Linus.

"A parting gift from Claudia," said Tullius with a nod of appreciation.

"We have to buy some provisions."

"I have enough for both of us," assured Lucius. "Now let's be off before the troublemaker gets here. I am sure he is on his way back by now."

As if bringing the herbalist's last words to life, the sound of hooves suddenly resounded in the village square. Tullius and Lucius looked at each other.

"Behind my house, nodded Lucius. Both turned their horses and quickly took cover behind the house."

Brutus and three men galloped past in the direction of the big house up the hill.

'Poor Claudia,' thought Tullius. 'Lord, please help her.'

"Let's be off," said Lucius spurring his light grey horse into a gallop.

Tullius followed.

Brutus, Trosinius, and the other two men, shouted at the guards as they approached the house. The gate was quickly opened, and riding into garden, they made straight for the stables.

Claudia hearing the commotion, hastened to greet her brother. They met in the hall as Brutus entered by himself.

"At last you are here," said Claudia with tears in her eyes. "Where have you been all this time?" she asked, embracing him.

"I went to Phoenix," he said.

"What's happening? Did you manage the funeral all by yourself?"

"Yes, with Sixtus and Tullius' help."

"Where is Sixtus? I have to find out what money Father left us, and all about our finances."

"He will be back tomorrow morning. He also needs to bring two official witnesses to sit in on the opening of the last testament scroll." said Claudia with some confidence.

"Oh bother that," retorted Brutus impatiently, and walked back to the main door.

"Trosinius!" He called out. The man came running and seeing Claudia, gave her a sickly smile.

"You know where Sixtus lives... Go fetch him."

Brutus turned to Claudia.

"Where is the physician?"

Claudia took a deep breath, and walking away towards the kitchen as if unconcerned, she said as nonchalantly as she could.

"He's gone... Come, have something to eat."

He followed her into the kitchen.

Before Brutus could ask the question she did not want to answer, she began a conversation with Viviana who was busy preparing the cena.

"Good to have you home again Brutus," said Viviana with a smile. "I am so sorry about your father's passing...Would you like me to make you something special, or are lamb chops to your liking?"

"No. The lamb chops will be fine."

Claudia busied herself in the kitchen. Brutus went to his room to wash and get ready for the cena and his meeting with Sixtus. He was dying to know how much the family was worth. His father would never tell him. For the moment he had forgotten to ask when Tullius had left; which is what Claudia was afraid of since he had not had much of a head start.

Brutus and Claudia, were in the middle of the cena when Trosinius and Sixtus walked into the dining room. The latter approached the new master of the house and extended his hand for him to press.

"I am quite distressed at the death of your father my boy," said old Sixtus as Brutus pressed his hand, and nodded his acknowledgement.

"Sit with us and have your cena." said Brutus with a smile. He turned to Trosinius who had his eyes on Claudia.

"Go back to the garden with the boys, I'll have your cena sent out to you. We don't want to be disturbed."

Trosinius, somewhat disconcerted, nodded and left.

Brutus called out to Viviana. She came quickly.

"Take some food out to my three men who are in the garden, they are tired and hungry."

The cook made a shallow bow and went back to the kitchen in a glum mood. She had not expected all those extra mouths to feed, but being the resourceful person that she was, she quickly organised her little army of three and began the culinary battle.

The meeting around the dining room table was in full swing. The siblings absorbed with great interest the disclosures that the old accountant presented to them. Neither had the least idea how their businesses were being run; and there were a number of them.

Kallinikus had been a very capable administrator and investor. He had amassed quite a fortune, but neither his son or his daughter had taken the least bit of interest as to where the money was coming from much to his disgust. Both had been satisfied with having enough money to spend on whatever took their fancy.

As Sixtus lectured them on their responsibilities, they looked at each other with much concern in their eyes. The old man, with great gravity in his manner, acquainted them with the inevitable truth, that unless properly managed, all their wealth could come to nothing very quickly.

"I am an old man," said Sixtus. "Like my dear friend, your father, I could be gone tomorrow also. What would you do then? There is no one you can trust to ensure your prosperity." He looked at the two siblings whom he had known since the day they were born. He loved them as though they were his. Even though he knew Brutus to be a scoundrel, he still felt some love for him knowing it was partly Kallinikus" fault for having spoilt him during his formative years

Sixtus, a widow of many years, had no children of his own and was now in his seventy-fourth year.

Claudia braced herself for the task ahead. She was intelligent and responsible enough to be concerned for the sake of her two children, whose welfare would depend on how she managed her affairs. Brutus was quite shocked by the responsibility the situation was forcing on him, and where before he could not wait for his father to die, now he wished he was still alive.

He got up from the table and thanking Sixtus, left him to continue the meeting with his sister, promising to meet with them again in the morning for the opening of the scroll.

Brutus having joined his men in the garden, was soon drowning his sorrows in wine. He kept all that he had learned to himself and avoided prying questions that the astute Trosinius kept throwing at him.

Soon they all decided to go down to the village and have some fun, terrorising the people. Now, they had no one to answer to.

As they walked uncertainly down the dark forest path, a man emerged from the trees, and approached Brutus.

"Greetings new Master," he said; his thick lips spreading in an evil smile.

"What do you want?" asked Brutus with little interest.

"Just a little of your money."

"I don't give my money away to everyone that asks me, you fool. But I can give you the point of my boot," said Brutus, preparing to do just that.

"Hold! Master! I have something to sell you that will certainly be of interest to you, or else I have been misinformed."

The 'Master,' checked his readied foot, and grabbed the man instead by the scruff of the neck. His men laughed, as the hapless victim squirmed.

"What are you selling?" asked Brutus, releasing the rascal.

"I have heard say that you despise Christians. Am I wrong?"

"So. What of it?"

"There is someone who is converting people in the village to Christianity."

Brutus was suddenly interested in this piece of news. It would give him much power over those unfortunate people whom he could abuse at will. Especially the women. He would not even have to go to the slave market in Phoenix to find them. Money he now had to spare. But power? Could he ever have enough of that?

"Do you know who that someone is?" asked Brutus.

"Oh, yes. And a few more too. I shall sell them to you one at a time if you like."

Brutus could see that this rascal had a brain in his head even if an evil one. He would pay the man for the leader, but once he had the leader, he had a better way of extracting information from the likes of him.

"Very well," hiccuped the 'new Master'. "Tell me."

"First show me two aureii."

"You don't come cheap do you?"

"One must live."

Reaching into his well filled purse, Brutus took a handful of money and picked out two gold coins, which he handed to the man. Trosinius simultaneously took a hold of him.

"Now! Tell me," said Brutus with some excitement in his voice.

"The physician! Tullius!"

Brutus could hardly believe his ears, he had never expected that. He had nurtured a hatred for the man, for keeping his father alive, of which the priest was well aware, though no words had ever been spoken in that regard.

"What proof have you got?"

"I have seen him perform a service sitting around a low table in front of a small wooden cross. There were some incantations said, and he then passed a small dish around with small pieces of bread in it. They all ate with bowed heads. A little later, a cup with what appeared to me to be wine, was passed around also, and all drank a sip off that. The words I could not make out."

"How come you saw this and where were they meeting?"

"I was curious about a group of people entering a certain house in the evening of the Dies Solis every week. I snuck into the garden of the house and saw the whole thing through an open window. They were praying around what looked like a cross. That I know, makes them Christians."

Brutus having now recovered from the surprise. Began to wonder just when the physician had left. Would he be able to catch him? He was fairly certain that Tullius was on his way to Phoenix if not already there. He knew that he could not go after him until the scroll had been opened, and he became very angry. He took a hold of the informer and held him by the throat.

"Who were the others?"

"You have to pay me first," blurted out the man, trying to free himself from Brutus grasp.

"Let's pay him boys." said Brutus. All four fell on the scoundrel.

The man lay still on the forest path.

"Let's wait till he wakes up," said Brutus, "I'll wager he will tell us now."

They had not given the village 'busybody' for so he was, a chance to tell the other names. In their drunken state, they had got carried away in their anger, and now, sharing their wine skins, they awaited the awakening of their victim. Presently, one of the men staggered over and gave the man a slap in the face. He did not stir.

Brutus went over and felt the man's face. It was cold. He listened to his chest.

"He's dead, you fools," shouted Brutus shaking his fist in the air, and looking daggers at his inebriated companions

"You da...d fools. You killed him. Now how are we going to find the rest of those rats?"

They were all so drunk, that they simply fell asleep right there among the trees, on the moss and leaves.

* * * * *

Tullius and Lucius had been galloping for the best part of an hour before slowing their pace to a canter. The spring weather was good, and they had met with no obstacle in their way. They could not relax however. They could not be sure if Brutus was following them.

"Why are we worried about Brutus chasing us?" asked Lucius, as they approached a fork in the road. He does not know that we are Christians. And even if he did, would it be worth his while with all the problems he has at home with his father's death, to come chasing after us.

"Your logic is flawless my friend. If it applied to any other human being, my mind would be at rest. But when the intensity of hate, such as Brutus is capable of experiencing comes into play, I cannot but wonder."

"Which way?" asked Tullius pointing at the fork in the road.

"To the left," said Lucius. It is much less travelled on than the right. It leads further up the mountain and the path which narrows considerably, is often blocked by goats which take a while to be moved out of the way. But by the same token it is better frequented with places to stay for the night. Many of the goatherds rent a barn for the night, and the food is usually good.

"That sounds encouraging said Tullius." He remembered the congenial peasants that he had stayed with on his way to Kallinikus' village and looked forward to his stop for the night.

The mountain path revealed some impressive and colourful landscapes. There were times when the pair of peace-loving travellers were somewhat apprehensive. Particularly when the path traversed a forest. They became very conscious of their money belts, which would be the main attraction for predators, who would leave them nothing; not even their horses.

Needless to say, they were not armed. Even if they had been, neither of them would have been proficient enough to use their weapons to advantage. Their only recourse was silent prayer, which filled a good part of their day.

As they travelled, the two friends spoke of many things. Tullius told Linus how generous Kallinikus had been in paying him sixteen gold aureii for his services, and which naturally he was carrying. The herbalist in his turn, made known to his friend the amount of money he was carrying, as a sign of reciprocating trust.

Tullius resolved to show Lucius the veil on their next stop for the night and told him so. In the meantime, he related some of the history of the veil, but made no mention of how it had cured Pontius Pilate. He advised him to keep the matter to himself, and Linus, if they ever met.

"Please do not tell Claudia," he cautioned. "I did not show it or mention it to her, since it did not as I suspected, save her father.

"I would like you at some future time," said Tullius, "To go to Rome, and look up my good friend Demetrius the baker, at the address I gave you. He will put you in touch with Linus, who will tell you what to do. Hopefully, Linus will be made a bishop soon, and he can ordain you into the priesthood. You will make a good priest. Tell him I said so. Then get yourself back here and continue to spread the good news in the villages.

"That would be wonderful," agreed Lucius, who being a bachelor could do as he pleased with no impediments whatsoever.

"If I am back from Cyrene by then, and you are still in Rome, I shall take you to meet my family in Umbria," promised Tullius. "In the meantime, look after the villagers and see that they do not stray from the teachings of Yeshua which I have taught you. Keep up the prayer meetings. Claudia will help you any way she can I am sure."

The sun was setting as they reached their stop for the night.

* * * * *

The morning sun filtering merrily through the trees in the wood above the village woke up the previous night's drunks.

Brutus quickly looked around him. His drowsy eyes fell on the dead man still lying where they had felled him.

"Wake up! Wake up!" He shouted, getting to his feet and shaking Trosinius and the others.

Slowly they collected their semi-dormant wits and got on their feet.

"We have to hide this corpse before it's found." urged the chief of the pack. "Come on get moving! People will be passing this way soon."

Between them they carried the man further into the wood and down a slope to where there was a cave; a swiftly running stream flowing merrily across its mouth. They dragged the body into the cave and tucked it away in a corner well away from the entrance.

"It will be a while before they find him," said Brutus retrieving his two gold pieces from the dead man's tunic. Trosinius searched the man further, extracting with some glee, another five denarii.

"Now people will think that he was killed for his money," he said, with a confident smile.

They cautiously left the scene and made their way back to the house. The guards saw them coming and opened the gate. Brutus went into the house with Trosinius. The other two went to the servant's quarters at the back, to wash up and try to recover from their murderous night.

Claudua was still asleep as was the whole household. The pair of delinquents tiptoed through the peristyle and into Brutus' room where they set about their ablutions.

The cocks crowing in the vegetable garden brought the big house to life, and presently, the servants began their day's work. When Viviana arrived a little later, the two slave girls had already begun preparations for the breakfast.

Claudia sat up in bed, stretched her shapely arms and got on her feet. A morning prayer escaped her lips as she whispered her dedication of the day to Yeshua, as Tullius had taught her to do.

'That way,' he had said, 'everything that you do during the day will become a prayer of praise to God, and Yeshua will surely guide your day and protect you from evil.'

She washed and dressed at a leisurely pace, suddenly realising that she had no reason for rushing. Her father no longer needed her: Tullius was gone: Sixtus, she imagined would not be arriving until late morning, seeing that he had to find and bring with him the witnesses.

She had no idea where Brutus was, but he would show up soon she guessed.

Viviana had been at her post in the kitchen for over an hour when Claudia traversed the colourful sunlit peristyle and entered the kitchen.

"Good morning to you all," she greeted. "We shall be having a few guests from the village for lunch."

"How many?" asked the cook.

"Allow for six just in case," said the mistress of the house with conviction.

Brutus and Trosinius had been discussing the pursuit of Tullius as they waited for the house to come to life. To Trosinius, who had no apathy for Christians, the whole venture of going after Tulliuswas nothing more than another exciting adventure. A game to fill his purposeless life. He had had a very unpleasant and loveless childhood and he was basking in the adventures and enticements that his wealthy friend created for him. He had not worked a day in his life. Brutus supplied all of his needs, and he was thoroughly committed to his friend regardless of the nature of the undertaking. He sat in Brutus' room awaiting his instructions for the day.

"Go out and stay with the boys. I have business to attend to here," said Brutus. Then observing a hurt look on his friend's face, he said. "But first come and have breakfast with us."

The two friends made their way to the dining room where they found Claudia mid way through her breakfast. One of the slave girls seeing them enter, hastened to the kitchen to bring their food. She returned shortly after and served the two men. They ate scantily, their stomachs being well on the queasy side.

"Wild night?" said Claudia, with a smile. "How's your head?

"Don't be funny," scowled her brother on behalf of the two.

Claudia chuckled, and having finished, got up and left them to themselves.

Sixtus arrived in mid morning as expected. With him were the two witnesses from the village. They were elders, well respected by the villagers, and being able to read and write, were accustomed to participating in legal matters. After partaking of some refreshments in the way of fruit and juice, they gathered in the reception room to perform their civic duty.

Brutus joined the party accompanied by Claudia, and the proceedings began.

It came as no surprise to anyone that the big house would go to Brutus as the male survivor. All the remaining holdings, investments, lands, businesses, etc. would be shared jointly by the siblings. Two parts to Brutus and one part to Claudia.

There were codicils to cover the inheritance of Claudia's children in the event of Claudia not being a survivor. But all that was irrelevant, since both children were alive to claim their inheritance.

Claudia and Brutus sat together in the reception room. Everyone had left. Claudia was quick to inform her brother that she would be building a house in town, where she could live with her children and in-laws.

"You and the children can stay here if you want," said Brutus.

"Thanks, but I have to think of my in-laws. They want to be near the children. I want them to be happy. They have a life of their own."

"By the way," said Brutus, looking at his sister.

"I have recently found out that Tullius the physician, is a dirty Christian priest."

Claudia was horrified. She said nothing. She simply stared at her brother.

"You don't believe me, do you?" he said with an evil smile.

"How did you find that out?"

"One of the villagers told me that he had seen him perform a service in front of a cross in one of the houses. They were passing pieces of bread around, which they all ate with their heads bowed as if in prayer."

Claudia thanked Yeshua that she was sitting down. She doubted that her legs would have supported her at that moment.

"Really?" she said, with as much control of her voice as she could muster.

"Now that our inheritance business is done with, I am going after the rascal. I shall catch him and give him up to the authorities in Phoenix. If I don't wring his neck first. They'll know what to do with him. The sneaky rat. He is probably going to board a ship to take him to Cyrene as he told Father when he first came." He got up and walked to the door.

"I'll let you know when I return. I shall be away for a few days."

She did not move. She was too wrapped up in prayer.

Brutus went to his room to collect his baggage.

A few moments later, he returned. She accompanied him to the door.

"Why don't you just let him go? He did us no harm, all he did was to help Father."

"Yea. That is how they cheat people into believing that they are harmless. Then they convert them and make slaves of them. They have to obey that God Yeshua of theirs no matter what he asks them to do. Kill, rob, cheat. And they hate the emperor and our gods. "I'll get him. He won't be able to trick any more people."

Hurriedly embracing his stunned and speechless sister, he went off to the stables.

A few moments later, he rode out with his gang, leaving her to commune with her beloved Yeshua, whom she asked not for her brother's safety, but for that of her beloved Tullius.

* * * * *

The second day of Tullius and Lucius' journey was well on its way. The weather however was not cooperating. It was raining and because of the altitude it was cold. They had had a good night's rest after a satisfying cena in one of the goatherd's houses. But now, up in those mountains they were soaked and cold. The path had become somewhat treacherous, visibility was poor, and their rate of progress was slow. There were sheer precipices on their right-hand side, and the narrow, muddy path felt soft under the horses' hooves. It could they feared, give way at any time.

Things became less hazardous by early afternoon, as they descended into a valley and the rain stopped. Reaching the valley floor, they got their horses into a canter and began at last to make some headway. The sun dried their clothes as they rode. Stopping was out of the question other than to rest and feed the horses. Man and horse alike drank from the crystal-clear streams they constantly encountered, especially up in the mountains.

A market in the valley gave them the opportunity to buy some food, which they hurriedly ate in the shade under a large tree beside a river, allowing at the same time their mounts to rest.

A little later, they resumed their journey following a path that led up another mountain and which proved to be not only narrow but strewn with small pieces of rock from a recent landslide somewhere further up. Not only did it slow them down, but it occasioned Lucius' horse to drop a shoe. He was forced to dismount and walk it for the remainder of the day; irreparably hindering their progress.

Nightfall found them still up in the mountains, though to their relief, descending. There was however, no house or shelter in sight. Their only consolation was the full moon, which by virtue if its soothing light, gave the two friends some solace. It was becoming very cold and they were feeling quite miserable.

Haunted by the time that had inevitably been lost, Tullius began to get a little nervous about their situation. He looked at Licius.

"You said when we took the road on the left of the fork yesterday, that the road was safer because it was less travelled on. But you did not tell me if it was a longer route that we were following,"

"Yes, it is a longer route, but if they are following us they will probably take the more popular, faster one. Chances were that if they were in actual fact after us, they would catch up with us if they mercilessly pushed their horses which they probably would have done.

"Well," said Tullius, "your idea was a good one. Unfortunately, we have been plagued with bad weather and now this problem with your horse's shoe. Incidentally, come and ride my horse for a while, you are tired. I shall walk it for you for a while.

The herbalist gratefully accepted his friend's proposal and they exchanged places.

They continued at a walking pace for some time. A faint light peeking feebly through the mist ahead caught their attention and gave them some hope of shelter. As they approached the light source, they encountered a barn and some men sitting outside around a camp fire.

"Good evening to you all," said Lucius forcing a smile amid his misery.

Tullius followed his friend's example.

"Good night to you also," came the reply. "Come sit with us and warm yourselves. It's a cold night."

The pair tied their horses to a tree, and going over to the campfire, sat down.

"My horse has dropped a shoe," said Lucius, "and it has really delayed us."

"Tough break," said one of the men. "There's a small village at the foot of the mountain that has a blacksmith.

"Yes," agreed another, "but it will take you four or five hours to get there at a walking pace.

"I see," said Tulius. "Thank you for telling us." He stared at the flames in front of him for a few moments, scratching his wet head through his soaking shawl. Of a sudden he looked at Lucius, and with some excitement in his voice, said.

"I have an idea. I don't know why I didn't think of it before. You can ride with me, and your horse can trot behind us. I think he could manage that without hurting himself. We can get there in half the time."

"That sounds like a good idea," agreed someone else.

"Yes," said Lucius, with an approving nod. "Let's try it. We have lost too much time already."

Now that our two heroes had warmed up a bit, they felt better, and bidding the party good night, mounted Tullius' horse as agreed, and off they trotted.

"I didn't fancy staying the night with that lot," said Tullius when they were out of ear shot.

"They were probably harmless, but why take a chance?"

Their experiment worked for a good while, and then the horse began to show some resistance. Lucius dismounted once more, and they continued at a walking pace. Good progress had been made however, and half an hour later much to their relief, they reached the village.

It was deathly quiet, everyone was asleep. They looked at each other and wondered what to do next.

"We shall have to wake up someone," said Lucius almost in a whisper.

"Maybe there is a barn nearby," suggested Tullius, "and we can slip in there for the night. At least we will get some sleep."

"They walked for a while around the village, and finally found one.

The door was closed. Tullius lifted the iron bar and swung the door open. But the screeching sound caused by the rusty door hinges was enough to wake up the village.

Presently, a light could be seen in a house directly across from the barn. It came from a torch, and as it approached, a dog's growling could be heard. A hefty young man of average height holding back a strapped and collared dog, appeared carrying the torch.

"Why are you trying to break into my barn?" asked the man, still holding back his snarling dog.

"We apologise for that, but we are two exhausted travellers," explained Tillius. "We did not want to disturb the sleeping village. We found your barn and thought of resting there for the night. We will pay you for your hospitality. We mean no harm."

"My horse dropped a shoe up in the mountains, or we would have reached the village much earlier in the day," said Lucius in an apologetic tone of voice.

"Very well," said the farmer, "you are welcome to stay. But you will need a light. I don't take torches into the barn. I shall fetch you an oil lamp." He started to walk away and stopped. Turning around he asked. "Do you have food and water?"

"Yes. Thank you," they answered.

Presently the man returned carrying the oil lamp and showed them into the barn. He hung the lamp on a post which lit up the place quite well. He showed them where to put the horses, and giving them a pitch fork, told them to help themselves to the hay that surrounded them for their beds and for feeding the horses.

"There is water for your horses here," he said pointing to a trough. "You can drink your own water. Tomorrow you can fill up you skins in the house before you go."

They thanked the man, who calling the loose dog after him, walked back to the house and left them to themselves.

Shortly after, having eaten some of their rations, and fed their horses, they tumbled onto their warm hay beds and promptly fell asleep.

The sun's rays filtering in through the cracks in the boards on the side of the barn, woke the two friends up. They immediately realised that they had slept in, and hastened to prepare for their departure. Pulling their horses behind them, they left the barn only to run into the farmer who had come to meet them.

"I let you sleep in. I hope you don't mind," he said. "I looked in on you and you were snoring your heads off. I reckoned you must have been real tired."

"Thank you. No harm done, but we have to hurry and get that horse shod. What do we owe you?" asked Tullius.

"You don't owe me anything. I'm glad to have been of help. If you give me your waterskins I shall fill them for you."

Tullius handed him the water skins and the young man took them away.

Two boys suddenly appeared and came running to meet them. One was around six, and the other four. The dog was with them and came to sniff the strangers whilst the boys stood admiring the beautiful black horse.

"My daddy is going to get me a pony when I am seven," said the older one with a big smile.

"You are a lucky boy," said Tullius, ruffling the boy's hair, and remembering his own baby boy.

"I'm going to ask him to get me a black one like this one," he said with great enthusiasm.

Tullius took two denarii out of his pouch.

"This is to help your daddy buy you the pony," he said and gave the boy the silver coins.

"Oh, thank you," said the boy with another lovely smile. His little brother looked at the coins in his brother's hand with a touch of envy.

"And this one is for you," said Lucius handing the other boy a denarius.

The farmer then rejoined them with the water skins.

Look daddy said the excited boys showing their father the coins.

"You are too generous my friends, I told you that you owe me nothing."

"We are only contributing to the pony your little fellow is expecting from you when he is seven," smiled Tullius.

A warm leave taking followed, and our two heroes went off in search of the blacksmith.

* * * * *

Lucius, standing in the blacksmith shop, watched the smithy shoe his horse, and awaited Tullius' return from the local marketplace where he had gone to buy the day's provisions.

The thunder of hooves, suddenly heard over the clanging of the smithy's hammer, peeked Lucius' curiosity, and stepping to the front of the shop, he was just in time to see Tullius riding 'hell for leather' past him, followed by Brutus and Trosinius riding into the cloud of dust created by the priest's horse.

Horror stricken, he exclaimed: "Lord have mercy!"

"Did you say something?" asked the blacksmith, stopping his hammering.

"No," he answered, pulling himself together.

* * * * *

Tullius who had suddenly been surprised by his pursuers, had barely had the time to mount his horse. He was now pushing his black mount to the limit of its ability, as he began to gain distance on Brutus who was closest to him. Trosinius was being left well behind, as Tullius continued to kick his heals into Negrus' sides.

He had not had time to purchase any food. The only thing he carried was the water skin that the young farmer had filled for him that morning.

The horse began to slow up as he climbed the mountain path, but so did Brutus' horse; he was quick to observe as he looked back. He soon realised, that to stay on the path would solve nothing. He would have to keep racing Brutus indefinitely, and when night came, he would not be able to tell how close the others were, and he would get no rest. His pursuers would have the advantage.

As he climbed further up the mountain he came to a forest. He studied it for density and found that the trees were close together offering him good cover. Losing himself in the woods was his best chance of escape. He could even double back to the village and stay in the barn for a few days. The young farmer would hide him he knew. He would then masquerade as an old man and sit near the market until he saw them pass on their way back home. He could then use the fast route to Phoenix with little chance of encountering them again.

Tullius continued to climb until he reached the summit an hour later. He could still see Brutus far behind.

'He is in no hurry of course," he said to himself.

Once at the summit, Tullius could see the winding path descending, and he pinpointed the place where he would diverge into the woods and lose himself before doubling back up the hill under cover of the trees and back down to the village.

His horse was tired, but finding itself going down, allowed the priest to prod it for some speed. As he turned into the wood, Tullius checked to see if Brutus had reached the summit.

The path was clear. Presently, he led Negrus into the woods, and as soon as he had found himself sufficiently immersed, he began to make his way back up the hill but more slowly, and cautiously. There were no paths he could follow, and the chances of his horse tripping on tree roots were considerable.

Once they regained the summit he dismounted. And walked in front of his horse to scrutinise the ground ahead of them as they walked. Occasionally Tullius' foot would sink into the mossy soil, and he would have to circumvent the patch and find firmer ground before he could continue. He could hear Brutus calling out to Trosinius to go into the forest, but the voices seemed to be getting farther away each time, and the clever priest new that they were continuing down the mountain and distancing themselves more and more.

For the first time in the last two hours, he began to feel more at ease as he descended towards the village. He thought of

Lucius and hoped he would go back to the Kallinikos village and tell Claudia that he had lost track of him.

'Since Brutus had not seen him with me,' he said to himself, 'he will not suspect him of being a Christian. He could simply go back to his shop, continue his life as a herbalist, and look after his flock.'

A small mountain stream suddenly appeared in his path and he stopped to allow Negrus to drink his fill. He drank also and sat down on a rock to rest. As he rested he thought of the veil.

If he were apprehended or killed, the veil would be lost for ever. He began to regret not having given it to Lucius who would eventually have taken it to Linus. He was glad however that he had shown him the veil. At least Linus would have some idea of where it had been lost. Not that it would be of much help of course.

From that thought his mind travelled to Umbria and his beloved Rufina, and his son whom he had seen but once. There was a good chance that he would grow up without a father.

The thought greatly saddened him and made him realise how vulnerable and in danger he really was. He stood up again and perceiving that the horse was ready to continue, he led on with a continuous prayer to Yeshua in his heart.

Not a sound could be heard. The noon hour approached, and he felt a bit hungry. He walked the horse a little faster and began once again to find the way back to the path. He presumed that by now he had given his hunters the slip.

He began to notice however, that he was no longer descending, but had in fact levelled off. Somewhat perplexed he continued forward. Presently he began ascending again. Suddenly, he caught the sound of voices again. They were not so far away anymore.

Then it hit him. He had overlooked a very obvious thing. The soft mossy ground of the woods showed the horses hoof marks with great clarity. Brutus was a hunter and as such, he would be an expert pathfinder.

'I must get back on the road before they leave the woods, and race my way down to the village again,' he said to himself with some alarm. 'Help me Lord. Please.' he prayed.

Turning to his left, he directed his steps in the direction of where he felt the path would be. A quarter of an hour later, he came to a sudden and alarming stop. The forest stopped there, right in front of him, and there was a sheer drop into a canyon far below. It had a small river running through the middle of it. The terrain around him was quite rocky, and it was going to be very difficult to guide his horse around the rocks. In any event he could not see any path whatsoever. He suddenly felt trapped.

The voices of his pursuers sounded closer. Tullius racked his fertile brain for a possible solution. A practical route of escape. He tied the horse to a tree and scampered over the rocks to find one. It was difficult for him to see to his left where he assumed the path would be. His view was obstructed by a large rocky protrusion immediately in front of him. The rock face was far too sheer and smooth to climb. He spotted with some difficulty, a rocky ledge a little less than an average man's height down from where he stood. It was partially hidden by a heavy covering of shrubs and woodland plants. But to his relief, he noticed, as he scrutinised the surrounding ground more carefully, that there was a dead tree firmly anchored into a crevice in the rock face. Holding on to it, he began to climb down.

He heard the voices again. One voice which Tullius recognised as belonging to Brutus shouted. "I have found his horse. He has to be up here somewhere."

Tullius continued his descent onto the ledge. He had no where else to go. Once down, he could see the path he sought. He was dismayed to find that it was quite far below him. He had completely miscalculated his bearings. After all, he could not see the sun clearly through the trees he reasoned.

Suddenly he heard footsteps on the rocky face. Remembering the veil, he searched frantically for a place to hide it. There, on the rock face near him, was another crevice; quite deep and narrow, but enough to allow in an arm. He quickly pulled out the pouch with the veil and pushed it in as far as his elbow. Then seeing a shadow cast in front of him, he looked up to see Brutus' evil, smiling face.

"He's over here to your front and right," he shouted, and nimbly jumped onto the ledge with a knife in his hand.

Tullius side-stepped as Brutus landed, and the latter missing his victim, lost his balance and found himself helplessly sliding over the edge. The priest, with a lightning movement, took a hold of Brutus' hand, simultaneously grabbing the dead tree with his other hand, as the latter slid over the edge. Brutus let his knife fall and made a desperate grab at the ledge with his freed hand. Tullius held him firmly.

That was the situation when Trosinius, emerging from the forest, bow and arrow in hand, looked around for his quarry. Suddenly he saw Tullius; his arm in the air. He could not see the dead tree that the priest was hanging on to. A sudden cry for help came from Brutus. Trosinius, having only a partial view of the priest, and unable to see Brutus, erroneously surmised that the Christian had somehow overpowered his friend and was pushing him off the cliff.

Quickly aiming an arrow at Tullius' back, he let fly.

He rushed forward in time to see his quarry fall to his knees and slide off the ledge, as if dragged by some invisible force.

The silence of the forest was suddenly shattered by a bitter echoing cry. Brutus' desperate, rapidly distancing voice, yelled:

"Fool! Fool! Foooooo..."

EPILOGUE

Trosinius jumped down, falling prostrate on the ledge. He looked down at the canyon in horror and disbelief of what his eyes had seen and his ears heard. He was just in time to see two figures floating away in the river far below him. Presently he lost sight of them.

'By Jupiter! I have killed the two of them.' he said to himself. He sat up and leaning against the rock face behind him, attempted to reconstruct in his befuddled head, that final action scene.

'The Christian must have been holding Brutus from falling. But how?' he asked himself.

He then noticed the dead tree beside him. The whole episode suddenly became clear to him. His stomach retched, his head swooned, and he vomited violently.

His world had suddenly collapsed. He had killed his friend and now he had nothing left. No money, no friends, no family, no future.

Rising to his feet, he climbed back up from the ledge, and mechanically started collecting the horses that had been tied to trees at various locations. He walked all three of them carefully out of the forest, and on regaining the path to the village, he mounted his own horse and led the other two away with him.

There was great excitement in the village as a consequence of the discovery of the two bodies in the river. They were on display for all to see, lying in a cart in the market place. Among the on lookers were the two members of Brutus' gang who had been left behind in the market place when the chase for Tullius began. They had been on their own awaiting orders from their chief, when unbeknownst to them, Brutus and Trosinius saw the priest and chased after him.

Seeing their dead boss lying in the cart with the Christian priest, they realised that their services would not be paid for unless they found Trosinius who might be able to pay them something at least so that they could return to their country. They were both Corinthians.

There had been money found on both dead men. Their money belts had however, been surrendered to the Roman authorities by the fisherman who had found the bodies. He had been promised a handsome reward if and when the money was legally claimed. It would be impossible for anyone to claim the money without very good proof of entitlement, he was told.

Standing not far from them and unbeknownst to one another, stood a mournful Lucius; praying to Yeshua for his dear friend and mentor. He had recognised Brutus' dead face, and was quite befuddled as to how this tragedy had come about.

'They must have been wrestling on the edge of some cliff and both fell over,' he mused. 'But what about the arrow in Tullius' back?' Then Trosinius whom he knew to have taken part in the chase, came to mind. The fact that the man was nowhere in sight bothered the herbalist.

'Perhaps,' he said to himself, 'he shot the arrow whilst Tullius was wrestling with Brutus?'

Lucius decided to stay and see if Trosinius would show up. He withdrew to a quieter part of the market where he sat on a bench with his horse beside him at the ready, in case he too, had to make a run for it.

That was the state of affairs, when Trosinius arrived at the village. He found the streets almost deserted, as he directed his steps to the market where he hoped to sell the two horses.

On entering the market place and seeing the crowd, he suspected that the bodies had been found. He tied the horses to a tree, and giving a boy who was nearby, a farthing, asked him to watch them for him until he returned.

He was about to push through the crowd to where the cart was standing when he spotted the two Corinthians near the cart. He turned around and quickly returned to his horses. The boy told him what had happened at the village, and how the bodies of the two rich men had been recovered. And how their fat money belts had been taken by the authorities.

Trosinius was livid at what the boy told him. All that money, some of which he was entitled to was going to be lost to the Romans. Taking the horses again, he distanced himself from the market and hid behind some houses to think.

Lucius who had been on the look out for Trosinius, saw him arrive and again quickly leave.

He knew that the rascal did not know him, and so leading his horse he followed him to where he was hiding. He walked right past him on his way to the Legion's headquarters, where a lone couple of Legionnaires kept order in the village.

Lucius lost no time denouncing Trosinius, who was immediately arrested on the grounds that he was in possession of Tulius' horse. The herbalist also disclosed to the keepers of the law, the identity of the two dead men, and since he knew exactly the amount of money his friend was carrying in his belt. His testimony was accepted.

The herbalist had both bodies buried in adjoining graves. He claimed both horses and all monies, and one of the Legionnaires was to escort him back to Kallinikus' village, where Claudia would verify his story.

Trosinius remained in custody awaiting trial on suspicion of murder and the stealing of Tullius' horse.

The two Corinthians, not being able to find Trosinius, disappeared; taking their horses as their only payment with them.

Two months after the tragedy that befell Tullius, Lucius travelled to Rome to meet Linus and give him an account of the beloved priest's sojourn and adventures in Crete.

Linus, was greatly grieved to learn of his favourite priest's demise, and insisted on accompanying Lucius to Umbria, where he would personally break the tragic news to Rufina.

You my dear reader can well imagine the sorrow that befell those good people at the vineyard. Linus was truly amazed at the way that the broken-hearted Rufina resigned herself to the will of God.

Holding her little son in her arms after a beautiful service by a tearful Linus, she proudly said for all to hear.

"Your father, my son, was a great man! And now," she continued, looking at Marcia with tears in her eyes, but a lovely smile on her lips, "he is a martyr just like your brave parents. They are all in heaven with our beloved Yeshua."

* * * * *

Veronica's veil, resting in its rocky Cretan shrine, became a mystery awaiting discovery.

"Perhaps, at some future time?"

Joseph L. Cavilla is a writer and visual artist.
He lives and works in Hanover, Ontario.